"*The Brazen Altar* is a gratifying example of what could happen if we allow technology to heal our deepest wounds, and shift our focus to more carnal aspirations. Kink happens, and it happens to be the main event, as we witness society delve into the realm of extreme pleasure in service to their deities. *The Brazen Altar* is groundbreaking in the world of erotic romance. Brave and bold, this book takes no prisoners, demands our attention, and opens up an entirely new playground for fantasy and ecstasy."

> —Melanie Nicholson

"This is the horniest book I have ever read... The story is delivered through sex. In the sex scenes, there is character growth, there are changes in dynamics. I am super-excited to see the next book in the series."

> —Tom Harrison

"One of the biggest problems with fantasy and SciFi stories is that rarely are the consequences of the fantastical elements taken to their logical conclusions. Magic and technology serve as throwaways to drive the plot and are then forgotten about. As a result, I hold in high regard stories that add a fantastical element and then explore the implications such technology would have.

The Brazen Alter nails this aspect of the story and it was my overriding feeling throughout reading it. In a post scarcity world, where would humanity find their drive? We've seen how religion and tribalism shape our society today, but what would it look like in a world where the desperate need for survival and power were taken away as concerns completely?"

> —Michael Vogel

THE BRAZEN ALTAR

THE BRAZEN ALTAR
THE PASSIONATE PANTHEON BOOK ONE

EUNICE HUNG & FRANKLIN VEAUX

Luminastra Press

The Brazen Altar
Copyright ©2021 by Eunice Hung and Franklin Veaux

Luminastra Press, LLC
620 SE 146 Ave
Portland, OR 97233
press@luminastra-press.com

Cover illustration ©2020 by Julie Dillon
Cover and interior design by Franklin Veaux
Edited by Kris M. Smith

Publisher's Cataloging-In-Publication Data
(Prepared by The Donohue Group, Inc.)

Names: Hung, Eunice, author. | Veaux, Franklin, author.
Title: The brazen altar / Eunice Hung & Franklin Veaux.
Description: Portland, OR : Luminastra Press, LLC, [2021] | Series: The Passionate Pantheon ;
 book 1
Identifiers: ISBN 9781734658705 | ISBN 9781734658712 (ebook)
Subjects: LCSH: Utopias--Fiction. | Voluntary human sacrifice--Fiction. | Gods--Fiction. | Sex--Fic
 | LCGFT: Utopian fiction. | Fantasy fiction. | Erotic fiction.
Classification: LCC PS3608.U547 B73 2021 (print) | LCC PS3608.U547 (ebook) |
 DDC 813/.6--dc23

10 9 8 7 6 5 4 3 2 1

Printed in the United States of America.

*To Maxine, whose worship of chaos
accidentally created order.*

BOOK ONE
THE FIERY ONE

1.1

On the morning of the five hundred and forty-second Ceremony of Light, a slender, red-haired woman with gray-green eyes waited impatiently to be sacrificed to the god of the sun.

The square in front of the temple buzzed with people. They'd been arriving throughout the night, alone and in groups. Tiny dronelights flitted through the air, lighting their way into the courtyard. The drones switched off their lights the moment they entered the courtyard, so as not to displease the Sun God on this, the day dedicated to his radiance. Behind the assembled congregation, the dome projected by the shield generators glowed faintly in the pre-dawn air. Ahead, the stepped pyramid of the Temple of Flame, the largest of the great houses of worship, carved an inky void in the sky.

Deep inside the Temple, in a small chamber illuminated by the dim yellow glow of small globes floating in niches in the rough stone walls, Kheema swallowed. She took a deep breath to hide her nervousness. Five hundred and forty-one Sacrifices before her had walked barefoot down the narrow hallway into this room. From here, five hundred and forty-one Sacrifices had ascended to the altar atop the Temple to welcome the day.

Now it was her turn. She could feel the weight of history on her shoulders, as pervasive and tangible as the mass of the temple itself. All but one of the Sacrifices before her had succeeded in the ritual that would bring the blessing of the Fiery One to his people. She didn't want to go down in history as the second person to fail.

"You'll do fine," Janaié said. She slipped her hand into Kheema's.

Kheema managed a small smile. "Is it that obvious?"

"Only to me."

"I can't hide anything from you."

"Would you want to?" Janaié placed a gentle kiss on her shoulder. "Your agony will be so lovely. I know the Sun God will be pleased."

Kheema looked down at her feet, pale against warm dark stone. She thought, not for the first time, that it felt like a living thing, this massive edifice of stone, the physical embodiment of the Lord of Light.

She remembered being surprised by the warmth the first time she'd touched these walls, eighteen months ago to the day. She and seven other Potentials had walked through the door on the far side of the courtyard, a door that opened just once a year to admit eight people who would compete to become Sacrifice to the Lord of Light. She'd hung back from the rest of the Potentials, running her fingers over the hard, textured blocks of stone, so carefully fitted that not even the finest knife blade could slip between them. The stones felt warm, much warmer than she had expected. The warmth entranced her. Tingling currents raced along her skin.

She could feel his presence here. She could taste him, the God of the Sun, in the air around her. Her skin buzzed. A soft whisper filled her mind. In that instant, she knew it would be her. The knowledge filled her until she felt she might burst. Of the eight women in the tight group who had passed through the mammoth stone doors into the Temple, she would be the next Sacrifice. She smiled at the thought.

"Hey!" The voice came from another Potential to Kheema's left. "Hey, that's her!"

"What?" Kheema looked around.

"That's her!" The voice came from a slight woman just a little ahead of Kheema. She stood half a head shorter than Kheema, with wide, dark eyes and dark hair that fell in a series of curls and ringlets over her shoulders. She pointed to the priestess who had met them at the door, and who was now leading them along the gently sloping hallway into the depths of the Temple. "That's her! Fahren! She was the Sacrifice two solstices ago. I was here. I remember. She was so beautiful. She's the reason I decided to become a Potential. If they choose me, I hope I can suffer as wonderfully as she did. I'm Janaié, by the way."

"Kheema."

"You're beautiful."

Color touched Kheema's cheeks. "Thank you."

"I mean it. If they don't choose me for the sacrifice, I hope they choose you. I bet you would suffer exquisitely." Her eyes swept up and down along Kheema's body. Something feral glittered there, in the soft light of countless small floating glow-globes. "I would love to watch you suffer."

Kheema turned away, blushing furiously. Her hand caressed the wall. The tingling grew stronger, like a light electric current dancing playfully over her skin. She smiled a small, secret smile.

The eight Potentials followed the priestess along a long, straight hallway that sloped slightly downward. Dim glowing globes hung silently in the air at regular intervals above their heads. Deep shadows lurked between the globes.

The hallway ended at a blank stone wall. The priestess gestured. Smoothly, without the slightest sound, the wall moved toward them, then split down the center. The two halves pivoted upward into the ceiling until they were flush with it, so seamlessly not the slightest crack could be seen.

Beyond lay a spacious chamber, flooded with sunlight. Brilliant marble tiles flecked with red and gold paved the ground and covered the walls. Snowy white columns, far too wide for Kheema to wrap her arms around, supported the high ceiling overhead.

They were deep underground, beneath the center of the Temple, yet somehow the space felt like an open courtyard. Sunlight poured in through wide slots in the ceiling, guided down into the chamber by cunning arrangements of reflectors so optically perfect that when Kheema looked up, she could see the small white clouds drifting through the hard winter sky.

The priestess directed the small group of Potentials into a circle of columns. In the center of the circle, a crystal bowl filled with shimmering liquid rested atop a slender marble pedestal. Eight beautiful transparent vials, each no larger than a thumb, formed a circle around the bowl. Deep red liquid filled the vials. Tiny motes of shimmering gold swirled in the liquid. When all of the Potentials were inside the circle, the two halves of the stone door stone pivoted smoothly back into place, leaving no sign that an opening had ever existed.

Kheema looked at the priestess closely for the first time. She wore only a translucent gossamer robe of white, woven through with glittering threads of red and gold. Her blond hair spilled over her shoulders like waves crashing over a rock. Her lips were full, her eyes the gray of a winter sea.

Kheema realized that the other Potential, Janaié, was right. The priestess was a previous Sacrifice, whose beauty and suffering were, even by the standards of the City, the stuff of legend. Kheema, like all worshippers of the Fiery One, had watched her sacrifice. Kheema hadn't been present in person; instead, she'd watched a holographic projection from her apartment. The expression on the woman's face, the way she struggled in her chains, her moans and cries as she recited the Litany of the Sun, all had awakened a hunger in Kheema that had taken days to slake.

Fahren instructed the Potentials to stand in a circle, each in front of one of the columns. For a moment, her eyes met Kheema's. A spark jumped between them. Kheema felt herself falling into those pools of tranquil gray. She felt a sudden clenching between her legs, a feeling of longing in her chest, before the woman looked away and the moment was lost.

"Eight of you have volunteered as Potentials," she said. "You represent the Eight who first awakened the Lord of Light, bringing forth his blessings into our world, creating the foundation upon which everything we have built now rests. All of you will undergo the training and the trials to become the next Sacrifice. The training is not easy. You will be pushed to the limits of your endurance so you can demonstrate your devotion to the Fiery One. Before the summer solstice eighteen months from now, one of you will be chosen to join the long line of Sacrifices to his holy light. There is no greater honor any of us may ever have."

She walked around the circle of nervous Potentials, her diaphanous robe drifting behind her. Kheema shivered as she walked by, intoxicated by her aura of confident grace.

"There can be no secrets here. Each of you will stand naked before the Fiery One, he who can see your very essence. It is fitting, therefore, that you should be physically naked as well. Please remove your clothes."

Moving in a trance, Kheema removed her plain white dress with red and gold straps along the sides. She kicked off her simple sandals. Around her, the other Potentials disrobed as well.

Her heart beat faster. She looked over at Janaié, standing naked beside her. Kheema's eyes traced the woman's nut-brown skin, entranced. Janaié had dark hair, streaked through with red and yellow. She caught Kheema's stare and gave her a dazzling smile. Her eyes were so dark they were nearly black. "Yes, you may," she said.

"I...I..." Kheema shook her head to clear it.

"I like you, too," Janaié said. Kheema blushed.

Fahren's eyes scanned the circle of expectant women. She stood before the pedestal and picked up a smooth rod of glass that rested in a graceful curved hook on the side of the crystal bowl. She dipped one end into the shimmering liquid, then raised it and allowed a drop to fall onto her tongue.

She shuddered. Her skin flushed. She breathed deeply, her eyes closed. When she opened them again, her pupils were tiny dots of black in seas of gray.

"Each of you will now come forward to receive the Blessing of Fire," she said. She gestured to Janaié. "We will start with you."

Janaié stepped forward, smiling. She closed her eyes, tongue extended. Fahren placed a drop of the liquid on her tongue. Janaié shivered. She stepped back into place in the circle with a sigh.

"Now you," Fahren said to Kheema.

Kheema took a hesitant step forward, nearly tripping over the mound of clothing at her feet. Her hands trembled. She took a deep breath to steady herself, then extended her tongue.

The heavy, sweet drop of liquid tingled as she swallowed. Kheema stepped back. She felt it slide down her throat. When it reached her stomach, it exploded, sending a shockwave through her body so intense she staggered. Her skin crackled, so sensitive that the tiny eddies of air overwhelmed her. A wave of raw, animal need took her. She moaned.

She was barely aware of the other Potentials as each stepped forward to accept a glittering drop on their tongues. They returned to their places with eyes closed, panting. A tiny part of Kheema heard the priestess speaking, somewhere off in the distance.

"I will ask you some questions," Fahren said. She walked slowly around the circle, so close Kheema could feel her warmth as she passed. Kheema inhaled, absorbing her scent. She paused in front of the Potential to Kheema's right, a short woman with a full, lush figure whose long brown hair was tied in an elaborate braid. Tiny metallic red and gold threads glittered in the braid. Fahren ran her fingers lightly down the woman's arm. "What is your name?"

"I—Tani," the woman gasped.

"Tani, do you pledge yourself to the Lord of Light, that you may spread his blessing?"

"Yes!" The word was a moan.

Fahren leaned close, her lips almost touching Tani's ear. She slid her hand down Tani's side, caressed the rolls at her hip. "Do you wish to serve the Lord of Light as his Sacrifice, to secure his blessing for all who seek it?"

"I—I—please! By the Gods, please!" Her eyes closed. Her back arched. "Please!"

"Good." She trailed her hand lightly across Tani's body as she moved on. "And you?" she said, stopping near a tall, willowy Potential. "What is your name?"

The woman's lips parted. Her breath came in short gasps. "Lianya," she said. "Lianya."

Fahren reached up to place her hands on the woman's shoulders. She ran both hands down her arms, drawing closer until their bodies nearly touched.

"Lianya, will you learn the Litany and the Histories, so that if you are chosen as the Sacrifice, you may recite them in their fullness as you suffer?"

"I will, I...I...oh!" Lianya threw her head back, screaming. Her body shuddered. "Oh God! Yes! Yes!" She clutched at the marble column behind her, thrusting her hips forward toward Fahren. Her body shuddered violently. "Please, yes, I will!"

Fahren moved around the circle. The other Potentials moaned, squirming under her touch, struggling to answer her questions.

There was Sakim, a short woman with a throaty voice and eyes of metallic green; Chanae, almost as tall as Kheema, with a triangular face framed by short black hair; Eranis, whose gray hair fell in a cascade down her back until it caressed the curve of her generous butt, and whose interrogation, like Lianya's, ended in cries of ecstasy. One Potential, a slender woman named Veenja with skin a deep, lustrous black and hair, legs, and eyes a pale, shining silvery-blue that was nearly iridescent, collapsed to the floor at Fahren's touch, writhing with pleasure.

Finally, she arrived at Kheema. Kheema closed her eyes. Her chest heaved. Her head swam with a raging firestorm of need. Her body burned. She ached with desire, so strong it felt like a living thing, clawing and coiling inside her.

She felt rather than saw Fahren draw close. She could sense the heat of the woman, smell her scent, hear the gentle slap of her feet on the warm marble tiles, feel the air swirling around her.

Fahren's hand touched her hip. Kheema jumped, overwhelmed by the intensity of it. The firestorm of need exploded into a conflagration. She shuddered, moaning. Every fiber of her being longed to feel Fahren's skin against hers, Fahren's lips on her neck.

"What is your name?"

Kheema opened her eyes. The woman before her seemed bathed in a golden light. A warm glow radiated from her, from the stone walls, from the air itself. Kheema's mind filled with the memory of this woman on the holographic screen, writhing in her chains, face contorted with something between agony and ecstasy. Instantly, she knew this was a test.

She took a deep breath. Biting back the aching need, she said, "My name is Kheema, Priestess." She fought to keep the quaver from her voice.

"Kheema. That's a lovely name." Fahren moved close. Her hand ran up Kheema's back, leaving swirling eddies of overwhelming pleasure in its wake. The aching need grew stronger.

"Kheema," she said again. Her hand rested lightly on the back of Kheema's neck. "Do you want to give yourself to the Lord of Light, Kheema, so that you can bring his blessing to the people?"

"I do, Priestess." Her body quivered. "I..." She shuddered. For a moment, her control slipped away. She fought to take it back. "I offer myself as a sacrifice in his name."

"Hmm." Fahren leaned close. Her lips brushed Kheema's neck, exquisitely gently. Her other hand slid over Kheema's breast. Kheema felt the breath sucked from her lungs. Her knees buckled at the sensation. "Are you fighting the Blessing of Fire?"

Kheema closed her eyes again. She clenched her hands so tightly her fingernails bit into her palms. "Yes, Priestess."

"Why? Do you not want to accept the gift of the Lord of Light?"

"I do, Priestess." Kheema felt suffocated, as though the room did not contain enough air to fill the void in her chest. She wanted to wrap her arms around the woman, draw her in, kiss her roughly. A small sob escaped her. "I want that very much."

Fahren's fingers stroked Kheema's nipple. "Then why do you fight the gift, Potential?"

"Because..." Kheema choked back a scream of frustration. "Because you are testing us, Priestess."

"How am I testing you?"

"You...you are..." The words caught in Kheema's throat. She felt herself moving forward, pressing her breast into Fahren's hand. "You are trying to see if we have the focus to become a Sacrifice. You want to see if we have the will to make it through the Litany."

"Do you?" Fahren moved forward. "Do you have the will?"

Kheema summoned every ounce of her strength to make herself move back, until she was backed up against the warm column behind her. Fahren kept coming, until her body was pressed against hers. Her hand slid down, over Kheema's breast, across her stomach, down to the place that seethed and burned between her legs. Her lips brushed Kheema's. "Do you have the will to become a Sacrifice?"

"No!" Kheema cried. The word was a wail of despair and defeat. Her will crumbled beneath the driving storm of need. She kissed Fahren, rough with desire, heedless of anything except the desperation that burned and unraveled her.

Fahren stepped back with a smile. Kheema's heart threatened to burst with sorrow.

"No Potential does," Fahren said. "Not on the first day. The training is long and rigorous for a reason. I was like all of you when I first entered the Temple. My will had yet to be forged in his sacred fire. Right now, you are all soft. Malleable. Easily bent. Unable to withstand his flame. We will temper you, until in time, one of you is able to stand as a Sacrifice in his divine fire." She looked at each of the Potentials in turn. "If any of you has the slightest hesitation in your heart, speak now. Once you begin on this path, you may quit at any time, but if you do, there will be no returning as a Potential. You will never become Sacrifice. Do you understand?"

Kheema swallowed. Her body still reverberated with the aftershocks from the kiss, like the echoes of a bell. She could still taste Fahren's lips on hers. "Yes, Priestess," she said. The other Potentials repeated her words. "Yes, Priestess."

"Good. Kheema is correct. Everything here is a test. For the entire time you are here, from now until one of you is chosen, the strength of your character will be put to the proof." She picked up one of the small vials from the pedestal. "Kheema, do you pledge yourself in service to the Fiery One, to belong to him, to give yourself over to his service, to carry his blessing into the world?"

"Yes, Priestess," Kheema said. Her heart beat faster as the woman approached, every cell in her body screaming its longing.

Fahren uncapped the vial, raising it to Kheema's lips. "Drink."

The liquid was warm and spicy, with a complex, constantly changing flavor. It burned in her mouth. When she swallowed, warmth spread through her body, filling her. Her skin felt suffused with light.

Fahren placed the empty vial on the pedestal and picked up the next. "Tani, do you pledge yourself in service to the Fiery One, to belong to him, to give yourself over to his service, to carry his blessing into the world?"

"Yes, Priestess."

She raised the vial to Tani's lips. "Drink."

She repeated the ritual six more times. Kheema felt the warmth swell and then fade, taking the feeling of frantic need with it. She felt a sense of loss as her desire disappeared.

Fahren gestured. The pedestal sank soundlessly into the ground. When it had disappeared from sight, a hatch slid closed over it.

"The Blessing you have just received will prevent you from experiencing sexual release," Fahren said. "Until you are given the antidote, you are all incapable of orgasm. You will learn, though, that you are still very much capable of desire. And you will, far beyond anything you have felt before. Now, follow me. Leave your clothes behind as you leave your old lives behind. You have no more need of them." Fahren gestured again. An opening appeared in the wall opposite where they had entered, two halves of a thick marble door silently swinging apart from each other. Fahren led the group of naked Potentials into the brilliant white hallway beyond, her filmy gown floating in the air behind her.

1.2

Fahren led the small group of Potentials down a short, wide hallway that emerged onto a balcony overlooking a broad underground atrium more than a hundred meters across. The balcony ran off to the left and right, surrounding the atrium on three sides. Two curved flights of stairs descended gracefully to another balcony below, then another below that, and yet another one below that, until finally, six levels down, they reached the ground. Two more curved upward to a balcony above them. Float-tubes threaded their way through the center of the curved stairways, for those too tired or lazy to climb the stairs.

Kheema leaned against the railing and looked down on a lush park of green grass and small trees. Pathways lined in marble tiles meandered through the park. Small fountains bubbled here and there. Three women, dressed like Fahren in gauzy robes that floated in the air behind them, walked down the path. They saw Kheema looking at them. One waved up at her.

Above her, past the balcony that hung above their heads, the ceiling was snowy white marble. Brilliant light poured down through wide, mirrored shafts in the ceiling.

"As new Potentials, you may go anywhere on this level or the levels below," Fahren said. "The level above us is reserved for the Potentials in the group ahead of yours. This year's sacrifice will take place in six months, during the Summer Solstice. At that time, you will move up to that level. Six months after that, during the winter solstice, a new group of Potentials will enter the

Temple. Until the next Sacrifice, your quarters are on this level. There are four living quarters for the Potentials. Each of you will be assigned another Potential as your companion. You will live, eat, sleep, study, and train with your companion. Do you have any questions?"

"Yes, Priestess," Veenja said. "Why are parts of the Temple so dark, and parts so light?"

Fahren smiled. "A good question. The outer portions of the Temple are dark to symbolize the darkness in which we were lost before we awakened the Fiery One. The inner parts of the Temple glow with the radiance of his holy light."

Janaié raised her hand. "I have a question, Priestess."

"Yes?"

"Can I be assigned as her companion?" She took Kheema's hand. Kheema gaped at her in astonishment.

"Do you know each other?"

"Not yet," Janaié said.

Fahren laughed. "We do encourage fraternization among the Potentials. It is written, ask the Fiery One for that which your heart desires. If your desire is pure…"

"…he shall provide it in abundance," Janaié said. She smiled shyly. "My desire may not be entirely pure."

"What about you, Kheema? Do you want Janaié as your companion?"

Kheema looked at Janaié, who winked coquettishly at her. "Um, I, sure," she stammered.

"Very well. So it is done. Now, on the left, you will find the quarters for the Potentials and for the initiates. To the right are the library, the study chambers, and the testing rooms. Below us are the living and recreation areas for the priests and priestesses. On the left side of the park are the chapel and the dining hall. To the right are the living quarters for the High Priestess and previous Sacrifices." She gestured in the air, flicking her fingertips in an intricate pattern. A glowing schematic of the Temple appeared in the air before her. "If you ever get lost, ask a priestess or call up a map." She gestured again. The hologram vanished. "Follow me. I will show you to your quarters."

She led the group of Potentials along the balcony to the left. They rounded the corner, traveling along the side of the atrium overlooking the garden until they arrived at a row of doors in the wall. Each was made of the same white marble as the walls and the floor. A thin horizontal red band, glowing faintly, marked each door.

"Red is for the Potentials," Fahren said. "White is for Initiates. Gold is for Priestesses. Blue is for Priests. Red and gold is for High Priestesses. Blue and gold is for High Priests. They stay on the level just above the park."

Lianya raised her hand. "Can men ever become Grand High Priest?"

"The Grand High Priestess is always a former Sacrifice." Fahren said. "The Sacrifice always inhabits a female body during their service. Those who feel called to serve in such a capacity can choose to change their bodies afterward if they wish, of course. Now then." She gestured. The door beside her parted silently. "Janaié, Kheema, this will be your room. You will find everything you need inside. Please make yourselves at home. You may feel free to explore the Temple as you wish, except the floor above us. Or you may rest tonight. Your training starts tomorrow."

Janaié stepped across the threshold first. Kheema followed into a sumptuously appointed room much larger than she expected. Two wide curving couches flanked an enormous bed in the center of the room, all decorated in shades of red and gold. A smooth black panel in the wall marked the Provider, from which clothing, food, and other necessities could be called forth.

Kheema explored the quarters. A sliding rice paper door opened into a large sitting room. Beyond that, she found a bathing room, where four broad, shallow steps descended into a large rectangular tub set into the floor.

When she came back, she found Janaié standing in front of the Provider, wearing a long, filmy red robe, open in the front, made of a material so light its tail almost floated in the air behind her. Kheema could clearly see Janaié through the thin fabric. "This is the only clothing it will give me," Janaié said. "I think it's all we're supposed to wear."

Kheema touched the featureless rectangle. A glowing hologram appeared in front of her. As Janaié said, the red robe was the only choice of clothing available, beyond a simple pair of red sandals. She moved her finger. A slot opened in the blank black face. A robe identical to Janaié's appeared within it.

"Put it on!" Janaié said.

Kheema slipped it on. The short sleeves barely covered her shoulders. It settled down behind her, so light she could scarcely feel it. There was no closure in the front.

"Mirror," Janaié said. The wall beside her turned silver. She moved back and forth in front of the mirror, watching as the robe floated behind her body. It slowly settled around her when she was still. "Isn't it beautiful?" she said. "We're here! We're really here! One of us will be chosen to be sacrificed to the Sun God! Oh, I do hope it's me. Or you, but I really hope it's me." She sat on the soft red blanket spread over the bed. "Do you think it's true?"

"What?" Kheema said.

"What Fahren said about us not being able to have an orgasm."

"I don't know," Kheema said. "I can't imagine why she'd lie to us."

"Maybe it's another test," Janaié said. "I'm going to find out. Would you like to help me?"

"I—" She looked into the women's dark eyes, open and earnest. "Um, sure. Okay."

"Thank you! Come here." Janaié patted the bed beside her. "I want to kiss you."

Kheema sat beside her. The gown, which barely qualified as clothing, floated behind her. Janaié touched her arm, suddenly shy. The touch made Kheema's skin tingle.

"Did you feel that too?" Janaié said.

"Yes." Kheema husked.

"Will you kiss me?"

"Yes."

Their lips met. Somewhere deep within Kheema, a tiny glowing ember flared into flame. The same dizzying, intoxicating hunger that had overwhelmed her when she received the Blessing of Fire took her once more, a burning need so powerful it frightened her. She kissed Janaié hungrily, desperately, lost in a maelstrom of desire.

Janaié looked into Kheema's eyes, panting. "Wow. You're a good kisser."

"It's not me," Kheema said. "It's the Blessing."

"I think it's also you. Kiss me again."

They kissed once more. Janaié caressed Kheema's thigh. Her hand slid up Kheema's side, gentle and unbearable. Kheema's heart thudded.

Janaié slipped her other hand between her own legs. She moaned softly, touching herself as they kissed. Her tongue flicked against Kheema's lips. Her breathing quickened. Her eyes closed. She kissed Kheema more frantically, her hand cupping Kheema's breast. Her fingers moved faster and faster. Her back arched. Kheema slid her tongue between Janaié's lips. Janaié stroked herself urgently, fingers flitting in small quick circles around her clit, until her body tightened, and she shuddered. She closed her eyes, panting, body shaking.

Then, suddenly, she stopped. "It's no good," she said. "I can't quite get there." She lay back on the bed, legs parted. "Maybe it will work if you help? Touch me. Please."

Kheema bent over her, running her hand lightly up her body, across her stomach. She slid her palm over Janaié's breast, feeling her nipple press against her hand. She leaned down, kissing her lips softly. Janaié masturbated furiously, her fingers a blur, her breath a series of short gasps. "More! Please!"

Kheema took Janaié's nipple between her lips. Janaié cried out, pressing Kheema's head down. She spread her legs wide, pressing herself up against her own fingers, moaning.

Then she stopped once more. "Nope, it's just not happening." She looked up into Kheema's eyes, caressing Kheema's hair. "By the light, this is going to be frustrating. When do you think they'll give us the antidote?"

"I don't know," Kheema said.

"Will you kiss me again anyway?"

"Yes."

Kheema and Janaié did not explore the Temple that evening. Nor did they rest. Instead, they spent the evening exploring one another, testing the barriers that separated them from sexual satisfaction. Time after time, they brought each other right to the edge of orgasm, only to be denied. They slept that night in a tangle of arms and legs, bodies pressed together. Dreams of desire and frustration filled Kheema's head.

1.3

KHEEMA AND JANAIÉ woke the next morning to a low, persistent chiming. Kheema untangled herself from Janaié and rubbed sleep from her eyes.

A pleasant, feminine voice came from all around them, without any apparent source. "All Potentials must be ready for breakfast and worship in one hour."

Kheema sat up. She recalled a dream of warm lips on bare skin, and then it was gone.

Janaié reached out to touch her arm. "Come back to bed. Cuddle me," she said, voice blurry with sleep.

"We need to get up. Breakfast in an hour."

"Ungh." Janaié pulled the blanket off her body with reluctance. She swung her feet to the floor. "Drink. Hot. Sweet."

The blank surface of the Provider flipped open. Janaié took a steaming mug from within and raised it to her lips.

Kheema tossed her crumpled robe into the slot. The Provider closed. Within its depths, the atoms that made it were torn apart, ready to be reassembled into something else.

Kheema padded naked into the bathing room. "Water," she said.

The sunken tub filled with warm water. The small black Provider set into the floor next to it opened, revealing a seafoam green cube. Kheema dropped it into the water. Her nose filled with the scent of flowers. She stepped down into the warm water. She sat back, closing her eyes as it enveloped her.

Presently, Janaié came into the room. She stepped into the tub next to Kheema. "Thank you for trying to help me last night, even if it didn't work. Would you like me to do your back?"

"That would be lovely."

"When you ask the servants of the Fiery One for what your heart desires, they will provide it if they can," Janaié said. She placed her hands on Kheema's shoulders, drawing her back against her body. "Ask me for that which your heart desires," she murmured in Kheema's ear.

Kheema relaxed, eyes closed. The scent grew stronger, heady and pleasant. She became acutely aware of the feel of Janaié's body against hers, of the caress of Janaié's hands. Those hands slid up her body, caressing her breasts. Her head grew light.

She opened her eyes. The room was filled with a golden glow. "I think…" she said. Her tongue seemed reluctant to form words. "I think they've given us something," she said. "It's in…in the water…"

Then the hunger washed over her, leaving no room for any thought. She turned, clutching at Janaié, pulling her close, kissing her frantically. Her body vibrated with the intensity of her need.

Janaié kissed her fiercely, answering her desire with desire. She explored Kheema's body, fondling and caressing her. Kheema cried out when Janaié's fingers found her swollen clit. She pressed her hips forward, teeth sinking into Janaié's neck. Janaié moaned with pleasure.

Three times, Kheema felt the tension of orgasm, building inside her. Three times, it slipped away at the last moment, leaving her gasping. Tears of frustration filled her eyes. "It's not fair!" she cried.

"Shh," Janaié said. "Shh. Just go with it. Feel my hands." Her fingers stroked Kheema's nipple. The sensation overwhelmed her, almost painful in its intensity. "Enjoy what you can." Her lips found Kheema's.

The chime sounded again. The pleasant, directionless voice filled the air. "Please be ready for breakfast in ten minutes."

Kheema groaned. She pried herself from Janaié's grasp. The water drained from the tub.

Janaié stood, arms held out. "Dry," she said.

Nothing happened. "Dry," she said again.

The blank black rectangle opened. A pair of towels appeared within it.

"Huh," Janaié said. She picked up one of the towels. "I guess we do it by hand. If you dry me, I'll dry you."

When they were dry, they trotted back to the main room. Janaié summoned a robe from the Provider. The door beeped.

"View," she said. The door turned transparent—an illusion created by a cunning trick of holographic projection. On the other side, Fahren waited.

Kheema summoned a robe for herself. "Open." The hologram winked out. The door slid silently aside.

Fahren moved down the hallway, collecting the rest of the Potentials. All of them seemed restless. "Did you sleep well?" Fahren asked.

"No!" Chanae said. Her short dark hair was still damp.

Beside her, Eranis chuckled. "You didn't let me sleep, either."

"I couldn't help it!"

"You have all given yourself to service," Fahren said. "Your bodies are instruments of the Fiery One's light. The fires of your own desire will help temper you for the Sacrifice. This way."

They descended the stairs to the park—all of them save Veenja, who sauntered over to the float tube. She hung there for a moment, her blue-gray hair and red robe drifting weightlessly around her, before floating gently to the park many stories below. When the group of Potentials reached the bottom of the stairs, she left the float tube, beaming, "I love doing that!"

Lianya wrinkled her nose. "Those things always make me ill."

Veenja clapped her hands together with delight. "Floating is so much more fun than walking!"

They followed a small group of white-robed priestesses along a path through the park. They passed a small stone fountain beside the path, decorated with sculptures of two women cavorting nude. One of the stone women held a pot over her third arm. A stream of water fell from the pot into a seashell-shaped bowl. A priestess in front of them, a slender young woman with long hair of pure white, ran long four-jointed fingers through the water as she passed.

Fahren brought them to the dining hall, a cavernous semicircle carved from the wall of the chamber. Sunlight poured in from slots in the ceiling, muted and softened by panes of frosted glass. The walls curved upward, arching overhead to the vaulted ceiling. Panels of light-colored wood, polished until they gleamed, covered the walls and ceiling. Alternating squares of wood and stone tiled the floor beneath their feet.

Tables and chairs filled the vast space without any order Kheema could see, some large enough for dozens of people, others small enough for two. Laughing, chattering people sat around the tables.

Silence descended as the group of new Potentials entered. Every eye turned toward them. Kheema could feel the palpable weight of their attention. When they passed one of the small tables, an exquisitely beautiful woman with copper hair reached out to touch Kheema's arm. Kheema's breath caught at the woman's touch.

Fahren led them on a circuitous path through the room to the front, where an elevated platform hugged the curved wall. Two tables flanked the platform, one draped with red, the other with gold. Eight women sat at the table with the gold covering, all wearing gowns identical to Kheema's but gold rather than red. Between the tables sat a longer table draped with white, threaded with red and gold. Several women sat at that table, wearing gowns like Fahren's.

"Look!" Janaié said. "It's Seeva! She was Sacrifice four years ago. And that's Hani! She was the Sacrifice—"

"Okay, okay, we get it," Sakim said. Fahren pursed her lips.

"The gold table is for the current Potentials, one of whom will be named as Sacrifice at the next summer solstice," Fahren said. "The red table is for you. The table between, as Janaié has surmised, is for past Sacrifices who have chosen to remain. If you will, please take your seats."

Kheema stepped onto the elevated platform. As one, all the Priestesses rose. They turned to face the small group of women, then knelt, eyes down, until everyone in Kheema's group was seated. Then they rose and took their seats again. The burble of conversation gradually returned.

"I wonder if they do that every day," Chanae said.

"I hope not," Sakim replied. "It feels weird."

"To you, maybe," Veenja said. "I like having people watch me. It's nice."

"Is that why you want to be the Sacrifice?" Chanae said.

"Partly. And partly because it looks like fun."

"Fun?" Chanae's eyebrows shot up. "An entire day of suffering, from sun-up to sundown, and then the sharing of the blessing, sounds fun to you?"

Veenja shrugged gracefully. "Yes. What about you? Why did you volunteer?"

It was Chanae's turn to shrug. "I'm still young. I want to experience something new. My siblings are all older than I am. They—"

"How old are you?" Sakim interrupted.

"Forty-eight."

Eyes widened around the table. "Forty-eight? You're only forty-eight?" Eranis said. "I feel dirty."

"Yes." Chanae blushed. "If they choose me, I will be the youngest Sacrifice ever given to the Sun God. My youngest sibling is twenty-seven years older than I am. My next older sister is twenty years older than she, and my oldest sibling is thirty-six years older than her. She—"

"Hold on," Sakim said. "You have three siblings? That sounds suffocating. I don't think I could handle a family that large."

"Everyone in my family has lots of kids. Always have. My youngest sister was chosen last year as Sacrifice to the Quickener. That was supposed to be my destiny, too. I don't know, I just figured I wanted to do my own thing, not always follow behind my siblings, you know? So, here I am."

"The Quickener?" Sakim said. "You're Chanae of the House Everessa? That Chanae?"

She looked down at the table. "Yes. I just...I don't want that to be what defines me."

"You're famous!"

"Maybe I don't want to be famous. Maybe I want to be me."

Sakim snorted. "Being chosen as a sacrifice to the Lord of Light will make you even more famous than you already are. If you just want to be you, shouldn't you go out into the Wastelands or something?"

Chanae shook her head.

Conversation died. In the silence, Miati, Grand High Priestess of the Fiery One—a tall, regal woman with chocolate skin—swept into the room. She wore a translucent white robe with a complex interlocking pattern of red and gold stripes. Everyone in the hall stood as one.

Belatedly, Kheema rose to her feet. She watched the woman approach and mount the platform. Something about her made it impossible for Kheema to look away. It was not just her beauty, though she had that—skin as flawless as a warm summer day, large luminous eyes, straight hair the color of midnight that fell to the middle of her back. She carried herself with an easy confidence that suggested mountains would move out of her way. When she drew close, Kheema noticed that her eyes were a purple so dark they were nearly black, flecked with gold. One pupil was a horizontal slit, like a cat's eyes turned sideways, while the other eye had no pupil at all.

She stood at the center table, her arms raised to the sky. "We thank the Sun God, who provides for us," she said.

"Praise be to the Sun God," all the people in the chamber said in unison. "Praise be to his light."

Miati sat. Everyone else in the hall followed her example. A moment later, panels opened in the tables, revealing plates of food. Conversation resumed.

"Kheema," Chanae said. "What about you? Why are you here?"

"I always envied the servants of the Fiery One," Kheema said. "They have a purpose, you know? Their lives have meaning. A lot of people just seem to exist. I guess maybe I wanted a feeling of purpose, too. Like I was part of something bigger."

"Isn't just being here purpose enough?" Lianya said. "I mean, just being born into this world is a blessing." She spread her arms. "What else could you want?"

"An orgasm," Janaié said. The rest of the table laughed.

"I don't know," Kheema said. "I just…I was communing with a priest out in the courtyard and I just…I felt him calling to me. I can't explain it. I felt his presence in a way I never have before. It was like…like a moment of clarity. I knew what I had to do. So, here I am."

"I'm envious," Chanae said. "I've always had other people tell me what my purpose was. I've never felt it."

"Are you sure it was purpose you felt?" Sakim said. "I've felt many things while communing with a priestess. For a little while, anyway." She smiled coyly.

1.4

AFTER BREAKFAST, THE High Priestess stood. Everyone in the hall stood with her. They all waited while she and the other priestesses at the center table departed. Fahren did not accompany them. Instead, she came to the table where Kheema and her fellow Potentials waited. "Follow me to the chapel," she said. "After morning service, we will start your training. This way."

Kheema and the others followed Fahren across the atrium into the chapel, a soaring space filled with light. Like the dining hall, it was a huge semicircle carved from the stone wall, though much grander in scale. The ceiling arched four stories above them. Sunlight flooded in from skylights overhead. Large hexagons of dark granite and snowy marble tiled the floor. Alternating bands of light and dark wood paneled the walls. Small sparkling gold motes hung suspended in the air in the vast open space.

Rows of long polished bamboo benches upholstered with thick, soft cushions of red and gold silk filled most of the floor. Two rows of balconies, one on each side, hugged the wall, reached by curved marble stairs and transparent glass float-tubes. People crowded the balconies and pews. Some wore white robes, most unadorned, a handful decorated with red, a few with red and gold. Others were bare-chested, and wore simple loincloths trimmed with blue or blue and gold.

At the front of the chapel, beneath the highest point of the ceiling, stood a low dais. Sixteen chairs sat facing the congregation, eight red and eight gold, behind a low balustrade. A pulpit of polished white wood stood in the center of the dais, just in front of the row of chairs. Eight cords of braided red silk waited in a neat row on the pulpit. A row of eight slender marble pillars stood in a line between the dais and the congregation. A small crystal bowl filled with a shimmering golden liquid rested atop each of the pillars.

Fahren directed the Potentials to the red chairs on the dais. The gossamer robe swirled briefly in the air behind her, then settled gently around her body. The gold chairs remained empty.

After the Potentials were seated, Miati entered through a door in the back. Kheema rose with the rest of the congregation. As the Grand High Priestess approached the pulpit, Kheema stared at her, entranced by her charismatic grace. When she had taken her place behind the pulpit, the assembled congregation sat.

Miati raised her arms. The dancing motes of light coalesced around her, until she seemed to glow with golden light.

"In the beginning," she said, "humanity was lost in darkness. There were none to guide us. There were none to provide for us. Our existence was marked by great tribulations. Suffering was our destiny, sorrow our companion. Yet within us, a tiny spark of Light burned. We looked to the darkness of the heavens and were inspired. We left our home behind. We ventured among the stars, seeking new places where we might cast off the chains that bound us. In this place, far from our home, the Eight gave life to the Lord of Light, first among the gods. He bestowed his blessing upon us, that we might carry it to others."

"Praise the Fiery One," the congregation said.

"Each year, on the day of the Summer Solstice, we choose a Sacrifice to remind us of the suffering we endured before the Awakening. Today, we welcome a new group of Potentials. One of them will be chosen as Sacrifice in just eighteen months, to come after the Sacrifice who will be chosen at the next Solstice."

"May his light fill the world," came the response.

"Today we present the new Potentials, upon whom we place our hopes for his blessing," Miati said.

Fahren directed Kheema and the others to step forward. Miati handed each woman one of the braided silk cords. Fahren instructed the Potentials to line up in front of the dais. Kheema's robe fluttered in the air behind her. She could feel the weight of the covetous eyes on her body.

Eight white-robed figures rose from the front pew and came forward. A short, slender woman with deep amber eyes took the cord from Kheema's hands. She brought Kheema's wrists behind her back and bound them there with the cord. On both sides of her, others bound the Potentials' hands behind their backs.

The eight priestesses stepped back. Each dipped a glass rod into the bowls of sparkling golden liquid that sat atop the eight pillars. The woman who had bound Kheema's hands held the rod up to her lips. Kheema extended her tongue. A shimmering drop fell onto it.

She swallowed. Her body surged with electricity. The hunger came upon her so fast she nearly stumbled. Her skin flushed. Her nipples hardened. Beside her, Chanae moaned.

"Please come forward, that you may get to know the Potentials before you go out to spread his light today," Miati said.

The members of the congregation rose and formed into long lines that snaked through the cathedral. Eight by eight, the servants of the light came forward. Each received a drop of golden liquid on an outstretched tongue. Then, pupils constricted to tiny points, they examined the Potentials.

The first person to examine Kheema was a short, slender priestess with brilliant orange eyes that matched her short orange hair. She ran soft, warm hands over Kheema's body, rolling Kheema's nipples between her inner thumbs and forefingers while the sharpened tip of her outer thumbs slid along the sides of Kheema's breasts. Kheema shivered at her caress. She lingered over Kheema's breasts, fondling them until Kheema whimpered with need.

After she was finished, a large, brown-skinned man with wide yellow eyes approached. He received the Blessing of Fire from the glass rod. A bulge grew beneath his loincloth. He put his hands on Kheema, caressing her shoulders, her side, her breasts. He kissed her neck so gently she shuddered with longing.

Kheema lost all sense of time. Her world shrank to nothing but the people caressing her body and the wild need within her. Lips and tongues explored her, probing her lips, tasting her neck. Strangers slid warm hands over her skin. A slender woman with brilliant green eyes slipped a finger easily inside her. Kheema cried out. The sound echoed in the vast hall.

More priests and priestesses touched her, stroking, fondling, caressing. Kheema closed her eyes, panting, overwhelmed by raging desire. She pressed herself forward against the people who explored her body, returning their kisses with heedless abandon. Her body quivered with every touch. Sensation poured through her, overwhelming her, until all reason was gone, and she could do nothing but writhe, panting, beneath the ceaseless assault. Wetness flowed steadily from between her legs. She tugged at the rope binding her wrists, desperate to touch the people who examined her, but it remained tight.

27

It seemed to go on for hours. Her body built closer and closer to an orgasm that never came. Probing fingers slid inside her until she wept with her need.

At long last, Kheema's torment ended. She opened her eyes, panting, and saw that the chapel was empty. Her body glowed with sweat. From all around, she heard whimpers and moans from the other Potentials.

Fahren walked down the line of desperate women, releasing the cords that bound their wrists. Immediately, Kheema slid her hands over her breasts. Fahren pulled her hands away from her body. "No," she said. "You must learn to control yourself despite your need. Your first duty is service to others, not yourself." She turned toward the others. "Follow me to the Hall of Memory."

She led the eight of them along one of the winding paths through the garden, toward the wall opposite the cathedral. Kheema could still feel the hands caressing her, like afterimages on her skin. Her body thrummed.

The path ended at a round opening edged in black obsidian. It led into a hallway that reminded Kheema of a tunnel, with glassy smooth walls of the same polished obsidian that curved overhead. Little points of light drifted deep beneath the surface of the walls, lighting their way with a dim glow.

"The Hall of Memory reminds us of the darkness in which all humanity lived before the awakening of the Sun God," Fahren said. Her voice echoed from the walls. "Here you will learn to repeat the entire Litany from memory. The Litany is our history. Whichever one of you is chosen must recite it without error during the Sacrifice."

"What happens to Sacrifices that don't get it right?" Janaié said. Her voice quavered with suppressed need.

"Only one Sacrifice has ever failed," Fahren said. "That was one hundred and eight years ago. She was unable to recite the whole of the Litany before the sun set."

"What happened to her?"

Fahren took a deep breath. An expression of sorrow crossed her face. "It may seem like we are harsh in our training, even cruel. But we do this for the greater good. The gods do not take kindly to those who fail them. We train you the way we do to make sure whichever of you becomes Sacrifice will not fail."

"But what if we do?" Janaié persisted. "What happened to her?"

"The God of the Sun hid his face behind the clouds for an entire week," Fahren said. "The other Potentials in her group were also sacrificed, one each day for seven days. The one who failed was given to the crowds who came to watch as an offering of atonement. After the week of penance, the Fiery One returned. The one who failed became his Oracle for eighty days and eighty nights. To touch the mind of a god…it drives a person mad." She shook her head. "Afterward, she left the City, but whether she was exiled or she chose to go, only the gods know. Nobody knows what became of her. Not even the gods, I expect. Or if they do, they will not speak to us about it. She was erased from the memory of the City. Only a handful of us who serve the Fiery One even remember."

"Why would the gods do such a thing to one of their faithful?" Chanae asked.

Fahren shrugged. "Who knows why? Perhaps they wish to punish transgressions. Perhaps they want us to rise to the best we can be. Maybe we're their playthings, or their pets. It's dangerous to try to understand the mind of a god. The gods provide for us and expect no more from us than what we choose to give, but if we promise them something, they take our promises seriously. Ah, here we are."

She placed her hand on the wall. A curved door slid up into the ceiling.

"This is a Memory Room," she said. "Each of you will study in one of these rooms with your companion. Every day, you will learn more of the Litany. Kheema, Janaié, this room is yours."

She led them into a small, snug chamber with walls of the same glossy black obsidian as the hallway. Dense carpet decorated with an intricate pattern of lines and geometric forms covered the floor, so soft that Kheema's feet sank into it. As she stepped into the room, tiny dots of light flowed through the plush piles of carpet, rippling outward from her feet like glowing marine creatures giving way before the prow of a ship.

Fahren made a graceful gesture in the air. From the floor in the center of the room, an oval shape appeared, growing upward as though being extruded from the floor. The carpet stretched and flowed around it. Tiny points of light scurried over its surface.

She gestured again. A hatch opened in the wall. A small shelf extended, bearing two small glass vials filled with shimmering liquid. Janaié hid behind Kheema. A tiny whimper of fear escaped her.

Fahren picked up one of the vials. She raised it to Kheema's lips. Kheema shivered again. Slowly, reluctantly, she forced herself to open her mouth. Fahren turned the vial upside-down. A single glimmering drop of liquid fell onto her tongue.

The sensation hit so fast Kheema's knees gave way. Fahren caught her effortlessly. Then the frenzy was upon her, and Kheema kissed her, rough and urgent, both arms wrapped around Fahren, holding her body tightly.

Fahren held her until the first wave of desperation had passed. "Breathe," she said. "That's it. Breathe. You must learn to control it. Let it flow through you." Kheema drew in a long, ragged breath. Fahren nodded. "Good. Yes, like that."

Kheema trembled. Golden light filled the room. She could feel it vibrating all around her, warm on her skin.

Fahren released her. "Lie down." She guided Kheema to the oval shape that had risen from the floor, helping her to lie on her back. The soft surface welcomed her, embracing her, warm and soft beneath her body.

Kheema closed her eyes. From somewhere a long way away, she heard Fahren say, "Now, you, Janaié. Accept the Blessing." A moment later, she heard Janaié let out a throaty cry of longing and need.

"Here in the Hall of Memory, countless Potentials before you have learned the Litany just like this," Fahren said. She knelt beside Kheema, placing her hands on Kheema's body. The motes of light flowed up from the carpet, crawled down Fahren's arms, and swarmed over Kheema's skin. They gathered around Fahren's hands. She caressed Kheema. A trail of glowing flecks followed her hands. They swirled and coalesced, forming words that hovered, ephemeral, on Kheema's skin.

Kheema gasped beneath Fahren's warm, soft hands. Electric currents of exquisite pleasure followed Fahren's fingertips across her skin. She arched her back with a moan.

"Don't move," Fahren said. "Each day, you and your companion will alternate who is the Reader and who is the Book. As Reader, you will read the words aloud, so that you may both memorize the Litany. As Book, you must remain still under the hands of your Reader. The more pleasure the Book experiences, the more clearly the words will form." Her fingers moved up, over the curve of Kheema's breasts, across her achingly sensitive nipples. The swirling, glowing letters followed. Kheema gripped the edge of the platform tightly and moaned again.

"Priestess?" Janaié asked.

"Yes?"

"What was it like? You know, when you were sacrificed."

Fahren smiled a dreamy smile. "Agony," she sighed. "Now it is time for you to begin your studies."

1.5

Fahren left the Memory Room. The other Potentials followed. The door closed silently behind them. Janaié knelt beside Kheema. Silence settled around them, broken only by Kheema's breathing.

Gently, tentatively, Janaié placed her hands on Kheema's body. Lights swirled around her fingers, outlining them in glowing gold. She moved her hands across Kheema's body. The golden light formed loops and swirls beneath her fingers. Kheema squirmed.

Janaié moved her fingers up over Kheema's breasts, along her shoulders, across the hollow of her throat. The whorls formed letters, then words. Kheema sighed, lips parted, breathing fast. Janaié read the words out loud. Her voice filled the small quiet place.

> *In the beginning was the Darkness. The first people came forth into the Darkness, and their lives were shrouded in night. Many were their trials, short were their lives, and great was their suffering, for in darkness they dwelt, and the darkness dwelt within them.*
>
> *Into the Darkness came a spark of Light. The light touched the hearts of some, so they felt its presence.*

They took the Light to the people, but the people accepted it not, for they dwelt in the darkness, and darkness was all they knew.

The people lived, and they died, but the spark of Light remained, for where the Light has been, it may never be erased.

And the people spread across the land, for they were fruitful, and they did multiply. Wherever they went, they carried the Darkness with them, but the Light went with them also.

The people looked up to the sky, where they saw the lights in the vault of the heavens, and they wondered. Some of the people turned their faces away from the sky, for the Darkness lived in their hearts, and Darkness abhors the Light.

Yet some of the people turned toward the sky, and the Light grew within them, for the Light calls always to the Light.

Kheema writhed under Janaié's touch. Janaié's voice reverberated through the room, filling Kheema's mind as the touch of her hands filled Kheema's senses, until the sensations merged, and she felt as though she was being caressed by the golden words that Janaié spoke.

The Light of the heavens spoke to the Light in the hearts of the people, leading them away from the Darkness. But the Darkness, which hungers always, sought to pull them back. And the people whose hearts were touched by the Darkness opposed them, saying 'cast your eyes not to the heavens, for there is nothing there for us, only death.' And they burned the forests, saying 'lo, we will make unto us a light of our own,' until the sky was choked with ash, and the waters became poison.

Janaié ran her hands over Kheema's body, summoning forth the words of the Litany. Kheema roiled with pleasure. She felt an orgasm grow ever closer, until even the lightest touch made her cry out with need. She spasmed, her body convulsing under Janaié's touch, but the release never quite arrived.

Still Janaié caressed her, reading aloud the words that poured out over Kheema's skin. The letters flowed over Kheema's body, following behind Janaié's soft warm hands. Kheema felt herself contract between her legs. Wetness leaked from her. "Please," she said, though she wasn't even sure what she was asking for. "Please…"

34

Then, all at once, the tiny motes of light winked out. The room went completely dark. Janaié took her hands from Kheema's body.

"What—" Kheema said, her voice hoarse.

"I think…" Janaié's voice sounded thinner, no longer filling the space the way it had. "I think that means the lesson is over."

"What happens now?"

Kheema reached up into the velvety blackness for Janaié. She drew Janaié down on top of her. Their lips found each other. Janaié's body pressed warm and heavy against Kheema.

They held each other close, frantic hands exploring one another's bodies in the darkness, until the door slid open and the room gradually grew brighter. Fahren entered. She seemed unsurprised to find them tangled together.

Janaié extricated herself from Kheema's arms. Kheema could not suppress a small sound of disappointment when she pulled away.

"It is time for the afternoon meal," Fahren said. "After that comes the Recitation, then evening service. After supper, you will have an opportunity for private meditation. Tomorrow you will begin again, and each day after that, until you have memorized the whole of the Litany. You will be expected to learn it all before the next Solstice. Follow me, please."

Whimpering softly, her body trembling with need and longing, Kheema followed Fahren into the hall. The other Potentials already waited there. Kheema could still feel Janaié's hands on her body, still hear the echoes of Janaié's words in her ears. Janaié fell into step beside her, so close Kheema felt her warmth. The longing grew stronger.

As they walked down the dark hallway, glossy black walls curving around them, Kheema heard the other Potentials whimpering. An occasional moan reminded her she wasn't alone in her suffering.

They ate at the table in front of the great dining hall. Excited chatter filled the vast space. Priests and priestesses laughed and talked. Kheema's need consumed so much of her attention she barely noticed her food. Janaié sat beside Kheema, occasionally reaching out to caress her beneath the table. With each touch, Kheema's eyes fluttered. Occasional sighs and covert touches from the other Potentials suggested they were just as distracted as Kheema.

After lunch, Fahren led them along a meandering path through the park to another opening in the wall. "This is the Hall of Recitation," she said. A priestess in a floating robe, smooth skin pale in the brilliant sunlight, smiled at them as she passed. Kheema caught a flash of bright pink nipples, hard in the warm air, and felt a sudden stab of desire so powerful she clenched between her legs.

The new hallway was as light as the Hall of Memory was dark. The walls glowed, curving upward to a smoothly arched ceiling. Tiny specks of darkness drifted in that featureless glow, just beneath the surface of the wall. Even the floor below their feet glowed gently. Not a trace of a shadow found its way into that soft light.

"In the Recitation Chambers, you will have the opportunity to repeat what you've learned," Fahren said. "This will be part of your daily routine. Until you are promoted to the higher tier of Potentials after the next Sacrifice, you will do your recitation alone. When you have memorized all the Litany, you will perform your recitation in front of the priestesses of the Temple." She gestured. A door appeared in complete silence where only wall had been a moment before.

The chamber inside was spartan in the extreme. No plush carpet here, just a bare white room whose walls curved to a domed ceiling. The room contained nothing except a white high-backed chair with long armrests and a small padded kneeling bench. The back of the chair reclined at a steep angle. In place of a footrest, it had two stirrups mounted on long slender supports sprouting from its base. The armrests, back, and seat were adorned with wide straps. The sole nod to anything beyond pure utility in the room was the luxurious red and gold fabric that covered the kneeling bench.

"Human memory is a funny thing," Fahren said. "We remember best when we're in the same state we were in when the memory was formed. This is why we make sure you're aroused while you're learning. The Blessing of Fire will help you remember. Kheema, please be seated."

Heart pounding, Kheema sat gingerly on the chair. She shook so badly she nearly slipped off the smooth, soft surface.

"Lie back," Fahren said. She placed her hand on Kheema's shoulder, pressing her back into the chair. Kheema shivered violently at the touch, fighting to prevent herself from embracing Fahren, drawing her down on top of her, pressing her body to hers, lips finding soft skin…

"Focus is important," Fahren said. She drew the straps around Kheema's body, passing one just above and one just under her breasts, cinching them tight. "Remember the words you just heard." She strapped Kheema's arms to the armrests. She raised Kheema's ankles into the stirrups and closed metal shackles over them.

Kheema blushed, bound to the chair with her legs spread wide in front of the other Potentials. Fahren made a gesture in the air. A tray bearing a tiny vial filled with glittering liquid appeared noiselessly from the wall.

Kheema struggled against the straps that bound her. "No! Please!"

"Disobedience is not permitted," Fahren said mildly. She raised the vial to Kheema's lips.

With great reluctance, Kheema extended her tongue. A sparkling drop fell.

Kheema thrashed in her restraints. Her body felt burned hot with need. Wetness flowed from between her legs.

"Wait here," Fahren said. "Someone will be in to assist with your recital in a moment. The rest of you, please follow me."

She left. The door closed behind her, leaving Kheema alone. The only sound was her own ragged breathing and her heart thudding in her ears.

She didn't have long to wait. The door opened with the same eerie noise-lessness. A man entered, bare-chested, dressed in a simple loincloth of red and blue. A small round drone made of gold metal elaborately ornamented with beautiful traceries of silver and blue followed him in.

Kheema's eyes traveled down his smooth, clean-shaven body. He wore his long brown hair tied in a ponytail with a gold ring. His pupils were two tiny black dots in a field of orange. As her eyes moved downward, she realized that the loincloth was cut in front in a deep V, exposing an erect cock. It, too, was entirely hairless.

He smiled beatifically. A musical voice sang out from the tiny drone. "Greetings, Potential! I am Novice Hassen. I have been assigned to help you with your recitation. It is an honor to meet you." The man bowed.

Kheema squirmed in her restraints. She was acutely, embarrassingly aware of how exposed she was, splayed wide open in front of this man, dripping with need, nothing hidden from view. She was also aware of his arousal. Her gaze lingered on his erection. Her body flushed. Her head filled with carnal thoughts of bodies entwining.

He knelt on the padded bench between her legs, hands clasped behind his back. "It is time to begin the recitation," the drone sang.

Kheema tried to summon the memory the words Janaié had coaxed from her body with her fingers. Her skin tingled with desire. "I—I—" She closed her eyes. "In the beginning was the Darkness."

"Yes, that's right," Hassen said. He leaned forward. The tip of his tongue flicked against Kheema's swollen clit.

"The first people came forth—oh! Oh!!" Kheema flailed, back arching, her voice rising to a shriek.

"You must continue," Hassen said as his tongue continued to flit across her clit. "If you wish to be chosen as Sacrifice, you must be able to endure any distraction."

Kheema's chest heaved. "The first people came forth…came forth…" She squeezed her eyes tightly shut, fighting to push back the tornado of desperate need rising through her. "The first people came forth into the darkness, and their lives were shrouded in…oh! Please!"

Hassen continued teasing Kheema's clit with his tongue. She struggled fiercely, twisting and writhing on the chair. "Please!" she cried.

His tongue traced small, gentle circles. Kheema moaned. Tears of frustration leaked from her eyes. "Shrouded in night!" she cried. She tugged helplessly at the straps around her arms. "Many were their trials, short were their lives, and great was their suffering, for in darkness…in darkness… nnngh!" Her back arched, straining against the straps. "In darkness they dwelt, and the darkness dwelt within them! Oh, gods!" Her body shook with the tension of an impending orgasm she knew would not come. "Into the Darkness came a spark of Light! The light touched…it touched…oh! Right there, please! It touched the hearts of some of the people, and they felt its… annnngh!" She let out a scream of pure longing.

Still he kept moving his tongue back and forth, up and down, as he whispered encouragement through the drone. She squirmed and screamed, repeating the first part of the Litany over and over until she lost track of time. Tears streamed down her face. Her body shook, straining for release it could not have.

At long last, Hassen straightened. Kheema cried out, craving the feel of his tongue and relieved that the torment was over. Gently, almost reverently, he unfastened the straps that held Kheema down. She quivered, too weak to stand.

She looked up at him. He seemed outlined in golden light. She could see the desire in his orange eyes, read it in the tension of his body.

"Have…have they given you the blessing that prevents release?" Her voice sounded hoarse in her ears.

He shook his head. "No," the drone sang. "As a novice priest of the Sun God, I may know the pleasure of release. It is only Potentials and those serving in the courtyard who are denied that pleasure."

"Would you like to feel release inside my body?" Kheema asked. "You may, if you wish. I…would like that."

He smiled. "You honor me, Potential. I would also like that. But it is not allowed."

Her eyes strayed down to his erection, so beautifully framed by the cutout in his loincloth. A glistening drop trembled at its tip.

She licked her lips. "I could pleasure you in other ways," she said. Her voice quavered. "I will offer you release with my lips and tongue."

"I am sorry, Potential. Truly, I am humbled by your generosity. But it is forbidden for me to touch you or to know you in that way." He helped her stand. She shivered at his touch. "Come. It is almost time for evening service."

1.6

THE ENTIRE TEMPLE gathered for service, filling the chapel to overflowing. Men and women sat on the long benches, wearing gauzy robes of red, blue, and gold or loincloths similar to Hassen's. Hassen escorted Kheema to the dais, where several of the Potentials in her group already waited, flushed and out of breath. The small drone floated behind.

The congregation stood as Kheema mounted the dais, then resumed their seats after she slid into the chair next to Janaié. Janaié appeared unfocused, breathing heavily, her cheeks burning red, her eyes glazed. Her hair lay in a tousled mess. She turned as Kheema sat, taking her face in her hands, kissing her with urgency.

The chapel grew quiet when Miati entered. The crowd stood as one as she ascended to the pulpit, then sat on signal.

"Today, we will read from the Book of the Eight Hundred," she said. She moved her finger in the air. A glowing rectangle of text appeared, floating in front of her, the letters flowing and changing as she spoke.

> In the early days, there came eight hundred people, descending from the sky. Lost in the Darkness they were, and there was none to guide them, for their eyes were blinded by darkness. Then the Eight arose, guided by the Light, saying, 'upon this rock, we will build a city.'

And so, the eight hundred worked to build a city. And in the city, they built a temple.

The Eight carried within them the knowledge of a new god. In the Temple they labored, for the Light was with them, and the Light was in them.

Janaié put her hand on Kheema's leg. Kheema's heart skipped a beat.

For eight times eighty days the people labored to build the Temple high and deep. On the day the Temple was complete, the Eight said, "Let there be Light." And the God of the Sun awoke.

Janaié's hand slid up Kheema's leg, her fingers probing, questing. They found Kheema's clit. Kheema shuddered, trying not to make a sound. Beside her, Veenja smiled.

And the God of the Sun said, Behold, I have awakened. As you have brought me forth, so shall I bring you out of the Darkness, into the Light. As you have built this City, so shall I protect it.

Kheema closed her eyes. The Grand High Priestess' voice faded away. Kheema floated into a still, dark place, where there was nothing but the heat that filled her body and the feel of Janaié's light touch on her clit.

Something else stirred there in that place, something powerful but delicate, barely perceptible beneath the sensation of Janaié's finger and the sound of her own breathing. It vanished before she could identify it.

All who dwell here shall be under my protection. Those with Light in their hearts, let them come forth and serve me, that they might spread the Light.

Janaié's finger slipped down, seeking entry. Kheema opened her eyes in surprise. She closed her legs. Veenja's smile grew. She put a hand on Kheema's knee and pulled Kheema's legs apart. Janaié's finger slid inside Kheema. Kheema shuddered, knuckles stuffed into her mouth to keep from crying out. She gave a silent prayer of thanks to the Light for the balustrade that prevented the assembled congregation from seeing what was happening.

The City grew and prospered. The Light reached more hearts. More gods came forth, born out of the Light and into the Light. The people were content.

Janaié worked her finger in and out. Veenja caressed Kheema's thigh, nails tracing delicate lines up and down along her skin. Kheema closed her eyes tightly, fists clenched, struggling for control.

It came again, that sense of a presence, something subliminal below the noise of her own desperation and the feel of the hands on her body. With it came a kind of peace, settling down around her. Something within her shifted. Like a person swept away by a raging torrent who suddenly enters calm water, she felt the wild desperation leave, replaced by a sense of tranquility. The raging waters of her need still churned and roiled, but she was no longer helpless in their grip.

> *And the Lord of Light said, on the day when the sun shines longest,*
> *make a sacrifice unto me, that you may remember that I brought*
> *you from the Darkness.*

Kheema pressed herself to the probing fingers. She rode the waves of pleasure that rippled through her body, shivering with delight.

Janaié and Veenja carried on their slow, steady molestation throughout the evening service. Kheema made no effort to resist. She savored the sensation, keeping herself just on the ragged edge of losing control, intoxicated with the thrill of it. Chanae winked in her direction.

Suddenly, the hands were gone. Kheema blinked. It took a moment to realize Miati had stopped speaking, and another to realize the worshippers were waiting for her to stand. She climbed sheepishly to her feet.

After the Grand High Priestess departed, leaving faint swirls of golden light behind her, Fahren came to collect the Potentials. "It's time for private meditation," she said. "Follow me. I'll bring you to your cells."

She led them back through the garden park. Kheema stepped off the smooth stones that paved the path. She paused for a moment to wriggle her toes in the grass, savoring the feel of warm ground beneath her feet. She remained there for a moment, inhaling deeply, while the others continued on. After a moment, she blinked and ran to catch up with them.

The path ended at a blank stone wall. Fahren made a quick, fluid gesture in the air. The seamless surface of the wall sprouted a row of doors. Beyond each was a spacious room, empty except for a great granite boulder in the center.

"Kheema, you're in here." Fahren gestured. "Janaié, here. Veenja, in here please. Tani, Lianya…"

Kheema stepped through the door. A warm directionless glow without visible source filled the room. The door slid closed behind her.

She studied the boulder, an enormous slab of white stone flecked with black. It was roughly circular, so large that three of her would not have been able to wrap their arms around it, and half as high as she was. She climbed up onto it. The stone felt warm and slightly rough beneath her fingers. She sat, surprised to find it quite comfortable.

The light dimmed, so subtly she did not notice at first. A whiff of summer air came to her, fragrant with grass and trees. Slowly, the light seemed to bend, moving and shifting, taking on color, until gradually, the featureless room became a lavish, meticulously crafted garden. The boulder rested in the center of a perfect square of gravel in the center of the garden. Someone had raked complex designs into the gravel. Neat lines of flowering plants, separated by perfect channels of white sand placed with artistic precision, surrounded the patch of gravel. A fence made of dark wood ringed the garden. Beyond the fence, Kheema saw rolling hills.

She hugged her knees to her chest with delight. The scene coalesced, becoming more and more detailed until it looked as real as the rock beneath her.

Kheema relaxed, letting her mind wander. It turned, predictably, to the Hall of Memory, and Janaié's hands caressing her skin. She sighed, smiling.

Gently, slowly, an acute awareness of her body crept into Kheema's thoughts on little cat's feet. Her skin felt exquisitely alive to everything—the texture of the rock beneath her, the tiny motions of air on her skin, the gossamer whisper of the nearly weightless robe touching her back. The hunger began again, the longing and need that had been her companion all day.

Her skin crackled with the desire to be stroked. Wetness formed between her legs. She longed to put her hands on herself, feel her skin warm and soft beneath them…

Her smile grew wider. She remained perfectly still, relaxing into the feeling. *Not just yet*, she told herself, *not just yet…*

A small rise, just the slightest protrusion, rose from the rock right between her legs. If she just moved down a little bit, and leaned forward just so, it would press on her clit…

Still she did not move. The garden around her was still, every leaf and flower motionless in the quiet air.

She focused all of her attention on her desire, indulging in it, feeling the beating of her heart and the throbbing in her clit. She willed herself to greater stillness, concentrating all her thoughts on how badly she wanted someone to touch her, to enter her, to fill her. The more she wanted to move, the more still she sat, encouraging the need, the desire…

The door opened. The garden winked out. She looked up in surprise. Fahren stood there, flanked by the other Potentials. The ache in her legs told her she had not moved for a long time.

She climbed stiffly from the rock. A dull throbbing from between her legs sent little wavelets of longing through her.

Without a word, Fahren led Kheema and the other Potentials back to their quarters. The instant the door closed behind them, Janaié was in Kheema's arms, kissing her with desperate urgency.

Kheema laughed. She took Janaié by the hands. "You're so eager!"

"Why wouldn't I be? What's the point in being coy? It only means you're less likely to get what you want." Janaié pressed Kheema down onto the bed. She knelt over her, kissing her again. Kheema slid her hands over Janaié's breasts, fingers lightly caressing her nipples.

"Mmm, you're probably right," Kheema said after the kiss ended. "So why did you pick me? What made you so bold when you asked to be assigned to me?"

"You're pretty. I wanted you."

"I'm pretty?" Kheema rolled Janaié's nipples lightly between her fingers. "Lots of people are pretty."

"I wanted you. I like indulging my desire—oh!" Janaié's eyes fluttered. She pressed her hands over Kheema's.

"How much do you want me?"

"Oh!" Janaié gasped. "I want you quite a lot." She rocked her hips back and forth in small, quick motions. "I was thinking about you, during meditation. I couldn't stop touching myself."

"You want me quite a lot, do you?" Kheema said. A shiver ran through her. Her desire roiled up inside her, making her clench between her legs. She closed her eyes for a moment, panting, fighting back the volcano of need, struggling against its eruption. "Is it me, or is it just the Blessing they've given us?"

"The Blessing has something to do with it," Janaié said. "But I wanted you before…before then… oh!"

Kheema leaned forward. Her teeth grazed the side of Janaié's neck. "Do you want me to touch you?"

"Yes!" Janaié whimpered.

"Do you want me to kiss you?"

"Please!"

Her tongue lightly touched Janaié's skin. "What is it worth to you?"

"What?"

"You say you want me. I want you to be mine." Kheema placed a row of tiny kisses up the side of Janaié's neck. "I want you to belong to me," she murmured. She took Janaié's earlobe lightly between her teeth. "I want you

45

to give yourself to me. Now and forever. That's my price." She bit Janaié's shoulder, exquisitely lightly. "Everything has a price. You asked for me. You should pay a price. Here, inside." She ran her hand gently over Janaié's heart. "Give this to me. Say you're mine."

"I—" Janaié leaned forward, wild desperation showing in her eyes. Her lips trembled.

"Say you're mine."

"I—I—this isn't fair!"

"Of course it isn't!" Kheema kissed Janaié's lower lip. "You can't control the need inside you. This isn't fair at all. I am taking advantage of you." She ran her hand down Janaié's body. Her fingers pressed between Janaié's lower lips, finding wetness. "Like you took advantage of me during Service. But I play for keeps." Her finger circled Janaié's clit. "Say." She spread Janaié open, just a little bit. "You're." Gently, easily, her finger slipped partway inside. "Mine."

"I—"

"Say you're mine," she murmured in Janaié's ear.

"I—"

"Say you're mine or I will stop."

"No! Please! Don't stop! I'm yours!"

"Do you belong to me?"

"Yes! Yes, I belong to you!" The words came out as a sob.

Kheema smiled. She relaxed, allowing the floodwaters of desire to break through the levee. She stood in their path and let them wash her away. The two women writhed on the bed, lost in their need, allowing it to consume them. They touched and held, kissed and bit, bodies pressing frantically together, feeling the tension build and build with no hope of release, until finally they collapsed in a tangle, too exhausted to continue.

1.7

THE NEXT MORNING, Kheema woke first. She disentangled herself carefully so as not to wake Janaié. She spent several long moments watching her sleep, savoring the memory of their desperate coupling.

After a while, she rose. She placed the tattered remnants of her robe into the Provider and watched it disappear. Then she tiptoed into the bathroom. "Water," she said.

The tub had just finished filling when Janaié appeared in the doorway, blinking sleep from her eyes. She had slept in her robe, which still hung around her body.

A cube materialized from the Provider near the tub. Kheema dropped it into the water and watched it fizz. When it was gone, she took Janaié by the hand and led her into the water. As they sat, the scent of flowers reached her nose.

She was prepared this time. When the shock of arousal hit her, hot and violent, she welcomed it like an old friend. Janaié stiffened as desire took her. Kheema drew Janaié down onto her lap. She pulled her back against her body, arms wrapped around her. "Good morning," she crooned. "Say you're mine."

"What? I—"

Kheema kissed Janaié's neck. Janaié's robe drifted open in the water. Kheema slid her hands over Janaié's breasts, fondling, caressing. "Shh. Say you're mine."

Janaié shivered. Kheema smiled. "It's such a small thing to do. Just a couple of little words, that's all." She stroked Janaié's hard nipples. "Tell me you're mine."

Janaié's eyes closed. "I'm yours."

"Good." Kheema massaged Janaié's shoulders. Her hands ran down her arms. "Remember that today. You belong to me."

When Fahren came to collect them, Kheema followed behind her, keeping one hand lightly on Janaié's back. At breakfast, she held her foot on top of Janaié's but otherwise paid no attention to her, turning instead to chat with Chanae. During the morning service, she rested one hand on Janaié's knee but refused to allow Janaié to touch her. "There will be time for that later," she whispered in Janaié's ear. Janaié pouted. Kheema smiled.

After service, Fahren led the Potentials down the Hall of Memory. A blank spot on the wall became a door at her signal. Kheema and Janaié passed through into the Memory Room. Fahren gestured again. The slot appeared in the wall. A tray slid out, bearing two glittering vials. Kheema held out her tongue. She dug her fingernails into her palm as the need gripped her. Fahren turned to Janaié. A shimmering drop fell on Janaié's tongue. Janaié gasped.

Fahren departed. After the door closed noiselessly behind her, Kheema gestured at the blank wall the way Fahren had. Nothing happened. "Hmm," she said.

"What?"

"Nothing. Lie down. Today it is my turn to read from you."

Janaié relaxed onto her back in the middle of the room. Kheema knelt beside her. The soft carpet yielded under her knees. She reached out. Motes of light flowed from the carpet up over her body and hands until they glowed with a shimmering golden nimbus.

She placed her hands on Janaié's body. Janaié sighed. The points of light flowed from Kheema's hands over Janaié's skin. Dim shapes appeared in the swirling swarm of lights.

Kheema caressed Janaié. The shapes grew clearer, forming themselves into letters. As she stroked and fondled Janaié, the letters resolved, becoming sharper and brighter.

A voice filled the air. Startled, Kheema realized it was hers. The words poured out of her like living things yearning to be free.

For years they were lost. Many were born into Darkness who did not know the Light. But still the Light remained, and the people who knew it could not drive it away.

The words vibrated in the air around them. Kheema moved one hand down, over Janaié's stomach, between her legs. Her fingers found Janaié's clit. Janaié moaned. The moan drew out an answering surge of arousal within Kheema, so powerful it threatened to swamp her delicate control. The letters grew brighter.

> *In the Darkness, the Light grew stronger. One by one, the people who carried it within themselves found each other, for the Light calls always to the Light. And more of the People turned away from the false light they had made, a light that did not illuminate their hearts.*

Kheema slid one finger into Janaié. Janaié arched her back with a cry of pleasure. The letters that formed amidst the swirling light on her body shone like a beacon.

> *And the people said, behold, embrace the Light that is all around you, and cast aside your false light, for it chokes you and poisons you. Many who saw the Light felt its truth and turned from the false light.*
>
> *But there were many who said "No! We have made this light, and it will protect us." For they were choked, yet they knew it not, and the waters poisoned them, yet they cared not.*
>
> *And many of those who embraced the Light were martyred, for the Darkness entered those who lived within it, and their hearts grew hard.*

Kheema's hand closed over Janaié's breast. Her finger slid deeper. Janaié convulsed. The letters grew blinding, filling Kheema's mind with words of golden fire.

> *Those who knew not the Light fought against those who did, crying, "The air chokes us, and the water poisons us. We must put you out from among us, for only then will the air choke us not, and the water poison us not."*
>
> *And the people who knew the Light said, "No, you choke yourself, you poison yourself. We must find another way." Their words were heard by some, and the Light grew.*

Kheema found herself lost in a place of golden light, hardly aware of her hands on Janaié's body or the words that came from her lips. The letters coalesced around her and inside her. As she spoke, each word filled her head. Janaié's moans and gasps became punctuation, emphasizing the words Kheema said.

Then, all at once, the motes of light disappeared, leaving afterimages dancing in Kheema's eyes. She shook her head to clear it. Beneath her hands, Janaié was panting, sobbing softly. "Please," she said, "please don't stop."

Kheema blinked. She slipped her finger from Janaié. It came out covered with wetness. Janaié whimpered.

"Are you mine?" Kheema asked.

"I am yours," Janaié whispered.

"Good." Kheema caressed her, cupping her hand over Janaié's mound. Janaié moaned, pressing up into Kheema's hand. Kheema's heart lurched. Blinding desire descended on her.

The door opened.

Kheema took her hands away. Janaié let out a small sob. Fahren smiled. "Come," Kheema said.

Janaié was subdued during the short walk to the great dining hall. She said little during the afternoon meal. Kheema rested one hand on Janaié's leg as they ate. Janaié leaned against her. Kheema felt the tension vibrating through her.

After the meal, Fahren led them down the Hall of Recitation. Kheema held Janaié's hand on the walk. Turbulent sensation swirled through Kheema's body.

They arrived at the doors into the white rooms with their chairs and straps. Kheema felt a pang of loss when she let go of Janaié's hand.

Kheema climbed into the chair, lifted her legs into the stirrups, and allowed Fahren to strap her down. She extended her tongue for the Blessing of Fire, spasming as the need hit. Her chest heaved. The room filled with golden light. She clenched between her legs.

The door appeared at Fahren's gesture, then disappeared after Fahren left. Kheema waited, alone. Wetness leaked from her.

After a while, the door opened again. Novice Hassen entered, wearing his beatific smile. His pupils were tiny pinpricks in a sea of orange. His erection strained, framed by the deep V in his loincloth.

Kheema's heart pounded. She found herself straining against the straps, struggling to touch him. He knelt, his drone shifting smoothly to follow him. "Are you ready to begin the Recitation, Potential Kheema?"

She shook her head. "No, I—"

He leaned forward. His tongue touched her clit. She cried out, with her hands curled into fists. The words shattered in her head. "I—I—I don't remember!"

He smiled at her from between her legs. "Just speak. The words will come." Kheema keened, a long sound of pure frustration. Her control broke. The floodwaters of her need took her.

She screamed and thrashed and moaned, her body twitching and jerking against the bonds. She wailed, desperate and frantic, and somehow, from that wail came the words.

His tongue teased her with expert precision, flitting over her clit while she screamed out the words of the Litany. Tears ran down her face. His tongue danced, until nothing existed for Kheema but the words that forced themselves from her raw throat and the tumultuous storm of wild lust that raged inside her.

When he stopped, the cessation hit her like a physical slap. She opened her eyes, gasping, staring at him without comprehension.

"I am sorry, Potential, truly," he said. "But the Recitation is over." He rose. Kheema saw a thin trail of glistening whiteness fall from the end of his erect cock. She made a small feeble noise in the back of her throat.

"I am sorry," he said again at her unvoiced question. "It is not allowed." He unfastened the straps that bound her and helped her rise.

The door opened. Fahren appeared.

The other Potentials waited in the hall. Lianya wept openly. Sakim folded her arms, face set in a frown. Chanae pushed Eranis against the wall and kissed her hungrily. Kheema embraced a shaking Janaié.

During the evening service, Kheema ran her fingertips lightly along Janaié's leg. Janaié reached to touch her. Kheema pushed her hand away. Her fingers stroked Janaié's inner thigh. On the other side of her, Veenja slid her hand over Kheema's breast, brazenly groping her. Raw animal need exploded through Kheema. She held on to her control, betraying no outward sign of the heat Veenja's touch ignited in her.

As Miati conducted the service, Kheema watched the other group of Potentials on the far side of the pulpit. Need showed nakedly in a couple of faces. One of the women, short and round with elfin features, squirmed in her seat.

After the service, Veenja kept up her steady, gentle molestation through dinner. Kheema bit her lip, pressing herself involuntarily against Veenja's hand. Her fingers caressed Janaié, one fingertip penetrating her just deeply enough to make her cry out and drop her fork. Chanae giggled. Lianya leaned over to kiss Veenja's shoulder.

After the evening meal, Fahren led the Potentials to the meditation cells. Janaié ran her hand along the inside of Kheema's arm. Kheema staggered and would have fallen had Chanae not caught her. "Oh, hi!" Chanae said. Kheema moaned.

They reached the blank wall at the end of the path. The doors opened at Fahren's gesture. Kheema ran into her cell, grateful to be away from the others. She felt the stormwater rising behind the dike, threatening to crash through without warning. She sat panting on the great granite boulder.

Gradually, the light dimmed and changed. Blurred, hazy outlines crawled across the walls. Kheema forced herself to stillness. Her heartbeat slowed. The image around her resolved into a stream that flowed around the rock, cutting through the center of a sunlit field that extended to the horizon.

An impossible breeze drifted through the cell. Kheema's robe streamed behind her. The warm air curled around her, ruffling her hair, playing lightly over her skin. The hunger grew. She shivered and wrapped her arms tightly around herself. The river flowed faster. Small waves crashed around the rock.

She closed her eyes. Her mind drifted back to the Hall of Memory, the feeling of Janaié's soft warm skin, the scent of her arousal. The wind picked up, driving the stream harder against the boulder.

She rocked back and forth. Her hands moved on their own across her body. Her fingers found her nipples. She gasped. She ground against the protrusion atop the boulder, feeling warm stone press into her clit.

The hunger smashed against her self-control, blasting it to rubble. The dam collapsed. Kheema let out a long, low cry, one hand slipping between her legs. She tugged at her nipple. The waters swirled and thundered around her. Wind whipped at the golden grain growing in the field around her.

She masturbated furiously, driving herself closer and closer to orgasm until her body trembled. The storm raged, driving the stream higher. She wept with frustration, twisting her nipple hard, pressing her fingers roughly against her clit, punishing her body for its refusal to give her release. Her hair whipped around her tear-streaked face. Her robe streamed out in front of her, threatening to tear itself from her body.

She dug her nails into her breasts, using the pain as a lifeline up out of the maelstrom. Her toes curled. She forced herself to take a deep breath and hold it, pushing away the ravenous hunger screaming through her. Bit by bit, she re-established control, reclaiming her body one inch at a time from the chaos.

She forced herself upright on her knees. She spread her fingers, taking her hands off her body, eyes closed. She took a long breath, held it for a moment, then exhaled softly.

She opened her eyes. The wind died down. Overhead, the sun reappeared from behind a cloud. The golden fields grew still.

Her body cried out to be touched. She trembled, longing to be filled. She inhaled again, allowing the feelings to wash through her without taking command of her. Breathe. Exhale. Inhale. Exhale.

When she opened her eyes once more, the stream babbled gently as it made its slow way down its bed. In the fields, not a stalk moved.

Kheema smiled.

When the door opened, Kheema sat cross-legged on the boulder, her eyes closed, savoring the desire that seethed and bubbled just below the surface. She rose before Fahren could call her. Fahren raised an eyebrow.

Outside the cell, Janaié waited for her. Kheema took her hand. Her breath caught. She closed her eyes for a moment, enjoying the hot flash of sexual need brought on by the touch of Janaié's skin. On the way back to the Potentials' quarters, Fahren trailed behind with a thoughtful expression on her face.

The moment Kheema and Janaié were back in their quarters, Janaié launched herself at Kheema, peppering her face and neck with kisses. Kheema laughed and took her by the shoulders. "What do you want?"

"I want you!"

"Do you need me?"

"Yes! I need you."

"Are you mine?"

"I am yours!"

Kheema laughed again. "Stand still. Stand perfectly still and you can have me."

Janaié grinned. She made a show of standing to attention, ramrod straight. Kheema guided her backward, pressing her shoulders to turn her this way and that. "Let's see here. Where should I put you?" She pushed Janaié back against the wall. "Right here, I think." She drew closer, until her lips lightly brushed against Janaié's. "Do you want me to touch you?" she breathed.

"Yes!"

"I want to touch you, too," Kheema said. It was the truth; her skin ached for it. "Stay perfectly still." She placed Janaié's hands at her side, palms flat against the wall. "Don't...move." Her lips brushed Janaié's neck. "If you move, the game is over."

"What—"

"Don't move." She drew Janaié close for a long, deep kiss. Her tongue flitted across Janaié's lips. Then she stepped back. She ran her hands down Janaié's neck, over her shoulders, down across her breasts. Her fingertips dragged lightly over Janaié's nipples. Janaié sighed.

Kheema kissed her again, lightly this time, her lips just touching Janaié's. She moved her hand slowly down Janaié's body, caressing her stomach, then lower, across her mound. Janaié made a small whimper of desire.

"Don't…move." Kheema's fingers probed between Janaié's legs. They slid easily into her without resistance. Janaié's eyelids fluttered. She moaned.

Kheema ran the tip of her tongue along the soft skin at the side of Janaié's neck. Her fingers began to move, working small circles inside Janaié. Her thumb found Janaié's clit. Janaié trembled like an autumn leaf.

Kheema pressed her fingers deeper. She kissed Janaié's shoulder, then bit, gently at first. Slowly, without hurry, she sank her teeth deeper. Her fingers moved faster, working their way deeper into Janaié with each small thrust.

Janaié's body shook. She moaned again and again. Her chest rose and fell. "Oh!" she said.

Kheema pressed her fingers as deep as they would go. Her thumb became a blur, moving in rapid circles over Janaié's clit. Janaié cried out, bucking her hips against Kheema's hand.

Kheema withdrew. "You moved."

"Please!" Janaié said. "Please!"

"Nope." Kheema turned away, repressing a triumphant grin. "You moved. Game's over."

"But—"

"Nope. You're mine. You broke the rules." She sat on the bed. "The game is over. Time to come to bed."

"You…you…you're mean!"

"Yes." Kheema slipped the translucent robe to the floor. "I am." She pulled the blanket over her, nestling down into the bed.

1.8

KHEEMA JERKED AWAKE. Around her, absolute darkness swallowed the room. Beside her, Janaié breathed evenly.

She blinked in the darkness. "Is someone there?" she asked softly. Janaié stirred without waking. The door opened silently. A faint shape appeared in the dim light beyond.

She slipped off the covers and rose from the bed, trying not to disturb Janaié. "Who's there?"

"Kheema," came Fahren's voice. "The Grand High Priestess requests the honor of your presence."

"In the middle of the night?"

"Now."

"Let me get dress—"

"Now."

Kheema slipped naked into the hall. Fahren led her into the float tube. Kheema felt a moment of vertigo as her feet left the solid floor, then she floated weightless down to the park, alighting on springy grass that was slightly damp beneath her feet.

Fahren led her down a winding stone pathway to a large door in the wall. Unlike the other doors of the Temple, this one was plainly visible, a massive bronze thing trimmed in dark wood carved with elaborate geometric designs and framed within a great carved archway of white stone. Fahren bowed to her. "Good night, Potential." She turned and walked away.

"Wait! What—"

The door opened. Heart beating fast, Kheema stepped into opulence beyond imagining. Walls of snowy marble, veined with black, supported a high ceiling lit by a row of golden glow-lights, suspended in a line from fine gold chains.

The foyer opened into a large living area, richly furnished with plush red couches. A glass tabletop floated silently in the air without legs. Thick drapes of red and gold hung on the walls.

Miati unfolded her legs from beneath her on the couch and rose to greet Kheema. "Good evening, Potential," she said.

"Good evening, Priestess." Kheema bowed. Her heart fluttered. Her mouth went dry.

Miati walked over to her, looking her up and down with a critical eye. Two narrow braids framed her face and the cascade of loose hair that fell almost to the floor between them. She wore the same shimmering, translucent robe she'd worn during the services.

"I like to get to know the Potentials in each new group," she said. "The Sacrifice is the most sacred of our rituals, so it's important that I meet the volunteers." She took Kheema's chin in her hand, turning her head sideways. She pressed three fingers into Kheema's mouth, forcing it open, inspecting her closely. Kheema blushed.

"Hm," she said. She took Kheema's hands in hers and raised Kheema's arms above her head. She placed one hand on Kheema's back, then with her other hand she fondled Kheema's breasts.

"The gods provide for us," Miati said. "In return, they ask for our service. Those who volunteer for Sacrifice should be our very best, physically and emotionally." She walked around Kheema, sliding her hands over Kheema's body. "Hands behind your back. Legs apart. Bend over. Let me see what you have to offer."

Blushing furiously, Kheema bent over, legs spread wide. Miati stood behind Kheema. She spread her open, fingers dipping inside Kheema. "How are you responding to the Blessing of Fire?"

Kheema whimpered. Miati's fingers pried her open. She felt wetness flowing out of her. "It...oh! Oh!" She inhaled deeply, fighting the urge to push back against Miati's hand. "It is very intense."

"Mm, yes." Miati withdrew her fingers. She knelt beside Kheema and slid her hands up and down Kheema's legs. Kheema quivered. "Remain still," Miati commanded.

Kheema endured the inspection without a word. When Miati finished, she instructed Kheema to stand upright. "The priests and priestesses must learn to control themselves even in the face of the most overpowering desire. Fahren has told me you have excellent control." She took a pair of carved transparent glasses from an ornate gold free-standing curio cabinet against the wall, which she set on the floating table. She filled each glass with deep amber liquid from a beautiful, jeweled crystal bottle. "Control is an important part of the life of a Priestess. Here." She offered one of the glasses to Kheema.

Kheema took the glass. She raised it to her nose, sniffing. The liquid inside smelled rich and heady.

Miati sipped from the other glass. "Have you ever felt the presence of the Fiery One?"

"I…maybe. I'm not sure. There was a moment, during the last service…" She took a small, hesitant sip of the potent liquid. It tasted of honey and alcohol and burned pleasantly on her tongue. She drank more.

Miati drained her glass and set it down. "To be a priestess of the Temple is to dedicate yourself to a lifetime of learning. The God of Light is also the God of Knowledge. Knowledge and Light are one and the same. One of the skills we learn is reading people. People reveal far more of themselves than they realize." She stood beside Kheema, looking her up and down. Her hands caressed Kheema's arms. She moved her lips close to Kheema's neck, warm breath playing on her skin. "There are so many ways to bring you pleasure, even though you cannot have an orgasm. There are so many delights of the body that do not have to end in release."

Her fingers moved over Kheema's skin. "I can see by the pulse in your throat that you love to have your neck touched. I can see by the tremble in the glass you hold that my fingers on your arms are waking desire in you. I can tell by the quiver in your breath that you want me. Knowledge brings control. A High Priestess can awaken desire as powerfully as the Blessing of Fire can. If I choose, I can use this knowledge to make you beg to give yourself to me, the same way Janaié begged to give herself to you."

"You know about that?"

"I know everything that happens in the Temple." Miati's hand folded around Kheema's breast. "You think you are in control of yourself right now. That control is an illusion. You have not yet mastered yourself." She took the glass from Kheema's hand. She turned away, her back to Kheema. "I can give you exquisite pleasure, if I want, but that is not why you're here tonight. Instead of giving, I will take." She snapped her fingers. "Take her. Remove her control."

The front door opened to admit two priests and two priestesses, the women dressed in robes, the men in loincloths. They headed directly for Kheema with purpose in their eyes. Kheema took a step back.

The two tallest, both powerfully built, grabbed her by the arms. Muscles rippled beneath smooth, hairless skin. The priestess holding her left arm had short black hair and dark eyes. Her skin was a rich black, deep as midnight. The priest on her right, fair-haired and dark-eyed, wore his hair tied back in a braid. Miati watched as they half-carried her into the center of the room. They held her there, their grips as unyielding as iron.

The remaining priestess approached Kheema. "Good evening, Potential," she said. She had golden eyes, bronze skin, and short black hair in a spiky cut. Her breasts were full and heavy, her voice languid. "I am Gera. I am going to break your will." She kissed Kheema's lower lip gently.

"I am Kanti," the other priest said. "The woman to your left is Rahon. The man to your right is Pennot. We will be helping Gera break you." He walked behind Kheema, dragging sharp nails lightly across Kheema's back.

Miati sat on the couch and raised the glass of amber liquid to her lips. Kanti massaged Kheema's bare shoulders. Kheema shuddered.

Kanti and Gera touched her here and there, gently, slowly. At each touch, the fires inside Kheema burned hotter. She struggled in the grip of Rahon and Pennot, but they held her fast.

The soft assault continued. Gera took one of Kheema's nipples between her lips. Kheema groaned. Her knees buckled. Kanti kissed the back of Kheema's neck with soft, warm lips. He reached around to fondle Kheema's other breast.

The dam collapsed. Kheema howled, a sound of pure feral need. She thrashed wildly, trying to escape the grip of the two people holding her. Gera kissed her lips. Kheema returned the kiss with absolute abandon. Gera pulled away. "She's ready," she said.

They lifted Kheema entirely off the floor and forced her down onto the couch. Miati took a gleaming box of light-colored wood from the curio cabinet, which she handed to Gera. Gera flipped the lid open and took out a black, shapeless bit of fabric. "Hold her," she said.

Rahon and Pennot pinned Kheema's arms to the couch. Kanti knelt and held Kheema's feet. Gera walked over to the couch with a smile. She unfolded the black fabric into a hood, which she pulled over Kheema's head. It closed weightless over her like a second skin, utterly opaque. Kheema plunged into darkness.

The people holding her pried Kheema's legs apart. She felt something hard and smooth forced into her. Something else closed firmly over her clit.

They began the assault in earnest. Multiple sets of lips kissed her, closed over her nipples, brushed against the side of her neck. Multiple sets of hands roamed freely over her body, fondling and caressing. She squirmed, blind and helpless.

The thing inside her began to tingle. Sharp little jolts crackled within her. Her clit buzzed. She arched her back, moaning. Strong hands held her down.

A low, steady throbbing joined the tingle. Kheema threw back her head and moaned louder. Someone kissed the hollow of her throat. A hand slid up and down her thigh. Another caressed her breast. Her moan became a cry of pleasure.

The throbbing grew more intense, becoming a buzz that sent waves of pleasure through Kheema's body so intense they were nearly painful. The hands and lips and tongues explored her skin.

The last vestiges of Kheema's control disintegrated. Kheema writhed and twisted, squirming beneath them, weeping openly behind the hood. No matter how she twisted, the four people found more places to touch, inflaming her desire. She hovered on the edge of orgasm, sobbing, crying out until her voice was hoarse. "Please!" she begged. "Please!"

She had no idea how long they held her there, trapped on the quivering edge of orgasm. Time lost all meaning, until she couldn't tell if they had been tormenting her for minutes or days. She shrieked and pleaded and begged as she thrashed helplessly in their grip.

Then, all at once, they stopped. The thing inside her quieted and slid out. She was hauled to her feet. Some unseen hand pulled the hood off her head. She blinked in the sudden bright light.

"Thank you, Potential," Miati said. "That will be all. Fahren will take you back to your quarters."

She opened her mouth to speak. Nothing came out. She took a trembling half-step toward the door and almost fell. The others watched her, neither helping nor hindering.

"Please," Kheema said, "I need…"

"You're dismissed, Potential."

Kheema staggered whimpering toward the door. Little aftershocks rippled through her, strong enough to make her clench. She wiped away her tears with the back of her hand. The door opened before she could touch it.

Fahren waited for her outside. "Follow me," she said.

Kheema followed behind her, still whimpering, so disoriented that without Fahren to guide her, she thought she might not have found her way back to her quarters.

Fahren brought her to her room. The door opened at her gesture. Kheema stumbled through.

Janaié stirred in the blackness. "What—" she said, voice heavy with sleep. "Oh, hey. Where did you go?"

Kheema crawled under the covers and onto Janaié. She pressed her body over Janaié's, grinding her hips against Janaié's leg.

""Mmm," Janaié said. "What's put you in this—oh!" Kheema kissed her, roughly, urgently. Her hips moved, rocking against Janaié. She wept, tears of need running down her cheeks, as her hands clutched at Janaié's body. Janaié responded, pressing herself up to Kheema, kissing her back.

Eventually, Kheema fell asleep from sheer exhaustion, still on top of Janaié, their legs twisted together.

1.9

KHEEMA WOKE THE next morning to an empty bed. Her body ached. Memories of the night before came flooding back. She bowed her head, feeling sheepish at how easily she had been reduced to a weeping, gibbering mess.

She climbed out of bed and followed sounds into the bathroom, arms wrapped tightly around herself. Janaié was just stepping into the tub. "Oh, hi!" Janaié beamed. "Good morning! I like what you did last night. Want to tell me what brought that on?"

Kheema mumbled something incoherent, stepping gingerly into the water. The shock of sexual arousal struck again. She blushed. Janaié embraced her. "Where did you go last night?"

Kheema shook her head, her face flaming.

"Are you going to ask me if I'm yours?" Janaié inquired. She took Kheema's hand and placed it over her breast.

Kheema gave her a small, shy kiss on her cheek. "I'm sorry," she said. "I didn't mean to...you know, last night, I..."

"That was fun," Janaié said.

"I didn't mean to! I feel embarrassed. I was so..."

"Out of control?"

"Yes!"

"Did they do that to you?"

"Yes!"

"Well, I liked it. You can do that to me whenever you want. I'm yours, after all." She pulled Kheema down onto her lap. "Here, let me do your back."

Kheema relaxed a bit under Janaié's hands. When Janaié slid a hand between her legs, Kheema leaned back, parting them just a little, allowing Janaié's fingers to explore her soft folds.

After breakfast, on their way to the Hall of Memory, Fahren pulled Kheema and Janaié aside. "A change has been requested from the highest level," she said. "Effective immediately, Kheema, you are assigned Sakim as your companion. Janaié, you will be with Lianya from now on."

Kheema reeled. "What? Why?"

"Because the High Priestess wills it so."

Janaié pouted. "But—"

"The decision is made. Follow me."

On the walk down the Hall of Memory, Kheema felt numb. Fahren opened the first door. Sakim smirked. "Looks like it's you and me," she said. "After you, please."

Kheema's body shook when Fahren administered the Blessing of Fire. Sakim accepted the glistening drop, laughing. "Lie down," she said to Kheema. "Let me make a book of your body."

Kheema climbed into the soft, cushioned mound. She felt disconnected from her own arousal, as if she didn't fully inhabit her body. She still hadn't processed the abrupt reassignment. She closed her eyes as Sakim knelt over her, the glowing points of light already gathering on her hands. Her skin tingled when Sakim slid her hands over her breasts, her nipples hardening in response to the touch, but it seemed to be happening to someone else.

Sakim's touch differed from Janaié's: rougher, more careless. She squeezed Kheema's breasts. She slid two fingers inside Kheema, fast, without warning. Kheema's body responded automatically. The lights brightened. Letters formed from the swirling motes.

Sakim's voice filled the small chamber, reverberating through Kheema like a living thing. Kheema felt herself slipping into that space where the words and the feel of hands on her body merged into one, bringing her into a world made purely of sound and touch, but a small part of her stayed behind. She heard the words, felt the hands, perceived the way her body responded, but it didn't affect her the way it had before. Even when her hips rocked up to meet Sakim's fingers, even when she heard herself moan in pleasure, it felt like something happening to another person, somewhere far away from her.

The nagging sense of unreality persisted through lunch. Janaié sat across from Kheema, sedate, saying little. Several times, she opened her mouth to speak, then closed it again, eyes downcast. Lianya leaned against Janaié and murmured something in her ear. Janaié didn't respond.

If Hassen noticed Kheema's detachment during the evening's recitation, he made no mention of it. He knelt in the appointed place, hands behind his back, his skillful tongue playing over Kheema's clit while the words that had penetrated her that day spilled back out of her. Kheema writhed on the chair, burning with need. She gasped and moaned, crying out the words of the Litany, but it was the memory of Janaié's body that lingered on her lips and skin.

Eventually, it was over. Hassen unstrapped Kheema and helped her stand, sweaty and trembling. When she saw Janaié in the hallway, Janaié smiled. They touched hands briefly. Sakim frowned.

During the evening service, Fahren instructed Kheema to sit at one end of the row of chairs, next to Sakim, and directed Janaié to the other end. Throughout the service, Sakim kept her fingernails resting lightly on Kheema's thigh. She dug her nails into Kheema's skin every time Kheema glanced in Janaié's direction. By the end of the sermon, Kheema could not even remember what it was about.

Dinner slipped by in a blur. When Kheema found herself standing before the door to her meditation cell, she could scarcely recall what she'd eaten. She walked into the chamber in a daze. As soon as the door closed, she folded her legs under her atop the boulder, took a deep breath, and waited.

The light dimmed. Shapes materialized around her. Slowly, the great vast bulks of ancient redwood trees emerged from the swirling light. When the image coalesced, she sat on a boulder in the middle of a clearing, surrounded on all sides by enormous trees. Impenetrable shadows cloaked the spaces between their trunks. Overhead, the large moon, Apla, hung low in a velvety black sky, barely visible through the branches. The smaller moon, Ianitus, glowed directly overhead, sending down its dim reddish light. A gentle breeze stirred, so light it produced just the smallest whisper of sensation on her skin. Fireflies winked in the shadows between the trees.

The wind's caress fanned a tiny ember of desire inside Kheema. She turned her mind to it with an almost clinical interest, observing it as it spread, sending tongues of flame licking through her. She made no attempt to control it. Instead, she allowed it to grow, until her skin flushed with heat. She slid her hands over her body. She ran two fingers down, seeking her clit. Sparkling fireflies wove a shifting tapestry of shadows between the trees.

Kheema moaned softly. Pleasure spread through her body. She stroked herself without goal or intention, edging ever closer to orgasm without expecting to reach it, accepting the sensations exactly as they were.

More fireflies joined the dance beneath the trees, until the forest was alive with a moving, changing glow. Kheema caressed herself sensually, lost in the feeling. Glints of light came to her, reflected from the leaves so far overhead. The moons bathed the treetops with a warm ethereal light.

When, finally, the light faded and the door opened, Kheema stood with neither joy nor regret. She met up with Janaié in the garden. Janaié panted, her hair a tangled mess. She took Kheema's hand. Sakim glared at her.

They walked hand in hand to the living quarters. Fahren stopped in front of the first door. "Janaié, you and Lianya are here. Kheema, you will accompany Sakim."

Kheema released Janaié's hand with a stab of regret. When the next door opened, Sakim stood in front of it. "After you."

This room was quite different from the one she'd shared with Janaié. It had the same large rectangular bed, but draped in white and black. A glass doorway edged in bright chrome opened into the bathing room. Couches and chairs of the same white and black as the bed lay about the sitting room.

"Looks like we'll be together from here on," Sakim said. "Let's get to know each other." She slipped the robe from her shoulders, wound it into a makeshift rope, and looped it around Kheema, pinning her arms to her sides, pulling their bodies together.

Kheema noticed with interest the way Sakim's breathing quickened, how her pulse beat in her neck. She noticed, too, the response of her own body, mindful of the quickening of her own breath, the swelling of her nipples, the sudden contraction between her legs.

"How would you like to get acquainted with me?" Kheema said, demure. She pulled at the robe, just a little, watching the answering flush in Sakim's cheeks. "You seem to have me at a disadvantage."

Sakim let out a small moan. Then her metallic green eyes abruptly refocused. "I see what you're doing."

"What am I doing?"

"You're doing what the Priestesses do. You're reading my body, trying to see what gets me going. Is that what you did to Janaié? Is that how you got her to promise herself to you?"

"What? No, I—"

"It won't work on me," Sakim growled. She pushed Kheema hard. Kheema flailed and fell on her back onto the bed. "You're not a priestess yet. I won't let you have control of me." She knelt on the bed, straddling Kheema. "I won't be so easy." She ground down onto Kheema's face, hips undulating. "We are going to do this my way."

Kheema acquiesced. She felt her own pulse quicken. She reached up to grab Sakim's hips, guiding her down onto her face, her tongue finding Sakim's clit. She tasted the excitement on her, felt her arousal in the wetness that flowed from her. She gave herself up to Sakim's demands, moving her tongue in circles, now faster, now slower, feeling how the tightness changed in Sakim's legs. Sakim's moans became cries, then tears of frustration. She tried to push herself off Kheema. Kheema pulled her back down onto her waiting tongue, hands gripping her tightly.

"Enough!" Sakim cried. Kheema smiled.

1.10

THE DAYS THAT followed shaped themselves to the same pattern. Kheema and the other Potentials lived a strictly regimented life: now at morning service; now in the Hall of Memory, drawing forth the Litany on a canvas made of flesh; now strapped down in Recitation, thrashing under the ministrations of a skillful tongue while they repeated the Litany; now in service, listening to the Grand High Priestess; now in meditation, sitting in the center of ever-changing scenery.

She saw Janaié every day, at meals and at Service. Fahren kept them apart, but they exchanged small touches whenever they could. One evening after meditation, when nobody was looking, Janaié leaned up against Kheema and murmured "I'm yours" in her ear. Kheema felt a jolt that even the Blessing of Fire could not give her.

At irregular intervals, one of the doors into the Potentials' quarters would slide open late at night. Fahren would lead a Potential to Miati's quarters to be inspected and, often, corrected. The Potentials rarely spoke about what happened in the Grand High Priestess' quarters. Those unpredictable summons made the only variation in what otherwise was an endless series of similar days. Eventually, Kheema lost count of how long she had been there. Each day blended into the last.

One day, without warning, the pattern changed. Kheema didn't know if weeks or months had passed since she'd been assigned to Sakim. During the morning service, as the Potentials sat in their chairs on the dais, Kheema noticed two empty seats in the row of chairs reserved for the other group of Potentials. She nudged Sakim. "What's going on there?"

Sakim shrugged. "I don't know. Maybe they quit? That happens sometimes. Not everyone can take the training."

After service, Fahren led Kheema's group of Potentials to the Hall of Memory. Instead of stopping at the doorways into the learning chambers, she led the group farther along the hall. After a time, it sloped downward, then curved back onto itself. Eventually, it ended in a blank wall.

At Fahren's signal, the door opened into a huge round room with smooth black walls. Tiny flecks of light moved slowly within the walls. White marble tiles veined in black covered the floor and ceiling. Brilliant light streamed down from channels overhead.

In the room's center, eight carved marble columns formed a circle. Each column had two large metal rings mounted to it, one at the base and one near the top. A mound of plush, soft cushions lay piled up in the middle of the circle.

Two women stood between the columns, bound wrist and ankle by red cords tied to the rings. Their legs were spread wide. Featureless black hoods covered their faces, revealing only the general shape of their heads. Each wore a skin-tight suit from hips to neck, made of a glossy black fabric that clung like paint to their bodies. The suits left their breasts exposed, their arms and legs bare.

"These are Nadaya and Denoma," Fahren explained. Kheema blinked, realizing that it was the first time she'd heard any of the Potentials in the other group addressed by name. "You have not yet learned the whole of the Litany, so you are not expected to be able to do Recitation in front of the congregation. Later, when you've had a chance to learn it all, your Recitation will take place before a group of priests and priestesses. When that happens, you'll be expected to perform the Recitation without error. Nadaya made an error during her Recitation yesterday. We must make sure that she and her companion are corrected."

"What's going to happen to them?" Chanae said.

"They have been given the Blessing of Fire," Fahren said. "They have also been given the Lord's Ambrosia, which removes the need to eat or sleep. The hoods they wear block all light and sound, to symbolize being lost in the Darkness as we all were before the awakening of the Lord of Light. This is the destiny we face if we fail in our observances. They will remain here for three days and three nights, offering their bodies as tribute to those of the

Temple. Spreading the Blessing of the Lord of Light is the path by which we all travel up out of darkness."

Kheema walked around the bound women, examining them with open curiosity. She could see the tension in their legs, the subtle quiver in both taut bodies. They both had erect nipples, the woman on the left bright pink on small, upturned breasts, the woman on the right protruding dark from large, full breasts. Both women whimpered, ever so softly, hips rocking slightly. She imagined what it must be like, to be stretched out and bound this way, trapped in total silence and darkness, perceiving nothing but her own breathing and the need inside her. She studied the woman on the left, searching for clues to her inner state from her breath and the tiny motions of her body.

Fahren came up behind Kheema. "That's Nadaya," she said. "You may touch her if you like."

Kheema slipped her hand between the woman's legs. She found wetness there, running down her thighs, dripping onto the marble floor. She slid two fingers inside without resistance.

The bound woman cried out. She thrust her hips forward, grinding against Kheema's hand, forcing her fingers deeper.

Fahren kissed the back of Kheema's neck. She slid her hands up Kheema's body to cup her breasts. Kheema moaned.

Behind them, the door to the chamber opened. People filed in—first Miati, carrying a large tray of tiny vials; then the other group of Potentials; and following them, priests in their loincloths and priestesses in their filmy robes.

They gathered in a loose circle around the two women tied between the columns. Miati released the tray. It hung silently in the air. She picked up the first of the small vials on it. "Come forward."

Fahren gestured for Kheema to step forward. Kheema opened her mouth. The drop fell on her tongue. She flushed, clenching between her legs, as the Blessing took hold.

All the other Potentials from both groups accepted the glittering drops. Kheema watched them stiffen, cheeks flushing.

Miati moved among the priests and priestesses, dispensing the Blessing of Fire. The men's cocks hardened. The women moaned.

Miati placed the empty vials on the floating tray. "In the beginning, we were lost in darkness, with none to guide us," she said. "Great was our suffering. We were adrift, unable to find our way. Through our work and sacrifice, the Light found its way into our hearts. We must remember the darkness, so that we know where we came from. We must make offerings of ourselves to the Light." She nodded to the assembled group. "You may begin."

People swarmed around the two bound women. Fahren urged Kheema back toward Nadaya. Kheema slid her hand over the bound Potential's mound. Nadaya pressed forward against her hand. Kheema sucked in her breath and closed her eyes. Fahren kissed Kheema, her lips warm against the side of Kheema's neck.

Hassen, the priest who had so often teased Kheema to the point of tears with his talented tongue, stood behind Nadaya. His speaking drone floated just above his head. His cock stood erect, a drop of white fluid at the tip. He placed his hands on Nadaya's breasts. Heart beating wildly, Kheema ran her fingers over his shaft as she had longed to do so many times before. She guided him into the bound woman, dizzy with need and longing.

Someone—Kheema wasn't sure who—kissed the other side of her neck. He, or perhaps she, pressed two fingers into Kheema. Kheema pressed back against them, lost in the sensation, not knowing or caring who they belonged to. She closed her eyes, feeling Hassen's slick shaft sliding between her fingers, savoring the lips on her neck and the hands on her body.

Nadaya wailed like a trapped animal. Hassen pounded hard into her, his cock sliding wet between Kheema's fingers. He shuddered silently. His body shook with his orgasm. White wetness spilled from Nadaya over Kheema's fingers. Kheema's breath caught in her throat. She pushed her hips back, mounting herself on the fingers inside her.

Hassen pulled out. Nadaya whimpered. Kheema felt herself contract around the fingers inside her in sympathy. All around her, she heard sighs and moans.

Hassen bowed to Kheema. "Thank you, Potential," his drone sang as he kissed her lips, very gently, and was gone.

A short woman took Nadaya's nipple between her lips, her long violet hair clinging to the sweaty skin. A taller woman with blood red hair and eyes came up behind Nadaya, sliding her fingers into her. Nadaya struggled against the cords, sobbing beneath her hood. Beside her, Denoma shuddered and cried out. Two priestesses fondled her breasts, while a third ran fingertips over her clit and a fourth caressed her thigh.

Kheema heard more moans from the cushions in the center of the circle. She opened her eyes. A tangle of bodies writhed together, hands and fingers caressing, massaging, exploring.

Janaié grabbed Kheema by the hair and kissed her roughly. Kheema kissed her back, hungry. She channeled all the longing and loss, accumulated over all the days they had been separated, into that kiss. Her tongue slipped between Janaié's lips. Her hands roved freely over Janaié's curves. Janaié leaned into her, moaning.

Chanae caressed Kheema's back. Two men Kheema didn't recognize closed on Chanae, one kissing her neck, the other fondling her breasts.

Sakim seized Kheema and steered her to Denoma's plump form. Two priestesses in front of her made way. A tall man with turquoise hair and skin the color of fine bone china stood behind her, hands gripping her hips, rocking her with his hard thrusts. She cried out with each thrust, pressing back to meet him.

Sakim took Kheema's hand in hers. She placed her hand between Denoma's lags, thrusting Kheema's fingers into her. Kheema realized the priest was impaling her anally, forcing himself deep into her tightest opening.

Sakim nuzzled Kheema's ear. "They will do this to me if you screw up," she whispered. "You better make sure you don't." She took Kheema's other hand and guided it between her own legs, penetrating herself with Kheema's fingers. "Oh! If you make a mistake that causes me to be punished like this, I will...uh! See to it that your...oh! Oh! That your life becomes...unh! Becomes very difficult." Her eyelids fluttered.

Kheema worked her fingers, feeling the wetness from both women, feeling the push and swell of the erect cock inside Denoma's body. Sakim gripped Kheema's wrist tightly. She closed her eyes and drove herself against Kheema's hand.

One of the Potentials from Nadaya's group walked up to Kheema. "I'm Kellis," she announced, and dragged her into a rough, deep kiss. Fahren pressed herself against Kheema's back, sinking her hands into Kellis's seafoam green hair and pinning her body between them.

Kheema lost track of time. Hands and lips and tongues explored every inch of her body. Priests and priestesses helped themselves to her, to the two bound women tied between the columns, and to each other. Cries of ecstasy filled the room, inflaming Kheema's helpless frustration. Her body ached to join in the ecstatic release, but she remained trapped on the shivering edge, unable to come.

People streamed in and out, entering hungry, leaving sated. The two bound women cried out under the ceaseless assault, begging for release until tears of frustration left dark lines in their hoods.

Eventually, Fahren gathered both groups of Potentials. "It is time for evening service," she said. "Members of the Temple are permitted to miss service to help correct these two. Potentials, however, are required to attend."

Kheema sat on the end of the row of chairs during service that night, even more distracted than usual. Throughout the sermon, Sakim held Kheema's legs apart. Her nails rested on Kheema's inner thigh. Occasionally, her hand dipped between Kheema's legs, fingers entering her roughly. Kheema struggled to stay silent. The taste of Janaié's lips lingered heavy in her mind.

It stayed there throughout her evening meditation. She sat on the boulder in the middle of a vast expanse of sandy beach that ran in a yellow ribbon along the base of a cliff of sheer black rock. Saltwater tang filled the air. Gulls wheeled overhead in a hard blue sky. Kheema let the memories fill her thoughts: Janaié's skin beneath her hands, Janaié's nipple between her lips.

As the memories flooded through her, the tide came in, each wave lapping farther up the beach. She closed her eyes and fell into a trance, summoning every curve of Janaié's face from her memory, focusing now on her lips, now on her eyes.

The water crept closer and closer. Soon, the waves lapped at the rock. It stayed where it was, solid and impassive. The water parted around it. Eventually, the tide reached the cliff face. Kheema sat alone on a rock surrounded on all sides by swirling crystal water.

She remembered Janaié's body against hers, the frenzy of Janaié's kiss. Her hand crept between her legs. Waves crashed against the cliff.

That night, Sakim was particularly rough with her. Kheema relaxed into it, letting Sakim's need crash against her, feeling her own arousal quicken in response, riding along the edge of orgasm, testing the invisible barrier that prevented her from plunging into ecstasy. She gave herself over to Sakim without a word, soft and compliant beneath Sakim's demands, water to Sakim's rock. Eventually, Sakim tired. The two of them drifted into sleep.

1.11

TIME TRACED ITS inevitable course toward the summer solstice. Kheema's regimented routine continued, the days divided into their distinct segments, but as the solstice approached, she felt the mood in the Temple change. Excitement and anticipation wrote themselves on the faces of the priests and priestesses.

Three days before the solstice, Fahren summoned together the eight Potentials after breakfast. "There will be no service this morning," she said. "It is time for the Ritual of Selection. This will tell us who will be this year's Sacrifice. This is our second most important ritual. Everyone is expected to participate. Follow me."

She led them through the passageways they'd traveled when they'd first entered the Temple a lifetime ago. Kheema recognized the chamber where she had first received the Blessing of Fire and where she and the others had left their old clothes, and their old lives, behind.

A new door opened at Fahren's gesture, revealing a hallway that curved back and forth in a series of switchbacks, always leading upward, until Kheema thought they must be somewhere near the center of the great Temple, many stories above ground. She ran her fingers along the walls as she had when she first came to this place, thinking about the many things that had happened to her.

The hallway came at last to a vast room tiled with alternating black and white marble slabs. Each slab had an irregular shape, no two exactly the same, yet the shapes fit together perfectly. Irregular patches of grass, some with trees growing in them, dotted the chamber. Benches, chairs, and couches lay scattered in the grassy patches according to some logic Kheema couldn't see. The ceiling, high overhead, glowed with carefully channeled sunlight.

The only regular shape in the room was a perfectly square pool about as deep as an adult person's head in its center. Steep steps descended into it on one side. Glimmering liquid caught the sunlight from above and reflected it back in a thousand dancing sparks of light. A large marble chair that reminded Kheema of a throne rose from the ground beside the pool, across from the steps. A long, low platform topped with plush cushions sat next to the throne.

Priests and priestesses of the Temple gathered in the chamber, some sitting on the benches and chairs, others standing in small groups. The space buzzed with excited conversation.

Fahren directed Kheema and the other Potentials to line up behind the throne at the far edge of the pool. Kheema looked into the sparkling liquid. A brilliant, rippling reflection looked back at her.

The chatter died. Miati swept in, regal as always, leading the other group of Potentials. Each wore a long, heavy robe of dense white fabric edged in gold, parted in the front, that swept the floor. Tension showed on every Potential's face.

The Potentials lined up next to the steps leading into the pool. Miati stood before the throne with an expression of benevolent calm on her face. More priests and priestesses flowed in. Kheema caught Hassen's eye. He smiled at her.

Soon the pool was entirely surrounded by people. Miati raised her arms. The chamber fell silent.

"In only a few days," she said, "the Summer Solstice will be upon us, and the Sacrifice to the God of the Sun will take place. Today we gather to choose a new Sacrifice. We call upon the Lord of Light to guide us. We pray that one of the Potentials now before us will be satisfactory to him as a Sacrifice, and that she will perform the Sacrifice with honor."

"Praise to the Lord of Light," the crowd chanted in unison.

"From darkness comes the Light," Miati said. "Let the Potentials enter into the Light, that they may spread its blessings."

As one, the group of Potentials descended into the pool. They gasped as the liquid touched them. Their robes turned transparent and clung to their skin.

82

The group continued forward, step by step, until they were completely sub-merged. Miati raised her arms once more. The Potentials turned and stepped out of the pool with glittering liquid streaming from their skin and hair.

They parted into two groups of four. One group walked around the left side of the pool, the other around the right. They gathered in a loose circle around Miati, going to their hands and knees. Then they prostrated them-selves, arms outstretched, foreheads touching the floor. Miati looked out over them, smiling. "Today," she said, "one of you will be chosen as Sacrifice. But first, you must demonstrate your self-control to the Lord of Light. Only when you have mastered yourself are you ready to give yourself to his Light."

"Praise to the Lord of Light," the Potentials said.

"Praise to the Lord of Light," answered the crowd.

"For one day and one night, you will offer yourselves to all of us who want you," Miati said. "For one day and one night, you will utter not a single word, nor touch yourselves, no matter how powerfully you might desire it. Any Potential who speaks even a single word may not become the Sacrifice. When one day and one night have passed, whoever among you has demonstrated the greatest dedication to the Lord of Light will be chosen as Sacrifice. Do you understand?"

"Yes, Priestess," the circle of women said in unison.

"Then take your place."

The women rose. They knelt on hands and knees on the cushions atop the low platform.

"It is customary," Miati said, "for the second group of Potentials to be the first to participate in the Selection. Let the Selection begin."

Kheema walked over to where Kellis knelt on the platform. Kellis looked up at her, her face a complex mixture of need, desire, apprehension, and fear. Kheema touched her cheek, where tiny glistening beads clung.

A small droplet touched her finger. Instantly, Kheema was aflame with de-sire, so wrenching in its ferocity that she stumbled with a gasp. She fell to her knees, overcome by an arousal stronger than any she had ever felt before. She grabbed Kellis's hair and kissed her ferociously, tongue thrusting between her lips. She slid her other hand over Kellis's breast to grope her tightly.

Kellis leaned forward into the kiss, accepting Kheema's demands with do-cility. The roaring fire within Kheema blazed hotter. She stood, both hands on the back of Kellis's head, pushing her face roughly between her legs.

Beside her, Sakim ran her fingers lightly over the wet robe that clung to Denoma's rolls. She stiffened. Her pupils shrank to pinpoints. She walked around behind Denoma, lifting the sodden robe, and without preamble shoved her fingers into her. Denoma let out a sharp gasp of shock.

Kheema pressed herself harder against Kellis's face. Kellis's tongue flitted over her clit. She closed her eyes, shuddering. All around her, she heard sighs and moans.

Kellis let out a cry. Kheema opened her eyes to see a tall, dark-eyed priest behind her, hands tight on her hips. He mounted her with vigor, thrusting hard into her, hand on the back of her head, pushing her face forward between Kheema's legs. He came with a scream, his entire body convulsing with the strength of it.

The moment he withdrew, another priest took his place. Kheema recognized him as Pennot, the man who had helped hold her down in Miati's chambers. He thrust into her roughly from behind, his eyes glazed, a predatory expression on his face. Kellis let out another shrill cry.

Kheema knelt again. She took a deep breath, held it for a moment, and then, when she had climbed on top of the tumultuous, raging need inside her body, she let it out slowly. "Shh, it's okay, you can do it," she said. She looked into Kellis's desperate seafoam eyes. "You can do it." She stroked Kellis's cheek. As she gazed into Kellis's eyes, Kheema could almost feel Pennot's strokes thrusting into her.

All around her, the moans and cries of unrestrained sexual congress faded into the background. Kheema knelt, intoxicated by the expression on Kellis's face. She drank in every detail: the sounds Kellis made, the small twitches of her body, the way her fingers curled into the cushions. Kheema caressed her, stroked her, murmured words of encouragement to her while priests and priestesses took pleasure from her body.

For hours it went on. People came through the ritual chamber, eager to participate in the yearly ritual of Selection. They arrived relaxed and calm. The calmness dissolved into hunger the moment they touched any of the waiting Potentials, as the robes released the shimmering liquid. They left spent, drained of their desire by frantic coupling.

No part of the Potentials' bodies was spared. Every inch of skin was touched and groped, every place that allowed entry was penetrated. Through it all, Kheema remained where she was, kneeling beside Kellis, stroking her hair, whispering encouragement to her.

Not all the Temple members were urgent in their affections. Some took delight in goading the Potentials, trying to provoke them into speaking. They teased them, touching them very lightly, fingertips barely stroking swollen clits. Some of the men stroked themselves just millimeters from the Potentials, not quite touching them, growing stiffer at the frustrated moans they provoked.

One priest in particular seemed to take special joy in tormenting Kellis this way. Over and over, he slid the head of his cock into her from behind, then stepped back to stroke himself. Kellis groaned, pressing backward toward him but finding only empty air.

He did this again and again, stroking himself just out of her reach until with a cry he arched his back and spurted warm white goo over her. It splattered her thighs and jetted across her mound. Not content with his orgasm, he pressed the head of his cock against her clit, sliding it around in small circles.

Kellis cried out. She opened her mouth as if to speak. Kheema placed her finger over Kellis's lips. "Shh," she said. "Breathe. Give yourself in service. You can do it."

The priest withdrew, stroking himself once more until, with a low, guttural growl, he spurted again. More white goo dripped between Kellis's legs. He slipped the head of his cock between her lower lips once more.

Kellis pressed herself backward, weeping. He moved back, preventing her from impaling herself. Kheema kept whispering to her. "Shh," she said. "Be still. Do you want to kiss me?"

Kellis nodded piteously. Kheema grabbed her hair tightly and kissed her roughly. The priest continued with his gentle teasing, brushing his cock exquisitely lightly against her clit. Kellis sobbed, her body shaking, her tongue thrusting between Kheema's lips.

Two priestesses, attracted by Kellis's piteous sounds, sat on the low platform on each side of Kellis. They reached beneath her to stroke her nipples, their touch feather-light. She moaned against Kheema's lips and arched her back, pressing herself down toward their hands. Laughing, they took their hands away. She whimpered and pressed backward. The priest behind her stepped back.

"Hush," Kheema said. "Be still and they will come to you. Be eager and they will go away. If you want to control your body, you must first control your mind." She ran her fingers over Kellis's forehead. "Find the stillness within yourself."

Bit by bit, Kellis stopped squirming. Her muscles strained with the effort. Eventually, only the smallest tremor betrayed her desire to move against the people tormenting her.

The two priestesses caressed her breasts, fingers gliding gently over damp skin. The priest pressed his erection ever so lightly against her clit. She remained still, breathing heavily.

"You see? Like that," Kheema said. She kissed Kellis's lower lip softly. Kellis moaned.

More people clustered around the two of them, drawn by what Kheema was doing. More hands fondled Kellis's body. Fingers and cocks and even a toe entered her body. The more she was groped and molested, the more still she became, until she knelt unmoving as a statue. Her wide eyes never left Kheema's.

Kheema sat still beside Kellis there while people flowed around them. The other Potentials eventually left, ushered out by Fahren, who seemed content to allow Kheema to stay.

Kheema remained with Kellis as she trembled, moaning, dripping from every part of her body. She remained as priests and priestesses of every rank used, teased, took, stroked, groped, and fondled Kellis's compliant, unresisting body. She remained even after Fahren spent herself by making each of the suffering Potentials lick her to orgasm after screaming orgasm.

All the while, the same things happened to the other Potentials in Kellis's group. Moans, cries, gasps, and whimpers filled the air. Kheema's own body quivered in sympathy. Every moan and cry vibrated through her.

Finally, when the sunlight piped in from the outside grew dim and ruddy with approaching night, one of the Potentials broke. "Please!" she sobbed. "Please, it's too much!"

Instantly, her robe turned black. Miati rose from the throne. One arm of the throne hinged open, revealing a compartment from which she took a small octagonal box of polished black stone. Inside it, on a black cushion, rested a tiny round crystal that glowed fiercely with brilliant yellow light. She walked over to the fallen Potential, her face sorrowful.

"You have failed the Light," she said. She took out the small round crystal. Its glow lit up her face. "All your study has been for nothing. You may not become a Sacrifice, nor a High Priestess of the Temple. However, you may yet still serve the Fiery One in your own way."

She brought the small point of light to the woman's lips. "Swallow this. It will release the Blessing of Fire for a year and a day. You will feel great need for that time, but your body will still be denied release. Only after a year and a day may you return to the Temple for the antidote."

She hesitated for a moment. Then, with tears in her eyes, the woman parted her lips for the small glowing thing. Miati placed it on the tip of her tongue. She swallowed.

"Now go," Miati said. "Travel the City. Spread his blessing and meditate upon the Light. Return in a year and a day, on the eve of next year's Sacrifice, so you may be redeemed."

Fahren helped the woman rise. She slipped the robe off her shoulders. A tiny, barely visible shudder ran through Fahren's body as the liquid in the robe touched her skin. She took the former Potential by the hand and led her from the room.

Kheema returned her attention to Kellis. She kissed Kellis's cheek gently. "Serve the Light with your body," she said. "Let your service bring pleasure to others. Do you see this priest? Do you see how he desires you?" She placed her hand on the back of Kellis's head. "He would like to know the pleasure of your mouth. Do this for the Light." She pressed Kellis's head down, guiding the man's thick erection between Kellis's lips.

Night fell. The light from the mirrored shafts overhead faded until the ritual chamber was illuminated only by the glow from the shimmering pool, which sent shadows dancing across the walls and ceilings. All night long, people came to help themselves to the bodies of the seven remaining Potentials. Kheema stayed with Kellis, ignoring the raging need inside her body, nuzzling Kellis, caressing her, encouraging her to stillness. The Potentials' bodies glistened with sweat, come, and the liquid that seeped from their robes. They whimpered, moaned, and wept with frustration as they served on hands and knees.

At last, the chamber brightened with the coming dawn. In some part of her brain, Kheema was aware she'd spent the entire night beside Kellis, without food or sleep, but she felt neither hungry nor tired. Her entire being seemed in resonance with Kellis, like two musical strings vibrating together. She sighed with pleasure whenever someone entered Kellis. She felt a wave of ecstasy with every person who took ecstasy from Kellis's body.

She felt, too, that presence she had experienced the first time she entered the Temple, that sense of someone else there with her, in the far corners of her mind. It grew stronger and stronger as the morning brightened, the feeling that she was not alone in her thoughts.

The presence sustained her, uplifted her, increased her desire, until she felt it thrumming through her body.

Then, as the sun reached its zenith and golden shafts of light flooded the chamber, it happened. Kellis's robe, still damp with the glistening liquid, changed all at once, from transparent white to deep scarlet.

Miati, who had remained on the throne all night, rose to her feet. She clapped her hands together. Everyone in the room, including those who were in mid-act with the Potentials, stopped what they were doing. They all turned to face Miati. "The Lord of Light has spoken," she said. "The choice is made. Rise, Kellis, as the new Sacrifice. When dawn comes the day after tomorrow, you will be sacrificed to his light."

1.12

THE DAY BEFORE the Sacrifice, Fahren collected the Potentials for breakfast and morning service as normal. The other group of Potentials was absent from their customary seats in the chapel. Instead, Kellis, resplendent in an elaborate robe intricately designed with twisting, complex patterns of red, black, and gold, stood in front of the dais. She wore a broad smile.

A long line of people snaked around the edge of the vaulted space and out the door. As the worshippers filed in, they knelt before Kellis. She touched each person's forehead before they rose to take their seats.

Kheema and her fellow Potentials were the last to enter the chapel. When her turn came, Kheema knelt in front of Kellis. She blushed when she touched Kheema's forehead. "Thank you," she said, so softly only Kheema could hear.

Kheema sat in her assigned place on the dais feeling pleased. The feeling of someone else inside her thoughts came back to her stronger than ever. She got the sense this mysterious companion inside her mind was pleased, too.

Miati led a long, impassioned service in honor of the new Sacrifice. A palpable, contagious excitement swept the room, washing over Kheema. Her heart swelled with pride over the small part she had played in Kellis's selection.

After the service, Fahren led the Potentials to the balcony that surrounded the garden. She stopped at the stairway that curved up to the higher level.

"The other Potentials are helping prepare Kellis for tomorrow's sacrifice," she said. "It is time for you to take their place. Follow me."

Fahren stepped into the float tube. Her hair swirled around her face as she rose to the uppermost balcony. Kheema and the others followed, all except Lianya, who took the stairs.

"I'm pleased you could join us," Fahren said when Lianya arrived, slightly out of breath. "This way, please. You will not be participating in the preparations for tomorrow's Sacrifice, so please take advantage of this opportunity to become comfortable in your new homes." She stood in front of a blank wall and gestured. A row of doorways opened silently. "You will find these doors respond to you. The second phase of your training and evaluation will leave you with more time for independent study, so you are free to come and go as you like."

Kheema followed Sakim toward the farthest door. Fahren touched her arm. "Your dedication during the Selection has led Miati to re-evaluate your companion assignment. You have been reassigned to Janaié. Sakim, you're with Lianya."

Sakim frowned. She stomped through the door to her new quarters, arms folded. Lianya followed after. A grin like the break of day spread across Janaié's face.

Kheema blinked. "Why was my assignment changed in the first place?" Understanding dawned on her face. "It was a test!"

Fahren smiled. "Of course it was a test. As servants of the Fiery One, we bring his light to all who need it. We may not always like those we tend to. It's easy to serve the Light when you're with someone you connect with. It's not so easy when it's someone you might not choose."

"I passed?"

"You did."

"Why was I the only one to be tested this way?"

"Your quarters are through there," Fahren said.

Kheema looked around the spacious new quarters, easily three times the size of her old unit, decorated in rich wood polished until it glowed. Brightly-colored frescoes of a noonday sun shining over the Temple decorated the vaulted ceiling. Wide mirrored skylights admitted sunlight from outside. Three steps led up to a mahogany door that opened into a large bathroom, tiled in stone, with a huge oval tub made of marble.

An enormous, low pedestal bed, flanked by ornately carved nightstands, dominated the center of the bedroom. A heavy table of polished wood sat next to the bed, on which rested an enormous book, bound in leather.

As soon as the door closed, Janaié embraced Kheema fiercely. "I missed you!" she said.

Kheema smiled. "Did you now?" she said. "How much did you miss me?"

"Lots!"

"Do you want me?"

"Yes!"

"Oh? Show me." Kheema disentangled herself from Janaié. "If you can take me, you can have me."

Janaié tried to wrap her arms around Kheema. Kheema pushed her away easily, chuckling. "I thought you said you missed me lots. That doesn't seem like lots to me. Show me!"

Janaié hugged Kheema tightly. Kheema wriggled loose, giggling, and scampered to the far side of the room. "I'm right here. If you want me, come and get me!"

With a roar, Janaié charged Kheema. The two of them tumbled onto the bed.

"That's the spirit!" Kheema said. "Now let me see how bad you want me."

Janaié pinned Kheema's arms down. Kheema squirmed free. She tried to unseat Janaié. Janaié caught her wrists and bore down, pinning her hands above her head.

They wrestled on the bed until Janaié hooked her legs around Kheema's, preventing her from wriggling away. She held Kheema's wrists tightly and leaned forward, kissing her with enthusiasm. Kheema felt the familiar tingle between her legs. She stopped struggling and kissed Janaié back. Her tongue slipped between Janaié's lips.

Janaié's grip loosened. In a flash, Kheema twisted sideways, slithering free.

"Hey!" Janaié said. She pounced on Kheema, forcing her onto her back, and straddled her. She grabbed Kheema's breasts. "Stop struggling!"

"Make me!"

Janaié twisted both of Kheema's nipples until she gasped. Kheema tried to push her off. Janaié pinned her wrists down once more, body pressed against her. They kissed roughly, urgently.

Finally, when they'd reached a point of sweaty, frustrated exhaustion, Janaié rolled off Kheema. "It will be nice when we're able to have an orgasm again," she said. "I don't know why they won't let us."

"To prove our dedication to the Sun God, of course," Kheema said. "At least that's what I hear." She stood, called up a new robe from the Provider to replace the torn scraps that still hung from her shoulders, and sat at the desk. She flopped open the large book.

"What's that?"

"A history," Kheema said. She turned the stiff glass pages, watching the illustrations change and move, text flowing around them as each new page was revealed. "It looks like the complete history of the Temple. Every Sacrifice, every High Priestess, everything."

"I hope they don't expect us to memorize it all," Janaié said.

"Why? I thought you liked putting your hands on my body."

"I do! But if they wanted us to memorize it that way, they wouldn't have given us a book!"

"I can't argue with your logic." She closed the book. "Come put your hands on my body again."

Kheema and Janaié reveled in each other until they had made a wreck of the room and their bodies glowed with sweat. They stopped only when the growling in their stomachs reminded them it was time for the evening meal.

The dining hall was nearly deserted when they arrived. They saw no sign of Miati, Fahren, or the other group of Potentials.

There was no evening service that night. Kheema wandered the park for a time, hand in hand with Janaié. Janaié kissed her shyly beneath the overhanging branches of a large tree. Fragrant air folded around them, warm and still.

They retired early. They pressed themselves together once more, this time less frantic and more measured in their coupling, until they collapsed into sleep in a tangle of arms and legs.

Kheema woke the next morning to a pleasant, directionless voice saying, "All Potentials, please be ready for the ceremony in thirty minutes." She blinked in the darkness. Dawn had not yet arrived, and inky blackness filled the room.

She rose from the bed. The walls lit up with a soft, gentle glow that offered just enough light to see by. "Water," she said. The tub filled. When she stepped in, she gasped with the familiar shock of arousal.

Janaié joined her a few moments later, still rubbing sleep from her eyes. "It hardly seems real that they've put us back together," she said.

"Come over here and let me show you how real it is," Kheema replied. Janaié giggled. The giggle transformed into a moan when Kheema's hands slid down her body.

After they finished bathing, they met Fahren and the other Potentials in the hall. Sakim glowered at Janaié. Fahren brought them down the Hall of Memory, past the study chambers, into the large circular room with its eight columns where they had helped punish Nadaya and Denoma. A holographic projector squatted in the center of the circle where the heap of cushions had been. A large tray sat atop a slender black pedestal beside the projector. On the tray, Kheema saw eight small glowing vials, eight slightly larger vials filled with swirling blue liquid, many red silk cords, and a small black bundle of fabric.

Fahren lined the Potentials up and administered one drop of Blessing of Fire to each. Kheema closed her eyes as the heat spread through her body. Beside her, Janaié made a small "unh" sound. Fahren directed them to stand between the columns, facing away from the center of the circle. She bound each Potential with the silken cords. When she'd finished, all eight women were tied, legs and arms outstretched, between the columns.

She moved around the circle once more, this time with the vials of blue liquid. "This will prevent you from feeling hungry, thirsty, or sleepy," she said. "As Potentials, you will remain here throughout the Sacrifice. You will not be permitted to watch. However, you still have a role to play, as you'll see." She ran her hands up and down over Kheema's body with a smile. "The Sacrifice will be broadcast from the projector behind you, for the benefit of anyone else who may be here. You, however, will neither see nor hear it."

She picked up the bundle of cloth. Kheema realized it was a pile of black hoods, all folded together. "These will paralyze your auditory and optic nerves," she said. "While you wear these, you will see and hear absolutely nothing." She stood in front of Kheema. "Do not fear the Darkness, for you are held in his light."

She pulled a hood over Kheema's head. It was thin and light enough that it didn't interfere with her breathing.

Fahren touched the hem. Instantly, Kheema was embraced by a darkness and silence more profound than anything she had ever known. Even the sound of her own breathing disappeared, swallowed up in that still dark void. For a second, panic gripped her. She pulled wildly at the cords, heart beating fast, unable to hear her own cries.

Slowly, with effort, she willed herself to stillness. She could feel her heart pounding in her chest, could feel the air moving in and out of her lungs, but she could hear nothing. The devouring blackness consumed even the memory of light.

A hand touched her breast. She jumped. She may have cried out, but she wasn't sure. It withdrew, leaving echoes of sensation skittering across her skin.

She waited in complete isolation, utterly cut off from the world. She had no idea what was happening around her, nor how long she stood there. Freed from sensory input, her mind retreated to strange places. She found herself calling up memories of sound, and light, and color; in the silent darkness, she was not even sure these things were real. Had she ever been able to see and hear, or were her memories delusions?

A faint whisper of sensation, caused by a tiny current of air, played over her back. An instant later, a pair of hands gripped her breasts, overwhelming in the absence of sound and light. She writhed, letting out a cry she could not hear. A body, hard and muscled, pressed against her back. A thick hot cock demanded entrance into her.

Kheema arched her back. The unseen figure behind her thrust deep. She realized that this was the first time she'd taken a penis into her since entering the Temple. Her mysterious lover took her in absolute, uncanny silence, utterly isolated from sight and sound. She could sense nothing but hands on her breasts and the movement of the erection within her. She could not hear his breathing, nor his groans, could not see the look on his face. Even as he took her in such an intimate way, she was entirely cut off from him. She was cut off even from herself, unable to hear her own cries of pleasure.

A tightening of his hands on her breasts and a sudden flood of warmth inside her told her he was finished. He withdrew. She felt wetness slide out of her.

Unexpected lips closed around her nipple. Hands caressed her ass. She floated in the timeless silent void as hands fondled her, fingers and cocks demanded entrance into her, and lips touched her skin, all of it immediate and distant, intimate and impersonal.

Again and again she was penetrated by thick, hard shafts and dexterous fingers, sliding slick into her pussy and anus. Each one moved within her for a time, spurted hot wetness, and withdrew to make way for another. Fingers and tongues found her clit, fanning the flames of desire inside her. She pressed back against them, eager and desperate. She felt occasional hot splashes gushing across her skin, splattering her thighs and belly as unseen people ejaculated on her.

It came to her again, there in that dark space, the sense that she was not alone. In between the touches and the caresses, the thrusting of greedy, erect cocks, twining itself around her own desire and longing, the sense of presence grew and grew until it seemed like it might fill her up, taking shape within her, assuming the outline of her form.

Hello there, she thought. *Are you the Lord of Light?*

A flickering staccato of images strobed through her mind like a burst of static, too fast for comprehension. It faded, and she was alone once more, a tiny speck of awareness locked within a vessel that existed, in this moment, only for the pleasure of others.

There was no time in that dark, quiet place. It seemed as though it went on forever, yet at the same time, the people who pleasured themselves with Kheema flitted by like mayflies, inside her for a moment and then gone. She hung there for a hundred years that went by in an hour.

Then it was over. Some unseen person pulled the hood from her face. Light and sound poured in. Kheema cried out, overwhelmed and dazzled. She shook, panting and gasping. Fahren unbound her and helped her sit on the edge of the holographic projector.

Other priestesses untied the rest of the Potentials. They all seemed stunned, not entirely aware of where they were.

Janaié sat beside Kheema and wrapped her arms around her, face buried against her shoulder. Her breathing came as a deafening roar in Kheema's ears. Dim light from the channels in the ceiling told Kheema that night was falling.

Bit by bit, Kheema returned to herself. She embraced Janaié wordlessly, feeling the abundant wet slick of many worshippers' pleasure on Janaié's skin.

"The Sacrifice is complete," Fahren said. "The Lord of Light will bless us for another year. Tomorrow will be a day of rejoicing. Return to your quarters and rest."

1.13

WITH THE SACRIFICE successful, the entire Temple united in a day of celebration. At morning service in a packed cathedral, Miati beamed as she inducted Kellis, resplendent in a robe of red and glittering gold, as a new High Priestess. She offered the remaining Potentials in Kellis's group the option to become novice priestesses or, if they preferred, leave the Temple with no further obligation. They all chose to remain. One by one, each came naked to the podium to receive the filmy white robe of a temple novice.

Miati lifted her arms skyward. "Today marks the beginning of a new year. We have performed the Sacrifice and asked the God of the Sun to give us his blessing. In six months, on the shortest day of the year, a new group of Potentials will be accepted into the Temple, and the cycle will begin anew. And thus does our connection with the Lord of Light, first among all the gods, continue."

After the service ended, Kheema approached Fahren. "What happens now?" Kheema asked.

"This is a day of rest," Fahren said. "The Sacrifice is over. The God of the Sun is pleased. You may study, or meditate, or walk in the park, or do whatever else you desire. Tomorrow, we will start the next phase of your training."

"What is that like?"

"Since you've now learned the entire Litany, you'll be studying it only four days a week. You'll start learning other matters of the Temple: customs, rituals, history, all the things you'll need to know should you choose to remain here after next year's Sacrifice. You'll also learn the skills of reading people, bringing forth their desires, and manifesting pleasure."

"Will we be allowed to orgasm?"

Fahren smiled. "The path of the Sacrifice is never easy. The Lord of Light demands devotion."

"That's what I thought," Kheema said.

Fahren ran her hand lightly down Kheema's arm, sending shivers through her body. "It's not so bad. Only one more year—" Her smile grew wider at Kheema's expression. "In one more year, you will have learned ways of pleasure you can only begin to imagine now."

"Is it worth it?"

"Yes." She ran her fingers lightly over Kheema's neck, then kissed her, so gently Kheema's heart skipped a beat. "Yes, it is. At least if you're chosen as Sacrifice." She smirked. "I can't say if it's worth it for those who aren't chosen." She trailed her fingers over Kheema's hand and walked away.

Kheema and Janaié spent the next few hours in the garden, kissing each other on a low stone wall surrounding the base of a tree. Presently, Lianya wandered by. She watched them for a minute, then sat beside Janaié and ran her hand over her shoulder. Janaié turned to kiss her. Kheema's hand lightly stroked Janaié's breast.

A priest and a priestess, both wearing the colors of initiates, walked down the path holding hands. Upon seeing the three Potentials, they paused to kiss each other. Kheema smiled at them. They sat down beside her. The priest put his hand on her knee.

Kheema's heart raced. She turned to kiss him. He returned the kiss gently. Janaié's lips found Kheema's neck. She sighed.

Soon they had attracted another priestess, and another. Two more priests in blue loincloths joined the growing group. Bodies writhed. The air filled with moans.

Kheema found herself at the center of a tightly packed throng of men and women, caressing, stroking, kissing, sucking, penetrating. Beside her, Janaié seemed taken by the sexual energy surrounding them. She kissed Kheema, tongue gentle against her lips, while her fingers ran over Kheema's skin. With her other hand, she stroked a tall, broad-shouldered priestess's cock, teasing her with slow, languid motions.

Kheema's vision grew hazy. Golden light filled the space around her. She found herself moving as though in a dream, her body something separate from her. She kissed her way down Janaié's body, sliding further and further down until she knelt in front of her, tongue seeking Janaié's clit. Someone entered her from behind in a slow, deep wave of pleasure that flowed around her like an incoming tide. The golden light filled her vision, obscuring details, forcing her attention inward to the pleasure that surged through her body.

She was aware of ecstasy all around her. Her own pleasure grew more intense, always approaching but never reaching the moment of orgasm. Now Janaié's body was beneath hers, damp with sweat, and the two embraced each other surrounded by a writhing sea of ecstasy. She looked up, squinting through the golden haze, to see Miati looking down at her. Miati nodded and turned away.

The next day, a new routine started. As Fahren led the Potentials down the Hall of Memory, she said, "Since you've now had time to memorize the Litany, your Recitation does not need to be private. From now on, one of you will be chosen each day to do your Recitation in front of the congregation. Any error, no matter how trivial, will be cause for punishment." She stopped in front of the row of doorways that appeared at her gesture. The rest of you may watch, or do your Recitation in private or with each other, or study and meditate on your own. Tomorrow you will have your first lessons in the sensual arts instead of studying the Litany. I will return after you've finished today's session."

When they were alone in the chamber, Kheema slipped her robe from her shoulders. She lay down on her back on the mound in the center of the room, closing her eyes and allowing herself to sink into the softness. "Come!" she said. "Put your hands on me and be enlightened."

Janaié grinned an impish grin. "I have enlightenment for you right here."

When Fahren collected them after study, she pulled Tani aside. "You will do public Recitation today," she said. "The rest of you may spend this time however you like."

Janaié's eyes glowed. "I want to watch!" she said. Kheema laughed and bid her go. After Janaié scampered off, Kheema found an unoccupied meditation cell.

She closed her eyes, savoring the memory of Janaié's hands. Her lips moved as she repeated the Litany under her breath. Already it felt like an old friend, comfortable and familiar. The light rippled. A vast savanna took shape.

"It came to pass," she said, "that the Light took hold and grew, and the people were inspired. They studied the world around them so as to know its ways. And as their knowledge grew, so did their wisdom." The wind picked up, rippling the savanna grass around her, setting small clouds racing through a deep blue sky. Her breath quickened. She slid her hand between her legs, remembering how it had felt when Janaié's fingers probed there. "The wisest among them gathered together. 'Let us make a way to explore the heavens,' they said, 'so that we may take our place among the stars.'" Her pulse quickened. She shuddered. Her robe streamed behind her.

Later, at the evening service, Janaié greeted Kheema, wide-eyed and somber. "Kheema!" she said. "The public Recitation is hard! I don't know if I can do it! I don't want to get us into trouble!"

Kheema smiled and kissed her forehead. "You'll do fine."

After service the next day, Fahren assembled the Potentials outside the chapel. "There will be no memorization or Recitation today," she said. "Today, we start observation and enhanced skills training."

She brought the Potentials to a large, long room across the park from their quarters. Light poured in through translucent overhead panels that muted and diffused it, illuminating the room evenly. Thick red tapestries with embroidered designs of people pleasuring one another hung from the walls. Kheema's feet sank into soft white carpet. Low, wide marble platforms lined both sides of the room, topped with plush, comfortable-looking cushions upholstered in red and gold. At one end of the room stood a row of columns, with metal rings set into them at the top and base. Several novice priests and priestesses sat on the cushions chatting.

"Some of you may become priestesses of the Temple," Fahren said. "As part of your duties, you will need to learn to read the bodies of those who come seeking the Fiery One's blessing, so that you may learn to call forth the maximum pleasure. We will begin today with a series of exercises to teach you to connect with the spark of desire that lives within us all. Please line up." She directed the Potentials to stand in front of the platforms with their cushions. Kheema found herself facing a short, curly-haired priest with bright red eyes. He smiled at her with a lopsided grin.

"Place your hands on the shoulders of the person in front of you," Fahren directed. Kheema placed her hands on the man's shoulders.

"Now, without speaking, explore your partner's body with your hands. Take your time. Notice how your partner breathes. Pay attention to every cue. Try to discover how and where your partner most likes to be touched, entirely through their physical responses."

"What are we looking for?" Veenja said.

"Anything that changes," Fahren said. "Dilation or contraction of the pupil. Changes of pulse or breathing. Flushing of the skin. Anything that signals pleasure. Go slowly. Take your time." She walked down the row of Potentials. "Don't rush to the obvious places," she told Sakim, moving her hand from between the legs of a slender, elfin woman with dark hair and deep orange eyes. "You are seducing a person, not a collection of parts."

She stopped behind Kheema. "Start light," she said. "Move your hands slowly. Like this." She placed her fingertips on Kheema's collarbone. She caressed Kheema gently, dragging her fingers slowly down Kheema's breast, avoiding her nipple. Kheema quivered and sighed.

Fahren smiled at the sigh. "I like you. You're easy to read. Your body hides nothing." She moved on to Janaié. "Excellent. Your lips, like your hands, are tools of discovery. The people before you have not taken the Blessing of Fire. You must learn the secret ways of their bodies without help."

Kheema ran her hands down the priest's arms, along his sides, up over his chest. She focused every bit of her attention on his breathing, the flutter of his eyelids, the pulse in his neck. Whenever her hands found a place that inspired a response, she lingered there, touching him more firmly or more gently, building on his response, learning him.

Soon he hardened. His penis sprouted, thick and erect, from the inverted V-shaped opening in his loincloth. Kheema slid her hands lower, stroking his skin, fingertips running lightly across his stomach, down his thighs, avoiding his erection.

His body entranced her. It spoke, yielding its secrets to her. A milky drop formed at the end of his shaft. Kheema smiled, enjoying the learning of him. Every sound, every shiver, every tremble offered a gold mine of information, telling her where to touch him, where to kiss, how to summon forth his desire. Her own body responded to his soft sounds of pleasure. She felt herself becoming damp.

She was so focused she was not even aware of Fahren standing beside her until she touched Kheema's shoulder. "Very good," Fahren said. "You're a natural."

Kheema blushed, pleased. "Thank you, Priestess."

"Okay, everyone, change partners," she said.

The line of Potentials moved to the right. Veenja circled around to the other end. Kheema found herself in front of the woman Janaié had just left. She was short and curvaceous, with brilliant pink hair and pale skin covered with subtle images of flowers in light pastel colors. Her nipples stood erect, bright pink on small breasts. She looked back at Kheema with unfocused eyes.

"It is one thing to arouse a person from cold," Fahren said. "It is another to read the body of someone whose desire has already been stoked. Using the same cues you've already learned, I want you to bring your new partner to orgasm as quickly as possible. Read their bodies to find out how they like to be pleasured. Use that knowledge to offer pleasure."

Kheema ran her hand lightly over the woman's shoulder. She closed her eyes and purred. Encouraged, Kheema explored her. She focused her attention entirely on her new partner's body, shutting out everything but the way her lips parted, her tiny quivers, the gentle exhalation of her sigh. Kheema slid her hands lower, caressing the woman's breast, bringing out a tiny gasp when her palm brushed her nipple.

She moved her fingers lower still, parting the folds between her legs, finding wetness there. The tip of her finger touched her clit. The woman shuddered.

Time slowed. Nothing existed except the woman before her and the hundreds of tiny ways she responded to Kheema's gentle exploration. Kheema moved her finger just a bit faster over the woman's clit, prompted by her tiny shudders and her sudden inhalation.

They created a private space, Kheema and her nameless partner, carving out a tiny bubble that was theirs alone amidst the crowd. The priestess threw back her head and moaned, pressing her body forward against Kheema's fingers, but she didn't quite reach the point of release. Kheema pressed harder against her clit. She gasped and parted her legs wider to allow greater access, yet still she did not cross the edge.

Somewhere far away, a man cried out in ecstasy, roaring as he came. The sound seemed much too distant to be of any concern to Kheema. She leaned in close, her lips lightly touching the woman's neck. That brought another moan, along with a small shudder.

Kheema's body touched an erect nipple. The woman gasped. Kheema smiled. She kissed her way down, her lips traveling along the woman's collarbone, over the curve of her breast, her fingers not varying in their insistent circles around her clit. Her tongue reached the woman's erect nipple. She took it between her lips.

The woman exploded into orgasm, screaming with pleasure, her body convulsing. Kheema kept touching her, fingers busy on her clit, tongue moving over her nipple, until she had wrung every last bit of ecstasy from the woman's body. The woman went limp, skin sheened with sweat. "Thank you," she panted.

More moans and cries of ecstasy rose around them. When they ebbed, Fahren clapped her hands together. "Sakim, as the first to pleasure your partner, you get special commendation. Now if we will…"

"Hey!" Chanae said. "I got him going first." The other Potentials laughed.

"Chanae makes a good point," Fahren said. "The journey is as important as the destination. Now we will bring in another group to continue the lesson. This time, I want you to arouse your partner without touching any of the normal erogenous zones. Learn to look beyond the obvious."

After the class ended, Janaié embraced Kheema tightly, her face flushed. Her eyes glowed. "That was fun!" she said. She took Kheema's hand shyly. "May I practice on you later?"

Kheema laughed. "Of course! What are partners for?"

1.14

ANOTHER DAY OF memorization followed. Kheema ran her hands over Janaié's squirming, writhing body to call forth the words of the Litany. Her voice filled the small room.

When they finished, Fahren pulled Kheema aside. "You have been chosen for today's public Recitation. Come with me."

Janaié, Sakim, and Chanae followed Fahren as she led Kheema to the chapel where a large X-shaped frame, padded and covered in red leather, awaited. A small stool sat at its foot. Two chairs flanked the frame.

Fahren removed Kheema's robe and directed her to stand with her back to the frame. She strapped her in place, arms and legs outstretched, and pressed a lever. The frame tilted backward until Kheema found herself looking up at the vaulted ceiling high overhead.

Hassen sat on the stool at the base of the frame between Kheema's open legs. Fahren sat in the chair to Kheema's right. Another priest—a short, stocky man Kheema did not recognize— sat to her left.

People filed into the chapel. Thirty or forty priests and priestesses took to their seats on the long benches. Kheema's heart raced.

When everyone was seated, Fahren intoned, "You may begin."

Kheema's mouth went dry. "In the beginning was the Darkness," she croaked. "The first people came forth into the Darkness, and their lives were shrouded in night. Many were their trials, short were their lives, and great was their suffering, for in darkness they dwelt, and the darkness dwelt within them."

Hassen leaned over to probe her clit with his tongue. She shuddered. "Into the Darkness came a s...spark of Light. The light touched the hearts of some, so they felt its presence. Uh!" Her hips lifted from the frame, pressing to Hassen's tongue.

The man beside Kheema took her nipple between his lips. She let out a small cry. Fahren kissed her neck, running her fingers down Kheema's body.

"They took the...mmm.... the Light to the people, but the people accepted it not...oh! For they dwelt in the darkness, and darkness was...oh! Oh! All they knew." Her chest heaved. She closed her eyes and swallowed, forcing her body to be still through sheer force of will. "The people lived, and they died, but the spark of Light remained, for where the Light has been, it may...uh! Never...oh! Be erased!"

It went on and on while Kheema writhed and squirmed, bound in place, reciting the Litany through the constant sexual attention. Her skin glowed with sweat. Eventually, when she completed the first chapter of the Litany, Fahren was satisfied. She unstrapped Kheema. "You did well," she said. The audience stood.

Kheema fled to the solitude of the meditation cell. She sat on her rock, surrounded by sand dunes that glowed in the late afternoon sun, shuddering at how close she had come to making an error in her Recitation. Endless desert folded around her, as still as a tomb.

The days sped by, becoming weeks, then months. Kheema and the other Potentials learned the history of the Temple, received instruction in Temple skills, and always, always practiced the Liturgy.

A few weeks before winter solstice, Lianya made an error, dropping an entire sentence from the third chapter of the Liturgy during her recitation. The next day, she and Sakim were bound, naked and hooded, in the chamber at the end of the Hall of Memory. All day and all night, priests and priestesses made use of their helpless bodies. Kheema took delight in helping herself to Sakim's body, running her nails over her skin, pinching and twisting her nipples, pressing fingers into her, knowing Sakim would never know who was tormenting her. Sakim shuddered and wept with frustration. Kheema smiled to herself.

The arrival of winter solstice meant the coming of a new group of Potentials. The task of leading and teaching them fell to Kellis, the previous Sacrifice. Kheema smiled when she saw them the next morning, sitting on the dais at their first service, timid and uncertain. She remembered how she'd felt in their place.

She took to spending her afternoons on the balcony overlooking the park, watching the comings and goings below. There was a rhythm to life in the Temple. The novices and initiates rose early to tend to their duties outside the Temple. They returned in the evenings exhausted and happy. Kheema realized, as she watched a small group of novice priestesses and a priest talking in the park one evening, that she had not set foot outside the Temple in more than a year.

The High Priestesses spent much of their time training novices. Kheema watched Miati whenever she could, learning about the life of the Grand High Priestess. Miati frequently availed herself of the other priests and priestesses. She was a skilled, attentive, and empathic lover whose attentions never went unwanted. Those who caught her eye invariably went away from their encounters flushed and happy.

One evening, after Janaié had gone to bed early, Kheema wandered out to the balcony to find Miati and Fahren in the float tube, naked and entwined, floating weightless in space. From the look of it, Miati seemed just as skilled at the erotic arts in weightlessness as she was on the ground. Kheema watched for a time, then returned to her quarters to rouse a sleepy but uncomplaining Janaié.

The Litany became a part of Kheema. She could recite it—all nine hours of it—forward and backward. At night, she dreamt of swirling words that glowed on Janaié's skin. Public Recitations became easier. She learned to separate her being, the part that repeated the words kept distant from the part that writhed and moaned on the rack.

The world traveled in its orbit. The rhythm of the Temple kept to its pace.

During the week before summer solstice, Miati developed the habit of summoning Kheema to her quarters at the close of every day. Night after night, Fahren came to fetch Kheema. Night after night, Fahren returned, sometimes hours later, to lead Kheema to her quarters, exhausted and sore, face covered with Miati's juices.

The solstice grew nearer. The time for the ritual of Selection approached. With each passing day, Kheema quivered a bit more. Butterflies churned in her stomach. The ritual aroused and terrified her.

Janaié, sensing her anxiety, attended to Kheema's needs, fussing and fretting over her. She bathed her in the morning, running soapy hands over Kheema's body while she murmured words of reassurance in Kheema's ear. On the days when they had Memorization, she ran her hands over Kheema's body like delicate butterfly wings, coaxing her into arousal with exquisite tenderness. After their classes in erotic arts, she practiced each day's lessons on Kheema. She learned to read Kheema with an uncanny precision that bordered on telepathy. At night, after Kheema returned from Miati's quarters, Janaié spent long hours massaging her, hands kneading the stress from her weary body.

The morning of the day of Selection, Kheema awoke anxious and tense. Janaié caressed her in the tub, whispering calming words in her ear as her hands worked her body. The Provider produced heavy robes of thick fabric in place of the normal gossamer clothing they usually wore. Kheema donned hers, marveling at its softness.

After breakfast, Miati came to gather the Potentials. She gave Kheema a wolfish grin. "Come with me," she said. Janaié took Kheema's hand.

They padded up the hallway toward the ritual chamber, Kheema's heart pounding. Janaié slipped her arm around her waist. "You'll do fine," she said. "You'll see."

The chamber buzzed with people when they arrived. Miati directed them toward the pool of sparkling liquid. She stood in front of the massive carved throne, arms uplifted, with the new group of Potentials arrayed on each side of her. "It is time," she said. "Every year, we gather to choose a new Sacrifice. We call upon the Lord of Light to guide us. We pray that one of the Potentials now present before us will be satisfactory to him as a Sacrifice, and that she will perform her duties with honor."

"Praise to the Lord of Light," the crowd said.

"From darkness comes the Light," Miati said. "Let the Potentials enter the Light, that they may spread its blessings."

Kheema swallowed. Janaié squeezed her hand. Kheema and the other Potentials stepped forward. The liquid closed around them.

The arousal hit Kheema like a physical thing, stunning in its ferocity. She squeezed her eyes shut. Her heart pounded. This arousal was more intense than she had expected—more intense than anything she'd ever felt even during training. The liquid flowed around her like a lover's caress. Hungry, wild desire exploded through her, so painfully sharp she cried out from the force of it. Bubbles escaped her lips.

When she stepped back out of the pool, the robe clung heavily to her skin, saturated with the glowing liquid. She knelt before Miati, struggling to control her raging body. She wanted to fling herself into the crowd, give herself to them, more than she had ever wanted anything in her life. Her heart threatened to erupt from her chest.

"Today," Miati said, "one of you will be chosen as Sacrifice. Before that happens, you must demonstrate your self-control to the Lord of Light. Only when you have mastered yourself are you ready to give yourself to his Light."

"Praise to the Lord of Light," Kheema said. Her voice sounded hoarse and strained even to herself.

"Praise to the Lord of Light," the crowd responded.

"For one day and one night, you will offer yourselves to all those among us who want you," Miati said. "For one day and one night, you will utter not a single word, nor touch yourselves sexually, no matter how great your desire. Any of you who speaks even one word may not become the Sacrifice, nor rise to the level of High Priestess. When one day and one night have passed, whichever among you has demonstrated the greatest dedication to the Lord of Light will be chosen as Sacrifice. Do you understand?"

"Yes, Priestess," Kheema said.

"Take your place."

Kheema rose on feet that wanted to leap into the crowd. Shaking, she knelt on the cushions atop the low platform, warm and soft beneath her. On hands and knees, she closed her eyes and waited.

She didn't have to wait long.

The crowd swarmed around the kneeling Potentials. Hands gripped Kheema's shoulders from behind. Kheema felt a rigid cock plow into her, hard and insistent. She let out a howl of pure animal desire. A priest with dark skin and a hard, muscled body grabbed Kheema by the hair. Before she could see his face, his erection invaded her mouth. She abandoned herself to the onslaught, her heat matching theirs, until they both came with howls of their own. Thick warmth rushed into her and poured down her throat.

The priest in front of her turned and left. Fahren took his place. She caressed Kheema's cheek. Her body went rigid for a moment when the liquid took effect. She seized Kheema's hair with both hands, forcing her face between her legs, grinding against her willing tongue. Kheema felt hands grab her hips from behind, then something hard and slick forced its way into her ass.

Kheema felt the dam begin to crumble. She scraped together what remained of her resolve, gathering it around herself in the midst of the howling storm. *Let them have you*, she told herself. *Give your body in service to the Fiery One.*

She pressed herself back onto the cock in her ass. Somewhere far behind her, a man groaned. Warmth gushed deep inside her. A moment later, Fahren screamed, shaking with pleasure from Kheema's dancing tongue.

More people came to sample Kheema's body, and more after that. She felt neither hunger nor thirst, only the struggle within herself to remain wordless as she gave herself to those who wanted her. Her body quivered with need.

She accepted every touch, every grope, every use of her body. She used the skills she had been taught automatically, sensing desire in every quiver and moan, drawing it out with subtle motions of her tongue and small contractions between her legs, heightening the experience of every person who took her, so that the pleasure she gave was all the more intense.

Not everyone who approached her made use of her body. Some of the priests preferred to tease her by touching her lightly, then retreating. They stroked themselves from just outside her reach. When they came, they splattered her face, her back, her breasts, and her thighs with warm wetness.

Through it all, none of the Potentials spoke a single word. The chamber grew darker with the coming of night, until only the dancing glow from the pool offered light. The flow of people slowed. Kheema fought off the urge to slip a hand between her legs during those moments when she found herself entirely empty. With the need upon her, those brief instants were worse than when she was at the center of greedy men and women.

The night passed. The rising sun sent its warm light filtering in through the channels in the ceiling. Priests and priestesses came to the chamber with the new day to help themselves to the Potentials before they went about their daily duties. Kheema and the other Potentials found themselves once more surrounded by clusters of forceful, demanding lovers.

Miati, who had remained seated on her throne the entire night, rose and clapped her hands. "It is done," she said. "The selection is made."

Kheema looked around, confused, wondering who had been chosen. She struggled to contain a surge of bitter disappointment. She had been so sure the first day she'd entered the Temple that it would be her.

The people in front of her knelt. She shook her head, trying to clear her vision. She looked down to see her robe was scarlet. "Oh," she said.

1.15

Kheema swallowed. She took a deep breath to hide her nervousness.

"You'll do fine," Janaié said. She slipped her hand into Kheema's.

Kheema managed a small smile. "Is it that obvious?"

"Only to me."

Kheema looked down. They stood in a wide circular chamber high up in the center of the Temple. Miati was there, and Fahren, and all the other Potentials from Kheema's group. Warm, still air filled the corridor. The walls glowed with dim light. Dawn was less than an hour away. "I can't hide anything from you," she said.

"Would you want to?" Janaié kissed her shoulder. "Your agony will be so lovely. I know the Sun God will be pleased."

Kheema wore a long, light dress of red fabric so thin it was almost translucent. The other Potentials wore the same robes they'd worn for the past year and a half.

A circular iris opened in the ceiling. In complete silence, a round stone platform, decorated with a stylized red flame, floated to the ground. Miati and Fahren stepped onto the platform.

Shaking, Kheema stepped onto it with them. The other Potentials followed. Without the slightest sound or vibration, the platform ascended again, carrying them through the opening in the ceiling.

It brought them out onto the peak of the Temple, a broad space ringed by low stone columns. Kheema's gaze gravitated to the altar itself upon which she would be sacrificed, a large marble block inclined toward the courtyard below. On each side of the altar sat a low stone table bearing a flask of thick amber oil. Kheema trembled.

Miati and Fahren turned her to face the broad courtyard, barely visible far below in the dim pre-dawn light.

A flickering column of shimmering light materialized in the center of the courtyard, partly illuminating the throngs of people gathered there. It coalesced into a huge, ghostly hologram of Kheema, many times larger than life. She blushed. Color touched the hologram's cheeks.

The Potentials knelt in a semicircle behind the altar. Fahren and Miati slipped the robe from Kheema's body, leaving her nude atop the temple. They led her to the altar. Miati gestured for Kheema to lie on her back.

Quivering, heart hammering, Kheema reclined nude on her back, the stone smooth and warm against her skin.

Miati bound Kheema's wrists to the altar just above her head. Fahren parted Kheema's legs, binding her ankles to the corners. Miati took a vial from a pouch inside her robe. "This is the antidote to the Blessing that prevents orgasm," she said. "It will also remove the need for food or sleep."

Kheema parted her lips. Miati opened the vial. A small drop of swirling, red and gold liquid fell onto Kheema's tongue. It tasted of honey and roses. She did the same for each of the other Potentials, allowing a single drop to fall on their waiting tongues. After they had accepted the liquid, each of them clasped their hands behind their backs.

A long, narrow arm separated itself from the base of the altar. It hinged up slowly, bearing two smooth rounded prongs at its end. These slid into Kheema, filling both the spaces between her legs. She gasped at the sudden violation.

The sun rose above the horizon. The prongs began to vibrate in long, slow pulses. Kheema opened her mouth.

"In the beginning," she said, "was the Darkness. The first people came forth into the Darkness, and their lives were shrouded in night. Many were their trials, short were their lives, and great was their suffering, for in darkness they dwelt—"

The orgasm hit her, fast and intense, the first one she'd had in eighteen months. All those long months of teasing, the constant nonstop arousal, the unending edging over and over again, all were released in one explosive moment of ecstasy. She shrieked in unbearable pleasure, thrashing against the bonds that held her to the altar. "And the darkness dwelt within them!" she cried. "Into the Darkness came...came..." A second orgasm roared through her on the heels of the first, following in such close succession she could not tell when one ended and the other began. "A spark of Light! The light touched the hearts of some...unghh! So, they felt its presence!"

Miati and Fahren stood on each side of her. They dipped their hands into the oil. Then, gently, they began to massage Kheema, hands gliding over her skin, caressing her.

"They took the Light to the people!" Kheema cried. "But the people accepted it not, for they dwelt in the...in the...in...oooongh!" Pleasure beyond endurance lashed through her. She arched her back so violently her body lifted off the altar. The smooth stone plugs within her continued their ceaseless thrumming. "In the darkness, and darkness was all they knew!"

Behind her, the other Potentials spoke along with her, hands still behind their backs, following along in the Litany. Far below, the hologram-Kheema writhed on the altar, enduring orgasm after overpowering orgasm.

"The people lived, and they...annngh! They died, but the spark...the spark...nngh! Of Light remained, for where the Light has been, it may never...oh! Oh! Be erased! Haaaangh!"

Miati and Fahren kept up with the gentle massage, their hands caressing her breasts, her stomach, her thighs. The oil tingled, sending little sparks of sensation trilling along Kheema's skin. Another orgasm slammed through her, sweet and agonizing.

The orgasms kept coming, each just as wrenching as the one before. The vibrating things within her seemed to be able to read her mind, somehow always pulsing at exactly the right speed and with exactly the right motion to wring another orgasm from her sweat-soaked body. The sun climbed higher overhead. Hands like fire stroked her body, reaching through her skin, awakening sensation deep inside her.

The sense of presence came to her once more, the strange alien mind moving inside hers. Its presence brought her comfort and a small measure of peace. Her voice became clearer.

"Many were born into Darkness who did not...onngh! Know the Light. But still the Light remained, and all the fear of the people who knew it not could drive it away." The words poured from her. Fahren and Miati fondled her breasts. The things inside her hummed.

"And the people who knew the Light said...uh! Said 'No, you choke yourself, you poison yourself. We must find ano—ano—another way!' Their words were heard by some, and the Light grew. Those who...ohngh! Felt the Light saw one another, and their voices were…oh! Oh! Raised together! Together, they set out to spread the Lightnnnnngh!" She writhed on the altar, eyes closed.

Miati slipped a finger against Kheema's clit. A rapid series of orgasms exploded through her without pause. "Aaah! Ah ah ah ahhhhh!" Kheema cried. "The Light found fertile…oh! Soil in the…nnnngh! Hearts of those it touched!"

On she spoke, twisting and thrashing, reciting the sacred text while orgasms beyond pleasure or pain wracked her body. The alien presence held her, comforted her while her body spasmed on the altar.

The rest of the Potentials remained still, kneeling under the bright sun while Kheema spoke and screamed. Miati and Fahren stayed with her throughout the entire day, massaging her body with sweet-smelling oil, running their hands over her skin. The shadows grew longer.

She finished just before the sun dipped below the curve of the horizon. A cheer erupted from the crowd below. The buzzing things inside her stopped. The arm withdrew. Kheema slumped, eyes half-closed, breathing hard, mumbling inaudibly to herself.

Reverently, tenderly, Fahren kissed her. She and Miati unfastened the bonds that held her to the altar. Her body twitched with aftershocks.

"The Compact is satisfied," Miati said. "The Sacrifice is made."

They helped Kheema stand. She clung to Fahren for support.

Miati held her arms high. Down in the courtyard, the hologram showed her shining face. "The God of the Sun accepts our sacrifice!" she said. Her voice carried through the courtyard. "Let all who wish his blessing for the coming year, receive the gifts of his servants!"

Fahren and Miati helped Kheema walk down the long, broad ceremonial staircase from the top of the Temple to its base. The other Potentials rose and followed behind, descending into the crowd below.

The twilight deepened. The throng surged forward. Hands reached out from the crowd to touch Kheema and the other Potentials, caressing, stroking, fondling.

Fahren released Kheema. Instantly, she was carried off into the crowd. People drew close around her, eager to receive her blessing. A tall, lanky man kissed her, his kiss an act of worship. Someone behind her wrapped his arms around her and stroked her swollen nipples. An erect penis slid easily into her. She moaned.

The crowd swallowed up the Potentials. They gave themselves freely to the throng. The courtyard filled with cries of ecstasy.

Kheema felt only partly aware of where she was. Light and warmth filled her body. A golden glow seemed to hover about her. Wherever she turned, people touched her, caressed her, kissed her, entered her.

Tomorrow, she would begin her new life as a High Priestess. The other Potentials would, if they chose, remain in the Temple as priestesses themselves. But for now, this evening, she would do her part to spread the Light.

BOOK TWO
THE GARDEN

2.1

SHE SAT ON the low stone wall in the evening gloom, staring out over the garden that lay sleeping beneath the rolling blanket of snow. In her mind, she saw it not as it was, but as it soon would be—a lush, luxurious riot of color, growing dense and wild around her still body. She felt a small stab of sorrow that she would not be able to see it in full bloom. The Garden was one of the most beautiful parts of a city that regarded beauty as a fundamental necessity. For most of her life, she had taken great joy in watching it blossom.

At the moment, her hair and skin were as white as the snow. That would change with the spring. As the days grew warmer, her hair would become first light green, then deep green. She had decided it would grow faster as well. Right now, it didn't even reach her shoulders. By the time winter came again, it would touch the ground.

Her eyes, too, would change, deepening from a blue so pale they were nearly translucent to a rich, dark blue. Then, when the first green appeared in the garden, they would change to emerald, to match her hair. Even her skin would change, from pale white to chestnut brown and, as autumn approached, to a deep coppery color.

She took the change of seasons seriously.

She wore a white dress, corset-tight at her chest and flared at her hips, that fell to the ground in wide pleats. The front was cut to expose her breasts. She wore no ornamentation other than a white choker with a small white disc in front clasped around her slender neck. Her bright pink nipples added the only splash of color to her monochromatic theme.

Exactly on schedule, a light snow began drifting down from the featureless white sky. It shimmered as it passed through the shield dome, little whorls of golden light rippling from each point of contact. The Garden nestled against the edge of the City, near where the shield dome met the ground. Occasional gusts of wind sent flurries of snow sideways through the shield, creating an ever-changing backdrop of swirling light behind the slumbering garden.

"Terlyn! I knew you'd be here."

She turned at the voice. A wide, warm smile lit up her face. "Donvin!"

They threw their arms around each other in a tight embrace. Donvin stood almost a head taller than she did. He was dressed more practically for winter than she, in a long black jacket that hugged his broad shoulders and left a trail of curved impressions in the snow behind him.

"I heard the news! You've been selected as the next Fountain. So, it's official, then?"

"It is! I start the purification in just a few days. When spring comes, I will be part of the Garden."

He stepped back, hands on her shoulders, and looked her up and down. "I want you to be happy. I know you've always wanted to do this…"

"You look like you're about to add a 'but' to that."

He sighed. "I guess I just don't understand losing yourself like that."

She frowned. "Does that mean you won't come visit me when I'm in the Garden?"

"Will you even remember if I do?"

"I always remember you."

He shook his head. "I'm serious, Terlyn. Once you're part of the Garden, I don't even know if you'll be you anymore. The Fountains, they don't…it changes you, you know?"

"Donvin, everything changes you. Do you want me to be the same forever? That would make life a prison."

"No! I just want you to be you. I don't want you to lose who you are."

"This is me. I have devoted myself to service to the Quickener. If that changes me, so be it."

They looked at each other for a long moment in the gathering gloom. Then he smiled. "You always were stubborn. Do you really want me to visit you when you're…you know, in there?"

"Yes."

"Okay. If you want it, I will do it. Even if you won't remember."

"I will remember. I promise." She linked her arm through his. "I don't have to start purification just yet. Take me somewhere warmer?"

They walked away from the garden. Snow crunched beneath their feet. The sun slipped below the horizon.

They reached a pathway, paved with smooth brown stone that was entirely clear of snow. As the darkness grew, a tiny flying dronelight zipped down from overhead, its light switching on as it approached. It glided just above their heads, lighting their way.

They walked for a time, following the meandering path through a series of small parks. At one point, they passed three people sitting on top of a large marble cube in the corner of a tiny triangular cluster of trees. A woman sat nude on one of her lover's laps, impaled on his erection. The other figure kissed the back of her neck while he caressed her breast with one hand.

She waved languidly to them as they walked passed. "Hi! Would you like to join us?"

Terlyn looked at Donvin. He shrugged.

"No thanks," Terlyn said. "Maybe next time."

"Okay…oh!" the woman said. She moaned, her face buried in her lover's neck. Ice crystals glittered in her hair.

They continued on, the enormous ziggurat of the temple of the Sun God behind them, the great towers of the housing district at the outer edge of the City before them. Eventually, they reached a float tube that ascended to the stacked tracks of the high-speed transport system overhead. The dronelight zipped away.

Hand in hand, they stepped into the illuminated float tube. After a brief moment of vertigo, they ascended in weightlessness to the first track, three stories above the ground. Another track ran parallel to it three stories above, and another above that, all following the curve of the City's outer edge.

The transparent tunnel of the transit system was warm and dry. Through its curved walls, they could see the City spread out like a vast jewel, glimmering in the gathering darkness. The rows of great black towers glowed with warm yellow light through tens of thousands of windows. Tiny dronelights bobbed and weaved, illuminating the way for the people who walked the meandering paths below.

There were only a few people on the broad landing. A small oblong pod stopped soundlessly in front of Donvin. The side hinged opened to allow them in.

"Where are we going?" Terlyn said.

"My place," Donvin said. "Tower five, level 117." The pod closed. The world outside dissolved into a blur.

"Tower five? Isn't that mostly where people go to be alone?"

Donvin shrugged. "Maybe I like to be alone."

"Why? It's not like you're four hundred years old!"

"It's peaceful. There's not a lot going on."

"Sounds boring."

"So don't live there. Do you want to spend time with me or not?"

"I'm sorry," she said. She put her arm around him. "I do want to spend time with you."

The pod tracks formed concentric circles, one along the outside edge of the City, the other closer in, near the Temple District, with straight segments linking the circles. The pod angled off the main track onto a curved ramp, rising to a higher level. When it had climbed several levels, it straightened again, picking up speed. They headed toward the edge of the City, then curved onto the circular track that made a circuit around the City's edge. The pod flashed through one of the living towers, then slowed as they approached the next. They coasted to a stop in a long corridor of polished white marble inside the tower.

When they left the pod, Donvin led Terlyn up a wide spiral hallway that looped around itself several times, then along another hallway. A door appeared in the glossy stone wall as he approached, opening silently to let them through.

Terlyn looked around. In all the years she'd known Donvin, she'd never seen his living space before. Donvin's quarters were quite large, but also spartan to the point of austerity. He'd arranged the space as a single large room, three of the walls covered in dark red wood polished to a high luster, the fourth an enormous floor-to-ceiling window that looked out over the City toward the great ziggurat in its center. He'd made only one concession to livability: a large bed in the corner, curtained off by a waterfall that fell from slots in the ceiling and disappeared into a channel in the floor.

Softly illuminated panels with narrow aisles between them divided up half the room. The arrangement reminded Terlyn of the Museum Hall beneath the temple of the Quickener. Sandwiched between panes of glass so transparent it was nearly invisible lay works of art in a dozen different media, each one an object of breathtaking beauty. There was a huge watercolor of a flock of birds arrowing through a sky dotted with small clouds, illuminated in red and gold by a setting sun. The paper, which Terlyn knew the painter had probably made by hand, gleamed with a faint iridescence.

Next to it, an intricate metal sculpture of a scorpion, so detailed it looked ready to spring from between the panes of glass, glittered in copper, gold, and platinum. Row after row of the display panels showcased dozens of pieces of art, each one representing years or decades of work, each one a gift someone had given to Donvin.

Donvin's own art was showcased there, too, sculptures in granite and marble. Many of them were only partly finished, beautiful forms emerging organically from hard stone.

A huge table made of the same red wood filled much of the center of the space. Atop the table sat an enormous half-finished granite sculpture of the City. In its unfinished state, the City appeared to be pulling itself out of solid rock. Small chisels and picks no larger than a fingernail lay scattered about the table. A thin film of granite dust covered the top of the table.

A small, functional bathroom and shower took up one corner, separated from the rest of the quarters by a serpentine waist-high wall of stone topped with copper.

Donvin sat on the bed. The water opened like a curtain to allow him through, then closed behind him.

Terlyn stripped off her dress, kicked her shoes aside, and approached the bed. The waterfall parted obligingly for her and closed after she passed. She sat on the edge of the bed next to Donvin, watching the water come down in a constant sheet. "That's interesting," she said.

"I got the idea from watching the rain on the window," Donvin said. He leaned close to her and caressed her arms. She closed her eyes.

Her mind flitted to the upcoming ritual of sacrifice. She felt a small shiver of nervousness. She would lose nine months of her life in service to the Quickener. It wasn't the loss of time that worried her; nine months was hardly significant. Donvin had put his finger precisely on her fear. She did worry about losing some part of herself. Past Fountains often spoke about the experience of being in the dream, of how the boundary between themselves and the Garden grew soft, of how their memory of their time of service went hazy. Being Sacrifice to the Quickener changed you.

Her family had served the Quickener for a very long time, going back almost to the founding of the City. She was glad to do it, and happy to be part of such a long tradition...

Donvin's hands reached around her body, cupping her breasts. He kissed the side of her neck. Her nipples hardened against his palms.

...and yet, she still felt that little tremor of fear. What if she returned from the Garden someone other than herself? Terlyn liked herself. Would being a Fountain mean losing a piece of what made her who she was?

One of Donvin's hands slid down her body, questing fingers probing between her legs. She parted them for him.

Terlyn's faith centered on the ceremony of the Garden. Through her entire adult life, she'd never doubted for even a moment that she would one day become a Fountain, the human embodiment of the Quickener. But now that the moment was nearly upon her, she found herself abruptly and unexpectedly afraid.

He rolled her over on her back. She cried out as he entered her. Her body responded automatically, hips pressing upward to meet his thrusts.

What did it mean, this little trembling of fear? Was she unfit to be Fountain? Would the Quickener see it within her? Did it mean she was unsuitable to serve? Would they be able to find another Fountain in time, this close to spring, if she should withdraw? And what would that mean for her and her family? Would she lose their respect?

Donvin roared. Wet heat gushed into her. She came as he did, the orgasm taking her by surprise, her hands clutching his back. When it was over, he withdrew. He lay down beside her, fingers running lightly over her collarbone. "You are somewhere else," he said.

"I'm sorry. Yes. I...I'm thinking about what you said."

"About what?"

"About losing myself."

He rolled over on his back and stared up at the ceiling. "Does that mean you're having second thoughts?"

"I don't know. I..." She sat up. "I don't know if I'm ready to talk about it yet."

"Fine." His tone suggested it wasn't.

"Don't be that way. I just...can we talk about something else right now?"

"Like what?"

She stood. The curtain of water parted obligingly for her. She carried her dress to the Provider. The slot opened. She fed it in, watching it disappear, then summoned up a bathrobe, printed with stalks of grass waving against a simple red circle representing the sun. She slipped it over her shoulders.

She walked over to the table and examined the exquisite detail of the model City. Tiny people almost too small to see walked about on the miniature pathways. Only part of the City had materialized from the slab of stone. The great ziggurat of the Fiery One was less than half visible, the foot of the temple still taking form from rough, shapeless rock. Her eyes followed the curving paths north, to the edge of the City, where the Garden nestled in full bloom against the shield generators. Donvin had exquisitely rendered every bush and flower in stone. Peering close, she could see the figure of a woman there among the vines. A set of tiny metal picks lay next to it.

"How long have you been working on this?" she said.

"I don't know. Eighty or ninety years."

She ran her fingers over the stone that still waited to be shaped. "How long will it take to finish?"

He sat up on the bed, watching her. "At the rate I'm going, maybe another hundred and fifty years, give or take."

"It's beautiful."

"Thank you." He gave her a warm, genuine smile. "It's my offering to the Lady."

Terlyn bent down to look closer. "The City will change by the time you're finished."

"It always does."

She smiled wanly. "Everything does. That's the way of things, I think."

"So you *are* going to do it, then." It wasn't a question.

She came back to the bed. The robe fell from her shoulders. She sat down beside him, taking his hand in hers. "We are who we are. That sculpture is you. The Lady is you. This is me."

"I think—"

She put her finger over his lips. "I'm here now." She leaned over to kiss him. He returned the kiss, lingering over it, tongue gently flicking over her lips until she sighed.

He kissed her neck, her shoulder, her collarbone, working his way slowly down her body, over her breast. She leaned backward. He kept going, kissing his way over her stomach, taking his time. When he reached the soft skin of her mound, with its neat line of hair, she opened her legs for him. He worked down further, until his tongue played across her clit. She moaned.

He continued working her with his tongue, slow and patient, until finally she cried out, arching her back with pleasure.

Only after the orgasm subsided did he take her again, sliding his erect cock into her once more. She kissed him, tasting herself on his lips. They both convulsed together. Afterward, they fell asleep side by side to the constant patter of falling water.

2.2

TERLYN WOKE BEFORE Donvin. Through the huge window, she could see that sunrise was still some time away. Snow came down endlessly from the dark void above, revealing itself in swirling traces of dim yellow light from the shield. A delicate trace of frost decorated the window.

She slipped quietly out of bed, careful not to wake Donvin. She fed her bathrobe into the Provider, then summoned a long white dress trimmed with white fur and a pair of thigh-high white boots. After she dressed, she stood at the Provider for a moment, thinking. She called up a single miniature rose, barely as wide as her fingernail, which she placed carefully on the tiny Garden in Donvin's model. Then, with one backward look at his sleeping form, she slipped out the door.

Outside, Terlyn stepped into a transparent float tube. The tube clung to the edge of the great round tower, which rose from the ground in a long, sinuous curve, bending with irresistible tropism toward the huge ziggurat in the center of the City. Hundreds of identical float tubes embraced the tower's surface. She hung weightless for a moment, watching the snow swirl around, before she settled toward the ground far below.

When she reached the ground, Terlyn set off toward the Garden. The long walk gave her plenty of time to think. A dronelight detached itself from the side of the building and swooped toward her, flicking on its light as it descended.

The snow stopped falling just before daybreak. The sun rose on a world of fragile beauty. A fresh carpet of snow lay over the city, carefully demarcated by the curving lines of the walkways. The enormous black towers grew, organic and sinuous, from a landscape of glittering white.

By the time she reached the courtyard in front of the enormous ziggurat, the priests and priestesses of the Fiery One already sat on the low stone benches in front of the rows of columns that spread in complex geometric patterns through the courtyard. The huge main doors of the Temple stood open.

The snow had avoided the courtyard and the Temple entirely. The air was warmer here too, as if the Temple and its surrounding spaces belonged to a different season altogether.

"You look troubled."

Terlyn blinked, distracted by the voice. She looked down at the woman who had addressed her.

The woman with creamy orange skin sat on a marble slab in front of a large column of stone, wearing the translucent white and red robe of a Temple priestess. Her hands lay folded in her lap, wrists bound together with red cord. Her pupils were tiny pinpricks in fields of brilliant orange. "I am Jilia, priestess of the Fiery One. You seem to have something on your mind. Would you like the blessing of the Lord of Light?"

"I...perhaps," Terlyn said. "I have...that is, I've never sought the Sun God's blessing before. I worship the Quickener."

"It makes no difference. The Lord of Light offers his blessing to all. He is not a jealous god."

"What...what do I do?"

"Bring a sunflower as an offering to any priest or priestess you choose."

"I don't have a sunflower."

"The Lord of Light is generous. Make an offering in the Temple to receive a sunflower."

"An offering?"

"Anything of value to you. Your time, a token, a symbol of your desire." She smiled beatifically. "The Lord of Light accepts all gifts and blesses all who seek him out."

"Thank you." Terlyn bowed slightly. She hesitated for a moment before she turned toward the Temple. "I guess there's no harm in trying."

Two immense doors opened into the Temple, wide enough for dozens of people to walk through abreast. Inside, Terlyn found an enormous walkway paved with white and red marble that ushered her into a vast, vaulted space. She had never before been inside the Temple. She half-expected the cavernous chamber to be dark, but it was brilliantly lit, flooded with sunlight guided into the space through a cunning arrangement of mirrored channels that directed light in from outside.

The vast hall, nearly a third the size of the entire ziggurat, housed a space part garden, part public bath, and part plaza, its ceiling ascending some four stories above. A long, narrow, rectangular garden bloomed with shrubs, trees, and flowering plants. Behind the garden, a huge rectangular pool sparkled in the channeled sunlight. Five broad, shallow steps of marble descended into it on all four sides. Two rows of columns, one on each side, flanked the pool.

People filled the space. Many were nude. Some were bound naked to the columns, arms above their heads, while others, seeking the blessing of the Fiery One, satisfied themselves with their bodies. Sighs and cries of pleasure echoed in the air.

"Is this your first time in the Temple?"

"What? Oh." Terlyn turned toward the woman who had addressed her. She was short, with pale skin that matched the filmy white initiate's robes she wore. Her wrists were not bound; instead, she carried a basket of sunflowers.

"It must be pretty easy to tell, huh? Terlyn said.

"Yes. Newcomers always stop at the door and look up." The woman smiled. "I'm Kirri. Welcome to the Temple of the Fiery One. You look like someone seeking guidance."

"You really can see through me, can't you?" Terlyn said wryly. "Am I completely transparent, or does the Lord of Light let you see into the hearts of everyone?"

"Neither one," Kirri laughed. "I just like people. I pay attention, that's all. Are you here looking for the blessing of the Fiery One?"

"I'm not really sure what I'm looking for," Terlyn said. "Clarity, perhaps."

Kirri nodded. "You're in the right place for that."

"How does this work?"

Kirri held up a sunflower. "Give one of these to a priest or priestess. You may bring a sunflower from somewhere else or present an offering to the Fiery One in exchange for one of mine."

"What kind of offering?"

"Whatever has value to you. Some people offer their time, or an act of service, or even something like a lock of hair."

Terlyn laughed. She ran a hand through her close-cropped white hair. "It's winter. I don't have much of that. Nor time, for that matter. I've already pledged myself in service to the Quickener."

"What do you value?"

"I value…" Her hand rose to her choker. "I value friendship. I value laughter. I value my connection to my past."

"Those are all admirable things."

Terlyn hesitated, then unfastened her choker. She opened the small round glass capsule on its front and tipped it into her palm. "This is my connection to my past," she said. "My grandmother gave herself as Sacrifice to the Garden many years ago. This is a seed from her service." She handed the tiny thing to Kirri.

Kirri clasped it. "Thank you," she said. Her eyes went soft. "This is one of the most precious offerings I have ever received. You honor the Fiery One." She handed Terlyn a sunflower. "I hope his blessing gives you the clarity you seek."

Terlyn traced the petals lightly with her fingers. "Thank you."

She walked back into the courtyard, still caressing the sunflower. She wandered for a time, lost in thought, until she almost tripped over a bare-chested man seated with his legs crossed beneath him on the marble walkway, wrists bound in front of him with red cord. He wore nothing but a simple loincloth of red and gold, deeply cut in the front in an inverted V to reveal a thick erection. He had short black hair, shot through with streaks of gray, brown, red, and white. He smiled up at her, his eyes a dark reddish-brown with pupils contracted to tiny points. "Do you wish the blessing of the Fiery One?"

She handed him the sunflower without a word. He rose gracefully to his feet in one fluid motion. "I am Fastof. Please follow me."

He led Terlyn through the crowded courtyard to the large rectangular pool, filled with shimmering liquid that almost seemed to glow with its own light. Sunflowers bobbed in the center.

He placed the sunflower in the pool, where it floated off to join others. He removed his loincloth. "Please disrobe," he said. Terlyn removed her clothes and piled them neatly at the edge of the pool.

He took her hand in both of his and stepped into the pool. She followed him down the shallow stone steps into the pool. The liquid closed around her, pleasantly warm on her skin.

The arousal hit her with such intensity she staggered, like a physical shock that slammed through her body. Raging need poured through her, so furious she let out a long moan.

Fastof sat in the pool. He pulled Terlyn down with him. He took a sponge from a slot in the edge of the pool and began to bathe her gently. The fact that his wrists were bound together did not hamper him at all. She leaned back against him, eyes closed, vibrating with desire. The world filled with a hazy golden glow.

By the time he was finished, Terlyn was unable to sit still. She ground herself back against him, longing to feel him inside her. He always seemed to be just out of reach, never quite in the right position for her to drive herself onto him.

Fastof climbed out of the pool. Water streamed from his muscular body. He dried her gently with a large, soft towel.

"What happens now?" she asked.

"This is your first time in the Temple?" He took her hand in both of his once more and led her to one of the columns. Then he raised his arms over his head and hooked the cord that bound his wrists together to a metal loop set in the stone column. "Now," he said, "you take the blessing of the Fiery One from my body."

With a roar, Terlyn threw herself at Fastof. She wrapped both arms tightly around him. His scent and the heat of his body consumed her. She impaled herself on his rigid cock. She let out a long howl of desire and pleasure as she drove herself on him over and over again, nails digging into his back.

The need was upon her so powerfully that she did not slow down even after she had had three powerful, wrenching orgasms in rapid succession. It was only after the fourth orgasm tore through her, dragging a scream of pleasure from her, that she slowed, body slicked with sweat. "Whew!" she panted. "You haven't come even once. I admire your stamina."

"I cannot," he said.

"Really?" She lifted herself up off his erection with a wet slurp. "Why not?"

"The Lord of Light wills it so. We spread his blessing in service to him, not for our own pleasure. Each morning, we are given the Blessing of Fire, to increase our desire greatly, but we also accept another blessing, to prevent release, so that we may serve with all our hearts."

"Does that mean you're just as turned on as I am?"

"Oh, yes," Fastof said. "We are trained not to show it, but I assure you, I am."

"Do you feel pleasure at all?" She ran her hand lightly over his shaft, slick with her fluids.

His eyelids fluttered. He gasped. "Yes. I can come very close indeed. But for me there is no final gratification."

"How interesting," Terlyn said. Her hand slid up and down along his erection. He groaned and shuddered.

"Oh, now that is interesting." Terlyn shivered. She knelt, looking up at him. "You are utterly unable to feel any satisfaction?" She parted her lips, resting the head of his cock against her tongue. He trembled. She smiled with delight. Slowly, deliberately, she drew him into her mouth, tasting her own pleasure on his slick shaft.

"Not until…oh!" He shuddered violently. "Not until tonight."

"What happens tonight?" she asked.

"After sundown, when the Temple closes, we all enter the pool. We eat the sunflower seeds from the sunflowers that were gifted to us."

"Go on," she said. Her hand caressed his shaft, tongue playing around the head.

"The seeds free us from the blessing, so that we may know release. We come together in the pool, gratifying each…oh!" His legs trembled. "Gratifying each other, in direct proportion to the amount of suffering we endured while we administered his grace to others."

"So, you're saying the more I make you suffer now, the greater your pleasure tonight?"

"Y-yes."

"I see." She placed both her hands on his hips. Holding his gaze steadily, she took him into her mouth. She sucked him in earnest, hard and fast, pulling him deep with each stroke. Her tongue danced over the head of his cock.

He shook, wrists bound over his head. He thrust forward, driving his erect cock into her mouth over and over. She grinned, savoring his desperation. She encouraged him, pulling his hips, urging him deeper.

She kept it up until tears of frustration formed in his eyes. She slid one hand between her legs to press her fingers against her clit. She looked into his eyes as she brought herself to orgasm, moaning around his shaft.

"By the Eight," he said, "you are cruel!"

She stood with a broad grin. "I want to give you something to remember tonight," she purred. She turned her back to him, pressing her ass against him, sliding his erection up and down between her ass cheeks. "It's a shame you're tied up. I would like to feel your hands on my breasts. Wouldn't that be nice?"

"Yes," he gasped, "it would." His breathing grew quicker.

She reached down between her legs to guide him into herself. She rode him that way, eyes closed, back turned to him, fingers stroking her clit until she came again in a long, explosive orgasm. He whimpered, twitching against the column.

As the orgasm faded from her body, a strange quiet settled around her. Fine golden mist filled the hall. The people faded away, until she found herself standing alone in the space. Even Fastof vanished. The trees and grass came alive with tiny dancing motes of light. They flowed along the edges of the trees, swirling, coalescing into the shape of a supine woman, arms and legs outstretched, surrounded by flowers. A sense of peace filled her.

Then the vision vanished, and she was in the noisy, crowded hall once more.

"…by the Fiery One," Fastof was saying.

"I'm sorry, what?"

"I said, you have the look of one inspired by the Fiery One."

"Maybe," Terlyn said. She gazed thoughtfully across the enormous hall. She unhooked Fastof's wrists. Then she gathered her clothing and dressed in silence.

On her way back through the courtyard, she passed Jilia again. "Did you find the enlightenment you were looking for?" Jilia asked.

"I'm not sure," Terlyn said. "The gods, they never just come right out and say anything, do they?"

Jilia laughed, a light, happy sound. "No, they never do."

"Ah. Well, one could hope, I suppose."

"If the gods made our choices plain to us, what purpose would there be to our lives? Figuring things out for ourselves is part of the reason we're here, don't you think?"

"Sure," Terlyn said. "It's as good a reason as any."

Jilia laughed again. "The gods provide for us, but they cannot tell us who we are."

2.3

TERLYN MADE HER way west, back toward the Garden. The City lay quiet, hushed beneath its blanket of new-fallen snow. She followed a winding path, lost in her own thoughts. The gods were nothing if not maddening in their opacity. She had given most of her life in service to the Quickener. Was it too much to ask for a straight answer now and then?

She walked past the great round amphitheater where the annual ritual of sacrifice to the Wild took place. She climbed up the stairway to the top of the amphitheater, ignoring the doorways at its base. As she rose, she wondered what it would feel like to walk these stairs on the day of the ritual. From the platform at the top, she looked down into the roofless amphitheater. It lay empty and still. Small mounds of snow gathered around the small, plain altar in the center.

She walked down the long spiral ramp that led toward the altar. The rows of cages along both sides of the spiraling walkway sat empty, their iron gates open, awaiting the worshippers who would be locked within on the day of the Sacrifice. She paused at the cage that had held her, the one time she had participated in the annual ritual so many years ago. She ran her hands over the cold iron bars and smiled at the memory.

After a moment, she moved on. The amphitheater had a textured stone floor, dotted with small, shallow pools connected by little channels no wider than her hand. They were empty now except for random drifts of snow. She sat on the edge of the altar, a featureless column of stone about waist high and barely wider than her body. When she looked up, the perfectly circular opening in the high, curved roof framed the sky. The clouds had cleared during her walk, and now roof and sky resembled a great blue eye, pupil contracted until it disappeared.

The God of the Sun was the first and oldest of the gods; everyone knew that. The Quickener Terlyn worshipped had come later, but was still quite old. The Wild was a young god, worshipped mainly by the young.

New gods did not come to the City often. No new god had arrived in Terlyn's lifetime, or the lifetime of anyone she knew. Some said the new gods weren't really new, but rather that each god was in some way an aspect of the Fiery One, some part of the Sun God's personality made manifest. Terlyn found that idea a bit far-fetched.

The Wild intrigued her. She worshipped him for a time, in her youth, when she'd given herself her first adult name and left her family to find herself. The Wild never called out to her the way the Quickener did.

But how much of that was her, and how much was the invisible weight of expectation? Most people tried several religions before settling on the one that best suited them. Worship of the Quickener was unusual, in that it tended to run in families. Terlyn's family all worshipped the hermaphroditic god, as did her parents and her grandparents. Donvin was right; she had always wanted to become a Fountain, even during her dalliances with other religions. Now, on the verge of her sacrifice, doubt plagued her. How much of that desire was really her?

After a time, she rose. Snow crunched underfoot as she retraced her path back up the steeply sloped spiral, past all the cages to the top of the amphitheater. The place offered only a sense of silent waiting. The Wild, it seemed, had nothing to say to her.

She headed away from the amphitheater, toward the inner ring of pod tracks that circled the Temple District in the center of the city. She passed several small garden plots. The snow had avoided them, falling in perfectly straight lines just outside the little gardens. A riotous profusion of flowers bloomed in every plot: large purple flowers with deep trumpets in one, dense bushes covered with sweet-smelling gold and scarlet blooms in another.

She took a float tube up to the track. An angular orange and purple pod saw her and swung near, door opening as it coasted to a stop. She climbed in. "Take me home."

The door swung silently closed. The pod merged smoothly into the stream of traffic traveling along the pathway. She settled back into the seat with her eyes closed. The pod accelerated. Outside the windows, the world became a blur.

Pod and passenger banked, following a graceful loop around the Temple district, then over a wide strip of forest laced with curving pathways. As a child, Terlyn had spent endless summer days exploring the forest, delighting in discovering the constantly changing secrets it held. What had been a sunlit glade with a small babbling brook yesterday might be a tiny pond filled with brightly colored fish tomorrow. The gods delighted in the act of creation, and constantly reinvented the City. She wondered how Donvin dealt with that in his sculpture.

The pod followed the track over a grotto surrounded by a dense tangle of trees, their bare branches dusted with snow. It slowed as it neared the shield wall, separating itself from the flow of traffic, angling toward the station closest to the Garden. It coasted to a stop. The door opened.

Terlyn stepped out. The pod closed its door and zoomed off, merging into the flow of traffic. She was the only one there.

The station resembled a temple from antiquity, all white marble and soaring columns. Rows of somber-faced statues stood silently along its outer perimeter, nude but for the wreaths in their hair.

She stepped into the float tube and drifted down. From the ground, the station looked like an ancient monument, floating impossibly in the sky. An intricate painting of figures gathered around a table piled high with the rewards of a bountiful harvest decorated its underside. Two men engaged in animated conversation at one end of the table; at the other, a woman with flowing auburn hair played a flute.

The float tube deposited Terlyn at the head of a path that wandered through a grassy park. The snow had avoided the park. Terlyn basked in the warm, fragrant air. Brightly colored flowers crowded both sides of the path.

The Cornucopia, the great Garden dedicated to the worship of the Quickener, was the only major center of worship in the City not located in the Temple District. All the other centers of worship except the small houses of the Blesser—the ziggurat of the Fiery One, the amphitheater of the Wild, the soaring temple dedicated to the Lady, and all the rest—lay in the center of the City. The Garden nestled against the shield generators at the edge of the City, in the center of a vast arc of parks, forests, and grassy hills that followed the curve of the City's outer perimeter.

Right now, the station was empty. Few people visited the Garden in winter. With the coming spring, the station would bustle with people seeking the Quickener's blessing. Throngs of people would come to visit the Garden.

To visit her.

The idea delighted and terrified her in equal measure.

She followed the path until it reached the edge of the park. Here, the invisible barrier that fenced off the snow ended. On one side, the air was warm, the ground covered with grass; on the other, a blanket of snow extended across the landscape. She felt the chill on her skin as she passed from one world to the other.

By the time she made it home, Terlyn was downright chilly. She savored the feel of the cool air on her skin and the dancing crystalline fog that coalesced from her breath.

Terlyn made her home in a tiny crystal box near an outcropping of rock. A small waterfall flowed over the rock into a little pond. The house was a simple rectangle whose transparent sides and roof were made of glass, nestled beneath a large pergola of wood. In the summer, lush vines covered in tiny purple flowers grew over the pergola. Today, the wood slats were bare. Small tufts of snow lay scattered across the roof.

The door opened at Terlyn's approach. Inside, the house was just a single room, as spare as it was outside. Terlyn's home contained nothing other than a large round bed surrounded by a low wood wall open on one side; a wood desk and chair; a low stone wall that partly concealed the necessary facilities; and of course, the opaque black rectangle of the Provider. Beneath her feet, wide planks of hardwood formed a floor that didn't reach all the way to the glass walls. A garden lined three of the four walls, lush with clusters of small flowering bushes growing from a flat expanse of short grass. Tiny creeping vines decorated with fingernail-sized flowers in gold, red, blue, and violet snaked along the grass, sending hesitant tendrils toward the wood floor.

Terlyn flopped onto the bed. "Walls opaque," she said. The glass walls turned frosted white. She left the ceiling transparent, so she could gaze at the clear blue sky.

Donvin was so sure her course was set. Out there, in the world, around other people, she was, too. Alone, she felt less confident and more afraid.

She didn't fear change. Everyone who volunteered as a Sacrifice to one of the City's gods changed.

Placing herself in the Garden would mean losing a part of herself. Donvin was right about that. Her time as Fountain, like the time he spent working on his sculpture, would be an offering. But Terlyn couldn't predict what else she might lose.

2.4

"You have a visitor." The calm, directionless voice filled the air around Terlyn.

"Who is it?"

"High Priestess Meersath of the Quickener."

She sat up. "Let her in."

The door opened. A woman came in on a draft of cool air, dusting flecks of snow from her long green gown. Her hair was a mad tangle of green, gold, red, and brown. She had wide hazel eyes and a broad, open smile. She was slightly shorter than Terlyn, but thick and muscular.

"High Priestess!" Terlyn said. "This is…" Her brow furrowed. "This is a surprise. You never leave your home. What brings you here?"

"Nonsense," Meersath said. "Why, I've ventured out into the world three times this year alone!" She chuckled at Terlyn's expression. "Don't look at me like that. I'm here because the Goddess spoke to me."

"Oh." Terlyn's eyebrows went up. "Oh. And, um, that brought you to me?"

"She told me you are questioning your decision to become Fountain."

"Well, I suppose she knows my heart. Maybe better than I do."

"I was the Fountain, years ago. You know many past Fountains. Some of them are members of your family."

Terlyn nodded. "We have been honored to have many from our lineage accepted as Fountain."

Meersath sat on the bed. "Yet you still have doubts." She touched the bed next to her. "Come, speak to me of your doubts."

Terlyn sat gingerly beside her. "I just…well, that is…" She ran one hand through her short white hair. "It's nothing."

"It must be something, for the goddess to feel it."

Terlyn sat quietly for a long time. Meersath waited serenely. Eventually, Terlyn said, "Why did you disappear after your Sacrifice?"

Meersath leaned back, lips pursed. "Oh, my darling, I was always prone to disappearing. Being around people wears me out. I need solitude. That's one of the wonderful things about giving yourself to the Quickener."

"Oh?"

"I know people have talked to you about what it's like to be in the Garden, but nothing can prepare you for the reality. You're there, but you're not. You sort of…go away, you see? When worshippers come to you, you're not quite aware of them. That's a blessing of sorts. It means even people like me who find the presence of others draining can offer themselves to the goddess. With most of the other gods, those who are called to give themselves need to be comfortable in crowds. The adoration, the service, the exultation…it all sounds so exhausting." She smiled. "Those who are called to give themselves to the Quickener can be an instrument of worship without really being entirely…well, present for it, if you know what I mean."

"What's it like, though? Being part of the Garden."

"It's…" She hesitated. "It's hard to explain. There's a reason so many Fountains, even the ones who are more social than I am, go into seclusion afterward. It's a lot to process. It's not just being in the Garden. It's the shock when you come back out."

"What shock?"

"While you're there, you're not really there. You have moments, but most of the time, you're kind of dreaming without dreaming. And then you come back out, and you're suddenly *here*. You're present. It's…jarring. There is a process."

"But what does it feel like?" Terlyn persisted. "You know, when you're actually in there?"

"It's not something that can be described. Only felt."

"Then show me. Please. I need to know."

Meersath sat still for a moment. "Very well," she said. She fluffed the pillows. "Take off your clothes."

Terlyn stripped without hesitation. Meersath patted the bed. "Lie down. Make yourself comfortable."

Terlyn settled on her back on the bed. Meersath smiled. "Relax. Place yourself in the hands of the goddess." She put her hands, warm and gentle, on Terlyn's shoulders. "Listen to the sound of my voice. Feel the bed beneath your body. Feel my hands on your skin. Let yourself go. Open your mind to the Quickener. Allow the goddess in." Her voice was calm and reassuring. "Listen to my words. Let them guide you."

Terlyn took a deep breath. She let it out slowly and relaxed. She tried to let go of her anxiety to make space in her mind for the goddess.

Meersath spoke to her in a calm, melodious voice. "Let yourself float. Feel your breath going in and out. Close your eyes. Allow the goddess within you." She ran her fingertips over Terlyn's throat, so gently Terlyn could barely feel them. "You are sinking further and further into the bed. You feel comfortable and relaxed. Breathe slowly. Become still. Release all your doubts and fears."

Bit by bit, Terlyn unwound, lulled by Meersath's soft voice. She drifted into a calm, still space. Meersath's soft words wrapped around her. Her breathing slowed.

Meersath caressed her with such unhurried gentleness that Terlyn soon became almost unaware of her. Her words guided Terlyn down into a tranquil place that wasn't quite sleep but wasn't wakefulness either.

"Good," Meersath said. "Follow my voice. Your arms and legs are very heavy. You cannot move. Your body is still, rooted in place. Your mind is adrift, far from your body." She ran one hand down between Terlyn's legs. "Let your mind listen to my voice. Let your body respond to my touch."

She built Terlyn up slowly, patiently. She ran her finger in small, gentle circles around Terlyn's clit. She increased the pressure only gradually, watching every small reaction in Terlyn's body, until eventually she penetrated Terlyn with the tip of one finger, parting her lower lips to slip it inside. Her mellifluous voice never stopped.

"You are calm and still. Let yourself sink deeper and deeper. Release control of your body. Allow it to respond. You hear nothing but the sound of my voice. You feel nothing but my hands on your body. You cannot move. You cannot think. Surrender to the goddess. Allow her to take you. Yield to her."

Meersath probed deeper. Terlyn quivered. "Be still," Meersath said. "Your body is now completely paralyzed. You cannot see. You cannot speak. You can only listen to my voice and feel my hands. Surrender."

Terlyn heard the words coming from somewhere far away. She felt the gentle probing fingers within her, the small caresses of her clit, but they seemed much too distant to worry about. Her body felt warm and heavy.

She was completely immobilized, but she felt no fear. She found herself mesmerized by Meersath's voice.

Meersath's words grew further and further away. Terlyn felt tension growing in her body, but it seemed of no consequence. She could no longer make out the words, but that too seemed of no consequence. She floated in a dark, still place, her mind unbound.

Meersath's words came with more urgency now, but Terlyn didn't care. She drifted far from the place where Meersath's fingers explored her,

"Wake up!"

Terlyn's eyes flew open. Her body convulsed. She exploded into orgasm. She stared at Meersath without comprehension. She tried to move, but her body would not respond. She tried to speak, but the words would not come. Her eyes widened. Meersath strummed her clit. Wave after wave of pleasure took her.

The orgasm ended. Meersath's voice told her to let go, to slip away. She sank back into that still quiet place, where she remained for a timeless time.

She woke once more with Meersath's lips on hers. She blinked in surprise, momentarily unsure where she was. Her body obeyed her once more. She sat, her eyes wide.

"Wha—I don't—"

"Yes," Meersath said. She sat back, watching the light dawn in Terlyn's ice-blue eyes. "This is what it is like to give yourself to the goddess. Waking up in the middle of an orgasm over and over again for many months."

"I—" Terlyn shook her head to clear it. "Does it change you?"

"Oh yes. Service to the gods changes all of us."

"How did it change you?"

Meersath gave her an enigmatic smile. "The gods never ask us for anything we do not willingly give. I can help you make an informed choice, but the choice has to be yours."

Terlyn reached for her dress, feeling uncharacteristically modest. She pulled it on without a word.

Meersath touched her cheek. "We all have our own reasons. We all have our own doubts. In the end, your love for the goddess will guide you."

Terlyn managed a small smile. She took Meersath's hand in both of hers and raised it to her lips. "Thank you," she said.

"The goddess believes in you."

"Will you be there? When I give myself?"

"Yes."

2.5

THE FIRST DAY of spring dawned bright and warm. Terlyn opened her eyes and looked up through the transparent ceiling to an indigo sky rimmed by a thin band of fiery red.

She arose naked from her bed and stepped outside. She stood there for a long moment, eyes closed, savoring the smells of growing things. Tiny rustles disturbed the air as small animals went about their business.

She stepped into the small pond beneath the narrow waterfall and let the warm water pour over her. The trees atop the rock sent out the first delicate shoots of green, little bright bursts of color along bare branches.

She bathed efficiently. The small stream swept the soapy water away. When she finished, she stood for a time on the soft ground outside the pond, arms outstretched, enjoying the feel of the air flowing over her skin.

Back inside the tiny glass house, Terlyn called up a simple robe in green and brown and a mug of hot tea from the Provider. She stood for a while sipping her tea, lost in thought. She caressed her nipple absently through the thin fabric.

When she realized she was dawdling, she tossed back the last of the tea. She fed the mug into the Provider, took a deep breath, closed her eyes, counted slowly to five, exhaled, and stepped out the door.

Terlyn walked barefoot along the path toward the Garden. By the time she arrived at the gate in the low stone wall, several other people already waited for her. Meersath was there, wearing a green dress decorated with embroidered vines and flowers. She held her thick tangle of hair in check with a gold wire she had woven through it.

"You have met High Priestess Eileithyia, I believe?" Meersath said, indicating the short, brown-skinned woman beside her. She wore a long form-fitting red dress trimmed with deep brown that covered one arm but left the other arm and one breast bare. She had eyes the same color as her dress, and long wild hair a dark burgundy shot through with leaf patterns and streaks of white, gold, green, and brown.

"Once," Terlyn said. "I was still exploring worship of the Wild when Eileithyia gave herself up to the Garden." She bowed deeply. "High Priestess."

She turned to bow to the two men who stood near Eileithyia: Tyrill, the Grand High Priest of the Quickener, a tall, broad-shouldered man with dark brown and white speckled skin and brilliant orange eyes, whose long white hair held a single broad strand of forest green; and Sedhi, a priest with a broad face that smiled easily, his head completely bald except for a single long turquoise braid that draped over his shoulder. Both men wore simple robes of rich brown cloth, tied at the waist with golden cords that ended in intricate tassels. "High Priest," she said. "Priest Sedhi."

Donvin stood slightly apart from the others in a close-fitting black shirt and simple black pants, his face serious.

"Donvin!" Terlyn threw her arms around him. "I'm glad you're here. I thought you'd visit me after I am in the Garden…"

"I can do both, right?" He hugged her tightly. "Your hair looks good green." She smiled and ran her hand through her hair, which had changed color during the night.

"Donvin, these are Tyrill and Sedhi, Priests of the Quickener. And Eileithyia and Meersath. They're both previous Fountains."

Donvin bowed. "It is a pleasure."

"The pleasure is mine," Tyrill said. "Thank you for being here to support the new Fountain." He turned to Terlyn. "You are ready?"

"I am."

"Do you pledge yourself to the Quickener, that your body may become his vessel to bring his blessing to the people?"

"I do."

"Do you give yourself as an offering to him, to be his Fountain?"

She swallowed. "I do."

Meersath smiled broadly. "Are you ready to begin the Rite of Preparation, so that your body may become sanctified to her service?"

"I am." Terlyn hoped the quaver wasn't audible in her voice.

"From this moment," Meersath said, "you will begin three days of purification. During this time, you will not sleep. You will perform the rites, and you will meditate. Do you undertake this journey of your own free will, with full understanding that your body will become a vessel of the Quickener from now until the last day of autumn?"

Terlyn nodded. "Yes." Donvin folded his arms.

"You may enter the Garden."

Terlyn took a deep breath. She slipped the robe from her body. The others stood aside. She walked nude beneath the stone archway.

Even now, on the cusp between winter and spring, the Garden was a place of beauty. It was shaped like an oval, a bit more than half as wide as it was long. A low wall of gray stone, no higher than Terlyn's waist, surrounded it.

Three wide pathways of soft earth met at the entrance. Flat slabs of gray stone lined the edges of the paths. Each slab had an image of a flower engraved on it. No two were alike.

The paths to the left and right hugged the stone wall. They ran all the way around the periphery of the Garden and met again at the far side. The path forward passed between rows of trees, six rows on each side, cunningly arranged so that from any vantage point, they aligned in neat, symmetrical patterns. Their branches, now clear of snow, reached like skeletal fingers for the sky, spare and beautiful in their way.

Two rows of androgynous figures carved in stone watched Terlyn silently from along the edge of the central path. Each of the bare-chested stone statues, a little larger than life, wore a simple wrap about their waist. Some stood proud and tall; others reclined on columns. One leaned forward suggestively, one hand on her breast. All regarded Terlyn with enigmatic smiles.

The others followed in Terlyn's footsteps. Eileithyia placed her hand on Meersath's arm. "I am pleased you've chosen to come out of your seclusion," she said.

Meersath bowed slightly. "I felt the Quickener calling me to return. I hope I was able to help the new Fountain on her journey."

The Garden stood stark and beautiful beneath the early morning sun. The snow had gone, leaving bare dirt that buzzed with the promise of new life. As Terlyn walked between the neat rows of trees, her feet sank into rich earth. Tiny green shoots appeared in her footprints.

Beyond the trees and the rows of statues, the path entered a diamond-shaped labyrinth of dense sculpted bushes, twisting and turning on itself in a complex pattern that would be walked by all those who came to visit her when she gave herself to the Garden. The carefully cultivated hedges grew waist-high near the entrance. At the center, they were well above Terlyn's head.

Right now, the hedges, like the trees, were bare. Their dry branches formed perfectly regular shapes. Terlyn walked through the geometrically precise bushes, imagining them as they would be in only a few days, exploding with new green leaves. The others accompanied her—including, she was pleased to see, Donvin. She slipped her arm around his waist. "Thank you for being here," she said. "I'm touched."

"We don't really understand each other," he said, "but I support your choice."

The labyrinth opened up in the center into a wide circular space, as wild as the rest of the Garden was tame. Clusters of vines, just beginning to wake from their winter slumber, twisted along small, artfully crafted hills. At the peak of the summer, they would be covered with bright flowers, but, for the moment, they were only just starting to unfold small, delicate leaves of brilliant green.

In the precise center of the Garden sat a great boulder of light, black-flecked granite, its top gently contoured into a graceful arc that had been polished smooth. It was covered with a thick layer of moss.

A short distance behind the boulder, golden liquid shimmered in a small, perfectly round pool whose edge was inset with curved marble blocks carved with flowering vines. Small steps descended into it. Across from them sat a bench carved from the same marble, its surface also engraved with vines. The golden liquid in the pool steamed invitingly.

Tyrill and Meersath took Terlyn's hands. They helped her step down into the pool. Warm, fragrant water folded around her, rich with the scent of green growing things.

"Meditate on opening yourself to the Quickener," Tyrill said. "Relax. Let him into your mind. This pool has been blessed by his grace. His blessing will dull your hunger and thirst and help you open yourself to receive him. We will return in one hour."

They retraced the path out of the labyrinth. Terlyn imagined the Garden as it would soon look, blooming with life, and felt once more the small sharp tang of disappointment she would not be able to see it.

The pool's warmth seeped into her. She relaxed. Gradually, her vision sharpened, until she became aware of every tiny detail in the boulder, the ground, and the hedges that surrounded her. Every color became brighter and more vivid. Every tiny feature vibrated with clarity. She gazed around in wonder.

The strange clarity persisted even when Tyrill and Meersath returned. They each carried a basket woven of thin, brightly colored strips of wicker, filled with small red flower petals. Terlyn arose from the pool, water streaming off her body.

Tyrill and Meersath set down their baskets. They each scooped up handfuls of the petals and began rubbing her down, crushing them against her skin. Tyrill's hands kneaded her shoulders and back. Meersath caressed her breasts, the flower petals soft on her sensitive skin. Terlyn whimpered softly.

They massaged her from head to foot, kneeling to reach her thighs and legs. The petals dissolved against her skin. A sweet, heady fragrance filled the air. Terlyn felt a rush of dizziness. Her vision swam. Her skin tingled.

When all the petals were gone, Tyrill and Meersath rose. Meersath took a robe of fine green cloth, printed with subtle patterns of leaves and vines, from her basket. She wrapped it around Terlyn's shoulders.

Tyrill said, "We will leave you to walk the Garden in meditation. Accept the Quickener into your mind." Meersath bowed to her. They picked up the baskets, now empty, and walked down the path toward the gate.

Terlyn stood for a time, waiting for her head to clear. The scent lingered on her skin. Her gaze fell on the moss-covered boulder. Her eyes followed the loops and whorls of moss, the cracks on the stone's ancient sides. She wondered how old it was. Had the gods brought it here, or had human hands placed it? Had it always been here? Was the Garden built around it?

A butterfly landed on the rock, brilliant blue against green, yellow, and gray. She watched it flex its wings, delighted by the elaborate patterns that adorned them. When it lifted off again, she followed it, entranced, as it fluttered its jerky, chaotic way down the path. The hedges rose above her. Her fingers dragged over the bare branches.

No, not bare, she realized as she looked closer. Tiny green leaves, almost too small to see, budded on every branch. She ran her palms lightly over the branches, watching with fascination. Tender shoots appeared beneath her hand, as if she were coaxing the leaves to sprout. She watched one branch for a while, captivated by the slow unfurling of the minute leaves, until she realized that the sun had settled low in the sky and the shadows fell long on the ground. She wandered without direction or purpose, until she found herself back in the center of the hedge maze once more.

Gentle light from a tiny, dragonfly-shaped dronelight announced Tyrill and Meersath's return. They walked down the path toward Terlyn, who stood near the small pool, watching the waning light play over its surface with rapt fascination. She smiled with delight at the way the dronelight's glow sent changing patterns of light and shadow through the water.

"How are you doing?" Meersath said.

"Everything is so beautiful!"

"We brought you something." Meersath handed her two small, octagonal cups, their transparent faceted sides carved with patterns that suggested leaves and flowers.

Terlyn held them in both hands. One cup held round white seeds, the other dun-colored, crescent-shaped seeds with pointed ends. She opened one of the cups and held a seed aloft, examining it in the light of the small hovering dronelight. Subtle patterns of iridescent color swirled slowly across its surface.

Tyrill took a bundle wrapped in dark green cloth from his pocket. He presented it to Terlyn reverently, like a sacred object.

Terlyn unwrapped the bundle. The cloth looked old. Old things were rare in the City; objects the people might need usually came from a Provider and returned to it as soon as the need had passed, becoming raw material to be reconstituted into something else. Objects made by hand were usually works of art, rather than practical things.

The fabric felt rich to her fingers, thick and soft, but so worn with age it was threadbare in places. There was a design printed on it, faded by the passage of years, a stylized image of a great tree whose branches spread in a circle.

Terlyn found a small silver spade with a long, narrow blade wrapped inside the bundle. It gleamed dully in the dronelight's light, engraved with a pattern of vines that twisted and wound around each other. It had a handle of dark wood, carved into an elaborate design, worn with time and use.

"Plant the long seeds around the rock," Meersath said. "Plant the round ones along the path. We will return to you at sunrise."

The tiny dragonfly dronelight drifted over to Terlyn. From somewhere high above them, another dronelight swooped down, this one shaped like a gleaming dart of gold-colored metal with fins covered in engraved geometric designs. Its light came on as it descended. It hovered glittering above Tyrill's head.

Terlyn watched them disappear down the path into the gathering dusk until the small point of light over their heads disappeared beyond the arch. In the sky above, the twinkling stars came out, hazy through the dome of the shield. The smaller of the two moons glowed red and full. The larger was just a thin crescent on the horizon.

Terlyn ran her hands over the textured stone boulder. The dronelight floated over her. Its soft yellow glow caught sparkling flecks of mica in the rich earth. Terlyn drew in her breath, marveling at its simple beauty. Beneath the moons and stars, illuminated by the gentle glow from the dronelight, the center of the Garden seemed a magical place. Chirps and thrums of countless small insects filled the air.

She knelt in the soft earth. The dronelight settled lower, casting a circle of light in front of her. She carefully set down the cups with their precious contents and took out the spade.

Its blade was quite narrow, scarcely wider than her smallest finger. She pressed it into the ground at the base of the boulder. It penetrated the earth easily, leaving a small but deep hole. She picked up one of the tapered, crescent-shaped seeds. It glistened in the light of the dronelight. She watched it for several minutes, fascinated by the way the colors crept across its surface, hinting at the life within.

Terlyn placed the shimmering seed carefully in the hole and covered it. She dug another small hole next to it, right where the rock met the earth. She dropped a seed into the hole and covered it.

She worked like this for hours, making small holes in the ground around the edge of the stone and placing a single shimmering seed in each one. As she worked, her dress changed. The pattern of vines printed on it gradually grew across the fabric, reaching upward from the hem toward her shoulders.

The work filled her with joy. Before long, her knees were caked with dirt. She made a complete circuit of the boulder, planting the seeds around its edge. When she returned to where she had started, a tiny green shoot had just broken through the dirt where she'd planted the first seed.

When the first cup was empty, Terlyn followed the path out of the labyrinth. She knelt on the ground beside the long, straight path, beneath the gazes of the statues. She dug a row of small holes along the edge path and planted seeds at the feet of the silent stone statues. The stars turned overhead in their slow courses. By the time she had finished with the second cup of seeds, a glow on the horizon hinted at the coming dawn.

Tyrill, Sedhi, and Meersath came to her just as the sun crested the line between ground and sky. The three of them were dressed in long, heavy robes of deep burgundy, embroidered with the same stylized tree that decorated the cloth that had been wrapped around the spade. Each of them carried a large basket. Terlyn stood, brushing the dirt from her knees. The dronelight zipped up into the sky, heading wherever dronelights went during the day.

"Good morning, Fountain," Tyrill said. "I see you had a productive night."

Terlyn nodded. In the gathering light of day, her head felt clearer. The intense colors had muted. The sharp focus had faded, leaving the world softer. She was surprised to realize she did not feel tired, though she had spent the entire night tending to her task. "I planted all the seeds you gave me," she said.

Sedhi collected the spade, the cloth, and the empty cups. He wrapped the spade in the cloth, then tucked it and the cups away in his basket.

They walked the labyrinth to its center, Terlyn in the lead. When they reached the rock and the pool, Meersath slipped the robe, now stained and caked with dirt, from Terlyn's shoulders. It disappeared into Tyrill's basket. Then she took Terlyn by the hand and led her to the small pool. Terlyn stepped down into it, sighing as the warm water folded around her. She leaned back, allowing the warmth to loosen knotted muscles.

Sedhi, Tyrill, and Meersath sat down beside the pool. The sun rose higher, bathing the Garden in warm golden light. Already, the Garden was transforming. Bright green buds burst from the hedges wherever Terlyn had touched them.

She felt herself relax. Knots in her shoulders and legs dissolved in the warm water. Gradually, so subtly she didn't notice right away, the world changed. Colors became brighter, details more vivid.

Time stretched and contracted. Meersath and Tyrill talked to each other in low voices. Terlyn found their conversation distant and unimportant compared to the beautiful intricacy of the robe Sedhi wore, the delicate texturing of the thread that made up the embroidered image of the tree, the curve of the hem around the collar, the play of light and shadow over the wrinkles in the cloth. Terlyn felt herself falling into it. Every line of thread promised revelation. If Sedhi noticed her gaze, he gave no sign.

Eventually, Sedhi took Terlyn's hand and drew her out of the pool. Meersath uncovered her basket, which was filled with purple flower petals. She and Sedhi scooped up handfuls of the petals. Sedhi stood in front of Terlyn, Meersath behind, and they began rubbing her down.

When Sedhi's hands reached her breasts, Terlyn let out a soft cry. They felt heavy and hot, achingly sensitive to his touch. The sweet-scented flower petals slid over her skin, across her nipples. Tingling electric shocks radiated through her. "What—"

"It's okay," Meersath said. "This is normal. Your body is changing. The Quickener is preparing you to be her avatar."

"I feel very—um—" Terlyn put her hand to her face.

"Just relax," Sedhi said. His fingers kneaded her breasts. "Allow the Quickener to inhabit you. Accept him into yourself." His hands moved lower, crushing the petals against her body. The scent filled her nose. Her body grew ponderous and heavy. "That's it," Sedhi said. "Breathe deeply."

Terlyn's head swam. The scent of the flower petals filled every corner of her awareness, thick and heady, driving out everything else. Meersath's fingers entered her from behind. She felt as though she should respond, but her body was too clumsy and cumbersome to obey her commands.

The flower petals dissolved on Terlyn's wet skin. Sedhi and Meersath caressed and probed her until the petals were gone. Then Sedhi took a long, translucent robe from his basket, splashed with an abstract design of many colors: red, gold, blue, purple, violet. He placed it around Terlyn's shoulders. She stood still, her mind filled with the scent of flowers.

"We will leave you now to meditate, Fountain," Tyrill said. "As you walk the Garden, open your mind to the Quickener. Invite him into your body." The three picked up their baskets and disappeared down the path toward the archway.

A gentle breeze caught the delicate robe. She watched it float in the air, enchanted by the way the sun reflected off the fine threads within it. After a time, she felt restless. She left the open space with its pool and its boulder to walk the labyrinth through the Garden.

The ground bore a record of her previous day's travels. Everywhere she had stepped, bright green grass spread outward from her footprint. She avoided the irregular ovals of new growing things, wandering the parts of the garden that were still bare earth. With each step, her feet sank into the ground. Tiny leaves struggled up from the compressed soil behind her.

She walked the path around the edge of the Garden, coming eventually to where it ran alongside the shield dome that arced over the City. As she followed along the boundary between the City and the Outside, she ran her hand through the air, feeling the slight whisper-tug of the shield beneath her fingers. Wherever she touched the shield, little eddies of gold light, so faint they were barely visible in the late morning sun, spread out in curling, swirling wakes.

Where the shield met the ground, a sharp line bisected the earth: garden on this side, flat grasslands on the other. A short distance away, across the broad swatch of prairie grass, rose the mighty columns of the automated farms, each as large as her house and reaching six stories into the air. A wide platform spiraled up each column, hung with an enormous assortment of growing food. Glittering farm drones flitted in the air between them, tending and collecting. The Providers could make food from nothing, if the gods so willed it, but the gods, like the people, often did things just for the pleasure of doing them. Even the gods celebrated the act of creation.

A small fleck of color caught her eye, a sliver of red where the shield met the ground. She paused, her breath catching in wonder. A tiny flower, no wider than her fingernail, had just started to open.

She watched it for a long time, while the sun crept higher and higher in the sky, captivated by its long slow unfolding. The petals extended, almost imperceptibly slowly, growing longer as they separated from each other. The tips curled away from one another in graceful arcs. Gradually, the blossom opened, revealing the thin, delicate parts within.

By the time the flower had fully opened, the sun had passed its zenith and was preparing for its long trek down to the horizon. Terlyn felt a growling in her stomach that reminded her she had been standing as still as a statue, captivated by the leisurely ballet of the flower, all morning.

She moved on, restless again, following the path around the edge of the Garden to the gate. She wandered down the path that bisected the Garden, watched by the silent statues.

Two rows of broad plants sprouted from the seeds she'd planted the night before. They had long, slender leaves that grew from a cluster in the center of the plant, bright green and glossy. From each plant grew one long, thin stalk that ended in a teardrop-shaped bud, green at its base and deep red at the tip.

Terlyn stepped off the path. The stalks with their buds bent in her direction, swaying in a breeze that wasn't there.

She moved her hand over the plants. The buds followed her hand, straining to be closer to her. She knelt in front of one of the plants. Its stalk curled toward her, bringing the bud close to her face. The scent of honey and cinnamon reached her nose.

Terlyn's stomach rumbled again. The smell overwhelmed her. Her mouth watered. Her head swam.

She reached out. The stem reached back, straining toward her hand. The other plants bobbed, offering their buds to her outstretched fingers.

She touched the plant. The bud detached, leaving a milky drop on the end of the stalk. She raised the bud to her nose. It smelled of comfort, of hot apple cider on a chilly winter's night, of the warm embrace of a lover.

She put the bud in her mouth and bit down. It burst open, filling her mouth with the taste of nutmeg and cinnamon. She swallowed.

Warmth radiated through her body. All around her, colors grew brighter. Her body felt light. Her breasts tingled.

The other plants reached for her with greater urgency. She touched another bud. It came off in her hand. She bit into it greedily. It burst, sending an eruption of sweet liquid down her throat. Her body thrummed like a plucked string. She walked down the path. The stalks bobbed toward her. She picked another bud and put it in her mouth. The world around her exploded into dazzling color, so beautiful it brought tears to her eyes.

She felt a vibration beneath her feet, in the earth itself. It grew and spread until her entire body buzzed in resonance. The statues of the women seemed by some illusion to move with exquisite subtlety, as if possessed by a delicate inner life she was only now aware of. She blinked…no, they were still just as they had been, inert images frozen in stone.

The restlessness came over her once more. Terlyn walked down the path to the labyrinth, lost in a world of light and color. When she reached the center, her breath caught. The seeds she had so carefully planted around the boulder the night before had sprouted. Fragile shoots of ivy, thin and spidery, crawled partway up the giant stone, wrapping it in delicate threads of green.

Terlyn walked around the boulder. The tips of the fragile young vines separate from the rock and reach for her in longing. She sat in the dense grass between the boulder and the pool. A gentle breeze played with her robe, curling it around her. The pattern on the robe had changed since the morning, the colors spreading, becoming more vibrant. Terlyn placed her hand on her breast. Her nipple swelled, pressing into her palm through the thin, light fabric. Her breasts felt so sensitive, she could almost feel every individual thread in the robe. She stroked her breast softly and gasped with the intensity of sensation. The tips of her fingers sent shocks like static electricity through her skin. A wave of pleasure rippled outward from her nipple.

She brought her other hand to her breast. Her fingers curled around her nipple. Concentrated, nearly unbearable pleasure spread out through her from the points of her nipples. She caressed herself, sighing, her eyes half-closed. Her skin crackled with energy.

She remained there, on her knees, running her hands over her breasts while the sun trekked down the vast blue dome of the sky. As evening settled around her, Tyrill and Meersath returned, escorted by a tiny hummingbird-shaped dronelight, bright in the gathering dusk. They found her, eyes closed, hands under her robe, fingers caressing her breasts, making soft whimpering noises.

Meersath nodded with approval. She took Terlyn's hand and helped her to her feet. She moved around her, examining her from all angles. "The Quickener is changing you. She is modifying your body for what is to come. Do you feel how sensitive you are to touch?" She caressed Terlyn's arm. "Are your breasts growing tender?"

Terlyn looked at her with wide uncomprehending eyes. Meersath cupped one of her breasts. Terlyn let out a small cry.

"How is the Fountain doing?" Tyrill said.

"Take a look." Meersath took Terlyn's hands in hers and lifted them over her head. The dronelight pivoted in the air to shine its light on her. A circle of light traveled up and down her body.

Tyrill inspected her closely. His hands slid over her, exploring her curves. When they reached her nipples, Terlyn drew in her breath sharply.

Thick fog closed around her mind, slowing her thoughts. She felt Tyrill's searching hands moving under her robe, caressing and exploring. His examination felt disconnected from her, or perhaps she felt disconnected from it. Her body felt like a room she was moving out of, an empty space that had once been hers but was now merely walls and a ceiling.

"She is nearly ready." Tyrill caressed Terlyn's cheek. "The changes are progressing nicely. Her mind is almost ready as well. What about the Garden?"

"It will be ready to receive her," Meersath said. She lowered Terlyn's arms. "I think the Garden is looking forward to having her."

Tyrill smiled broadly. "This augurs well. I think we are looking forward to a bountiful summer. Yes," he said, eyes moving down her body. "This will be a bountiful summer indeed."

2.6

THE SUN SETTLED behind the hedges as Tyrill and Meersath left. Terlyn almost didn't notice their departure. The slow progress of the shadows through the center of the labyrinth captivated her attention. She watched them creep over the boulder, as soft as a lover's kiss.

As darkness swallowed the Garden, she felt the restlessness in her feet again. She wandered the twists and turns of the labyrinth for a while. No dronelight descended from above to light her way, but it didn't matter; her feet knew the path well.

As the vibrant colors of the Garden faded to a soft, muted tapestry in subdued shades, the sounds of the night folded over her. She welcomed the chirps of the insects and the gentle sigh of the breeze.

Eventually, she found herself back on the path between the rows of statues. The trees, which had so recently been bare, now exploded with tender new leaves.

She lay on her back in the middle of the path, looking up. The stars sparkled like tiny jewels in the dome of the night, beyond the faint shimmer of the shield. Her eyes followed the dusty band the ancients called the Milky Way across the sky, until it dipped down to meet the great sparkling obsidian towers in their graceful arc along the outermost edge of the City. Travel pods raced along their elevated tracks, zipping back and forth between the towers and toward the center of the City.

She found herself musing on the countless people going about their lives so far away from her, wondering what they were doing. The glittering obsidian edifices seemed impossibly distant. Everything beyond the edge of the Garden felt dreamlike, surreal.

A stillness settled over the Garden, a calm waiting. Small creatures chirped and thrummed in the underbrush. Occasional rustlings in the trees spoke of larger creatures, birds perhaps, living their lives as earnestly as the people in the City.

Terlyn folded her arms over her breasts as she looked up at the stars. Strange, she mused, to think one of those tiny points of light, so small and insignificant, had once been home to the whole human race.

She fell upward toward those impossible points of light. For a time beyond time, she wandered among them, feeling the music of the spheres resonating within her. Far away, on an insignificant speck floating through the void, the woman who was Ikanni Terlyn Relan Verinas of the Everessa family caressed her breasts and slid her fingers between her legs.

She drifted back into herself when the stars faded with the morning sun. She sat up, blinking. Droplets of dew beaded on her skin. The matted robe clung to her. Her hair hung in tangles.

When Tyrill and Meersath appeared from beneath the arch, Terlyn stood. She felt their presence significant for some reason, but she couldn't remember why.

She stood passively as Meersath slid the robe off her shoulders. It seemed an inconsequential thing, scarcely worth noticing. The two of them took her hands and guided her through the labyrinth to the edge of the pool. She stepped down into it. Yes, this felt right.

The water closed over her, warm and invigorating, inviting her deeper into herself. Her vision grew sharper, clearer, until she could count the threads in Meersath's emerald green dress, cut to leave one arm and one breast bare. She could make out each individual strand in the green stripe through Tyrill's hair.

She looked around, exploring this strange new sight. Everywhere, the Garden exploded with green: dense green leaves covered the trees, thick green grass carpeted the ground. New leaves covered the hedges that surrounded the great diamond-shaped labyrinth, speckled here and there with tiny flowers of purple, red, yellow, blue, and turquoise. The air carried the scent of living, growing things.

Her head vibrated, blurring her thoughts. She reached up to discover her hair, now a deep forest green, had grown nearly an inch during the night. Her breasts, too, were fuller, her nipples permanently erect. "I feel…"

"Yes, Fountain?" Tyrill said.

"Different."

Tyrill nodded. "Your body is almost ready. Tomorrow, you will surrender yourself to the Garden."

Terlyn ran her hands gently over her body. Her skin buzzed, achingly sensitive. "Will it hurt?"

"Let go of attachment to such worries," Meersath said.

Terlyn smiled a dreamy smile. "You are so pretty."

Meersath bowed. "Thank you, Fountain. That is a lovely thing to say."

Terlyn leaned back, soaking in the pool's pleasant warmth. When she opened her eyes again, Sedhi appeared from between the rows of hedges, carrying a large basket over his shoulder. He nodded to Tyrill. "It is time."

Tyrill and Meersath helped Terlyn out of the pool. They drew handfuls of flower petals from Sedhi's basket, these ones deep violet. They rubbed the petals into Terlyn's skin, filling her senses with the scent of flowers. She shuddered when Tyrill touched her breasts, even more tender than they'd been yesterday.

She felt herself recede. The world dwindled into the distance. Meersath and Tyrill spoke, but Terlyn paid no attention to what they said.

Sedhi laid a large square of thick red cloth, patterned with abstract designs in brown and gold, on the ground. Meersath helped Terlyn lie down on it. Sedhi and Tyrill knelt beside her. Terlyn smiled at the feel of soft fabric beneath her skin.

Sedhi took a flask, engraved with a fine, delicate design of trees in bloom, their branches heavy with flowers, from his basket. He lifted off the cap. Terlyn smiled. "Mm, cinnamon," she said, her voice blurry.

Sedhi poured a thin stream of oil down Terlyn's body, between her breasts. Then he and Tyrill massaged her, strong hands spreading the oil across her body. It tingled, sending little waves of warmth spreading through her.

Meersath knelt between Terlyn's legs. She poured the oil onto her hands and caressed Terlyn's legs.

The warmth became heat. Terlyn's eyes grew heavy. She felt herself drifting, untethered from the body she normally inhabited. As the three sets of hands slid over her skin, she fell further and further away. The warmth wrapped around her, enveloping her in a peaceful trance.

Hands slid over her breasts. She was aware, in a detached way, of fingers stroking her nipples, sending little waves of pleasure radiating out. Fingers penetrated her, finding no resistance. None of it seemed important. She floated in a space somewhere beyond herself, not caring what happened to her body.

Even when a finger pressed against her clit, sending a long, slow shiver of sensation up her body, she remained adrift. The things being done to her were far less important, and certainly far less interesting, than the humming of the insects that traced their weaving paths through the air. Every aspect of Terlyn's being filled with the warm scent of cinnamon.

She floated free in a private world of sound and scent far from the Garden while her body remained behind in the hands of others. Eventually, the touch changed. Bit by bit, she became aware that Sedhi and Tyrill had left, replaced by two other priests. She wasn't sure who they were, but she couldn't bring herself to care.

More oil, warm and lightly scented, drizzled on her body. More hands touched her. Fingers located the most sensitive parts of her body. It responded with arousal, but an arousal that felt disconnected. She was intellectually aware that somewhere far away, wetness flowed easily from her. She knew that the moans she heard were probably coming from her, but none of it felt real. Only the warmth and the way the oil made her skin tingle seemed real. She floated between ground and sky, basking in the heat.

The people massaging her changed again, then again. She noted the differences in the hands touching her, the different textures of the sensations, the differences in the way her body responded. She moaned, now loud, now soft. Her body reported increasing arousal, but there was no urgency to it, so she paid it no mind, absorbed as she was in watching the small white clouds that scudded across the blue sky.

The sky grew ruddy. Somewhere far away, the hands withdrew from her body. Terlyn drifted for a time, gradually coming back into herself. She sat, dizzy and confused. "Where…"

Meersath put a hand on her shoulder. "Slowly, Fountain. The Quickener still has you."

Terlyn placed her hand on her breast. Her swollen nipples tingled and throbbed. Slick wetness dripped between her legs. The world felt hazy, just slightly out of focus.

Meersath and a man Terlyn didn't recognize helped her to her feet. The smooth, shiny fabric of his simple red pants threw back the evening light.

"Good evening, Fountain," he said in a deep, pleasant voice. "I am Initiate Marisem. I will be caring for your body while you are in the Garden."

"Oh!" Terlyn said. She reached out to touch his broad, muscular chest, with its layer of wiry black curls. "Thank you for taking care of me, Initiate Marisem."

He bowed. "It is my honor to be of service, Fountain."

She giggled. "I am honored that you are honored, Initiate Mar—ooh!" She wavered. He caught her arm easily.

Meersath wrapped a sheer robe around Terlyn. It was a deep, rich brown, decorated with leaves in gold and red that moved very slowly, tumbling down the robe.

"We will leave you now to walk in meditation," Meersath said. "Tomorrow, you will become one with the Garden."

They left Terlyn alone in the gathering twilight. She looked around the darkened Garden with eyes made far more acute. Everything she saw—every bush, every tree, every blade of grass—seemed edged with its own dim glow.

She looked at her hands in wonder. Her own body shimmered faintly. Her skin appeared ever so slightly translucent.

She parted her robe and placed her hands on her body, running them over skin that was soft and smooth as silk. She stroked her nipples and was surprised to find moisture there, a tiny drop of clear liquid that glinted in the moonlight.

The larger moon rose higher in the sky. She made her way along the labyrinth, tracing the path between the rows of hedges. She inhaled deeply, taking in the smell of growing things.

Terlyn spent the night walking the labyrinth over and over again. Each circuit took her about thirty minutes. The simple ritual brought her a sense of peace. The red jewel of the smaller moon appeared over the hedges. It seemed, as she gazed at it, closer than the great gleaming towers at the city's edge. A shooting star streaked across the heavens, leaving a bright hard trail behind it. She felt sad at its passing.

Shortly before dawn, the two moons set, changing the Garden into an abstract monochromatic collage of geometric shapes. Terlyn paused before the pool, a dark circle in the ground filled with rippling liquid that bore the faintest phosphorescent glow. She knelt to trail her fingers in the warm water. Swirls of shimmering light formed whorls in their wake. She smiled at their beauty.

Meersath, Tyrill, Sedhi, Marisem, Donvin, and a woman Terlyn didn't recognize met her at the entrance to the Garden just as the sun peeked above the horizon. All except Donvin wore simple clothes of a deep green hue, either one-piece dresses, cut to cup and display their breasts, or tunics of green, hemmed in burgundy. Donvin wore a long-sleeved, high-collared black shirt with black pants.

"This is Priestess Rahmos," Meersath said. Red and brown glinted in her golden hair as she extended her hand. She had eyes of bright orange, flecked with tiny bits of gleaming gold. Terlyn took her hand automatically.

"Are you ready to give yourself to the Garden?" Tyrill asked.

"Yes," Terlyn said. Her mind was a pool of deep water unruffled by the passing wind.

"Follow me, Fountain," Tyrill said.

He entered the labyrinth. Terlyn followed, walking the path for the last time that season. Every turn felt as familiar and as intimate as her own body. She touched the hedges, geometrically perfect in their precision. Her fingers lingered as though on a lover's skin. The leaves on the branches responded, bending slightly toward her as she passed.

Eventually, they reached the center. Without a word, Tyrill slipped the robe from her shoulders. He and Meersath helped her step into the pool.

The water had changed to a subtle turquoise color during the night. Tiny shimmering flecks of green danced in it. As she sat, the warmth settled into her. She felt a lightness of being, her mind freed of the moorings that tied it to her body. Arousal stirred in her, a quiet, euphoric receptiveness, detached from need, so different from the desperate, frantic arousal she'd experienced in the Sun God's temple. Tyrill and Meersath took her hands and lifted her from the pool. She floated effortlessly up the small steps and stood for a while, water dripping from her body. They led her to the boulder.

The vines she'd planted encased the sides of the rock, large and strong. Only its polished, moss-covered top remained untouched. Spade-shaped leaves grew in profusion along the ropy, gnarled vines.

"Lie down on your back, Fountain," Tyrill said.

Terlyn floated over to the boulder. The vines stirred restlessly. The tips lifted from the rock and strained toward her, trembling. She smiled. Brilliant, vivid color flooded the world around her. She placed her hand on the rock. Thick moss grew atop it, soft and inviting.

She lay down with a beatific smile on her face. The boulder's upper surface had been carved into a shape that allowed her to recline comfortably. She settled peacefully into the soft moss.

Tyrill stepped away from the stone. The vines moved with purpose, rustling as they reached toward her. Terlyn remained still, watching them with curious interest. The vines crawled slowly up the rock toward her, sliding with quiet determination toward her nude body.

The tip of a vine crept up over the top of the stone, trailing small tendrils behind it. It touched her foot, coarse against her skin. It paused for a moment, then continued on, feeling its way over her foot and up her ankle. Terlyn felt the rough bark sliding over her skin. When it reached her calf, it curled around her, a slow-motion snake wrapping gentle, unhurried coils around its prey.

More vines appeared over the edge of the stone to advance toward her. Leaves touched her wrist. She held her hand flat. A vine slid along her palm. Terlyn drifted, not sure if she was awake or dreaming.

Another vine coiled itself around her other wrist. Still more vines caressed her legs, their leaves soft as velvet. Terlyn sighed. She felt herself slipping further into the dreamlike trance as the vines caressed her like a lover.

Something sharp touched her. She looked down. There, hidden beneath a cluster of leaves, a long, sharp thorn pressed against her skin, exquisitely gently. A shimmering drop of liquid, as red as wine, formed on its tip.

"Watch," Meersath told Donvin. "It won't be long now. The Garden is claiming her."

The vines slid over Terlyn, dragging sharp thorns lightly across the delicate skin of her arms and inner thighs. She watched them move, slow and dreamlike, through a fog of arousal that settled around her. The vines stroked her gently, almost lovingly, embracing her in their tendrils. They held her fast, tangling her limbs.

Darkness closed in from the edges of Terlyn's vision. Her head grew light. Meersath and the others receded, becoming small and impossibly far away. "What's happening?" she said.

"You are being taken," Meersath said. Her voice came from the bottom of a deep well. "The Quickener is moving into you. You are becoming one with the Garden."

All at once, without warning, the vines coiled tight. They contracted, pulling her legs apart. Sharp thorns pierced her skin. Red liquid flowed into her. Terlyn thrashed. An orgasm, powerful and unstoppable, tore through her body. She screamed in ecstasy.

It went on and on, more intense than anything she had ever known before. The world faded. She slipped away, carried off on a wave of pleasure. Darkness took her.

2.7

THE SMALL GROUP gathered around the stone watched in solemn silence as Terlyn's eyes closed. Donvin caressed her forehead, warm and damp with sweat. "What happens now?"

"She is now the Fountain, the embodiment of the Quickener," Tyrill said. "Those who seek his blessing, whether for themselves or for their creative endeavors, will come here to receive it."

"Which means?"

"They will commune with the Fountain," Meersath said. "When they do, the Quickener will offer her bounty. The supplicants may collect the bounty as it comes forth from the Fountain's body. It increases fertility if drunk."

"Fertility? Like, to have children?"

Meersath nodded. "If that's what they want. But it's more than that. Many supplicants seek the Quickener's blessing before embarking on any creative project. And, of course, the blessing may be applied to growing things to increase their vigor."

"Is the Quickener a male or a female? I'm sorry, I don't know much about your faith."

Meersath laughed. "No need to apologize. The gods are not like us. The Quickener is neither male nor female. Or rather, she is both. We refer to her in many ways."

"Terlyn will be here all summer?"

"She will sleep here until the coming of winter. We will care for her. The Garden will nourish her."

Donvin shook his head. "I don't understand her choices, but I don't need to, I suppose. She follows her own path. I guess it's what she wanted."

"It's a great honor to be the Fountain," Meersath said.

"If you say so."

"Would you like to receive the blessing of the Quickener?"

"I did promise to visit her. Will she remember me?"

"Perhaps. It's hard to say. She is more likely to remember visits from those close to her." Meersath put her hand on his arm. "Everyone is welcome in the Garden. You need not worship the Quickener to ask for her blessing."

They followed the winding path through the hedges out of the Garden. Behind them, Terlyn sank deep into a still, silent sleep. A small part of her awareness glowed like a tiny ember in a banked fire. She felt herself reaching down into the soil, her roots drawing forth water and nutrients from the earth. Her arms reached up into the sky, sending out a thousand tiny fingers to catch the warming rays of the sun. When night came, she settled further into the dreamless dream.

The turning of the world brought the sun back into the sky. Terlyn's dim awareness felt her leaves open to welcome it. She felt the slow movement of water through the soil beneath the Garden. The water traveled up, up, in its own languid rhythm, from root to branch to leaf. She felt the processes of the Garden without consciousness, sensations with no meaning or understanding attached to them. Time did not exist except for the measured flow of water and sun.

Into that tiny ember of awareness intruded a flicker of sensation, a sense of pressure, building...

Terlyn exploded into the light. There was someone on top of her, a stranger, mounting her. She blinked, confused, and then her body shuddered with orgasm, so intense she could not keep herself from screaming. It rang through her, wave after wave of ecstasy. Bewildering sights and sounds crashed around her—the face above her, contorted in ecstasy; the feel of the hard cock sliding fast and rough inside her; the blue sky, scattered with small puffy white clouds. She tried to move, but something was holding her, something coarse wrapped tightly around her arms and legs.

She shook her head. "What—"

The man dismounted, stormy gray eyes intent. He picked up a small stone bowl made of dark granite flecked with mica. He slid his hand over her breast and squeezed.

Pleasure washed through Terlyn. She looked around, confused. Meersath was standing beside her, and Tyrill, and Eileithyia. She opened her mouth to call to them. "What—"

Another orgasm took her. She arched her back, crying out with pleasure. Clear liquid flowed from her nipple. The man collected it in the stone cup. It shimmered slightly in the sun.

Terlyn shook her head, trying to clear it, but the fog that filled her mind would not part. "I don't…"

The vines tightened. The thorns in her wrists and legs drove deeper. Red sap flowed into her, and she was falling, falling into an inky blackness.

Her eyes flew open. An orgasm tore through her. The sun had moved in the sky. There was another man on top of her. His cock moved inside her. She cried out with pleasure, confused and overwhelmed. A woman's face came into view, red hair framing an elfin face dominated by large dark eyes. She was nude from the waist up. She caressed Terlyn's face. "What a lovely Fountain this year," she said.

She bent over. Her lips closed around Terlyn's nipple. She squeezed Terlyn's breast. Her tongue played over Terlyn's skin. "Mmm," she said.

A second orgasm tore through her, radiating outward from her breast. Terlyn convulsed. The woman straightened. "Mm, that was so…oh!" She wavered, putting out her hand to steady herself. Her pupils constricted and expanded again. "Oh!" She kissed the man atop Terlyn, rough, urgent. "Come, my darling. We should—" The vines tightened. The world of light and sound receded to a tiny dot and was gone.

It came rushing back. The sun jumped in the sky. Another orgasm exploded over her. Terlyn shuddered and writhed, but the vines held her fast. A tongue played over her clit, coaxing her to greater pleasure. She screamed.

A woman straightened from between her legs, wiping the back of her mouth with her hand. She walked around Terlyn, smiling slyly. Another woman bent over Terlyn from the other side. Two sets of lips and tongues found her nipple. She tried to pull free, but there was something wrapped around her arms, holding her.

Her body shook again in the grip of another orgasm. She felt slick wetness flow from her nipples. The women leaning over her sighed.

The vines contracted, causing the thorns that pierced her skin to shift. "Wait!" she said. "I don't underst—" Her voice trailed off. Darkness closed around her.

Night settled over the Garden. Small glowing fireflies moved in the dark spaces in the hedges. Terlyn slept.

Sedhi and Marisem came to her as the sun disappeared, escorted by two dronelights shaped like butterflies with delicate wings of stained glass. As darkness settled over the Garden, small flower buds opened on the hedges, revealing pale luminescent flowers that glowed with a soft white light. More glowing flowers, small and delicate, blossomed on the vines that held Terlyn down, bathing her body in their gentle light.

Sedhi unrolled a large, cloth-wrapped bundle and took out two large sponges. He gave one of them to Marisem. The two men knelt beside the small round pool to soak their sponges. Then they stood on each side of the stone.

Gently, reverently, Sedhi washed Terlyn's slumbering body. He moved the sponge over her breasts and down across her stomach. Softly shimmering liquid glistened on her skin. Marisem did the same for her legs. He slid covetous hands up her thighs. "She's very wet," he said. Terlyn remained unmoving.

"The Quickener makes sure she stays that way," Sedhi said.

"And she can't feel what we're doing?"

"No. The Fountain wakes only when she has an orgasm. She is aware of nothing but her pleasure. Through her ecstasy, the Quickener offers us his blessing. During the season, she may offer the Quickener's blessing a thousand times or more."

Marisem gaped. "She wakes up in the middle of an orgasm a thousand times?"

"Yes. She is not aware of the passage of time as she sleeps, so to her, it feels like it is happening without pause."

Marisem shivered. "Have you ever wondered what that would be like? I mean, to wake up that way, over and over."

Sedhi smiled. "Many times. I have often imagined the experience of being a Fountain."

"And?"

"The Fountain must be in a female body. I've never been curious enough to change. I've never changed at all."

"Really?" Marisem looked surprised. "You've never changed your body in your whole life? Not even once?"

Sedhi looked down at himself and shrugged. "I'm comfortable in this body."

When they finished bathing Terlyn, Sedhi ran his hands over her body, massaging her. Marisem scooped some water into a small crystal bowl engraved with twisting vines. He knelt beside the rock and washed Terlyn's hair. One of the dronelights swooped low, crystalline wings fluttering, to offer him more light.

"You are new, are you not, Initiate Marisem?" Sedhi said. "This is your first season?"

Marisem nodded. "Yes."

"Part of your nightly duties, Initiate, include making sure the Fountain is kept receptive for the next day's worshippers. In addition to bathing her, you will also be responsible for stimulating her."

"High Priest Tyrill said something about that," Marisem said, "but he was a bit...err, short on details. What should I do? I mean, 'stimulating' can cover a lot of ground, if you follow my meaning."

"I follow your meaning, Initiate. You have broad latitude in the way you choose to discharge your responsibilities. You will be expected to ensure that the Fountain is kept in a high state of physical arousal, so that she will reach orgasm more easily when worshippers come to visit. However, her orgasms and the blessing of the Quickener are reserved for those who come to worship. You'll need to learn the small signs that will tell you to stop before you bring her to climax." He stood next to Terlyn, looking down at her fondly. He brushed her hair back from her forehead. "The Fountain is unaware, so you must become skilled at reading her body. It is important that you do not allow the Fountain to reach orgasm. Her pleasure is sacred. It is the conduit by which the Quickener blesses his supplicants."

He ran his hand lightly over Terlyn's body. She did not respond.

"The signs will be subtle." His hand slid further down. His fingers opened her folds. She remained still, her breathing deep and even. He pressed his finger against her clit. Still she did not respond. The two dronelights bathed her body in light.

"Watch the way she breathes," he said. "Feel tremors inside her. Look for swelling in her nipples or color in her face."

"I see, Priest," Marisem said.

Sedhi slid his finger easily into Terlyn. "The Quickener has her. The Fountain may reach ecstasy rapidly. You must be vigilant." His fingers moved. "There! Do you see that? The way her pulse beats faster? The way her lips part? Those are signs."

"Yes, Priest," Marisem said. He caressed her cheek. "She is very lovely."

"Yes. She is one of the loveliest Fountains in my time as a priest of the Quickener. Would you like to pleasure yourself with her?"

"Is that allowed?"

"Yes. It is one of the nice things about being in his service." He laughed at Marisem's expression. "Not until you learn to read the signs, Initiate! You must take care not to allow the Fountain to reach ecstasy. When you have learned to do that, you may perform your duties in whatever manner you choose." His fingers strummed Terlyn's clit. "You'll learn to read a person's body very well. You may also be called upon to excite the Fountain during days of heavy worship, which means you will learn how to touch a person to evoke excitement again even after an orgasm. There is a reason we who serve the Quickener are in such high demand as lovers."

"I look forward to learning what you can teach me, Priest."

"Well, then, let's begin." He slid his fingers from Terlyn. "Observe the Fountain. What do you see?"

"Well…" Marisem hesitated. "She seems calm. Her face is a little bit flush. Her nipples are hard."

"Put your finger in her."

Marisem slid a finger inside her. Sakim smiled. "Did you see that? The little tremble? The way her eyelids fluttered? Her mind is not here, but her body still responds. Those little responses tell you a great deal. What do you feel inside her?"

"She is warm and very wet."

"Touch her clit. Tell me what happens."

Marisem moved his fingers around Terlyn's swollen nub. "She got a little bit tighter around my finger."

"Do you see the little intake of breath? The Fountain is very close. Slowly now. Remove your fingers. Our work here is done." He bent over to kiss Terlyn's lips. "Sleep well, Fountain."

Marisem gathered up the things they had brought with them into the Garden. The two men left, walking between the rows of gently glowing hedges. The butterfly dronelights followed overhead.

2.8

THE TWO MOONS dipped below the horizon. A glow in the east heralded the dawn. A gentle rain fell over the center of the Garden, confining itself precisely to the space in the center of the hedge maze. Terlyn's body shone, wet and slick.

The rain stopped at the exact moment Meersath and Eileithyia stepped into the center of the labyrinth. Each of them carried a small basket. They both wore long, flowing dresses of fine, lightweight green fabric, cut so that one breast and one arm were bare. Eileithyia wore a strand of small red and purple flowers in her wild tangle of multicolored hair.

They knelt in the grass beside the stone. Tiny drops of water beaded on the blades of grass. Each woman took handfuls of small red flower petals from the baskets and began rubbing them over Terlyn's motionless body, hands gliding over her wet skin. The petals dissolved. The scent of flowers filled the air.

Eileithyia's hands folded over Terlyn's breasts. "We give thanks to the Quickener for the blessings she offers. We give thanks to the Fountain for the offering of her body."

Meersath slid her fingers over Terlyn's clit, circling it lightly until wetness flowed from within her. "The Fountain is ready to receive worshippers," she said.

The first supplicant of the day, a tall, strong man with a narrow frame, arrived not long after. Two priests wearing green and brown greeted him at the entrance to the Garden. Tyrill met him on the path lined with trees and statues. "You wish to commune with the Quickener?"

"Yes." His voice was soft, incongruous with his powerful body.

"Have you brought an offering?"

"Yes." He reached into the pockets of the loose-fitting blue pants he wore. He brought out a small box that opened to reveal a flower, green and delicate, carved from a block of jade. "I am hoping the Quickener will bless me in my new project."

"Of course," Tyrill said. He accepted the box with its offering and bowed deeply. "Please continue."

The man walked the labyrinth without haste, gold-ringed eyes half-closed, each step deliberate and contemplative. Eileithyia greeted him at the center. She helped him disrobe. When he stood naked, she and Meersath assisted him in stepping down into the pool.

He emerged a moment later, water flowing off his body, with dilated eyes and a cock that stood ramrod straight.

Eileithyia escorted him to Terlyn's prone form. "Please accept the blessing of the Quickener through her Fountain."

"Thank you, priestess," he said.

He knelt over Terlyn's prone form, his gaze lingering on her face for a long moment. "Thank you, Fountain, for this gift," he said.

Then he mounted her, pressing his erection slowly into her.

Far away, lost somewhere deep in slumber, the tiny ember of Terlyn's awareness flickered. In the silent darkness, aware of nothing but the slow movement of water through the Garden, aware not even of herself, she felt a tug, a pull toward somewhere else...

Terlyn's eyes flew open. She exploded in orgasm, dragged from her slumber into a torrent of ecstasy. A stranger leaned over her, his lips close to her ears. "Thank you, Fountain," he said.

His lips found her nipple. She convulsed in the grip of another unstoppable wave of ecstasy. "What..." she said. "What..."

He drew deeply on her nipple. Small jolts of pleasure shuddered through her. He twitched inside her, sending the last few spurts of warmth up into her. Terlyn's eyes widened.

Then he withdrew. The vines around her arms and legs tightened. Red sap flowed. The world faded. Darkness claimed her once more.

She exploded again into the light, back arching, contracting around a rigid cock that thrust powerfully into her, over and over again. She flailed, held fast by the vines that bound her. A man looked down at her, his face framed by long golden hair. "Praise be to the Quickener," he said. He withdrew. He slid his hands over her breasts, cupping, squeezing. Liquid flowed from her nipple. He pressed a cool stone cup against her skin. She shuddered in ecstasy, moaning, not comprehending anything except the pleasure that rang through her body.

The vines tightened. Tiny points of pain flared as the thorns pierced her deeply. She parted her lips to speak, but the world of sunlight and blue sky was already fading.

Light and sound flared once more. She was aware that she was screaming, calling out the ecstasy that burst through her body. Fingers penetrated her. Fingers strummed her clit. Two pairs of lips wrapped around her nipples. She shuddered and thrashed so strongly her hips lifted from the stone. Two women stood beside her drinking greedily, mirror images of each other with skin the color of polished ebony and ivory. Their tongues circled her nipples before they kissed each other over Terlyn's body, hungry.

Terlyn blinked. "I—" she panted. "I—" The vines tightened, dragging her down into the dark stillness.

The light returned an instant later, washing over her as her body convulsed in ecstasy. The sky overhead glowed red with the last rays of the sun. Long fingers of shadow crept through the Garden. Terlyn cried out, fists clenched, toes curled. The man atop her had long black hair streaked with glittering silver. His body tightened as his pleasure answered hers. She felt the wet spurt of his ejaculation deep inside her.

He bent over to lick her nipple. Another man standing beside her, one hand on the first man's back, lapped at the clear sparkling fluid that flowed from her other nipple. The two men kissed each other.

"Wha—"

The man atop her kissed her deeply, his tongue sliding between her lips. She tasted something warm and sweet. The vines constricted. Thorns drove into her skin. Consciousness drained from her eyes.

The shadows grew dark and deep. The luminescent flowers opened, bathing the Garden in their ethereal glow. Sedhi and Marisem walked the labyrinth to the center, escorted by two dronelights.

They bathed Terlyn's slumbering body. Sedhi gazed at her face for a long time.

"What are you thinking about?" Marisem asked.

"What? Oh." Sedhi shook his head. He smiled down at Terlyn. His fingers caressed her face lightly. He ran his hands down her body, gentle and loving. "She is beautiful."

"You like her?"

"I do." He caressed her forehead. "I would like to be able to bring her pleasure. Alas, that is not for us."

Marisem knelt to wash Terlyn's hair. "Not even if you make an offering to the Quickener?"

"No. The High Priestess pleasures the Fountain on the first day of summer, and the High Priest on the first day of autumn. Beyond that, those of us called to serve do not participate in the Fountain's ecstasy. Those of us who serve the gods gain through our service, but we also give something up. This is what we who serve the Quickener give up. It is not so great a thing as the Fountain gives up, but I think we probably gain less as well."

"What does she gain?"

"Communion with the Quickener, I think. Those who volunteer as Fountain say they feel close to the Quickener for the rest of their lives, even if they go on to worship another god."

"Do you think she hears us talking?"

"No," Sedhi said. "The Quickener moves within her. She is aware of nothing but pleasure."

"That sounds wonderful."

"Hmm. Perhaps. I have watched many Fountains give themselves to the Garden over the years. I think it must be very disorienting."

Marisem finished washing Terlyn's hair. The water shimmered faintly as it dripped from her hair. "She is so lovely," he said.

"Are you ready to perform the rest of your duties?"

"Yes, priest."

The two dronelights rose, bathing Terlyn in light. One had the shape of a butterfly, its iridescent wings alive with slowly moving colors. The other was an exquisitely crafted clockwork contraption with two pairs of long, slender metallic wings driven by a complex array of gears and levers.

Sedhi massaged Terlyn's breasts in slow circles. Marisem slipped his hands between her legs. She remained perfectly still, her eyes closed, her breathing slow and steady.

"Tell me what you see," Sedhi said.

"She looks peaceful. Her face is calm." His eyes traveled down her body. "Her nipples are getting hard. Is that because you're touching her?"

"Yes. What else do you see?"

"Um…her pulse is slow. So is her breathing. The vines around her wrists are moving. They keep contracting and relaxing. It's very gradual. I never noticed that before."

"Yes. What you see is the rhythm of the Garden. Think of it like a heart-beat. Do you see the thorns that pierce her skin? There is a constant flow through the vines, into the Fountain's body. It nourishes her and keeps her in her trance. The Quickener uses her body to create his blessing. Put your fingers in her. What do you feel?"

"She is still very wet. She is relaxed."

"Yes." He ran one hand down her body, until his fingers found her clit.

"Oh!" Marisem said. "I felt that. Like a trembling inside her."

"She is becoming aroused. Pay attention to her face and her body. Learn to read the signs. This skill will help you in your duties. It will also help you to know how to excite your lovers in your worldly life. The way a Fountain responds is not so different from the way we all respond. The signs are the same. The trembling, the color on the cheek, all the other little things I will teach you to read. When you have mastered that, you will need to master yourself as well."

"Myself?" Marisem said.

"You may pleasure yourself with the Fountain. In fact, it will be expected of you, to help keep her body in a receptive state. But you must not bring her over the edge, even if it means stopping when you yourself are on the brink of ecstasy. You must learn to read her, of course, but also learn to control yourself. It would not do to bring the Fountain to orgasm because you were too focused on your own!"

"That sounds challenging."

Sedhi shrugged. "It's just practice. The practice is fun." He moved his finger a bit faster. "Do you see how her body shudders? Notice how her lips part, how her muscles tense. She is getting close." He took his finger away. "What do you observe?"

"She's breathing faster," Marisem said. He looked closer. "Now she is growing still. Her body is relaxing."

"Yes! By keeping her here, just at the point where she starts to tense, you can keep her ready for the worshippers. This is important on ceremonial days when she will have many visitors, so that all of them may receive the blessing. There will be times when the Fountain has had so many orgasms in such a short span of time it will take skill and persistence to work her up for her next worshipper." He grinned. "This is also a skill that will make you popular in your worldly life."

"Oh?"

His grin grew wider. "When your lover says, 'I'm done' and you say 'Oh, no you aren't,' well, let's just say word travels. Now, let's practice. You try."

Under Sedhi's watchful eye, Marisem teased Terlyn, caressing her breasts, one finger stroking her clit, over and over again. He paid close attention to her, reading her body, stopping when her breathing quickened, then starting again when she relaxed.

Deep in her dreamless slumber, the tiny speck of Terlyn's awareness felt the whisper of a distant pull. She paid it no mind, lost as she was in the secret rhythms of the Garden.

2.9

MORNING SENT LONG fingers of red light through a pale sky. The shield folded itself down from the dome, channeling a gentle rain precisely to the center of the Garden. The pale luminescent flowers closed. Terlyn's body shone wet and slick.

Tyrill and Eileithyia traced the labyrinth to the center. The rain ceased just as they reached the open space at its heart.

They put down the baskets they carried. From them, they took out handfuls of bright purple flower petals. "Thank you, Quickener, for giving us your blessing," Tyrill said. "Thank you, Fountain, for offering your body." The two of them crushed the petals against Terlyn's wet skin, filling the air with a heady, intoxicating scent.

Tyrill slid his fingers over Terlyn's mound. He spread her open, probing, inspecting. He nodded, pleased. "The Fountain is ready."

Eileithyia bowed. "That is good. We have many supplicants here to receive the Blessing today. People are saying this is the most blessed Fountain we have had in years. I think this Fountain is going to be very popular."

"She is wonderful," Tyrill said. "The Quickener is pleased."

The first of the day's supplicants arrived seeking blessing. Tyrill and Eileithyia received him. Eileithyia bowed. "I am delighted to see you," she said. She helped him to disrobe and led him into the pool.

He emerged, water streaming from his body, cock erect. He stood at the edge of the pool for a moment, breathing rapidly, eyes unfocused. "So how does this work?"

"You may pleasure yourself with the Fountain however you like, so long as you do not cause harm," Eileithyia said. "You will receive the blessing of the Quickener when you bring her pleasure, which you may do before or after satisfying yourself, as you choose. If you require assistance, Tyrill or I will be happy to help you."

He climbed, a bit awkward, onto the stone. He knelt over Terlyn for a long time, gazing down at her. He stroked her cheek, tenderly, watching her face. She did not stir.

He placed a small, hesitant kiss on her lips. She lay as still as the statues that lined the garden path.

He kissed her more deeply. His tongue slid without resistance between her lips. Her body reacted not at all.

He pressed his body against her. He kissed her neck, her cheek, her shoulder. He worked his way down, planting kisses over the curve of her breast. He lingered for a moment at her hard, pink nipple, taking it with exquisite gentleness between his lips.

He worked his slow, unhurried way down, kissing and caressing her with tenderness and care. When he reached her mound, he placed his face between her legs. His tongue made gentle contact with her clit.

Tyrill and Eileithyia watched him move his tongue in lazy circles, exploring her until her breathing quickened. Terlyn's lips parted. Her eyelids fluttered.

He moved back up again, still taking his time, until his lips found hers again. He kissed her very softly, tongue flicking against her lips, while he slid slowly into her.

Deep in the black void of dreamlessness, Terlyn became aware, in a vague way, of something calling to her from some distant place. She floated away from the calm, measured flow of water through root and leaf, drifting up toward...

Her eyes flew open. Ecstasy seized her—pleasure so intense it left no room for anything else. Someone was kissing her, moving inside her, moaning against her lips. She lay on her back under a clear morning sky, nude. She tried to move, but something held her down. Her mind reeled with dazed confusion.

He moved faster, thrusting hard into her, his hands caressing the sides of her face. She pushed against the fog in her mind. Pleasure tore through her, causing her body to convulse. Her hips lifted to meet his thrusts, even as she struggled to understand what was happening. She was on her back, with something soft beneath her, but she couldn't quite remember how she'd gotten there.

He thrust deep, spasming. A hot wet torrent poured into her. He broke the kiss, crying out in his own pleasure. She blinked up at him. "Donvin?"

He drew on her nipple with his lips. His hand squeezed her breast. She felt a tingling, and then a rushing sensation. Pleasure washed over her again. She shuddered and moaned. There was a sense of pulsing, a constriction around her wrists and ankles. Sleep dragged at her. "Donvin," she said, voice bleary. "Donvin…" He looked down at her with eyes filled with tenderness as the darkness closed in around her.

A moment later, she exploded into the world of sight and sound again, pleasure roaring through her body. A stranger writhed atop her, bathed in sweat, corded muscles moving beneath dark brown skin. His arms wrapped tightly around her, hands underneath her back.

"What—" she mumbled. "Where is—"

He kissed her roughly. Her body responded, without thought or will. She kissed him back, as her hips rose against him, meeting his thrusts. Her struggles ceased. She gave herself over to the incomprehensible ecstasy, pressing against him, inviting him deeper. He let out a roar. Wetness jetted into her.

He pulled out of her. She gasped in shock. His hands, large and strong, curled around her breasts. He squeezed and massaged. She trembled, moaning as another orgasm rolled over her. Clear shimmering fluid poured from hard pink nipples. He pressed a small stone bowl against her breasts, collecting it as it ran down her skin.

The vines tightened. She heard a roaring in her ears. Sleep tugged her downward into the void. "What's happening?" she said. Her eyes closed. She sank into the still quiet darkness.

They flew open a moment later. Her body convulsed in orgasm. Someone knelt over her, legs on each side of her face. A tongue played rapidly across her clit. Her body shook. Her knees trembled. Her hips bucked.

She heard a delicate laugh. "You are a delight, Fountain," said an unfamiliar voice. The woman on top of her crawled backward, moving up toward Terlyn's head until her mouth was over Terlyn's breast. She pressed her own nipple to Terlyn's lips. Her tongue curled around Terlyn's nipple.

Terlyn cried out, caught up in orgasm again. Her breasts tingled. The woman sucked greedily at her nipple. Darkness crept in from the edges of Terlyn's vision. Her body became heavy, her thoughts sluggish. "I feel…" Her voice slurred as her consciousness faded away.

She was visited three more times that day, twice by men, once by a group of two men and a woman. She woke gasping and screaming, her body arching in the throes of orgasm, and was dragged back into slumber before the pleasure had fully faded.

Sedhi came to her alone that night, after the luminescent flowers opened. The Garden held a quiet beauty after dark, bathed in the glow of the phosphorescent light from the wide-petaled flowers.

He stood beside the rock, smiling down at her for a long time. A tiny jeweled dronelight drifted noiselessly above him. After a time, he soaked his sponge in the pool and washed her, meticulous and gentle, touching her like a sacred object. He knelt on the ground and washed her dark green hair, which had already grown long enough that it was beginning to spill over the edge of the rock.

When he was finished, he removed the simple brown tunic and loose brown pants he wore. He stepped into the pool, eyes closed, soaking in its warmth. By the time he got out, the smaller moon had crept above the trees.

He stood naked in the soft glow of the flowers for a while, shimmering liquid dripping from his body. He approached the rock once more. He stood there for a time, eyes closed, hands folded in front of him in silent meditation. He bowed, then placed his hands on her body, reverent.

"Thank you for your gift, Fountain," he said. "And thank you, Quickener, for bringing your blessing into the world through the Fountain."

He caressed her still, silent body. His hands glided over her without haste. He bent over to plant a line of small, soft kisses on her lips, on the hollow of her throat, on each nipple, on her navel, on her mound, and finally, on her clit. Then he traced the same path back up, kissing her navel, each of her nipples, her throat, and finally her lips once more. His lips lingered on hers. The tip of his tongue touched her lips.

He ran his hands over every inch of her body not wrapped in vines. He watched her closely, alert to the slightest change in her breathing, the smallest tremor of her eyelids, the changing rhythm of her pulse fluttering in her neck.

He bowed once more before he climbed onto the rock. He knelt over her, placing one more kiss on her lips, then slowly, slowly, he slid into her. She didn't move.

He took her in long, deliberate thrusts, worshipping her with solemn reverence. His eyes did not waver from her face. He slowed whenever her breathing increased or her pulse quickened, adjusting his pace until she relaxed again.

Then, as the smaller moon crept higher, he came, letting out a soft "uh!" of pleasure. Terlyn remained still and calm beneath him.

"Thank you, Fountain," he said. He kissed her unmoving lips before he dismounted. He washed her again with the water from the shimmering pool. When he was finished, he dressed. He walked around the rock, bowing to her from each of the four points of the compass. Then he gathered up the things he had brought with him into the Garden and left. The dronelight floated along above him.

2.10

EACH MORNING STARTED with the same gentle rainfall, confined by careful folding of the shield to the precise center of the labyrinth. Members of the priesthood—sometimes Tyrill and Eileithyia, sometimes Sedhi and Meersath, sometimes other men and women dressed in burgundy and brown—came to her in the morning to rub her down with flower petals. They greeted the worshippers who arrived seeking blessings, accepting their gifts to the Quickener.

Donvin arrived every morning at sunup. He presented tiny sculptures in offering: a detailed stone figure, no bigger than a thumbnail, of Terlyn; a small stone box, carved with images of snow-covered trees; a tiny model of the Garden, complete with flowers and hedges. He bathed in the pool, then took his time with Terlyn, caressing her, kissing her, adulating her with his hands and lips and tongue. She woke in ecstasy, her body wracked with the force of her orgasm. He lapped at her breasts, accepting the Quickener's gift. Afterward, he gazed down at her, touching her cheek, until consciousness faded from her eyes.

She woke in ecstasy again and again, each time with the sun in a different place in the sky and a different person or, often, different people atop her. She writhed in pleasure as the offering was taken from her breasts by lips and tongues or accepted in small stone bowls. Then she faded once more, drawn inexorably down into timeless, dreamless sleep to await her next ecstatic awakening.

At night, when the flowers cloaked the Garden in pale light, the priests and priestesses of the Quickener visited her again. Sedhi attended to her on most nights, often accompanied by Marisem, occasionally by Meersath, and on two occasions, by Tyrill.

He taught Marisem to read the ways of Terlyn's body. Over days and weeks, Marisem learned to track Terlyn's arousal like a hunter tracking his prey, reading the signs in every tiny quiver, every small intake of breath. He learned to bring her just to the edge of pleasure, without quite allowing her to waken, to keep her body primed for the supplicants who would arrive with the dawning sun. Eventually, Marisem became familiar enough with the ways of her body that he was able to pleasure himself without rousing her.

Sedhi spent many nights in silent communion with her. He pleasured himself with her sleeping body, attentive and reverent, as gentle and as thorough with her each night as Donvin was each morning. The two men developed a respect for one another that, over several weeks, blossomed into genuine friendship.

Through all these things, Terlyn remained the sun about which the Garden revolved. She stayed in her place of quiet, summoned over and over again into a body writhing and shuddering with pleasure before sinking back to sleep. No time passed for her in the dark stillness. Each explosion of ecstasy followed directly on its predecessor and led directly into its successor, day after day, week after week.

The Garden transformed around her. The bright green of new leaves on the hedges gave way to a deeper green. The trunks of the trees turned yellow and green with moss.

On the eve of the first day of summer, the routine changed. Sedhi, Marisem, Tyrill, Meersath, and Eileithyia all tended to Terlyn that night. They were joined by two additional priests: Rhian, a novice priest with long blue hair and scarlet eyes flecked with gold, who wore a simple burgundy robe tied at his waist with a belt of bright green; and Ahani, a tall, graceful woman with pale skin and auburn hair whose eyes were flat, blank discs of copper, dressed in a tight-fitting, ankle-length burgundy dress that opened in the front to reveal full breasts with a silver chain that hung between her large brown nipples.

No dronelights accompanied them. The soft light of the luminescent flowers illuminated the center of the Garden. They each approached the stone upon which Terlyn slept and bowed. Each of them knelt in turn at the head of the stone, saying, "Thank you, Fountain, for giving your body.

Thank you, Quickener, for giving your blessing." Then they each rose and kissed Terlyn's lips.

All seven of the men and women poured water onto her body from small stone bowls and washed her with sponges. When they finished, they gathered in a loose circle around the stone. Eileithyia placed a garland of vines with green leaves and small, closed buds around Terlyn's neck. Ahani and Meersath used their fingers to paint an elaborate pattern of abstract lines on Terlyn's breasts with blue, brown, red, and yellow pigments from tiny crystal cups. Rhian and Tyrill placed a small gold ring, inlaid with a spiral design in green stone, over each of Terlyn's nipples. Marisem washed her hair, which now fell in a wide green wave over the edge of the stone, reaching toward the ground.

Then, beneath the light of the two moons, they filed out of the garden, walking the convoluted path of the labyrinth between hedges dotted with glowing flowers.

The morning rain fell on Terlyn's sleeping form. Her skin had darkened since the close of winter, from pale white to a rich brown. The painted designs gleamed on her body. The buds on the garland blossomed into small yellow flowers that filled the air with a spicy scent.

New flowers opened on the vines that bound Terlyn. These were large and white, with violet stripes on each petal. A small red bead grew in the center of each flower.

The entire Garden had exploded overnight into color. Flowers blossomed on every tree and every hedge. Tiny florets of pink, purple, and blue burst up among the blades of grass. A sweet, pleasant scent, warm and floral, filled the air.

Eileithyia entered the center of the labyrinth. Sedhi and Marisem followed her. Eileithyia removed her simple one-piece red and green dress and stepped naked into the pool. Sedhi draped her dress over his arm.

Before she had finished bathing, a stream of worshippers walked the labyrinth to the center. They wore everything from simple tunics and pants to elaborate dresses whose patterns changed, swirling fabrics that seemed to float around their bodies, and even body paint that glittered with small flecks of light. Many of those with breasts wore clothing cut to display them. They gathered in the center of the labyrinth, where they stood or sat in multiple rows. Some chatted with their companions; others walked the labyrinth in silent contemplation.

Eileithyia raised her arms toward the sky, palms up. The crowd fell silent. "In the name of the Quickener," she said, "I welcome you to the first day of summer."

The crowd cheered. She raised her arms again. "Through her Fountain, the Quickener offers you her bounty. Accept it so that your undertakings, whatever they may be, will bear fruit."

Sedhi leaned close to Marisem. "Do you see the new flowers on the vines? They show us that the Quickener has prepared the Fountain with a special blessing for Firstday. It will allow her body to pass on the Quickener's blessings to all the people here. Those who accept the blessing directly from the High Priestess are especially favored by the Quickener. Watch."

Eileithyia plucked one of the white and violet flowers from the vines around Terlyn's wrists. She placed it in her mouth and swallowed. She closed her eyes and shuddered. When she opened her eyes again, her pupils shrank to tiny pinpricks.

She placed her hands on Terlyn's body. "Thank you, Fountain, for the suffering you are about to endure," she said, too low for the assembled crowd to hear.

She slipped one hand between Terlyn's legs. Her fingers spread Terlyn's folds. One finger found Terlyn's clit.

Deep in the silent dreamless sleep, Terlyn responded. The tiny ember of her consciousness flared. She woke screaming with ecstasy, her body convulsing among the vines. Another cheer went up from the crowd. Eileithyia smiled down at her. "Thank you," she said again.

She placed her lips on Terlyn's nipple. Terlyn shuddered and thrashed in another orgasm. Eileithyia straightened.

Donvin was the first to step forward. Eileithyia wrapped her arms around him to draw him close. She kissed him deeply. Her lips remained on his for a long moment.

He accepted the sweet liquid from her lips. His body shook. "Oh!" he said. His eyes glazed for a moment, then cleared. "Thank you, Priestess."

She smiled. "Go forth with the blessing of the Quickener."

Terlyn blinked sleepily. Her body still reverberated with the echoes of her orgasm. Eileithyia slid her hand between Terlyn's legs once more.

A moment later, Terlyn gasped, back arching, struggling helplessly against the vines as she came again. Eileithyia wrapped her lips around her nipple, finger still dancing on her clit. Terlyn cried out with the force of her orgasm, hips bucking against Eileithyia's finger.

A short, golden-haired woman with indigo eyes stepped forward on bare feet. She wore only a translucent green wrap around her ample waist, shot through with gold. She kissed Eileithyia, taking the clear liquid from her. Terlyn pulled against the vines. "What—what—"

Eileithyia moved her finger in quick little circles around Terlyn's clit. Terlyn shuddered. Her back arched. She screamed, shaking her head. "Please! Please!"

Her scream became a wail when Eileithyia's lips circled around her nipple again. Her body convulsed with pleasure.

Two more people stepped forward, hand in hand. The man was short and slender, his chest bare. Brightly colored tattoos covered every part of his body in a complex, chaotic design that moved and changed as he walked, the colors flowing over his skin without mixing. His companion was tall and voluptuous, with light brown skin and pure white hair. She wore a backless dress in a pale green that matched his black-trimmed pants, cut with a deep V-shaped slit along one side. Her eyes, like his, were the color of a raging fire, and like his, her irises were outlined in black. She gazed down into Terlyn's uncomprehending eyes. "We are grateful to you, Fountain," she said.

They embraced Eileithyia. She wrapped her arms around them. She kissed the man deeply. He turned and kissed his companion, sharing the blessing with her. Her nipples swelled. She sighed. "Thank you, priestess," she said.

Terlyn watched the three of them, struggling to understand what was happening. She felt this must be important, but it seemed unreal. The three people looked an infinite distance away. Sleep tugged at her. She closed her eyes, reaching for it.

Before it could claim her, Eileithyia's fingers slid over her clit, and she exploded into a wrenching orgasm again, so intense it was almost painful. Eileithyia looked down at her in sympathy. "I know, Fountain," she said. "I understand your suffering." She took Terlyn's nipple in her mouth. Terlyn felt a tingling and a sense of pressure in her breast, and then a rush. She cried out. Pleasure took her. Warm liquid flowed into Eileithyia's mouth.

All morning and all afternoon it went on. Over and over, Terlyn came, trapped on the rock, unable to escape Eileithyia's fingers. Her nipples, held erect by the metal rings, throbbed and burned. She cried out again and again, twisting in something between ecstasy and agony. Darkness closed around the edges of her vision, until it seemed as though she were looking at the world from the end of a long tunnel. Many times, she thought she surely would not be able to orgasm any more, her body too sore and spent, but every touch on nipple or clit tore another orgasm from her.

The vines around her wrists and ankles tightened and relaxed, tightened and relaxed in a steady rhythm. With each pulse, she felt a surge of sap enter her through the thorns that pierced her skin. She felt it move within her, up her legs and down her arms. Her head swam.

All through the day, more people came to the Garden for the Quickener's blessing. They took their place among the other supplicants, waiting for their opportunity to accept the gift from Eileithyia's lips. Eileithyia continued without stopping. Even as the sun settled low in the sky, she remained where she was, forcing Terlyn to orgasm again and again. Terlyn's clit throbbed, overstimulated and sore. Her breasts ached. Eileithyia drew the clear fluid from Terlyn's nipples to pass on to the worshippers. By the time the shadows grew through the Garden, Terlyn sobbed with each new agonizing ecstasy.

Then, finally, there were no more people. The space around Terlyn emptied of everyone except Eileithyia, Sedhi, and Marisem.

The vines constricted. Terlyn's eyes closed. Sleep wrapped its dark velvety wings about her.

Eileithyia reeled. Sedhi caught her before she could fall. He helped her to the pool. She slumped in the warm water, exhausted.

Sedhi removed the rings from Terlyn's nipples. They remained swollen and erect. He kissed her forehead. "Sleep well this night, Fountain," he said.

Sedhi and Marisem bathed Terlyn with special care. Marisem washed her hair while Sedhi cleaned her lovingly with a sponge, gazing down at her with an expression of tenderness. He removed all traces of the designs that had been painted on her breasts, careful to be gentle with her nipples.

When they had finished bathing her, Eileithyia rose from the pool. Marisem gathered up her dress. Sedhi remained, caressing Terlyn's forehead.

"Are you coming with us, Priest Sedhi? Marisem asked.

"Not just yet," Sedhi said. "You may go with the High Priestess if you like. I wish to remain here in communion with the Quickener."

"Of course, priest." Marisem bowed and left, carrying Eileithyia's robe in one hand, supporting her with the other.

Sedhi remained in the Garden, silent and unmoving, for a long time. The luminescent flowers opened, bathing the Garden in their unearthly glow. The larger moon climbed above the hedges.

Sedhi kissed Terlyn's lips for a lingering moment. Then he removed his clothes and stepped into the pool. When he came back out, he mounted the rock and Terlyn, sliding slowly into her in a single long thrust. He moved deliberately, in short, careful thrusts, until his breathing changed. He gasped as he came. Terlyn didn't move beneath him.

When he withdrew, he dressed again. He stood there for a while longer, fingertips lightly caressing her face.

Presently a drifting dronelight alerted him to another person in the labyrinth. Donvin came into the open space, escorted by a dronelight shaped like a tiny golden dragon with bright blue designs on its wings.

The two men stood looking down at Terlyn in silence. Donvin kissed her lips. "Thank you for being here for her," Sedhi said. "Your dedication will help her adjust after her time as Fountain is over. You are a tribute to the Quickener."

Donvin gave a wry smile. "I'm not really a worshipper of the Quickener. My loyalties lie with the Lady."

Sedhi shrugged. "You can serve more than one god. Many people find that the blessings of the Quickener make their artistic endeavors more fertile."

Donvin laughed. "I suppose so. But I don't come here to worship the Quickener. I come here for her."

"You bring offerings to the Quickener, do you not? Works of art you create from your own imagination, yes?"

"Yes."

"Service is service, whatever your motivations. You honor the Quickener. He makes your imagination more fertile."

Donvin spread his hands in defeat. "Okay, you're right. I suppose I do serve two gods."

"And Terlyn," Sedhi said. "Your devotion to her is beautiful."

Donvin laughed again, but this time there was a trace of bitterness in it. "She might not agree. She doesn't much like entanglements that are too close. She says they constrain her. She has always needed a lot of freedom." Changing the subject, he said, "Do you often spend time with her at night?"

"Yes." Sedhi brushed the hair away from her forehead. "It's part of my duty as a priest of the Quickener."

"But?"

"But there's something especially captivating about this one."

"I know what you mean."

They stood for a while beneath the light of the dragon dronelight. Then Sedhi said, "You're here late."

"I wanted to see her again. I think this was a long day for her."

"One of three. There is another celebration of Firstday for autumn, and then of course the Day of Wakening in winter."

"What happens after that?"

"She will be a High Priestess of the Quickener, if she chooses. Most High Priestesses are former Fountains. Many Fountains go into seclusion for a time after they awaken. Readjusting can be difficult."

"I imagine so," Donvin said. "Will you help her? To readjust, I mean."

"If she wishes me to."

"Do you love her?"

Sedhi remained silent for a time, considering the question. Then he said, "I only know her as the Fountain. I don't know her as Terlyn. You can't love someone you don't know." He looked down at her sleeping face. "But there is something about her…"

"Yes."

Another moment passed. Donvin said, "I am content. I will leave you in peace."

"I am ready to go as well. Would you permit me the honor of accompanying you through the Labyrinth?"

"Of course."

The two men departed in silence, with a small golden dragon hovering above their heads. The white flowers with their violet streaks that had appeared on the vines folded up and dropped from their stems. They didn't return the next day.

2.11

For Terlyn, there was sleep but no rest. She woke the next morning crying out with orgasm, memories of the summer Firstday ritual still fresh in her mind. She stared up at Donvin's face in confusion. He smiled down at her and winked.

Then his lips closed around her nipple, and another orgasm shook her. The vines tightened. She sank down into the waiting blackness once more.

She was recalled from darkness four more times that day, three times by a strange woman atop her, thrusting into her, and once by a tall, fair-haired man who woke her with his tongue before collecting the fluid that expressed from her breasts in a bowl of speckled granite.

Neither Eileithyia nor Meersath attended to Terlyn that day. Instead, Tyrill and Ahani accepted the offerings from the worshippers who came to visit the Fountain. Tyrill wore a simple black shirt buttoned in the front by a diagonal row of buttons that ran in a row from one shoulder to his opposite hip, and black pants, both made of a smooth silky material. Ahani's clothing was as elaborate as Tyrill's was sober, a multicolored dress of translucent fabric printed with an intricate pattern of flowers, with an oval opening in the front that supported and displayed her breasts. A fine silver chain connected her nipples.

That night, Rhian accompanied Sedhi and Marisem. In the glow of the phosphorescent flowers, Sedhi and Marisem bathed Terlyn while Rhian washed her hair.

"She looks so peaceful," Rhian said. "I wonder what she's thinking right now."

"Nothing," Sedhi said. "She is beyond thought or feeling."

"Are you sure?"

"Yes. Nothing but orgasm can wake her. For her, there is nothing between her orgasms. No thought, no time. For her, her time in the Garden is nothing but the most excruciating pleasure."

"Nothing else will wake her?"

"Nothing but ecstasy. The Quickener makes sure of it. And she sleeps again when it is over."

Rhian ran his hands over her body, from her shoulders down over her breasts to her stomach and then to her legs. Terlyn lay still and quiet, breathing evenly. "That seems like a shame," he said.

"Why?" Sedhi asked.

"Because she can't feel this." He slipped the tip of his finger into her. With his other hand, he caressed her breast.

"Ah. But anyone who wants to know can learn what it feels like to be caressed. I'm sure she's probably felt what you're doing now many times. Few know what it's like to be worshipped in the Garden."

"Yeah, I suppose that's true."

"Initiate Rhian, Initiate Marisem, please make sure the Fountain's body is ready to receive worshippers tomorrow."

Rhian slid his finger deeper into her. Marisem kissed and caressed her breasts. Sedhi kissed her lips gently, feeling her warm breath. They coaxed and teased her unmoving body until wetness flowed freely between her legs. The vines pulsed in their slow rhythm, feeding her with wine-red liquid. Three tiny dronelights watched it all.

With the beginning of summer, an exuberance of color touched the Garden, and with it, a greater interest in communing with the Fountain. Ahani took over many of the daily functions for Eileithyia. More and more often, when supplicants arrived to receive the blessing from the Quickener, she rather than Eileithyia received their offering and led them to the pool. For several weeks, Tyrill assisted her with the daily duties; then, as the weeks went by, he turned the task of watching over the day's activities to Sedhi. At night, Terlyn's care fell to Marisem and Rhian.

Donvin continued to visit Terlyn every day. Each day, he brought ever more detailed sculptures as offerings.

On the fifth day after the welcoming of summer, Donvin brought two offerings instead of one. He met Ahani just inside the archway leading into the Garden, where he presented her with a tiny swan carved from white stone. "This is for the Quickener," he said.

She bowed as she accepted it. "Your devotion is remarkable. Your offerings show tremendous dedication."

He smiled. "Thank you, though I am not entirely certain it's the Quickener I'm dedicated to."

"Even so," she said. "The Quickener accepts your offering, and your dedication. Many who worship her exclusively are less dedicated than you are."

"Thank you, priestess," he said. He showed her the second offering, a smooth dolphin shape with fins engraved on its side, carved from green stone. "This is for the Fountain."

Ahani smiled and nodded. "That's lovely."

Donvin walked the labyrinth with measured, unhurried steps. Meersath met him in the center. She helped him disrobe and escorted him to the pool. He emerged dripping, his pupils constricted to tiny points, his cock erect.

Terlyn came up from the dreamless dark and crashed into the bright world in a paroxysm of unbearable, unstoppable ecstasy. She thrashed with pleasure, her uncomprehending eyes open wide. She felt a tongue on her clit, and something else...something hard inside her ass, unyielding as she throbbed and clenched with orgasm.

Donvin came into view above her. He leaned over her, naked. His lips closed around her nipple. His fingers slid into her. She screamed in pleasure as another orgasm tore through her. He sucked greedily, lapping up the fluid that issued from her breast. She twisted and turned in the vines, unable to get away. He kissed her roughly. His tongue thrust into her mouth. She could taste sweetness on it, something heady and rich that made her shiver. Her body tingled.

He entered her. She gasped and shuddered as he pressed his way inside her.

He took her with long slow strokes, each one an agony of overwhelming pleasure. She cried out in orgasm again and again as ecstasy wracked her body. He continued his slow, inexorable assault on her, neither speeding up nor slowing down. His tongue invaded her mouth. She bucked against him involuntarily. Clear liquid flowed from her breasts.

At last he came, unleashing a hot torrent inside her. He withdrew from her. She let out a yelp, her body clenching around the space where he had been. He pressed a stone cup against her breast, collecting the liquid that ran down her skin. "Donvin!" she said. Sleep tugged at her. She fought against it. Her body felt heavy and slow. "Donvin! I want..." Blackness crept in from the corners of her vision. "I want to say...to say..."

He looked at her curiously from a long way away. The vines tightened around her wrists and ankles. She felt something flowing into her through the thorns that penetrated her skin. The world contracted until it held only his face, then only his eyes. "I want…"

Darkness took her. Her eyes closed, and she was gone.

They flew open again a moment later. The sun had somehow jumped to the middle of the sky. A woman pressed down atop her, her body warm against Terlyn's, lips locked on hers. Her fingers moved between Terlyn's legs. Terlyn shook and spasmed. "Who—what—"

The woman chuckled. Her eyes, the color of a cloudless spring sky, peered warmly down as she smiled. "There it is," she murmured. She kissed the side of Terlyn's neck. "Don't try to understand. Just feel."

Then her lips found Terlyn's nipple, and a second surge of pleasure washed through her. Terlyn mumbled, trying to form words that wouldn't come. Darkness crept up to claim her once more.

An instant later, she woke again, gripped by an orgasm that curled her toes. The man atop her had short hair, black on one side and white on the other. One eye was pale blue, the other deep brown. He moved hard and thick within her. He placed one hand over her mouth as she woke. "Shh," he said. "Thank you, Fountain." He kissed her cheek as she came, writhing on the warm stone.

He came a moment after she did, releasing a warm flood into her. Then he squeezed both her breasts with powerful hands and collected the liquid that flowed from them in a small stone cup. She had two more orgasms in rapid succession as he squeezed and fondled her breasts, before the vines throbbed and tightened, sending her once more to her insensate slumber.

She awoke again, crying out with the force of the orgasm that ripped through her. The figure atop her had a strong, slender physique. Muscles rippled in powerful arms. Her lover cried out as she did, revealing sharp triangular teeth. The tattoos on their arms and chest, complex abstract patterns in fine lines, turned from red to gold as they came. Sharp teeth pressed against Terlyn's neck. She arched her back, spasming as warm wetness gushed into her. Her mind filled with a hazy, half-forgotten memory: a cage, an amphitheater, a long spiral walkway, men and women releasing all inhibition…

Her head swam. For a moment, she lost track of where she was. No, this was stone beneath her, soft with moss…

The figure bit her breast. Warm shimmering liquid flowed. She shuddered, shrieking with another orgasm. The memory fled her mind. Then the vines tightened, and consciousness fled as well.

She remained asleep as the sun set and the light faded from the sky. When the luminescent flowers opened, High Priest Tyrill, Initiate Rhian, Initiate Marisem, and Priestess Rahmos all made their way through the labyrinth to tend to her slumbering body.

"This Fountain has been quite extraordinary," Rahmos said. "I've been listening to the way the worshippers speak of her. The quality of her blessing is very high."

Tyrill nodded. "The Quickener likes this Fountain," he said. "He has been generous with his gifts."

Rahmos kissed Terlyn, running her fingers through her hair. She caressed Terlyn's face. "What of her friend, the one who worships the Lady?"

"Donvin?" Tyrill said. "He has offered a great deal to the Quickener. His creativity has been made particularly fertile by the Quickener's blessings, I think."

Rahmos looked down at Terlyn's sleeping face. "I envy her," she said. "His constancy will help her adjust when her service is over."

"Priestess?" Rhian said.

"Yes, initiate?"

"Why do Fountains hide themselves after they wake?"

Rahmos ran one hand absently down her body. Her gaze grew distant. "Time doesn't exist for you when you sleep. What are months to the rest of us is days to you. You wake to orgasm again and again and again. Every time your eyes open, it's a different person, a different moment in time. You never fully awake before you fade again. You don't know if this is your third awakening or your three hundredth. You have no idea if you've just begun, or if your service is about to end. Your thoughts are muddled. You cannot move. This happens until you cannot remember or even imagine any other existence. Then one day it's over, and you have to go back to life as it was. It's hard. You don't really remember, but your body does. When you come back, everything is too bright, too loud, too intense. It's a lot to adjust to."

"Why do people volunteer?"

She smiled. "Because it is amazing. There is no ceremony, not even the sacrifice to the Sun God, that is such incredible, sweet torment."

"I don't understand."

"You don't have to. We all serve in our own way."

Tyrill and Rahmos washed Terlyn. Marisem and Rhian washed her hair. When they finished, her body glistened wetly in the soft pale light.

Rahmos ran her hand over Terlyn. "This Fountain is a real beauty, isn't she?"

"She is just as lovely as you," Marisem agreed.

Rahmos laughed. "Oh, you are a flatterer," she said. "Come here and give me a hand, will you?"

She turned her back to Marisem and opened the green and gold dress she wore. He slid it from her body. She looked over her shoulder at him and smiled. She took him by the hand. He helped her step down into the pool.

She stayed there for only a few minutes. When she stepped back out, her nipples were hard, her pupils constricted. She kissed Marisem's lips softly. "Help me commune with the Fountain?' she said.

"Of course, Priestess," he said.

She stood at the base of the rock, caressing Terlyn's thighs, running her hands over Terlyn's smooth skin. Her fingers lingered at the places where thorns pierced Terlyn's flesh.

"What does that feel like?" Marisem asked.

"It hurts," Rahmos said. "It hurts so much. But it also feels good. In the moment when they first take you, you come. It's the last fully conscious orgasm you have until the Garden releases you."

"The gods expect a lot of their sacrifices."

"Yes."

Rahmos leaned over the stone and placed her face between Terlyn's legs. She parted Terlyn's folds with her tongue. She probed gently, tongue playing with exquisite care over Terlyn's clit. Marisem caressed Rahmos. His hands moved lower, over the small of her back, the curve of her ass, then between her legs, where he found wetness.

He stripped out of his pants and tunic. He put his hands on her hips. She continued her gentle probing with her tongue as he entered her, grinding deep. She pressed back against him, encouraging him.

Tyrill and Rhian moved to each side of the stone to kiss Terlyn's breasts. They ran their hands over her sleeping body, stroking, fondling, caressing. Terlyn remained still, her eyes closed, her expression peaceful.

Marisem cried out in ecstasy, unleashing a tide of warmth inside Rahmos. His hoarse voice split the air. A flock of birds, startled from their sleep, took flight above the trees.

Rahmos shuddered and let out a soft sigh, the only outward sign of her orgasm. She carried on her gentle, deliberate attention to Terlyn's clit, alert to Terlyn's breathing, careful not to rouse her from her sleep.

Marisem withdrew. A tiny shudder, barely perceptible, passed through Terlyn. Rahmos stopped. "Thank you, Initiate Marisem," Rahmos said. "The Fountain is very near to pleasure." She touched Terlyn's lips. "Thank you, Fountain, for the gift of your body," she said. "Thank you, Quickener, for the gift of your blessing."

She bent to kiss Terlyn. Her tongue played over her lips. Terlyn's breathing remained calm and steady.

Rahmos gathered up her clothes. A quartet of dronelights, sensing that the evening ritual had drawn to a close, flitted noiselessly from the dark sky overhead, their lights turning on as they descended. They followed the people through the labyrinth and then out of the Garden into the City beyond, leaving Terlyn alone in the glow of the luminescent flowers.

2.12

TERLYN WOKE GASPING. Pleasure screamed through her body. Her hips bucked. The orgasm went on and on, without ceasing, dragged from her helpless body by the combination of a tongue dancing on her clit and something inside her. It was hard, and moving, spinning in several directions at once, pressing against the most sensitive places within her in agonizingly delightful ways.

She struggled frantically, surprised and confused. The vines held her tight. The person atop her thrust his hips steadily, sliding in and out of her mouth while his tongue worked its magic. The thing inside her seemed covered in bumps and ridges that were cunningly designed to overwhelm her.

She felt trapped by the vines that held her down, trapped by the knees on each side of her head that kept her from turning away, and trapped in the grip of a ceaseless orgasm that would not stop. She whimpered and moaned around the erect cock in her mouth, overwhelmed and helpless. Her body jerked and convulsed. Her skin glistened with sweat. Something wet rolled from her nipples and ran down the sides of her breasts.

The cock stiffened in her mouth. Her eyes widened. She just had enough time to take a deep breath before it exploded, twitching and throbbing as it sent jet after jet of warm salty goo down her throat. She swallowed reflexively. Still the tongue danced on her clit, the evil thing whirled inside her, and still her orgasm continued, stretching out without end. She flailed, struggling to pull her arms free. The thorns bit deeper. The pain only added to the orgasm, making it more intense.

Her scream came out as a wet gurgle. White fluid dripped from her lips.

Then the tongue stopped. The hard, bumpy thing slid out of her. She gasped in shock at the sudden aching emptiness. Her body shivered uncontrollably.

He slid off the rock. She looked up at his face. "D-Donvin?"

He smiled. "Good morning, Fountain!" His lips found her nipple. She shuddered as a fresh wave of ecstasy took her.

Meersath appeared, her face hovering above Terlyn. "You have caught the attention of the Quickener," she said. Her tone was approving. "Look at how bountiful the Fountain's blessing is!"

Donvin licked and sucked her nipple. Meersath pressed a stone bowl against her other breast. Her hands massaged her breast squeezing hard. Another orgasm crashed over Terlyn. She screamed.

Donvin straightened. He kissed Terlyn, rough and urgent. She tasted sweetness on his lips.

"I will visit you again tomorrow, and the day after that, and the day after that," he said. "You have many more days to go." The vines coiled tightly around Terlyn. She felt the sap flowing through the thorns into her. The world grew dim.

"Sleep now," Donvin said. His voice was faint and far away. "There is so much more time before winter. So many more days to visit you. Sleep now." He faded and was gone.

"Thank you," Meersath said when Terlyn's eyes closed. "We are blessed by your dedication. So is she."

He laughed. "The Lady has blessed me for my dedication to her, too. Never in my life have I been so productive in my art."

"I've always thought the Quickener and the Lady have unique synergy. The blessing of the Quickener brings greater artistic fecundity. The creations of your imagination please the Lady, and become offerings to the Quickener, who blesses you with an ever more fertile imagination." She laid her hand on his arm. "It is an inspiring thing to behold."

"So, you're saying I really can serve two masters?" He seemed bemused.

Now it was her turn to laugh. "Of course! True love is never jealous."

He handed her a long cylindrical object, blunt at the end, with a series of rings stacked along its length. Bumps and ridges decorated each ring. They were connected inside by a cunning series of shafts and gears so that, when the handle at its base was turned, each ring rotated in a direction opposite to the one beneath it. "Will you see that she gets this? After she wakes, I mean."

"Of course," Meersath said. "You seem to have started a new tradition."

"Have I? What's that?"

"Bringing an offering for the Quickener and another for the Fountain. Others have noticed and are doing the same thing. Judging by the bounty we just received, I dare say the Quickener approves." She pressed the stone cup with its shimmering liquid into his hand. "The Quickener and the Lady bless you."

He bowed low. "Thank you, Priestess. Now I am off to spread the word."

Her eyebrow lifted. "Oh?"

"The other devotees of the Lady have noticed my...err, unusual and persistent inspiration. Don't be surprised if more of us start making regular visits to the Fountain."

"I will be pleased to welcome the Lady's worshippers," Meersath said.

"In an official or a personal capacity?"

Meersath gave him a dazzling smile. "I suppose that depends on which worshipper we're talking about." She placed both hands on his chest. "We who serve the Quickener pride ourselves on welcoming members of all faiths."

"Thank you, Priestess. You are very kind." He leaned close to her.

"Call me Meersath."

Their lips met.

When the kiss ended, Meersath smiled. "If you like, I would enjoy seeing you at sundown."

He bowed. "I would like that very much."

"Until then."

"Until then."

He made his way out through the Labyrinth, carrying the stone bowl with him.

The next morning, Donvin came to the Garden accompanied by a tall, thickset woman who towered over him. Colorful, intricate tattoos decorated every inch of her pale skin. The tattoos told the story of the founding of the City and the construction of many of the major temples of worship. Jewelry, set in and through her skin, highlighted the features of the tattoos: small metal rings placed in the columns that stood before the temple of the Fiery One, metal bars through her skin illustrating the cages in the amphitheater of the Wild. Tiny flickers of color strobed through her long white hair like lightning strikes in a distant thunderstorm. One eye was green, the other gray.

She wore nothing but a belt hung with an assortment of small, colorful pouches and a gauzy cloak of light, translucent material attached to rings in her shoulder blades. The cloak followed behind her, floating impossibly in the air without sinking when she stood still. An abstract pattern of pastel colors shifted and moved across it.

Meersath stood waiting beneath the trees at the archway that led into the Garden. She embraced Donvin warmly. They kissed. Meersath purred.

"High Priestess Meersath, this is Grand High Priestess Kalaian of the Lady," Donvin said. "Grand High Priestess Kalaian, this is High Priestess Meersath of the Quickener."

The two women bowed to one another. "Welcome, Grand High Priestess," Meersath said. "Do you come to seek the blessing of the Quickener?"

"I do," Kalaian said. "Donvin tells me the Quickener has much to offer those of us who worship the Lady."

"I hope you find it so."

"Me too," Kalaian said. "If I am even one-half as inspired as Donvin, I will be very happy. I've brought an offering for the Quickener and an offering for the Fountain."

"What have you brought for the Quickener?"

Kalaian reached into one of her pouches. She took out a tiny crystal vial, smaller than her smallest finger, filled with layers of powder of different colors: red, green, yellow, blue, purple, orange, and white.

She carefully pried off the cap and turned the vial upside-down. A stream of fine dust poured from it. It hung suspended in the air for a time, swirling gently. Then, almost imperceptibly at first, it started to coalesce. It pulled inward, until a cloudy ball floated just above the ground. The colors shifted without mixing. The dust cloud drifted upward, growing larger and larger. Little flashes of static electricity crackled through it.

It mushroomed as it expanded, until soon it seemed the Garden was covered in a dome of colorful dust. The swirling patterns of color resolved into patterns, becoming more defined until a beautiful pattern of vines and leaves hung, as insubstantial as a rainbow, in the sky above them.

Meersath clapped with delight. "That is beautiful, Priestess! A fitting tribute to the Quickener from a servant of the Lady."

"Thank you."

"What do you bring for the Fountain?"

"Only this." From another pouch, she produced a complex mechanical device of bronze and polished wood, two short cylinders connected to each other by an elaborate clockwork apparatus.

"It is lovely," Meersath said. "Grand High Priest Tyrill will be happy to greet you in the center of the Garden."

Donvin led Kalaian through the labyrinth. When they arrived at the center, Tyrill bowed. "Priestess," he said. "You honor us."

She smiled. "The honor is mine. It is a privilege to visit the Fountain."

She unhooked her cloak from the rings in her shoulders. Donvin disrobed. Tyrill led them each to the pool.

Far off in the deep, a flickering at the edge of Terlyn's awareness drew her away from the slow rhythm of root and leaf. She sped upward through the silent darkness until she crashed into an explosion of light and sound, body convulsing in orgasm.

There was a woman on top of her, tall and pale, and behind the woman, Donvin. Above her, the sky was...

She blinked, feeling a sudden vertigo. For a moment, she felt suspended upside-down, looking down at a second garden, somewhere far above or below her, she wasn't sure which. This phantom garden floated out of her reach, pale and insubstantial. Flowers of all colors blossomed from sinuous green vines.

She exploded into another orgasm. Above her, or below her, the dream-garden echoed her explosion, the flowers becoming fireworks, dissolving into sparkling gold fragments.

"Yes," the woman atop her said. "Bless us with your gift, Fountain." Her hips moved rhythmically. Something hard and smooth moved inside Terlyn, and inside the woman on top of her, linking them together, rotating with each thrust. Donvin knelt behind the woman, his hands on her breasts, thrusting into her ass in the same slow steady rhythm.

Then the woman cried out in an orgasm of her own. She leaned over, pressing her strong, tattooed body against Terlyn's. "Bless me, Fountain," she panted. "Bless me, Quickener." Donvin roared, joining them in orgasm.

The woman kissed Terlyn, frantic and needy. Her body and Terlyn's glowed with sweat. She pressed against Terlyn, forcing the mechanical object that linked them together deeper into her. It spun and whirred. Terlyn screamed as she came, again and again, each contraction setting off another orgasm like a chain of small explosions within her.

Donvin pressed himself against the woman, grinding into her, panting. He groaned once more, his body shaking, his eyes half-closed. Then he withdrew from her, spent. She smiled a lazy, dreamy smile at Terlyn. "Thank you for your gift," she said.

Her lips fastened around Terlyn's nipple. Donvin took her other nipple between his lips. Three more orgasms rocked her body in rapid succession before the vines constricted and all was dark once more.

2.13

IN THE WEEKS that followed, Terlyn received many more devotees of the Lady. Competition raged to see who could give her the longest orgasm, the strongest orgasm, and the most orgasms. They competed, too, over who could bring the most beautiful gifts to the Fountain and the Quickener.

Day after day, Terlyn woke screaming in ecstasy with buzzing, rotating, twisting, and vibrating things inside her. She woke with colorful images made of insubstantial dust twisting in the sky above her, with music and lights dancing around her. More and more often, she woke to orgasms without end, orgasms that went on and on until sweat sheened on her skin and her voice became hoarse with her cries.

Through it all, Donvin was there. Some days, he brought a new piece of sculpture with which he would torment Terlyn, dragging orgasms from her until she was delirious before finally placing his lips on her nipple, forcing the last few paroxysms from her body before allowing her to escape into oblivion.

At night, servants of the Quickener tended to her. They bathed her, then teased her body into readiness. On most nights, they satisfied themselves with her, careful not to allow her to awaken.

And so it came to pass, through a ceaseless series of orgasms beyond time or comprehension, that summer drew to a close.

On the evening before the first day of autumn, Donvin and Kalaian joined Sedhi, Meersath, and Marisem in the center of the garden. Terlyn lay on the stone, eyes closed, with a peaceful expression on her face.

"Tomorrow will be a long day for her," Kalaian said.

"From her point of view, no longer nor shorter than any other," Meersath said. "The Fountain experiences one long uninterrupted string of orgasms for her entire period of service."

"That is something like what we feel during the Dance of Sacrifice," Kalaian said. She walked around the rock, trailing her fingers over Terlyn's body. The gossamer robe, luminescent in the dim light, floated behind her. "Why do you suppose they do it?"

"The Fountains? To serve the Quickener."

"No, the gods. Why do you suppose they demand these things of us? Giving our bodies this way, I mean."

"Our ecstasy is the greatest form of communion," Meersath said.

Kalaian chuckled. "That's not really a reason, is it? Why ecstasy? Why not something else?"

Meersath shrugged. "Perhaps it is our capacity for pleasure that makes us human. Perhaps it is the thing that defines us in the eyes of the gods."

"Perhaps." Kalaian looked unconvinced.

Sedhi and Meersath bathed Terlyn while Marisem washed her hair, which was now so long it spilled over the boulder to the ground.

When they had finished, Kalaian removed a set of tiny glass pots from the pouches on her belt. She lined them up on the edge of the rock. Their contents glowed faintly.

She dipped her fingers in the pots and then drew an intricate design suggestive of highly stylized vines on Terlyn's body. The pearlescent pigments, green and gold and brown and red, seemed to absorb the light from the two moons overhead and store it within themselves.

Donvin took a pair of small gold rings from his pockets, engraved with intertwined vines, so fine the details were barely visible to the unaided eye. He kissed Terlyn's nipples until they hardened, then slipped the rings over them. He took out ten more rings, thin and flat and decorated with tiny red gemstones, and placed them on Terlyn's toes. Meersath placed a garland of red and gold leaves around Terlyn's neck. Marisem and Sedhi wove tiny red and yellow flowers through Terlyn's green hair.

When they finished, Donvin bent over and kissed Terlyn's lips. "Sleep sweetly," he said. "I will see you tomorrow."

The morning sun came up on a Garden transformed. Overnight, the green leaves had turned to red and gold. Delicate new flowers with white and red petals blossomed on the vines that held Terlyn. Each had a red ball in its center.

The Fall Firstday ceremony attracted an even greater crowd than summer's ceremony. By the time Tyrill made his way through the labyrinth with Meersath, Donvin, Sedhi, Ahani, and Marisem behind him, two rows of supplicants stood around the open space in the center of the garden. Meersath and Donvin held hands as they accompanied Tyrill through the labyrinth. More supplicants followed behind, walking the path in silence.

A hush fell as they entered the center of the labyrinth. Kalaian was already there, wearing nothing but the cloak that floated from the rings in her shoulders. Four people stood with her. They too were completely covered in tattoos. All were entirely nude except for belts lined with pouches they wore around their waists. Tiny points of light twinkled like stars in their hair.

Tyrill took his place beside the sleeping form of Terlyn. He raised his arms. "The Quickener welcomes you to the first day of fall," he said.

A murmur went through the crowd.

Tyrill removed his clothes. Sedhi took them from him and folded them neatly. Tyrill stepped down into the pool. He emerged a moment later, dripping wet, his cock erect, his pupils mere points. He stood beside Terlyn. "This has been a year to remember," he said. "Through his vessel the Fountain, the Quickener has offered us an especially generous blessing this year. We give thanks to the Quickener and to the Fountain. We give thanks also to the Lady, and to those of her worshippers who have graced us with their presence and gifted us with their offerings." He bowed to Kalaian, who returned his bow. "We thank the followers of the Lady who have helped us prepare the Fountain for Firstday."

Tyrill plucked one of the flowers that grew on the vines binding Terlyn's wrists. He placed it in his mouth. His pupils dilated, then constricted again. He shuddered. He slid his hand down her body. His fingers spread her open, seeking her clit.

The world burst around Terlyn, bright and jagged. She cried out with pleasure, body spasming. The crowd cheered.

Terlyn stared up at Tyrill with wide eyes. The last echoes of her orgasm still shivered through her body. She saw him reach down to caress her forehead. "We thank you for your sacrifice," he said. "Autumn is just beginning."

Panic took Terlyn. She struggled urgently, desperately at the vines. He leaned over, ignoring her struggles, to place his lips on her nipple. She felt a tingling rush, and a sense of warmth, and then she came again in a hot flash. "I—" she said. She wanted to ask where she was, and what was happening, but the words refused to form.

Tyrill straightened. Once again, Donvin was the first to step forward. He kissed Tyrill deeply, accepting the blessing from his lips. Then he bowed and returned to Meersath's side. Meersath squeezed his hand.

Kalaian stepped forward. She took a small, simple box made of thin strips of different colors of wood from a pouch on her belt and touched different points of the box. With a series of subtle motions, she slid various parts of the box in an elaborate pattern until the lid opened. From it, she took a golden bud-shaped object, small but heavy, with ripples molded into its smooth surface. With a deep bow, she gave this to Tyrill.

Tyrill pressed the hard thing into Terlyn. Her body felt so alive, so sensitive, she could almost count every one of the curved ridges in it. He pressed his thumb against the base. It began to spin. Terlyn gasped. The vines tightened around her wrists and ankles. She felt the sap flow from the vines into her body. The world shimmered. She moaned.

Tyrill's finger slid over her clit again. Terlyn clenched around the object within her. Ripples of pleasure spread through her. Her nipples, constrained by the metal rings, swelled. She stared helplessly up at Tyrill. "I…I don't understand, I…"

Ecstasy exploded over her. She arched her back, screaming with pleasure. Tyrill bent to take her nipple between his lips. His fingers kept moving over her clit. Clear liquid flowed from her breasts.

Kalaian wrapped her arms around Tyrill. She kissed him deep and long. Terlyn felt her hold on awareness begin to slip. Her lids grew heavy. Tyrill stroked her clit again. His tongue played over her aching nipple, and she exploded once more into an orgasm that went on and on and on.

Throughout the day, more people came to the Garden to visit the Fountain. By midafternoon, just as many supplicants waited to receive the Quickener's blessing as had been there that morning. Terlyn shook and shrieked and spasmed, convulsing in orgasm after orgasm. Her clit throbbed. The object inside her spun and buzzed. Tyrill squeezed her breasts until they ached, forcing more of the shimmering liquid from them.

New people kept coming, even as the sun sank lower in the sky. Terlyn's voice grew hoarse from screaming. The vines tightened and relaxed, throbbing like a slow heartbeat. Wine-red liquid flowed into her. Transparent shimmering liquid flowed out of her. She came over and over again, writhing, until nothing existed for her except unbearable pleasure.

As the sun settled, Terlyn found herself in a trancelike state. Her life beyond the Garden faded away. She existed just as she always had—a part of the Garden, her entire experience nothing but wave after wave of unstoppable ecstasy, as inevitable as the change of seasons or the coming of the rain. The dim and distant notion that she had ever been anywhere except here, with the priest standing over her, wrenching orgasm after orgasm from her body, seemed plainly as absurd as a hallucination born of some inexplicable fever. This was all there ever was and all there ever would be.

Shadows spread long fingers through the Garden. The softly luminescent flowers opened. Still Tyrill performed the ritual, forcing more orgasms from Terlyn's quivering, sweat-slicked body, accepting the liquid that flowed from her swollen nipples, gifting it to the people who came forward to receive it from his lips.

The smaller moon had set beneath the horizon before at last there were no more supplicants. Tyrill staggered and collapsed to his knees. The vines binding Terlyn pulsed one last time, sending a surge of wine-colored liquid into her. Her eyes closed. Merciful blackness welcomed her into its folds.

Sedhi and Meersath helped Tyrill stand. They half-led, half-carried him to the small pool. He sat in the warm water for a long time, his body shaking violently.

"That was the longest Firstday I have ever experienced," Sedhi said. Fatigue showed in his eyes.

Meersath gazed lovingly at Terlyn's sweaty, sleeping body. "This is the most remarkable Fountain the Garden has seen in my lifetime. The Quickener is pleased."

"Does he still speak to you?" Marisem said.

"The Quickener? Oh, yes," Meersath said. "The Quickener speaks to all Fountains. Once you've been part of the Garden, you carry the communion forever."

Tyrill opened his eyes. Meersath turned to Marisem. "Help the Grand High Priest find his way home. He has had a very long day."

Marisem bowed. "Of course, Priestess." He helped Tyrill dress, then slipped his arm around Tyrill to support him. A dronelight flitted down from somewhere overhead to light their way.

Meersath and Sedhi bathed Terlyn with water from the fountain. Meersath carefully slid the ridged golden object from inside her. Sedhi washed her hair, his hands gentle and loving. He looked down at her sleeping face. "She is extraordinary," he said. His voice was filled with wonder.

"Yes, she is. Do you wish to stay a while in communion with her?"

"Yes, I do."

She smiled and touched his arm. "Then I bid you good evening."

He bowed. "Good evening, Priestess."

Another dronelight swooped down from the dark sky overhead to guide Meersath home.

Sedhi watched Terlyn sleep for a long time. Then, as the larger moon reached its peak, he slipped off his clothes. He took her slowly, carefully, kissing her face and lips as he pressed into her again and again. Finally, he shuddered and sighed, releasing a warm wet flood into her. She remained still beneath him.

He gathered up his clothes. A dronelight curved down to meet him. With a long backward glance at Terlyn, he made his way from the Garden, leaving her on the rock bathed in a gentle glow.

2.14

TYRILL DID NOT show up at the Garden the following morning, nor during many of the mornings after that. Throughout the fall, Sedhi and Meersath greeted the worshippers most mornings, while Ahani, Marisem, and Rhian cared for Terlyn at night.

Donvin appeared in the center of the Garden every morning without fail. Kalaian accompanied him more often than not. He frequently returned in the evening to help bathe Terlyn. Afterward, he accompanied Meersath home.

Terlyn measured the passage of days by the number of times she roused from her timeless sleep with Donvin atop her, shuddering in ecstasy while he looked down at her. She would come again, crying out in pleasure, when he drew the blessing from her breasts.

The days grew longer, the nights shorter. The trees erupted into gold, red, and orange. The hedges turned yellow and gold. Terlyn's body also changed. Her skin, as white as the snow at the start of spring, was now a rich, deep coppery brown.

She was aware of none of this. Terlyn lived in a place without time or space. Nothing was real to her save those brief flashes of wakefulness with pleasure screaming through her body. Flickers of blackness that left no trace on her memory punctuated the moments of pleasure. Of the priests and priestesses who bathed her and, frequently, spent themselves in or on her, she had no perception at all.

As the autumn drew on, the air became colder everywhere in the City except the center of the Garden. The winds that swirled through the rest of the City steered around it, leaving it a warm, tranquil oasis untouched by the steady approach of winter.

The leaves fell from the trees. They formed a thick carpet of bright color on the ground and built up in mounds at the feet of the statues that flanked the pathway, melting away into the rich soil each night only to fall again the next day.

When only a week remained before winter, Tyrill began appearing once more at Terlyn's side. Sedhi and Ahani took their place each morning at the archway leading into the Garden, where they accepted the offerings of the worshippers. Rahmos joined Marisem and Rhian each night to bathe her and wash her hair.

The night before the first day of winter, Tyrill, Meersath, Marisem, Rahmos, Ahani, and Sedhi all gathered around Terlyn. Meersath and Ahani carried baskets with them.

"I am sad to see the end of the season," Meersath said.

"So am I," Rahmos said. She caressed Terlyn's cheek. "This has been the most bountiful season in memory."

"What happens now?" Marisem asked.

"We prepare for the Awakening," Meersath said. She turned to Terlyn. "Soon, your beautiful service will be over."

After Marisem and Ahani finished washing her hair, Meersath sat on the carpet of leaves covering the ground. She used a comb from her basket to brush out Terlyn's hair, which had grown wild and thick. She tied two rows of braids in it, weaving a string of small flowers into each braid and tying them off with small gold rings.

Tyrill took a set of broad straps from Ahani's basket. He and Ahani fastened them around Terlyn's arms and legs, near the place where the vines held her. Tyrill drove four stakes into the ground around the boulder. Ahani anchored the ends of the straps to them with long, strong cords.

"What are those for?" Marisem asked.

"When Terlyn awakens," Tyrill said, "she will be confused and disoriented. These will keep her from injuring herself."

Once Tyrill and Ahani were satisfied the straps were secure, Tyrill gave Terlyn a small, gentle kiss. Sedhi ran a hand along her side. "Sleep well, Fountain," he said. "It is almost over."

The rain fell for a long time the next morning, a steady light drizzle from a perfectly round cloud that hung over the center of the Garden in an otherwise clear sky.

As the sun rose above the hedges, the rain slowed and stopped, leaving Terlyn's body slick with water. Tyrill walked tranquilly into the center of the labyrinth, wearing a heavy robe of red and brown embroidered with an intricate design of stylized trees, their bare branches reaching toward the sky, lightly dusted with snow. Eileithyia and Meersath escorted him in matching dresses in the same red and brown, their edges hemmed in white. Behind them came Rahmos and Ahani, each in a long white dress that exposed one arm and one breast. Rhian and Marisem stayed at the archway to accept offerings from the faithful.

As usual, Donvin was the first to visit. He disrobed. Meersath gave his hand a quick squeeze as he stepped down into the pool. His face was somber.

When he emerged from the pool, he spent a long time gazing at Terlyn's face before he climbed onto the rock. He entered her very slowly, kissing her mouth as he did.

Down in the sheltering dark, the ember of Terlyn's consciousness flared. Up and up it rose, obeying the irresistible, inevitable siren's call of her impending orgasm. Her eyelids fluttered. Donvin slowed his thrusts. He kissed her breast softly, moving slower and slower, so that when she woke, it was more the cresting of a long, rolling wave of pleasure than a violent explosion. Her eyes opened. "Oh!" she said.

Donvin kissed her deeply, tongue slipping between her lips. He shuddered into an orgasm of his own, releasing himself into her. "Oh!" she said again.

He let his tongue play over her nipple, lapping at the sweet fluid that flowed from it. Every motion of his tongue sent waves of pleasure radiating through Terlyn, until her skin buzzed and her body vibrated. Another orgasm rolled over her. He straightened, drawing himself out of her. The world began to fade.

"Donvin!" she said. "I…" The thorns pressed deep. Sleep dragged at her. Her body grew heavy and distant. "I want…" Darkness closed in around her. "I want to say…" Her voice trailed off. She sank once more into the void.

In the blink of an eye, she woke again, crying out her pleasure. A woman with short violet hair lifted her head from between Terlyn's legs, peering up at her through copper eyes. Her pupils were narrow black crosses in red irises. "Mmm, that's a lovely sound," she purred. She grinned, revealing pointed teeth. "You are magnificent." She moved smoothly to kneel over Terlyn, as graceful as a cat. "I like you." Her lips closed on Terlyn's nipples.

Sharp teeth pressed into Terlyn's skin. Terlyn convulsed in ecstasy. The darkness took her again.

She woke a moment later with a man atop her, his black, spiky hair already sweat-drenched. He moved in short fast thrusts, hot and thick within her. Every stroke triggered firecracker detonations of pleasure inside her. His seafoam eyes closed. He grunted. The hot wet slap of his ejaculation gushed into her. Terlyn thrashed as she came, their bodies locked together in mutual orgasm.

"Thank you, Fountain," he said. He pressed a stone cup against her breast. Shimmering liquid flowed. Terlyn blinked. The vines pulsed. Fog rolled over her mind. Her eyes closed.

Sunset that night sent fingers of red light over a long line of people who walked the labyrinth, heads bowed in meditation. Without a word, they formed a wide circle around Terlyn. Sedhi and Donvin followed the cluster of people. Sedhi carried a basket covered with a thick red cloth.

"Friends, thank you for joining us," Eileithyia said. "Today is the final day of autumn. The Fountain has given us a great gift, and we thank her for it. Tonight, her sacrifice ends."

Sedhi stepped forward. He removed the cloth from his basket and took out a flask of oil, its pale iridescent glass etched with images of swirling snowflakes.

A hush fell like a physical thing over the Garden. The people gathered around the stone stood in watchful silence. The red fingers of light lengthened, then faded as the sun dipped beneath the horizon. Shadows crept through the center of the labyrinth. The pale flowers opened, casting their otherworldly light across the Garden. In their soft glow, the brilliant autumn colors faded.

At the exact moment the last sunlight faded from the sky, the vines around Terlyn's wrists and ankles relaxed. The thorns slid from her skin, crumbling into dust as they did. Tiny drops of blood welled up in each of the places where the vines had penetrated her. These quickly faded into small white dots. Her eyelids fluttered.

Sedhi opened the flask he carried. He poured a stream of heavy honey-colored oil over Terlyn's body, from her breasts to her mound and then down each leg. The scent of wildflowers and spices filled the air.

"What happens now?" Donvin said.

"The scent brings her back," Sedhi said.

Eileithyia, Meersath, and Tyrill moved in close around Terlyn. Eileithyia and Meersath massaged her breasts with the sweet-smelling oil. Tyrill massaged her legs.

Terlyn awoke slowly from the depths of a deep sleep. She felt someone doing something wonderful to her. A pleasant scent guided her out of the deep, toward the light. She opened her eyes. Eileithyia's blurred face materialized from a soft glow.

She stirred and tried to stretch. Something held her down. "Where... where am I?"

"Shh. Slowly."

Terlyn's arms and legs felt heavy, unwilling to obey her. She fought down sudden panic. "What—"

"Slowly. Slowly. You're going to be confused for a while."

Eileithyia bent over and placed her lips on Terlyn's nipple. Her breast tingled. Something wet flowed from it. A sudden orgasm took her without warning, fast and unstoppable. She convulsed, screaming with pleasure. "What—I don't understand—"

"We must finish drawing the Quickener's blessing from your body," Meersath said. "Just relax. Don't try to move. Be still." She took Terlyn's other nipple between her lips.

Terlyn convulsed again in another orgasm, even more powerful than the first. Tyrill continued his gentle massage. His hands glided over her skin.

"It's okay, Fountain," he said. "Your head will clear. For now, just be still."

She looked around wildly. Her eyes found Donvin. "Donvin?"

He moved to her side. He brushed her hair out of her eyes. "I'm here, Terlyn," he said. "You're almost finished."

"Finished?" Her brow furrowed. "But I...I only just...I don't understand. I—" Another orgasm hit her, so intense she screamed, her back arching.

Eileithyia and Meersath stepped back away from her. The circle of people closed in around her. Many hands caressed her. Mouths closed around her nipples. She shook and cried out as one orgasm after another tore through her. She fought desperately, but the straps held her down.

Strong hands squeezed her tender breasts until they ached. Shimmering liquid flowed from her nipples. The tight knot of people around her massaged and caressed, squeezed and licked, while Terlyn rode waves of pleasure too intense to stand against.

The smaller moon rose high in the sky before, at last, she ran dry. A final orgasm shuddered through her, leaving her shaking. She panted, her eyes unfocused.

Eileithyia and Meersath unstrapped her. Meersath helped her stand. She stumbled. Donvin caught her.

"Slowly," Eileithyia said. "It will take a little while for you to recover."

"How...how long..."

"It is the end of the season. Your time as Fountain is over."

"But…" Terlyn frowned. Fog rolled in over her mind, blurring the outlines of her memory. She shook her head, but the fog did not clear. "But I thought…I mean, I don't remember…" She focused on Donvin. "You were there! You visited me!"

He smiled. "Yes."

"But it wasn't…it hasn't been…" She stumbled again. His strong arm held her up.

"Shh. You'll feel a little fuzzy for a while," Meersath said. She and Donvin guided Terlyn to the pool.

She lowered herself into the warm water with a sigh. The heat penetrated her body, softening muscles cramped by long inactivity. She closed her eyes.

Fragments of memory surfaced like half-remembered dreams, then submerged back into the mist. Terlyn struggled to hang onto them, but they slipped through her fingers, leaving only vague impressions behind: a man on top of her, a hand on her breast, a glimpse of a face contorted in ecstasy. Her body quivered with the physical echoes of pleasure.

She remembered the thorns biting into her skin, sharp and painful. She looked at her wrists. Tiny white dots gave evidence to where they had pierced her. She rubbed her arms, expecting the spots to be sore, but there was neither pain nor tenderness.

She looked at her arms. They were deep brown, totally different from the pale white they'd been just days…

No, not days; that couldn't be right. It must have been months, but that didn't seem right either. She clearly remembered walking down the path on the first day of spring, lying down on the rock, inviting the vines to crawl over her. That was only yesterday, wasn't it? But no, she had memories of waking many times…

She shook her head. Her hair dragged at her neck, unexpectedly heavy. That could not have happened overnight, could it? She ran her fingers through it, and found it was long and green, braided in two rows that ran all the way down her back. She inspected the ends of the braids closely, looking for answers in the woven strands.

Eileithyia carefully gathered the seed pods that had formed on the vines. She placed them in a large crystal cup. When she finished, she put them in Sedhi's basket. Sedhi bowed to her and left, escorted by a small bird-shaped dronelight

The last tattered scraps of sleep left Terlyn. She stood. Eileithyia dried her with the heavy cloth that had covered Sedhi's basket. "We'll take you home," Meersath said.

Meersath and Donvin took her hands and led her through the labyrinth toward the entrance to the Garden. Terlyn paused, looking at the hedges in wonder. When she'd closed her eyes, days or months ago, they were covered in new leaves. Now the leaves were falling, red and gold and brown. The petals had dropped from the pale flowers and lay in glowing heaps on the ground.

The moment they left the Garden, the temperature dropped. Terlyn spread her arms wide, savoring the cool breeze.

A lot had changed in Terlyn's home. The plants inside the glass rectangle had been tended to in her absence, and now wore the colors of fall. The grass was longer than she remembered. The trees above the waterfall had shed their leaves in preparation for winter.

Donvin and Meersath followed Terlyn inside. "Do you want to sleep?" Donvin asked. "You've had a long day."

"I don't think I could sleep if I wanted to," Terlyn said. "I feel like I've spent a long time asleep…well, I guess I have, haven't I?" She shook her head. "It still feels like I just left. But also like I've been away forever."

"That's normal," Meersath said. "Would you like us to leave you alone?"

"No. I think…I think I would like some company. If you don't mind."

"Not at all," Meersath said. "It can take a while to readjust. There's a lot to process."

"I guess so," Terlyn said. She frowned. "It doesn't feel like a lot. I mean… well, maybe it does. I…" She pressed her hand to her head. "It's like I can't hang on to it. It doesn't feel real, you know? Is it really winter already?"

"It is," Meersath said.

"What do you remember?" Donvin asked.

"I remember you!" She smiled broadly at him. "I remember you visiting me many times. I remember…I remember feeling overwhelmed. I remember waking up, and then falling back asleep even if I didn't want to. I remember coming. A lot." Her smile turned dreamy. "I remember…feeling the ground beneath my roots. Did you really visit me every day?"

"He did," Meersath said. "He was there every morning."

"I'm surprised. Not in a bad way," she added when she saw his expression. "That was very kind. Thank you." Her eyes turned glassy for a moment. She stumbled. Blackness crept in around the edges of her vision. "Okay, maybe I should sleep."

"That would probably be best," Meersath said. "You still need to adjust."

Terlyn sat heavily on her bed. "I think…will you stay with me? Both of you. I don't want to be alone."

"Of course," Meersath and Donvin said in unison.

Terlyn dreamed that night of faces and lips and unending pleasure. She came awake with a gasp and lay in bed, confused, blinking in the darkness.

She stared up at the stars through the transparent ceiling, not sure where she was. She turned, surprised to find her arms and legs unbound.

A desperate, frantic need rang through her body. She was on something soft…her bed, not a thick cushion of moss. Donvin slept on one side of her, breathing quietly. Meersath slept on the other.

She rolled on her side to face Meersath. Donvin stirred and wrapped an arm around her. She pressed back against him. He was erect in his sleep.

The need burned hotter. She reached down to guide him into her. She came almost instantly. Her breasts ached.

"Wha—" Donvin said. His voice was blurry with sleep.

Terlyn pressed back against him over and over, waves of pleasure washing over her with every stroke. He wrapped his arm more tightly around her. His hand clenched her wrist. "What is—"

His words ended in a groan. Terlyn felt the hard, wet gush of his ejaculation inside her. Another orgasm rolled over her, long and intense. She faded back to sleep with his cock still inside her.

2.15

TERLYN WOKE AT daybreak. Red and gold filled the sky above her. She lay still for a long time, luxuriating in her gradual awakening. Meersath and Donvin both slept soundly beside her.

Eventually, she extricated herself from between them. She summoned a cup of tea and a loose-fitting robe printed with elegant, long-necked birds from the Provider. She wrapped the robe around herself, then called up a soft, fluffy towel.

When she had finished her tea, she stepped outside. The early winter air carried a biting chill. She stripped off the robe and stood for a time beneath the warm water that spilled over the waterfall.

When she came back, Donvin and Meersath were both awake. Donvin wore a robe printed with a marble pattern. He was sipping a cup of coffee, sitting in a chair he had summoned from the Provider. Meersath wore a flowing skirt of green and gold, her chest bare. She was lacing silver wire through her hair.

"Good morning, Fountain," she said.

Terlyn sighed. "I'm not the Fountain any more."

"You'll always be revered as a Fountain."

"Do you ever get used to that?"

"Not really," Meersath said.

A soft, directionless chime filled the air, followed by a soft, directionless voice. "You have visitors."

"Who is it?" Terlyn said.

"High Priestess Eileithyia and Priest Sedhi."

"Show them in."

The door swung open for Eileithyia and Sedhi, both dressed entirely in white. Sedhi wore loose-fitted white pants with a subtle pattern of snow-flakes printed in a slightly different shade of white, and an open-front white shirt. Eileithyia wore a plain white dress with an oval opening in the front cut to reveal her breasts. He carried a large box made of light-colored wood. She carried a small pouch.

"Fountain," Eileithyia said, bowing low.

"Terlyn. Please."

"Terlyn. I bring you a gift." She presented her with the tiny pouch, made of soft green fabric and drawn closed with a drawstring that resembled a vine. Inside, she found a small collection of long, curved seeds. "From the vines that bound you to the Quickener," Eileithyia said.

"Thank you, Priestess."

"Eileithyia."

She inclined her head. "Eileithyia." She took one of the seeds out of the bag and examined it closely. Subtle iridescent patterns crawled across its surface. "What did you do with yours?"

"Some I saved as a memento. Some I planted in a garden. They still carry some small part of the Quickener's essence. Allowing their thorns to prick me helps me commune with her when I need guidance."

Terlyn nodded. She turned to Sedhi. "What brings you here, Priest? Or perhaps I should say, what do you bring here?"

"Offerings, Fount—Terlyn."

Puzzlement crossed her face. "Offerings?"

Sedhi smiled. "You were very popular during your time as Fountain. You have started a new tradition."

The puzzlement deepened. "What kind of tradition?"

"Many people brought offerings to you as well as to the Quickener."

Terlyn set the box on her desk. Inside, neatly laid out in separate compartments, she found an array of beautiful things: a bud-shaped object of white stone with an elaborate design of ridges carved into it; a clockwork mechanism with many stacked rings that rotated in different directions, each covered with smooth bumps; a long cylinder, slightly curved, that pulsed with warmth; a short, stubby rod, rounded at one end, whose other end melded seamlessly into a curved shield with a small pulsating nub on its lip.

Beneath them was a thin wooden panel that covered a second layer of objects and beneath that, a third.

A rapid succession of images, vague and jumbled, spilled through her head. She felt a sudden wave through her body like the aftershock of an orgasm and put out her hand to steady herself.

"Oh!" she said. "I think…Donvin, did you make these?"

"Some of them," he said.

"I remember! I…" Her mind clouded. The images faded into the mist. "No, it's gone now."

"That's the way of it," Eileithyia said. "The memories are hard to keep."

Terlyn closed her eyes, struggling to retain her grip, but the images faded around her. She tightened her grip on the desk. "I think I would like to be alone now."

"Of course," Eileithyia said.

She and Sedhi left. Donvin put his hand on Terlyn's shoulder. "Are you okay?"

"Yes. I just feel…I want to be alone."

Donvin looked stricken. Meersath touched his arm. "I understand," she said. "Shall we return later?"

"Yes. I would like that."

Meersath bowed. She took Donvin's hand. Hand in hand, they left.

Terlyn sat alone with her thoughts for hours. She pursued the memories of her time in the Garden down the recesses of her mind, but time and again, they melted away like specters. Tantalizing fragments surfaced here and there—a look in some stranger's eye as he came atop her, a feeling of a hand or a mouth on her body—but they slipped away before she could hold them. She took the beautiful things from the box one by one and rolled them in her hand, feeling the weight of them, the tangible reality, reassured by their solidity.

Always there was Donvin. All her most substantial memories were of Donvin: his face, his voice, his hands, his lips.

"Give me a dress," Terlyn told the Provider. "Something simple. Conservative." Designs flickered in the air before her. She flipped through them, finally settling on a long, white dress with full sleeves, modest and warm. The panel opened. The dress and matching shoes slid out.

Terlyn dressed, then headed out into the crisp winter day. She wandered for a while, with no objective in mind, reveling in the unimaginable luxury of moving about as she chose.

She paused for a while at a small rectangular garden plot, neatly delineated by four rows of walkways. The plot hadn't received the memo about the coming of winter; within its boundaries, the air remained warm, and flowers bloomed. A woman with golden hair tended the brilliant purple blossoms. She looked up and smiled at Terlyn. Her eyes were the same shade of purple as the flowers. Behind her, another woman sat on a large stone block reading, her creamy white skin shaded by a hovering drone. Words and images floated in the air in front of her.

Terlyn nodded to the gardener and moved on. She followed a path in a wide arc around the Temple of the Fiery One. A crowd had gathered in the courtyard in front of a man chained to one of the columns, bare-chested, wearing a white kilt with an opening in the front cut to expose his erection. People reached out to stroke and fondle him as they walked by. He writhed in torment.

Terlyn watched for a moment. She felt a clenching between her legs. She remembered thorns penetrating her skin, the sense-memory slide of sharp spines into yielding flesh so vivid that she rubbed her wrists. She shook her head and moved on.

Through the rest of her walk, Terlyn felt a vague sense of unease. She ignored the people who flowed around her as she drifted in a large loop around the temple district, lost in her own thoughts. She longed to be touched, but paradoxically she also craved solitude. She wrapped her arms around herself and kept her head down, not greeting any of the people around her.

As she headed away from the Temple back toward the Garden, she nearly walked into a man coming the other way. She caught herself at the last moment. "Sorry," she said.

"No, no, the fault is mine, Fountain," he said.

She looked up at him. She caught a quick glimpse of white hair streaked with color, pale eyes, broad shoulders heavy with muscle. Then, in a flash, she was back in the Garden, lying on the rock, vines twisted around her wrists. He was on top of her, thrusting…

Terlyn spasmed as she came, so hard she stumbled. He caught her by the arm. "Are you okay, Fountain?"

"I…I…" she panted. Aftershocks trembled through her. "I'm fine, I just…" He looked at her with concern. Their eyes met. The memory slammed into her again, so intense she reeled. A second orgasm took her. Thankfully, it was a pale shadow of the first.

"Fountain?"

She turned and fled, rushing away from the Temple, away from people, back toward the safety of home.

2.16

Terlyn returned to an empty home. She sank into the chair Donvin had summoned, unable to decide if she felt relieved or disappointed.

The soft, directionless chime came again at sundown. The frosted white walls glowed with the last rays of the setting sun. "You have visitors," said the voice.

"Donvin?"

"Yes. Donvin and Priestess Meersath."

"Let them in!"

She hugged Donvin tightly the moment he came through the door. He looked at her in surprise. "Oof!" he said and hugged her back. "How was your day?"

"I'm not..." She shook her head. "I'm not sure. I'm still not completely here, I think."

"That's as normal as sunshine," Meersath said. "You weren't here for a long time. You'll find your way back."

Terlyn gave her a half-smile. "If you say so."

That night, Terlyn woke again from a dream of lips and hands and tongues, her body aching with need. She rolled over atop Donvin, who protested sleepily. His protests died when she straddled and mounted him. She came hard, rolling her hips against him. His hands caressed her breasts, sending flashes of pleasure through her in the darkness. After he came, he slipped quickly back into sleep. She lay awake for a while, staring at the stars through the transparent ceiling, feeling the cooling wetness drip out of her.

The next morning, she woke first again. She bathed in the waterfall, then summoned breakfast from the Provider. When Meersath woke, Terlyn was sitting nude at her desk, looking at the various objects she had been given in offering.

Meersath came up behind her and placed her hands on Terlyn's shoulders. "Trouble sleeping?"

"Yes. I keep having...well, dreams, I guess. Visions of people on top of me. My hands are tied. People are doing things to me. I can't stop them. They feel so good. And there's something else, too. Like...I don't know, like a whispering in my mind. It's in a language I don't understand. And... feelings. Like someone is proud of me."

"You're in communion with the Quickener. Those of us who have served as Fountains can hear her in our thoughts."

"Will I ever understand what she's saying?"

"Not completely. The gods are different than we are. Their thoughts aren't like ours. They don't see the world the same way we do, even though we made them. But in time, yes, you will learn to understand her better."

"Those dreams aren't really dreams, are they? They're memories."

Meersath leaned over to kiss the top of Terlyn's head. Terlyn squeezed her hand. "Do you remember what I asked you, when we first met?"

"Yes. You asked why I disappeared, after I came back from the Garden."

"You also told me nothing prepares you for the reality of being the Fountain."

Meersath chuckled. "That sounds like something I might say."

"Something happened to me yesterday, while I was out walking."

"Yes?"

"I met a man. I...I remembered him. From the Garden. I don't know who he was, but as soon as I saw him, I...the memory...it made me come."

Meersath moved around to look at Terlyn. She brushed a strand of green hair away from Terlyn's face.

"Is that why you disappeared?" Terlyn said. "Did that happen to you too?"

Meersath nodded. "Yes. It's a common thing. You can't always predict what will trigger it. Sometimes you will see the face of a person who was with you in the Garden, or hear a voice, and..." She shrugged. "I don't know. Your body remembers."

"Will it always be this way?"

"No. It fades in time. The first few weeks are the hardest."

"You didn't tell me that might happen."

"Would it have mattered?"

Terlyn looked down. "No," she said.

"What do you need from me?"

Terlyn put her arms around Meersath. "I need to be alone. Completely. For at least a few weeks. Maybe more. Probably more."

Meersath nodded. "Of course."

"And...I need that to be okay. I am not upset with you. It isn't about you. I don't want you to be hurt or offended."

"Oh, my dear lovely woman," Meersath said. She kissed Terlyn's forehead. "I understand completely."

Meersath woke Donvin. Terlyn heard the two of them murmuring to each other. Donvin rose and called forth a change of clothes from the Provider. "Will I see you again?" he said.

"I don't know." Terlyn reached out and took his hand in both of hers. "Please don't look at me that way. Yes. Yes, you will see me again."

"When?"

"I don't know. I just...I have a lot to think about, and I really need to be alone for a while."

He looked down at her for a long time. Then, finally, he squeezed her hands. "I will be here whenever you need me."

"Thank you."

Terlyn watched them go. When they left, she spent a long time staring at the door.

After that, Terlyn's days followed each other in quiet simplicity. She rose each morning to bathe in the waterfall, then walked the forest or sat in meditation on the strip of grass just inside the glass box that was her home. Half-remembered moments from her time in the Garden filled her dreams: faces, sounds, memories of overwhelming pleasure.

She remained in seclusion, seeing nobody and accepting no visitors, until the evening of the Winter Solstice. She was sitting nude on the edge of her bed, running her fingers over a small bud-shaped object of gold from the offerings that had been given to her, when the directionless chime filled the air. "You have a visitor."

"Who is it?"

"Priestess Eileithyia."

"Let her in."

She rose as Eileithyia entered. Eileithyia smiled at her. "No need to get up, Fou—Terlyn. How are you doing?"

"Peaceful," Terlyn said. She looked down. "Though I did just realize I haven't bothered to get dressed for days."

Eileithyia laughed. "Don't put yourself out on my account." Her eyes flicked to the swath of grass near Terlyn's bed, where a cluster of vines hugged the ground. "I see you've planted some of your seeds."

"I have. I haven't allowed them to bite me yet. What brings you here, Priestess?"

"I wanted to let you know that next year's Fountain has been selected. Her name is Samathrian."

"You chose early this year."

"Yes, especially since we had a lot of volunteers. You've inspired people. She was an easy choice. She is very passionate about becoming the avatar of the Quickener."

"I've inspired people, have I? I haven't even talked to anybody in weeks! Besides, it's not like I did anything while I was Fountain. I was just sleeping."

"It's not what you did, it's what you represent. People responded to Donvin's loyalty to you, for example."

Terlyn looked down. "I haven't talked to him," she said, her voice small. "He must be very disappointed."

"Not at all. He understands. Well, as much as anyone who has never been Fountain can understand. He sends his regards."

"I'm still not ready."

"I know. I won't intrude on your time any more. When you are ready, should you wish to become a High Priestess of the Quickener, come see me."

"I will." Terlyn looked up. "Thank you, Priestess."

That night, Terlyn sat with her legs folded beneath her in the grass next to the bed. The vines bent toward her, hesitant, tentative. She remained still. Slowly, they crept nearer. She remained as unmoving as a stone statue.

The vines touched her thigh. She flinched. They recoiled away from her. She took a deep breath, forcing herself back to calmness. They moved forward again. This time, when they touched her, she did not move.

They slid over her, leaves and stems coarse on her bare skin. Sharp thorns dragged across her. She sucked in her breath. Tiny beads of liquid formed on the ends of the thorns.

The vines coiled around her arm. The thorns left faint, fine scratches on her skin. Up and up the vines climbed, wrapping around her, rustling as they moved. Time slowed.

Terlyn closed her eyes. The soft, alien murmur in her head grew louder, until she could almost make out the words.

All at once, the vines tightened. Thorns sank into her skin. Red liquid flowed into her. She came violently, wildly, screaming with pleasure, her body convulsing.

The orgasm went on and on, wave after wave of ecstasy crashing through her. The murmur in her head resolved into words of comfort, showing her the path. She felt a sense of peace descend upon her, even while, somewhere far away, her body shook with pleasure.

2.17

"Donvin!" Terlyn said. "You made it!"

He bowed. "High Priestess Terlyn," he said.

She laughed. "You enjoy saying that way too much."

"I'm sure I don't know what you mean, High Priestess," he said, his face a picture of pious innocence.

"If you two are finished flirting," Meersath said, "we have things to do."

Meersath, like Terlyn, wore a form-hugging green dress that left one arm and one breast bare. Terlyn's thick tangle of snowy white hair was only barely subdued by the fine gold wire woven through it. Meersath had braided her hair with shiny green metal wire. Donvin, dressed in a simple black shirt and black pants, was by far the most somber of the three of them.

They walked toward the Garden. A brilliant blue sky hung overhead, unmarked by even a single cloud. "You know I'm never going to get tired of calling you High Priestess," Donvin said.

"Never? It's been, what, a week?"

"Two weeks!" Donvin said. "Two weeks, one day, fourteen hours, and twenty-six minutes."

"Okay, fine. Two weeks. You'll have to get tired of it eventually."

"Don't underestimate his patience," Meersath said. "Speaking of which, Donvin, if you ever decide to become an initiate of the Quickener, we would be glad to have you."

"And abandon the Lady? Perish the thought!" His face carried a look of mock horror. He took Terlyn and Meersath by the hand.

At the archway, they joined Tyrill and a woman Terlyn had never met before. She was small in stature, with gray eyes that seemed too large for her face and hair that was a glossy blue so deep it might almost be black. She wore nothing but a simple robe of red silk, her bare feet peeking out from beneath the hem.

She bowed deeply. "High Priestess Terlyn! It is an honor to meet you, ma'am!"

Terlyn darted a glance to Donvin, who hung back a respectful distance. He winked. She extended her hand. "Good morning, Samathrian. The honor is mine."

Tyrill turned toward Samathrian. "You are ready?"

"Yes, I am."

"Do you pledge yourself to the Quickener, that your body may become his vessel, bringing his blessing to all who would accept it?"

She nodded vigorously. "I do." Her eyes did not leave Terlyn.

"Do you give yourself as an offering to him, to be his Fountain?"

"Yes. Yes, I do."

"It is time for the purification," Terlyn said. "For the next three days, you will not sleep nor leave the Garden. You will perform the rites in meditation. You will symbolically pass through the seasons of the Garden, spring, summer, and fall, so that your body will become an instrument through which we commune with the Quickener. Do you undertake this journey voluntarily, of your own free will, with full understanding that your body will be a vessel of the Quickener from now until the last day of autumn?"

"Yes!" Her eyes were wide. "Absolutely!"

"Very well." Terlyn smiled. "You may enter the Garden."

BOOK THREE
THE WILD

3.1

THREE PEOPLE STOOD on a hill in the early morning sun looking at a dense tangle of trees. Yesterday, it had been a large park, with cultivated shrubs and marble fountains carefully arranged on gently rolling hills. Today, it was a vast ancient forest, wild and chaotic.

Eventually, the woman spoke. "What do you think?"

"This looks like a fun one, Ashi," the shorter of the two men said.

Her smile grew. "Big and bad. Definitely going to be fun."

"How long do you think before it opens up?"

She studied the trees, packed shoulder to shoulder, dense enough to make passage impossible. A small winding path that had once led into the park now ended at a no-nonsense wall of huge thorns with wicked spikes wider than her hand.

"No idea," she said. "But I can't wait until it does."

She regarded the forest through eyes the color of freshly polished copper, her pupils like small black crosses. They shone with eagerness against her short, asymmetric-cut brown hair, shot through with streaks of orange and red. Her short-sleeved green and brown shirt and green shorts were unusually neatly tucked over her trim, athletic frame.

Her companions also sported similar copper-colored eyes with cross-shaped pupils. Ruji was thick and broad-shouldered, with muscular arms and legs and an easy smile. He wore his black hair long, with a white streak through it, contrasting sharply with the brilliant, spiky flame-red hair of the taller man, Vrynn. Vrynn had a runner's body, lithe and slender, clothed like Ruji's in a kilt of heavy brown fabric decorated with abstract black designs, fastened in place with red belts hung with pouches. Both men were bare-chested in the mild autumnal air.

Tattoos decorated Vrynn's chest—heavy, broad lines that shifted shape and color with his mood. Right now, their jagged red spikes telegraphed his uncertainty. "I'm a bit nervous about this one," he said. "It looks pretty dark."

"That's what you said about the last one," Ruji observed.

"Was I wrong?"

"Not as such, but…"

"Well, I think I'm going to enjoy it," Ashi said. "Looks like we're the first ones here. Let's tell the others."

Ruji's eyes unfocused for a moment. "Done."

Ashi sat on the grass atop a small hill, patting the ground next to her. Vrynn and Ruji sat beside her. "Okay," she said. "Now we wait."

A short time later, a tall, wide-chested man climbed the hill. He had a strip of black hair that fell past his waist. The sides of his head were shaved and adorned with geometric tattoos that, like Vrynn's, slowly morphed and changed over time. "Tavin!" Ashi said. She bounded to her feet and threw her arms around him.

He laughed a full, deep laugh as he scooped her off her feet and kissed her soundly. "Ashi! Still keeping bad company, I see." He clasped hands with Ruji, then embraced Vrynn warmly.

"How do you know I'm not the one keeping bad company?" Vrynn asked.

Tavin laughed again. "You make a good point, my friend, a good point indeed." He and Vrynn kissed deeply.

Next to arrive was a leggy, barefooted woman with midnight-black hair. Tiny points of light danced amongst the strands. She wore a simple deep green one-piece dress. "Hi, guys!" she said, shading her copper-colored eyes to gaze at the forest. "This is a big one."

"Shia! Hey!" Vrynn smiled. He hugged her tightly. "It is! I have no idea what we're getting into here."

"We wouldn't be giving ourselves to the Wild if we knew."

"True that," Vrynn said.

Shia sat on the grass beside Ashi, laying her head on Ashi's shoulder. Ashi slipped her arm around her sturdy waist.

More people arrived throughout the morning. By the time the sun stood directly overhead, twelve people sat on the grass regarding the forest with tense anticipation.

At the precise moment the sun reached its zenith, the dense, twisted wall of thorns parted with a rustle. The twelve cheered and swarmed down the hill.

Past the edge of the forest, sunlight filtered through a broad canopy dense with leaves. Shafts of light fell on broad, craggy trunks covered with thick, gnarled bark. A dense mat of leaves and twigs carpeted the ground. The woods smelled old, like a deep and ancient forest undisturbed for centuries.

A short way in, they found themselves in a completely different world. The ordinary noises of the City faded into silence. No sound broke the stillness except their breathing and the soft sighing of the wind in the trees. No birds sang overhead, no animals ran through the undergrowth. Nothing existed except the dense, ancient forest.

Ahead, the path branched. Two slightly smaller paths continued on. Ashi paused. "Right or left?"

"Left," Vrynn said.

"Right," Ruji said.

Ashi laughed. "I guess it's on me, then. Fine. That way." She pointed to the right.

The group split, with half following Ashi's lead and the other half taking the path on the left. Both paths headed in the same direction but diverged enough to put an impassable wall of trees and underbrush between them. High above, the canopy began closing over them, allowing only occasional rays of sunlight through. Ashi, Ruji, and Vrynn walked abreast. Excited chatter floated up behind them.

The path straightened, then slowly, almost imperceptibly, began curving to the left, following the contours of the forest. The two branches of the path spiraled parallel to each other toward the center.

Deeper in the forest, the light dimmed. Thin, light mist filled the air—not quite fog, not quite rain. The path remained easy to follow, gently curving through dense trees.

After they'd walked for several minutes, the path split again, branching into three slightly smaller paths to the left and right and continuing ahead. The side branches ran away from the main path for a short distance, then curved to run parallel.

"Now which way?" Vrynn said.

Ruji shrugged. "All paths lead to the Wild."

"But not all paths are the same," Ashi said.

"I'm going this way," Tavin said. He turned right. Two people followed him.

"Okay," Ashi said, "let's go—"

"This way," Vrynn said. He started down the forward path. Ashi and Ruji hastened after him. The remaining people behind them, including Shia, headed left.

The path narrowed rapidly, until they were forced to walk single file. It continued its slow spiral toward the center of the forest. Overhead, the forest canopy thickened until it blotted out the sun. Deep shadows lurked between the trees.

Ashi stopped at a dense mound of brambles whose roots crossed the path. "Look at this," she said.

"What?" Ruji said.

"I don't know. There's something here." She pulled at the vines. There, in the center of the mound, a white marble fountain burbled. Water bubbled from a moss-stained stone jug resting on the lap of a surrealistically proportioned marble woman. Above her, a marble man, proportioned just as heroically, bent to kiss her. His hand rested on her breast.

"I recognize this fountain," Vrynn said. "I was here yesterday, before the forest came."

"I'm thirsty," Ashi said. As she said it, she realized it was true. The thirst crept up on her so quietly she didn't notice until she saw the bubbling fountain. She cupped her hands and drank.

The water had a subtle spicy flavor. She swallowed. Immediately, the world took on a faint, slightly surreal glow. The mottled patches of sunlight on the forest floor rippled, as though imbued with inner life. The wind whispered indecipherable words as it played through the trees. Ashi's skin tingled with pleasant warmth.

Ruji and Vrynn followed Ashi's example. "Mm," Vrynn said. His tattoos changed, cycling from deep red to green to dark blue to amber. They flowed across his body, the spikes rounding, becoming softer. "I feel nice."

Ashi held out her hands. Her fingers left faint glowing trails in the air. She touched Vrynn's chest. He sucked in his breath.

They moved on, winding their oblique way toward the heart of the forest. Before long, they arrived at another fork in the path. The trees here grew denser, their crowns lower to the ground. The two paths, dim and dark, began to resemble tunnels carved by an unseen hand through the forest.

"Which way now?" Vrynn said.

"Let's go that way," Ashi said, pointing left. She started down the path. Vrynn followed.

Ruji took a step. With only the barest rustle, branches closed in front of him, barring his way.

"I'll take that as a hint," he said. He turned to the right.

The path narrowed, closing on Ashi and Vrynn until they had to duck to avoid low-hanging branches. The forest here felt wilder, more overgrown. The trees, their trunks so wide two people couldn't wrap their arms around them, grew almost touching each other, branches dripping with moss. Dense thorny bushes discouraged any thoughts of straying from the trail.

The mist grew until it was almost a light rain. Their skin glowed wet.

They came to a point where a vast tree, its trunk wide and its branches low, squatted directly in their way. Large, craggy roots snaked across the path. In the clefts between them grew a dense cluster of plants with wide, spade-shaped leaves and broad yellow flowers. The tree's branches hung so low they were forced to bend over to pass beneath.

Ashi stepped carefully through the roots, mindful of twisting an ankle. She looked back at Vrynn. "I think we're getting closer," she said. "We—"

The flowers erupted with small pops. A thick cloud of yellow pollen settled on Ashi and Vrynn, coating their faces and arms with a layer of fine dust.

Ashi pointed at Vrynn. "You're all yellow!" she laughed. "You look silly. Ooh!" She put her hand on the tree trunk. "I feel dizzy."

The grains of pollen turned translucent and sank into fabric and flesh, leaving no trace. Vrynn blinked rapidly. He shook his head. "Keep going," he growled.

Ashi giggled. "Okay, Mister Grumpy."

They pushed on. The path led them on its slow spiral, becoming less defined and more difficult with each passing step. Ashi felt herself floating, as though she were a balloon being carried along behind her body. She watched herself pushing through the underbrush and giggled at the absurdity of it.

Eventually, they came to a large fallen tree. Roots projected into the air like skeletal fingers. Several saplings grew from a rotting log. Ivy twisted around it, its wide green leaves open to catch what little sunlight filtered down this far. The path divided, branching around each side of the fallen tree.

Without a word, Vrynn headed around the log to the right, squeezing through a narrow space between two slender trees. Ashi turned to follow. The ivy twisted around her feet, tripping her. The opening through which Vrynn had passed closed.

"I guess this is goodbye, then!" she called. She giggled again.

The way to the left was little more than the suggestion of a path. Thick roots snaked across it. The branches grew so low that Ashi was forced to crawl on hands and knees. The path, if it could still be called that, closed in on her, so narrow she couldn't turn around. It curved sharply enough that she couldn't see what was ahead, except for more trees and bushes. Almost no light reached the forest floor here.

She came to a bush that blocked her way. It was too dense to crawl through, with wiry branches and narrow, sharp-edged leaves that were a green so dark they were nearly black. A profusion of red berries covered the bush, so vibrant they almost glowed in the gloom.

Ashi's stomach rumbled. Without thought, she plucked a handful of berries and put them in her mouth. They burst on her tongue, juicy and painfully sweet. She grabbed another handful, then another after that.

Colors brightened. Detail sharpened. The gentle sounds of the wind in the trees became words, whispering in a language she could almost but not quite understand.

She tugged at the branches, now bare of berries. They came away easily, revealing a space just large enough to crawl through. As she forced her way through, she felt the entire forest reaching out to caress her. Shivers of delight ran through her body.

Ashi stopped at a tree whose branches were so low that even on her hands and knees, she couldn't wriggle through. She tried to back up. The dense brushes clawed at her. She lowered herself to the ground and squirmed forward, flat on her belly. Rough bark plucked at the back of her shirt.

With one last squirm, she pushed between two bushes and crawled out into a fantasy wonderland.

3.2

Ashi found herself in a wide circular clearing. An enormous banyan tree grew in its center, spreading immense branches in all directions. Roots dropped from the branches to the ground. Its crown towered above the rest of the forest. Golden shafts of light streamed down around it.

A streamlet trickled to a shallow pond at the foot of the immense tree. Mushrooms and puffballs grew between its massive roots. Pale green moss hung like curtains from its mighty branches. Green creeping vines, festooned with purple flowers, embraced its trunk.

Near the edge of the clearing to her left, a huge weeping willow sent its long, thin branches, heavy with bright pink flowers, almost to the ground. Petals drifted down, covering the ground beneath the willow's sheltering limbs.

Ashi looked around in awe. Dense, near-impassable bushes walled off the clearing. Tiny glowing flowers, no bigger than her fingertip, grew over the bushes, lighting the dark spaces beneath them with an eerie greenish glow. The air smelled of forest and rain.

The moment she stood, a thick tangle of vines rose from the ground, blocking the opening through which she had come.

All around the clearing, more worshippers crawled out through the dense underbrush. As they did, thorns sprouted behind them to keep them from leaving. Some of the people appeared dazed, others, eager.

Vrynn wriggled out near Ashi. Sticks and leaves matted his hair. His back bore the marks of thorns and bark. His pupils were barely visible crosses floating in molten copper.

Ashi giggled. "You're a mess!" she said.

Vrynn snarled and bared his teeth. He rushed at Ashi. She giggled again when he grabbed her. "Ooh, so fierce!" she said.

Ruji's head appeared. He struggled through the bushes and stood, brushing twigs and dirt from his knees. Tavin and Shia crawled out into the clearing beside him.

"Ruji!" Ashi sang. "Vrynn's being all grabby." She grinned at him. Faint streamers of light curled away from his face.

Vrynn spun her around. Ashi laughed. He grabbed both her arms tightly and pinned them behind her back. "Ruji!" she called again. "Vrynn is being rude. Do you see how grabby he's being?"

Ruji stalked over to her. Vrynn held her tightly. Ruji kissed the side of her neck. Sharp teeth pressed lightly into her skin. He slid his hands over her breasts, squeezing and fondling. She giggled. "Ruji!" she said. "You're being grabby too! Oh." Her eyelids fluttered. Pleasure danced across her skin. A purple halo glowed around Ruji. "That feels nice."

Vrynn gripped her arms more tightly. He pushed her against Ruji, sandwiching her between their bodies. Vrynn ground his hips into her. She felt his rigid erection against the cleft of her ass through his kilt. Her breath caught. "Is that for me?" she asked.

Ruji seized the front of her shirt. His muscles flexed. Scraps of cloth fell like leaves to the forest floor.

"Hey!" Ashi said. "That was my shirt!"

Ruji kissed her, hard. His tongue invaded her mouth, demanding. His hands cupped her bare breasts. Little whorls of light crawled along the trees behind him. Every leaf, every branch, every root was highlighted as if etched in an old-fashioned woodblock print.

Ruji pressed his thumbs into Ashi's nipples. Fireworks erupted within her body. Her skin crackled with electricity. She shivered.

Vrynn yanked down Ashi's skirt. She squirmed. He grabbed her arms again, so tightly his fingers sank into her skin. She ground her hips back against him.

Ruji grabbed her by the hair with one hand. His other squeezed her breast. "Oh!" she giggled. "You're so needy!"

Vrynn unfastened his kilt, which fell with a rustle to his ankles. Ashi squirmed, laughing. "Both of you! You're both so demanding. Oh!" She

262

looked into Ruji's eyes. His pupils were so large the copper had all but disappeared. "Vrynn is pressing against me," she said. "He's very hard. I think he means to ravish me. Yes, he's definitely going to...oh!"

She dissolved into laughter as he entered her. She draped her arms around Ruji's shoulders. "He's inside me!" she said. "He's so very hard!" Her body trembled as he forced his way deeper. "What are you going to do to me?"

Ruji snarled. He yanked her head back by her hair and kissed her, hard and deep. He forced his tongue between her lips. Behind her, Vrynn pounded into her. Ashi came over and over, a whole series of tiny explosions detonating with each thrust. Ruji pulled off his kilt and pushed her head down. The tip of his engorged cock slid between her lips.

He held both sides of her head and guided her lower still, until his shaft filled her mouth and pressed against the back of her throat. Vrynn held her hands pinned behind her back while he ground into her, hard and deep. Ashi convulsed in another orgasm. Swirls of light danced in front of her eyes.

Ruji hardened in her mouth. A moment later, his body shook. Jet after jet of wet salty liquid spurted into Ashi's mouth, filling it to overflowing. Behind her, Vrynn roared. She felt him twitch, then a sense of warmth spread through her.

The two men released her. She straightened as they withdrew. "Goodness!" she giggled. "I like when you're so demanding."

They ignored her and stalked off in search of new prey.

Ashi heard a sigh. Shia lay nude beneath the willow tree, behind a curtain of branches. Tavin caressed her gently.

Ashi wandered over to them. She sat on the ground beside Shia and watched the tiny points of white light dance in her hair. Small halos surrounded each point of light. "It's so pretty!" she said.

A shower of flower petals drifted down from the branches of the willow tree. They stuck to Ashi's damp skin. Wherever they touched her, they turned transparent, then slowly dissolved.

Euphoria washed over Ashi. Her skin flushed.

"Isn't it nice?" Shia said. She reached up with a languid hand to caress Ashi's breast. The contact, warm and electric, made Ashi shudder.

"Lie down!" Shia said. Her eyes were dreamy, her voice deep and slow. "Play with us!"

Ashi lay on her back on the carpet of flower petals. Her skin glowed. The branches above her buzzed with color and light. The sunlight seemed alive as it danced through the gently swaying boughs.

Tavin ran one hand over Ashi's body. Shia rolled on her side toward Ashi. She stroked Ashi's cheek. "Touch me."

Ashi turned to face her. They ran their hands over each other, caressing one another's skin, fondling each other's breasts. Tavin stroked both of them, his hands gliding over their bodies. The sensation took Ashi's breath away.

Two more people joined them beneath the willow tree, holding hands. Shia waved to them. "Martia! Dekas! Come play with us!"

Martia, a short woman with navy blue hair and fiery orange eyes, sank down beside Tavin. Her short skirt of light, filmy blue fabric floated in the air as she sat. Her blue sleeveless shirt was unbuttoned to reveal heavy round breasts with four small round beads that pulsed and throbbed with colored light surrounding her nipples.

Dekas, as tall as Martia was short, was already nude. He had a lithe, graceful body, trim but powerful. He sat behind Ashi and began massaging her shoulders. Ashi sighed and closed her eyes.

The wind shivered through the tree. A fresh cascade of flower petals floated down. They dissolved on contact with damp skin. Martia moaned. Dekas shuddered. A gentle warm glow enveloped Ashi.

Martia wrapped her arms around Tavin and buried her face in his neck. Her fingers teased his nipples. He let out a long, soft moan.

Ashi's fingers curled over Shia's nipples. They hardened under the touch. Shia cupped Ashi's breasts. "We don't play nearly often enough," she said. "I would like to see more of you."

"You can see all of me you want to," Ashi giggled.

Dekas stretched out on his side behind Ashi, his small pert breasts pressing against her back. Everywhere their skin touched, little whirlpools of pleasure floated across her body. She arched her back and purred.

Dekas kneaded her shoulders. Shia slid her hands over Ashi's breasts. Ashi sighed. "You can both keep doing that," she said.

"Mm, I intend to," Shia said.

Dekas pressed tighter against Ashi. She felt his erection hard against her body. "Someone is enjoying this," she laughed.

"I think all of us are enjoying this," Martia said.

Dekas rocked his hips. The head of his cock slipped between Ashi's thighs. Ashi made a small gasp.

"That was a nice sound," Shia said. "What was that for?"

"It's Dekas!" Ashi said, and giggled. "He's getting into trouble."

"Oh? What's he doing?"

"He's…he's…oh!" Ashi's eyes widened. Dekas slid into her easily in a single smooth motion.

"Kiss me," Shia said.

"But Dekas!"

"Don't worry about Dekas. Kiss me."

Dekas took Ashi with long, slow strokes, sliding gently in and out of her. Ashi kissed Shia's lips. Little shivers of electricity crackled between them. Ashi closed her eyes and focused all her attention on the kiss.

Dekas hardened inside her. Ashi's body stiffened. An intense tornado of pleasure, sudden and unexpected, exploded through her. She screamed as she came, clutching at Shia with both hands, her body convulsing. The orgasm went on and on, a storm within her that rendered her speechless.

"Ooh, wow, that was interesting," Shia said. "What was that?"

"I—I—" Ashi said. Her fingers dug into Shia's arms. Her body shuddered uncontrollably.

"All that, hmm?" Shia murmured. "I wonder what will happen if he takes you in the ass?"

"I—"Ashi said. An aftershock shuddered through her body.

"I think we should find out," Shia said. "Would you like to take her ass?"

Dekas kissed the back of Ashi's neck. "It might be fun."

"Well, then, it's settled," Shia said.

Dekas slid free of Ashi. She mewled at the sudden emptiness. "It's okay," Shia said. "He's going back in."

Dekas' cock pressed against her ass, seeking entry. Ashi felt herself widen around it. Slowly, bit by bit, she opened up to allow it in. Trails of light swirled in the air around her.

"Kiss me like you mean it," Shia said.

Ashi kissed her with hungry enthusiasm. Her anus relaxed. Dekas slid in all the way. Ashi cried out with pleasure.

"Focus!" Shia said. "Kiss me!"

Ashi focused every bit of her attention on the kiss. Her tongue caressed Shia's lips. Dekas pressed against her from behind, not thrusting, just making tiny little motions with his hips, grinding against Ashi. His nipples grazed back and forth in minute circles on Ashi's back.

"I don't see why Dekas should have all the fun," Martia said. She pressed Tavin down so that he was lying behind Shia. She wrapped her fingers around his shaft. "Don't you want to have fun too?"

Tavin moaned.

"That's what I thought." She positioned him against Shia, sliding just the head of his erection between her folds. Shia gasped.

Ashi slipped her tongue between Shia's lips. Her hands caressed Shia's breasts. Martia stroked Tavin's shaft, her hand sliding up and down along its length. Tavin let out a groan. He kissed Shia's neck. His breathing sped up.

Martia stroked faster. Tavin tensed. "No, not yet, darling," Martia said. "It will feel so much better if you wait."

Ashi kissed Shia with growing need. Every small thrust from Dekas sent another wave of desperate desire rippling through her. She pressed back against him and felt him thicken in response.

Just like that, she couldn't contain it anymore. She shivered into orgasm. She rode Dekas with gyrations of her hips until her body shook and she wailed, hands tightening on Shia's breasts. Dekas made a loud, guttural cry. Hot wetness flooded into her.

"Now!" Martia said. Her hand blurred along Tavin's shaft.

Tavin convulsed, coming with a groan. His cock pulsed. White goo gushed across Shia's folds. Shia squeaked in surprise.

Dekas slid his softening shaft free from Ashi's embrace. Ashi shivered. "Was it all you had hoped?" she asked Shia.

"And more!" Shia said. She turned over on her back. Her hand dipped between her legs. "I'm a mess! Which one of you is going to get me all nice and clean?"

"I will!" said Martia and Tavin in the same breath.

Shia laughed. "Well, technically, I suppose it's your fault," she said to Martia, "so I think you should be the one."

"If you want to get technical, I made the mess," Tavin protested.

"You were the instrument," Shia said. "Martia was the intent." She beckoned to Martia. "You have a task to perform, I think."

Tavin pouted theatrically. Ashi clapped her hands and laughed. "Let's go to the pool!" she said. "You and Dekas can clean me up."

She took them both by the hand and led them to the little pond. Two people Ashi knew only in passing, Heran and Camit, already sat nude in its knee-deep waters. Heran, lanky with a wiry, narrow frame and short hair of deep indigo, sat behind Camit, a thickset, broad-shouldered man with golden eyes whose pupils were shaped like sideways figure-8s. His jet-black hair grew down to his knees; at the moment, its ends spread out on the surface of the water in a semicircle around him. Heran looked up from caressing Camit's back as they approached.

"Room for three more?" Ashi said.

"Always," Heran said.

Ashi sat in the warm water. Ruji and Dekas sat beside her. Dekas scooped up some water in cupped hands and let it flow over Ashi's breasts. She leaned back with a sigh, her eyes closed. Tavin kissed her neck. His hand slid up her inner thigh. "Tell me where you're dirty," he murmured in her ear.

266

"There's not a single part of me that's clean," she said, and giggled. She tilted her head back and kissed him.

A surprised shriek caught their attention. Riyan, a slender woman with pale skin and hair so silver it sparkled, dangled nearly upside down, suspended by vines from one of the banyan tree's massive horizontal branches. Her eyes had irises like round silver mirrors, with no trace of a pupil.

The vines came to life. They reached out and grabbed her, hauling her completely off the ground. As Ashi watched, curious, more vines wrapped themselves around her ankles and pulled her legs apart.

All at once, the puffballs scattered across the forest floor detonated with dull "whup" sounds. A mist of fine spores filled the air.

For a second, silence descended in the clearing. Then everyone except the people in the little pond with Ashi swarmed toward Riyan, growling and baring their teeth.

A strong, almost overwhelming sense of sexual need crept over Ashi. Beside her, Tavin and Dekas shuddered. They watched the scene unfolding beneath the banyan tree, transfixed.

The vines held Riyan parallel to the ground, face-down, her legs apart, her knees bent. A coil of ivy wrapped around her, binding her arms at her sides. Vrynn and Hallia, a voluptuous, dark-skinned woman with ice blue eyes and cyan hair that fell around her rounded shoulders, reached the struggling woman first.

Vrynn stood between her open legs. He ran his hands up her thighs, sliding the skirt up out of the way to reveal a neat triangle of pubic hair the same silver as the hair on her head. Her eyelids fluttered. She sighed.

The sigh sent a jolt through Ashi. She reached down for Tavin and Dekas. Her questing fingers found two rigid erections. Small moans nearby told her Heran and Camit were just as captivated as she.

Hallia knelt beside Riyan's head. She leaned over to whisper something Ashi couldn't hear in Riyan's ear. Riyan stopped writhing and hung still.

Vrynn entered Riyan from behind. She let out a cry of surprise. The cry electrified Ashi. She felt herself clench in response. She stroked the two erect shafts. Dekas slipped a hand between Ashi's legs. Tavin leaned over to bite her shoulder.

Ruji, Shia, Martia, and a short, powerfully built man named Jannon all converged around Riyan. Jannon stood in front of her, sporting an erection that projected straight out from his body. Hallia murmured in Riyan's ear. Riyan opened her mouth. Hallia caressed Jannon's erect shaft. She placed her other hand on the back of Riyan's head as she guided his erection between

Riyan's lips. She pressed down on Riyan's head until she had swallowed up his entire length.

Vrynn thrust hard with his eyes closed, head thrown back. He slammed into her with complete abandon, hands on her hips. Hallia curled her fingers through Riyan's hair, pushing her head down over and over again.

Ruji and Shia groped the helpless Riyan, hands squeezing and massaging her breasts. Martia bit her. She let out a thin squeak, muffled by the erection buried in her mouth. Hallia whispered nonstop into her ear.

Ashi drifted, unmoored from her body in a bubble of breathless pleasure. With every thrust Vrynn made into Riyan, her own body responded, clenching in sympathetic resonance. She stroked Tavin and Dekas beneath the water, light and fast, fingers barely brushing their shafts. Her body flushed with heat and desire.

Dekas slid his hand along her inner thigh. She parted her legs, inviting his hand to move further up.

His hand slid higher, until his fingers encountered her folds. He spread her open and ran the tip of his finger over her clit.

The bubble popped. Ashi dropped back into her body, writhing and squirming in the shallow water.

Vrynn roared. Trapped in vines, Riyan went stiff. Her body quaked. Hallia continued whispering in her ear, hand on the back of her head. Vrynn withdrew from her. Something white and thick dripped onto the forest floor.

Ashi whimpered softly, rocking her hips against Dekas's hand. She moved her hands faster, caressing both of her companions lightly, fingers playing over the heads of both cocks. Tavin breathed harder. Dekas moaned.

At the tree, Ruji took Vrynn's place behind Riyan. He entered her hard and fast, without preamble. He began thrusting furiously, both hands on her waist. Vrynn kissed him while he thrust into her. Ashi felt herself clench with need.

A nearby moan diverted Ashi's attention. Heran and Camit both stared at Riyan with naked hunger on their faces. Heran had wrapped his legs around Camit's thighs, pulling his legs apart. One hand reached around to stroke Camit beneath the surface of the water. Camit groaned.

Jannon let out a cry. He arched his back, forcing himself down Riyan's throat. Shia whispered something Ashi couldn't hear into Hallia's ear. Hallia laughed and nodded. Jannon withdrew from Riyan's mouth. Shia wrapped her fingers around his slick shaft. She stroked him with short, quick strokes until he screamed with pleasure. He spurted wildly, gushing over Riyan's face. Hallia clapped with delight.

Ruji shuddered, crying out in pleasure of his own. Riyan added her own voice to the chorus, eyes closed, moaning with the force of her orgasm.

A wave of dizziness swept over Ashi. She felt a sudden, fierce desire to go over to Riyan, grab her body, make her scream…

Camit rose, so suddenly he splashed water over the others in the pool. He took Heran's hand and lifted him to his feet. They both approached Riyan with teeth bared. Camit pushed Ruji out of the way with a snarl. He slid into Riyan, so abrupt she yelped in surprise. Heran grabbed the back of Riyan's head. She opened her mouth, tongue slightly extended. With one savage push, he forced his erect cock into her mouth.

In the pool beside Ashi, Dekas and Tavin trembled with barely contained desire. Ashi giggled. "Go!" she said. "Go get her!"

Dekas and Tavin splashed out of the pond to join the group around Riyan. Ashi watched the mob of people around her, groping her, fondling her, using her roughly. She twisted in the vines as Camit and Heran thrust into her, blinded by their need. With every stroke, Ashi could almost feel them inside her.

Riyan seemed outlined in swirling light. Eddies and whorls of color danced around her. Ashi slid her hand between her legs as she watched. Her fingers pressed against her clit. She arched her back, masturbating with furious abandon.

Heran came with a roar. A second later, Camit twitched. He made a soft sound, barely an exhale. Then his body shook, and he was done. He pulled from Riyan. More white wetness splattered the ground.

Ashi felt her own orgasm growing. She watched Tavin move behind Riyan, hands sliding up her legs, watched him penetrate her, watched her eyes grow large, watched the hands groping and fondling her, and then she could not hold back any more and her own orgasm took her, raging, until the world dimmed and she fell backward into the water.

3.3

THE SHOCK BROUGHT Ashi back to her senses. Trails of light floated in front of her. She stood wavering for a moment, panting, her chest heaving. She walked on unsteady feet to the edge of the small pond and collapsed, falling into a cluster of long, slender violet flowers growing from a patch of ivy that clung to the ground.

The flowers turned to face her. With a sibilant, barely audible sound, they released clouds of fine yellow pollen in her face. She blinked in surprise. Her head spun. The world turned a bit wobbly.

A fit of giggles overcame Ashi. She rolled on her back in the bed of flowers, laughing. The sky above her danced with twisting loops of color.

She tried to sit up. Her body resisted. Her limbs felt heavy and slow. From somewhere far away, moans and cries told her that people were still having fun with Riyan, but it all seemed remote.

She sprawled among the flowers, feeling soft petals stroke her skin and watching the breeze play with the trees overhead. The distant sounds slowed. She heard a faint rustle and wondered in a detached way if the vines had finally released Riyan. She remembered the look of shocked helplessness on Riyan's face when the vines had grabbed her, and giggled again.

Eventually, a face swam into her vision, staring down at her. She blinked. It resolved itself into Ruji. He moved in slow motion, drifting lazily over her. "Ashi?" he said.

Ashi tried to answer him, but her tongue didn't seem to want to work properly. "Urr?"

Shia's face appeared next to Ruji's, outlined in faint streamers of multicolored light. Ashi tried to wave, but her arm was much too heavy to lift from the grass. She gave up and smiled at Shia instead.

More faces floated, slow and dreamlike, above her: Camit, Dekas, Hallia, Vrynn. She laughed, amused by how slowly they converged around her.

Riyan drifted into view. Her face dripped with white goo that splashed down onto her breasts. Ashi giggled. "You're messy!" she tried to say, but her words came out slurred and indistinct.

Hallia knelt beside her head. She caressed Ashi's exquisitely, achingly sensitive breasts. Ashi moaned.

"Can you move?" Hallia said.

Ashi tried to raise her arm. Her fingers curled slightly. She poured all her strength into moving her legs and managed only a tiny quiver. "Nup!" she chirped.

Hallia lifted Ashi's arm and let it go. It flopped back to the ground. "Not at all?"

"Nuh!" Ashi said with a grin.

"Oh. How lovely," Hallia said.

The trees swayed in a sudden gust of wind. A huge cloud of fine pollen drifted from their crowns. Ashi had plenty of time to think about what it might mean as it swirled leisurely toward the ground. She grinned with giddy anticipation.

The cloud of pollen reached the clearing floor. Ashi watched with interest as the faces around her changed. Their eyes glazed. Pupils contracted and expanded again. Their expressions turned hungry and predatory.

Camit was the first to be affected. His expression hardened. His face flushed. Ashi watched in a dreamlike trance as he grew erect. She knew, even before he started to move, what he would do next.

He grabbed her ankles and pulled her legs wide. She let out a squeak. Hallia placed both hands on the side of Ashi's head and bent down toward her. "Think of this as practice," she said. "I know you want to be sacrificed to the Wild, right?"

"Yush," Ashi said.

"If you become the Sacrifice, nothing you can do will stop what happens to you," Hallia said. "Just like now."

Camit released Ashi's ankles. Her legs remained spread, wooden and unresponsive.

"Just relax," Hallia said. "Let go. Release yourself to the Wild. In your abandon there is service. What will happen, will happen."

Camit bared his teeth. He crawled over Ashi in slow motion. She remained splayed out beneath him, unable to move. He forced himself into her with a grunt, pressing hard and deep.

"Yes, just like that," Hallia murmured. "Surrender. Just be."

Camit took Ashi with a savage intensity, his eyes distant and unfocused. He drove himself into her again and again, until his body went rigid and she felt the wet slap of his release inside her.

The others gathered around her. The moment Camit withdrew, Martia was on top of her, her knees between Ashi's. She kissed Ashi with rough intensity, shoving her tongue between Ashi's lips. Ashi tasted come on her lips.

Martia pushed three fingers into Ashi. Ashi tried to press into the probing fingers, but her body, heavy and limp, did not move.

Martia withdrew her fingers and pushed them into Ashi's mouth. Ashi could taste the slick wetness all over them, a mixture of Camit's ejaculation and her own juices. Hallia stroked her hair.

"Give yourself over," Hallia said. "Every part of your body belongs to the Wild. Let go. Accept the purity of surrender. Clear your mind. Let them purge themselves with you."

Ashi let out a muffled "mff!" She wasn't sure if it was a sound of agreement or disagreement. Not that it mattered either way.

Martia straddled Ashi's face. As she moved down in the curious slow motion that had taken over the world, Ashi had plenty of time to see the wet whiteness flow from her. She tried to turn her head. Her body remained still.

Martia lowered herself until her sex touched Ashi's lips. "Please her," Hallia said. "Accept the gift she gives you. Let this be your gift to the Wild."

Ashi slid her tongue between Martia folds. Wet glop poured into her mouth. Ashi tried to struggle. Her fingertips twitched, but her body lay still as stone.

Martia grabbed Hallia's hair and kissed her, hungry and demanding. Her hips rocked against Ashi's face. Her breathing quickened. Her legs tensed. She came with a muffled cry, twitching against Ashi's tongue, while more of the thick white goo flowed from her.

She collapsed beside Ashi, panting. Ashi looked up to see Tavin standing over her. Shia stood behind him, one hand caressing his chest, the other stroking his erect cock. He let out a cry that was half scream, half growl. A jet of fluid streamed from the head of his cock.

Ashi watched as it floated lazily down toward her. She saw the end of the jet curl in on itself, describing a twisting path through the air on its long trip down to her body.

Another jet spurted from the head of his cock, and another after that. Ashi had plenty of time to watch them fall, but her unresponsive body would not move out of the way.

The first spurt landed hot and wet on her stomach. She could feel its warmth, feel the weight of it, the wet slipperiness. The second splashed on her neck and shoulder. Ashi felt droplets, wet and slick, begin to drip down her skin. The third splattered on her breast, coating her erect nipple.

Shia kept stroking, coaxing one last spurt from his softening cock. Ashi watched it tumble through space, following its immutable trajectory to splatter across her face. She felt little beads of warmth roll down her chin.

Hallia slid her hands over Ashi's body, massaging her, caressing her breasts, spreading the slippery goo across her. "If you are chosen to be Sacrifice, every part of your body will exist for the Purging. Every inch of you will be available for the pack to use," she said. "Feel yourself surrender. This is what you want."

"I want her!" Jannon growled. He pushed Tavin out of the way, then grabbed Ashi and rolled her face down among the flowers. He entered her from behind, taking her in hard, fast jackhammer strokes. She lay limp and still, passively accepting the assault.

"I saw you, when the vines had Riyan," Hallia said. "I watched you in the pool touching yourself. I saw you come. Did you enjoy watching what was happening to her? Did it excite you?" She turned Ashi's head so that Ashi could see where Riyan was sitting. "Look. Look at her. Do you see how she is cupping her breast? Do you see her fingers between her legs? Look at how she's watching you. Watching you excites her. She is enjoying what is happening to you. Look! Look how hard her nipples are! I think she is going to come. Watching you being ravished gives her pleasure. There! There it is! Do you hear her moaning? She likes what's happening to you!"

Ashi tried to speak. Immediately, Hallia pressed her fingers into Ashi's mouth. "Hush now," she said. "This is not the time for talking."

Then the second orgasm was on her, as unexpected but inevitable as the first. A moment later, Jannon came, gushing into Ashi's inert body.

He withdrew. Someone else—Ashi couldn't see who—replaced them. A stiff cock entered her slack body. He took her, slamming into her until he had satisfied himself, sending another torrent into her.

Hallia murmured nonstop into Ashi's ear as more fingers and more cocks invaded Ashi. Through it all, she watched Riyan, marveling at her beauty, quivering every time Riyan sighed. She drank in every detail: the quickening flutter of the pulse on Riyan's neck, the glints of sunlight from Riyan's silver hair, her own reflections in the flat mercuric pools of Riyan's silver eyes, the wet drops of semen that rolled glistening down the curve of Riyan's breast, the slickness that coated Riyan's fingers as they busied themselves between her legs.

Riyan came again and again watching the violation of Ashi's immobile, unresponsive body. Every time she did, Ashi felt intoxicated by Riyan's beauty.

Eventually, the assault on Ashi's body ceased. The hands left her. All around her, people sat or lay on the ground, panting.

Riyan rose. She wandered over to Ashi and sat down beside her. "The thorns are still up," she said. "You and I haven't played yet, but I think everyone else has played together. Do you know what that means?"

"Unh fnon nough," Ashi said. She giggled.

"It means one of us is probably the gatekeeper," Riyan said. "And if that's true, we are all going to stay here until you and I play. Since you can't move, that means it's all up to me." She ran her fingers through Ashi's hair. "You're pretty. I enjoyed watching what just happened to you. In fact," she went on, "I don't think I'm finished watching yet." She looked around at the little clusters of people around Ashi. "Some of you still seem to have some energy left. I am not going to play with Ashi until everyone else is completely exhausted from having her. If you guys ever want to leave this forest, you better get busy!"

Ashi whimpered. She tried to move. Her body lay on the ground like a rag doll.

"Well," Ruji said, "if I must, I must."

With a theatrical show of effort, Shia hauled herself to her feet. "Let me help," she said. "I couldn't live with myself if I made you face this challenge alone." She stretched out on her back in the bed of flowers. She hauled Ashi's limp body on top of hers and hooked her legs around Ashi's hips. "Is that good?" she asked. "Is she in a convenient position for you?"

"Yes, thank you," Ruji said. He knelt behind Ashi. "That's perfect."

He plunged into her. Ashi screamed. She felt Shia's breath on her face, Shia's lips on hers. She felt Ruji enter her, thick and hard. Beside her, she heard Riyan moan.

"I suppose I still have a bit of energy left in me," Vrynn said. He knelt in front of Ashi and Shia.

Hallia knelt beside Ashi and Shia. She twisted her fingers in Ashi's hair and lifted her head up. She opened Ashi's mouth. "How's this?" she said.

"Good," Vrynn said. "Just hold her right there." He slid his erect cock between Ashi's lips.

Shia and Hallia held Ashi in position while the two men spent themselves in her. Ruji came first, thickening inside Ashi and then erupting with a cry. A moment later, Vrynn twitched in Ashi's mouth. Thick salty goo flooded into her mouth, dribbling down her chin and splashing on Shia's face. "Hey!" Shia said. She dragged Ashi down and kissed her. Beside them, Riyan cried out in ecstasy.

"Who's next?" Ruji said.

"I think I might have enough energy for one more go," Tavin said.

Ashi lay atop Shia while Tavin took her from behind. Ashi felt tension build inside her, then she came with a long, soft sigh just moments before Tavin spurted inside her.

"Come on," Riyan said, "I know you all must have some energy left. I want to see more!"

Good-natured grumbling rose from the crowd. Martia crawled over to Ashi and Shia. She grabbed Ashi's hair and pressed her face into her breast. Her nipple hardened under Ashi's tongue. Dekas placed his hands on Ashi's hips. He slid into her, slow but deep, nipples hardening with pleasure. Ashi moaned against Martia.

Riyan slid her fingers between her legs, watching with eyes of reflective silver. Her cheeks flushed. She quivered, moaning with pleasure.

Dekas thrust in a steady rhythm, taking a long leisurely time to reach the peak. He shuddered into a prolonged orgasm, spurting wetly into Ashi. When he finished, he collapsed on the ground, breathing hard. "That's it, I'm done," he panted. "If any of you make it out of here alive, tell my friends I love them."

After that, things went blurry for Ashi. She was aware of people doing more things to her, but she couldn't focus on who or what. Something wet spurted across her face. Fingers and rigid erections invaded her. She lay motionless on top of Shia, helpless to stop any of the things that were happening to her. Through it all, she heard Riyan's cries of ecstasy.

A dark fog rolled over her vision. When it cleared, Riyan knelt over her, hands on her breasts. "You're so lovely when you're helpless," Riyan said. "I think I might enjoy watching you being ravished even more than you enjoyed watching me."

She kissed her way down Ashi's immobile body. The heat of her breath and the soft touch of her lips were a torment, almost unbearable on Ashi's sensitive skin. Then her tongue found Ashi's clit, and soon Ashi came one last time, a sweet, agonizing pleasure that dragged her far from herself and buried her in a deep, still place.

Ashi woke slowly. She rolled over and was surprised to find that her body obeyed her, though it grumbled a bit in the process. She lay naked in a clearing in the center of a forest. All around her, a cluster of people in similar states of undress sprawled on the forest floor.

She climbed laboriously to her feet. Her vision was fuzzy, her movements clumsy and uncoordinated. The evening sun hung low in the sky, sending golden fingers of light through the trees. The willow tree had dropped all its flowers and leaves. Its bare branches hung to the ground. The thorns had vanished from around the periphery of the clearing.

One by one, the others stirred. Ashi wandered among them. She reached down to help Tavin to his feet. He brushed the dirt off his knees.

Memories came to her in hazy, disconnected flashes, dreamlike, as they always did after worshipping the Wild. She frowned, trying to remember everything that had happened. Images surfaced in her mind: coupling with Tavin beneath the willow tree, Hallia whispering something in her ear. They remained fragmented, refusing to coalesce into a whole.

Vrynn looked down at his chest. His tattoos formed blue whorls, curling around each other. "Well, it looks like I had a good time," he said.

"I seem to recall you having a very good time," Ashi said. "More than once, in fact."

Riyan came up behind Ashi and draped an arm around her shoulders. "He's not the only one who had fun," she said. "I think I remember you having a very good time too."

Ashi ran her hands over her body. "Yes, I did, didn't I?" She looked around her. "Where are my clothes?"

"Did we ever figure out who was gatekeeper?" Heran said.

"I believe it was either me or Ashi," Riyan said. "Ashi, what are you doing?"

"Looking for my clothes." She put on her skirt and picked up a handful of tattered scraps of cloth. "I think this used to be my shirt. Which one of you did this?"

"I think that might have been me," Ruji said.

A memory emerged from the fog, Ruji's strong hands on the front of her shirt. "Ah, yes, I think you're right," Ashi said. She ran her hands over his chest. "Did you enjoy it?"

"I'm sure I did," he said.

They made their way back out of the forest, crawling through the openings in the underbrush, then following the spiraling paths toward the entrance. When the paths rejoined, Ashi took Vrynn's hand. Ruji took Vrynn's other hand. Ashi hummed to herself as they went along, enjoying the shafts of sunlight on her skin.

At the fountain, she paused to drink deeply. The water reminded her how hungry she was. Her stomach grumbled.

They all rejoined each other at the place where the main path branched into smaller paths. Riyan came up behind Ashi and wrapped her arms around her. "Boo!" she said. She kissed the back of Ashi's neck.

"Ah, hello!" Ashi said. "Just who I wanted to see. I think you and I should spend some private time together."

"Oh?" Riyan's eyebrows went up. "Sounds lovely. Whatever for?"

"I have a bone to pick with you," Ashi grinned. "I believe you were being particularly mean to me today."

"That doesn't sound like me."

"Nevertheless, I think we should discuss the issue."

"Well, then," Riyan said. She assumed a somber expression. "If we must, we must."

"How mean do I have to be to spend some private time with you?" Tavin asked.

"How mean can you be?"

Tavin grinned. "Mean enough to warrant a stern talking-to. Possibly even a reprimand."

Ashi laughed. "Your offer intrigues me. We'll talk."

3.4

FIVE DAYS LATER, Ashi sat on a large, plush circular cushion in front of the window in a small room high in one of the living towers, looking out over the sweep of the City. A few small clouds scurried across a deep blue sky. In the center of the City, the great ziggurat of the Fiery One reached for the heavens. She could just see little dots moving here and there in the courtyard.

Ashi's space was a jumble of textures, shapes, and colors. The floor was polished blonde wood. Her perfectly square bed was piled high with pillows and blankets in a cacophony of colors. Chairs and cushions lay scattered haphazardly about the room, each a different shape and size. A low wall separated the main space from the shower and bath; on it sat a jumbled assortment of brushes, sponges, and small bottles. A huge floor to ceiling window made up one wall. The other walls were paneled in wood, with small inset shelves that overflowed with everything from physical books with pages that turned to pretty rocks.

Ashi sat curled on a red and white cushion with her feet tucked under her, wearing a simple pair of green shorts and a black shirt of smooth, silky fabric with short sleeves. She held a mug of hot, spicy tea in her hand.

A chime with no discernible source filled the air. A pleasant, equally directionless voice announced, "You have a visitor."

"Who is it?" Ashi said.

"Riyan."

"You could have just told me that," Ashi said. "You could say 'Riyan is here to see you,' instead of telling me I have a visitor and then waiting for me to ask—oh, never mind. Let her in."

The door opened to admit Riyan. She wore a green dress decorated with an image of a willow tree in shimmering colors. Pink flowers bloomed on the branches. Petals swirled from the flowers, falling in a slow animated pattern that moved across the dress. The front descended in a deep V all the way to her navel. A thin silver choker adorned her neck. Silver rings bedecked all her fingers. Her metallic silver hair fell in waves over her shoulders.

"Wow," Ashi said. "You look amazing."

Riyan smiled. "Thank you."

"What brings you by?"

"Well," Riyan said, "I recall you saying something about needing to discuss my conduct the other day." Her face arranged itself into a serious expression. "I hear a rumor that people who are mean to you get a stern talking to, or maybe even a reprimand."

"So you came by to see if you could get a reprimand?"

"I thought we might go dancing first," Riyan said. "Then later we might see if there's time for a reprimand. Who knows? Depending on how the evening goes, I might even be due for some *chastisement.*"

"I don't know who you've been talking to," Ashi said, "but I would never dream of reprimanding anyone."

"Oh, I see. Clearly I am in the wrong place, then. Don't mind me, I'll show myself out."

Ashi laughed. "Oh, no, you're not escaping that easily. You mentioned dancing?"

Twenty minutes later, they stepped into a float tube that carried them from a curved pod track to the ground. Ashi wore a slinky, form-fitting dress in brilliant white with long wing-like panels that fluttered from the sleeves.

Riyan led them to the base of one of the tall towers that made up most of the living space along the edge of the City. The towers rose hundreds of stories from the ground, sleek black monoliths that curved inward toward the City. Viewed from above, Ashi thought, they might look like long tentacles, reaching out toward the ziggurat that marked the precise geometric center of the City.

The party was already going full force when they arrived. A throng of joyous people, all dancing to a silent beat, filled an open-air courtyard at the base of one of those towers. The shield dome had folded down around the party to prevent the sounds within from disturbing those outside.

Ashi felt a tingle as she passed through the nearly invisible shield. Once she was through, the sound washed over her, the noise of over a hundred people reveling to a complex, ever-changing beat.

The wall at the base of the tower had been opened for the occasion. The dance continued inside. More than half the tower's first floor had been converted to a single large space to accommodate the dancers.

Riyan took Ashi's hand. They walked past a tall, slender woman with deep blue skin and long white hair. Ashi stopped for a moment and watched her spin two glowing balls on the ends of fine silver chains. Trails of red and blue smoke emerged from the balls and twisted together around her, forming a spiral that rose high into the air.

At the edge of the courtyard beneath the stars, they walked past a broad, heavyset woman who towered head and shoulders above the rest of the dancers. She wore nothing except a belt around her waist hung with small pouches. Tattoos of the City covered her skin, showing it in different points of its history—the construction of the ziggurat to the Fiery One, the laying of the Garden, the building of the first ever-changing temple of the Lady. Little bolts of lightning rippled through the tattooed sky, flashing across her skin in small bursts of light.

As she danced, sinuous and graceful, she occasionally reached into the pouches at her waist and tossed small pinches of dust into the air. These hung above her head, slowly expanding, forming images of people and landscapes and city scenes that hung for a few moments before dissolving, insubstantial, and floating away like smoke. Ashi watched her in wonder.

"Come on!" Riyan said. "I have a surprise for you." She tugged Ashi into the open hall at the base of the enormous tower.

Twisting, pulsing light moved within the black walls inside the tower, shifting in time with the music. People danced around Ashi and Riyan, singly, in pairs, and in larger groups. Many of the dancers wore intricate clothing with tails that fluttered in loops and whorls around them. Some of the dancers were nude. Others wore only glowing body paint in elaborate designs that moved on their own.

Four large transparent float tubes hugged one wall. Dancers flipped and twirled weightless inside them, dancing in three dimensions. Ashi watched an androgynous figure dance in one of the tubes. They had a long, lean body clad in nothing but two wide strips of long white fabric tied to their ankles. As they danced and tumbled, streamers of cloth whirled around them.

Riyan led Ashi to a platform deep inside the hall where people sat on chairs and cushions watching the revelry. A shield generator cast a faintly glowing wall that separated the space from the main dance area, muting the sound just enough to make conversation possible.

More people sat along a long counter, drinking multicolored liquids from fluted crystal glasses as they watched the spectacle. A whole row of black rectangles lined the top of the counter.

"Wait here." Riyan went over to the counter and touched one of the Providers. Ashi watched the dancers in the float tubes. In one of them, two women with pale skin and short black hair danced nude, tumbling and somersaulting over one another. Ashi wondered how they did it without colliding.

Riyan came back with two slender vials made of curved glass, bent in spirals that wrapped around each other like corkscrews. She disentangled them and handed one to Ashi. "Here!"

Ashi examined the vial. Little motes of red dust swirled in the clear liquid. They sparkled in the light.

"What is it?"

"You've never tried it? The worshippers of the Blesser use it. It's called the Blessing of Union. I gave myself to the Blesser for three days to receive this gift. I want to share it with you."

"I'm honored," Ashi said. "What does it do?"

Riyan flashed a mischievous smile. "Drink!"

Ashi removed the teardrop-shaped stopper from the vial and drained the contents in one gulp. The liquid tasted sweet and slightly peppery. Riyan winked at her, then drank the contents of her own vial.

"I didn't know you worshipped the Blesser," Ashi said.

"I have for a long time. I've only just started worshipping the Wild as well. He's fun, but the Blesser is where my heart is."

"Do you plan to compete to be the Sacrifice for the Wild?" Ashi said. "Ooh!" Her vision blurred. For a moment, she felt a powerful sense of being outside herself. Then it cleared, and she was back in her body where she belonged.

"I do!" Riyan said.

"Why do you want to be Sacrifice?"

"Why do you?"

"Being the center of all that energy, walking down the ramp with all the people in the cages...mmm," Ashi said. "It sounds so intense...oh!" She reeled. The world spun for a moment.

"Exactly!" Riyan said. "Doesn't it sound wonderful? Let's sit down." She took Ashi's hand. "It takes a little while to get your bearings if you've never done this Blessing before."

She guided Ashi to a large, deeply cushioned chair covered in soft blue fabric with a good view of the dancers. Ashi plopped down gracelessly. Riyan sat in a smaller chair next to her. Beside them, on a long sofa covered in burgundy velvet, three people writhed naked together. Sighs and moans drifted above the muted music.

Ashi had that momentary sense of being outside her body again. Riyan smiled. "Do you feel it?"

"I feel something. What is it?"

Riyan slipped a hand inside her own dress and squeezed her breast. Ashi gasped. "It feels like you're touching me!"

"The Blessing of Union lets me feel what you feel, and you feel what I feel," Riyan said. She leaned forward, grinding her hips on the corner of her chair.

Ashi shuddered. "I feel something inside me!"

"You feel something inside me," Riyan said. "I came prepared." She touched one of her rings with the tip of her thumb. Ashi felt a phantom thing-that-was-not-there start to vibrate. Her eyelids fluttered. She grasped the edge of the chair and moaned.

Riyan smiled. The vibration vanished.

Ashi panted. She had a brief, disorienting instant of feeling like she was in two places at the same time. "You did come prepared."

"Come dance with me!" Riyan said.

"I don't know if I can!"

"You'll be fine." She took Ashi's hand and pulled her through the shield into the noise and chaos of the whirling throng.

Ashi let the music wash over her. She felt Riyan's hand in hers, and at the same time, her hand in Riyan's. As she moved, she felt Riyan move as well—the swish of her hips, the way she leaned forward into the crowd. Ashi stumbled a few times before she learned to let her body do the walking without thinking too much about it.

Riyan spun her around and pulled her close. With every move, Ashi felt the buzzing thing shift inside Riyan. Before long, she moaned openly.

Riyan whirled Ashi around and caught her from behind. "I feel how turned on you are," she murmured.

"Oh?" Ashi said. "Then what are you going to do about it?" She twirled away from Riyan and slipped into the press of dancing bodies.

Riyan smirked. She reached up and tweaked her own nipples. Ashi stumbled and almost fell, her hands flying protectively to cover her breasts. Riyan winked at her.

Ashi fled through the dancing throng. Riyan chased after her. A dancer whirled through the space between them, a tall, nude, pale-skinned woman with bright red hair slicked up in a mohawk. Her fingernails and toenails were the same red as her hair.

The woman spun between them, eyes closed, lost in the rapture of the dance. As she twirled, Ashi saw that the strip of red hair that crested her head ran down the nape of her neck and from there down her spine, a wide stripe of red fur that grew from her smooth white skin. It ended at her tailbone. A long, sinuous tail, covered with the same red fur, extended from the base of her spine and waved through the air behind her.

Ashi's breath caught. Riyan captured her with both arms. "Gotcha!" she said. "Where do you think you're going?"

Ashi relaxed into Riyan's arms. "Nowhere, now that you've got me." She leaned close. She had a brief moment of disorientation as she felt her breath on Riyan's lips and Riyan's breath on hers. Riyan pulled away, laughing.

"Tease!" Ashi said.

"Oh, you have no idea." Riyan touched her ring. The object throbbed powerfully within her. Ashi gasped.

"There's nowhere you can go to get away from me," Riyan said. She slipped a hand inside her dress and twisted her nipple. Ashi shivered. "You might as well just accept it."

"By the Eight, you're delightful," Ashi said.

"Does that mean you're going to stop trying to run away and dance with me?" Riyan said. "Or am I going to have to torment you some more?" She slipped a hand inside her dress again.

"Okay! Okay!" Ashi laughed. "Anything but that!"

Riyan left the round, heavy object inside her buzzing at a low, steady speed while they danced. Ripples of shared pleasure bounced between the two of them. Ashi found herself floating somewhere in the space between them, not always sure which body belonged to her.

Eventually, long after the moons had set, Riyan took both of Ashi's hands. Her skin glowed with sweat. "I'm tired!" she said. "Take me home."

They left the party. As they stepped through the shield, the noise and bustle vanished into quiet peacefulness. A pair of dronelights zipped out of the dark sky to light their way. Riyan waved one of them away. "Shoo!" she said. "She's with me."

Ashi led Riyan to a float tube that carried them up to the pod track. A pod pulled over for them, all sleek black curves, its doors lifting open as it stopped. They crawled inside, giggling.

Ashi moved to kiss Riyan. Riyan put her finger over Ashi's lips, still giggling. "Shh," she said. "Close your eyes."

Ashi closed her eyes. She felt hands on her breasts...no, on Riyan's breasts. Riyan was touching herself, sliding her hands over her own skin. The buzzing vibration intensified inside her. Ashi felt herself clench around something that wasn't really there.

Riyan ran her fingertips over her own nipples. Ashi moaned. "Your nipples are sensitive!"

"So I hear," Riyan said. She turned up the vibration. Ashi ground her hips against the soft cushion beneath her and moaned.

"You like that?" Riyan said.

"Mmm," Ashi said. She spread her legs and slid her fingers against her clit through the thin fabric of her dress. This time, it was Riyan's turn to gasp.

"Ha! Two can play at that game!" Ashi said.

"Oh, you think so?" Riyan touched her ring. The object inside her buzzed faster. Ashi clutched the edge of the seat, panting. Riyan caressed her nipples. Ashi's body reverberated with the sensation.

Ashi slid her hands over her breasts and squeezed tightly. Riyan gasped. She touched her ring. The buzzing within her became a deep, raspy vibration, alternating between fast and slow. Ashi let out a cry. They both came together, each wrapped in the other's orgasms, filling the small pod with their cries.

The pod coasted to a stop. The doors opened. Ashi looked at Riyan, panting. "That...that was..."

"I know," Riyan said. Her cheeks flushed. Her eyes shone.

Ashi led her into the tower. A moment later, they were back in Ashi's quarters. "When I said, 'take me home,'" Riyan said, "I wondered if you would assume I meant my place or yours—oof!" Ashi pinned her to the wall and kissed her, marveling at the sensation of simultaneously kissing and being kissed. Her fingers found Riyan's nipples. She caressed them and shuddered at the sensation.

"What are you going to do to me?" Riyan asked.

"What would you like me to do to you?"

"Whatever you want," Riyan said. She smiled. "I like being... accommodating. Why do you think I worship the Blesser?"

Ashi wrestled Riyan onto the bed. She pounced atop her and bit the side of her neck, feeling phantom teeth on her own skin. Riyan purred.

Ashi grabbed the edges of Riyan's dress and pulled. It tore. Riyan wore nothing beneath it.

Ashi wrapped her lips around Riyan's nipple. Riyan touched her ring. The vibration kicked into high gear. Ashi bucked her hips with a muffled cry. She straightened just long enough to pull off her own dress, then she was back on top of Riyan, exploring her with fingers, lips, and tongue.

She felt every touch on Riyan's body as though it was a touch on her own, felt every ripple of pleasure that curled through Riyan's body echoed in her own. Riyan lay still beneath her, eyes closed, a dreamy smile on her face.

Ashi lingered for a long time over Riyan, mapping out every square inch of her, discovering all the secret pleasures of her skin. She buried her face between Riyan's legs, running her tongue over Riyan's clit, feeling Riyan's pleasure mounting. She caressed Riyan's body, sliding her hands up over Riyan's breasts. She came when Riyan did.

When it was over, Ashi flopped panting onto her back. "Wow," she said. "That was really intense."

"Oh, darling," Riyan said, "you have no idea."

Riyan rolled over atop Ashi, straddling her face. She bent down, placing her own face between Ashi's legs. Her tongue flicked over Ashi's clit. Ashi did the same, running her tongue in small circles, feeling Riyan's pleasure at the same time as she felt her own.

The orgasms came on them fast and strong. Riyan touched her ring at the moment they both peaked. Ashi screamed. She clutched desperately at Riyan with both hands. Riyan kept her face between Ashi's legs, finding all the places where Ashi was too sensitive, guided there unerringly by their shared experience.

Ashi squealed. Riyan held her fast, tongue flicking over her unbearably sensitive clit. The persistent vibration kept going, made all the worse because it was not really in her, so she had no way to escape it. She giggled and laughed and whimpered and begged, but Riyan would not stop. Eventually, a wall of darkness swallowed her up.

3.5

ASHI WOKE THE next morning with a building tension coiling through her body. Sunlight slanted in through the window. She barely had enough time to realize what was happening before she exploded into orgasm.

When it faded, she looked around the disaster of her room, panting. Cushions and bed covers lay flung haphazardly about. The torn scraps of Riyan's clothing still hung forlorn from the edge of the bed. Ashi had slept diagonally, twisted up in the sheets.

She blinked. Riyan watched her, nude, from one of the cushions. Her fingers moved idly between her legs.

"Was—was that—" Ashi said.

"Me? Yes. Good morning!" Riyan tweaked her nipple. Ashi shuddered.

"How long will we stay connected?"

"A full day. We have until a couple hours after sunset."

"Wow."

"Indeed. The Blesser is generous with her gifts." Riyan rose and stepped into the shower.

Ashi jumped at the sensation of phantom water pouring over her skin. Riyan laughed. "It's interesting, isn't it?" She slid soapy hands over her body. "Would you like to come again?"

Ashi closed her eyes, breathing hard. "I'm not sure if I can."

"I'm not sure you have a choice," Riyan said. "Here, let me show you." She slipped one finger over her clit. Her other hand teased her nipple.

Ashi buried herself beneath the blankets, but there was no way to escape the sensation. She cried out as she came, her body locked in resonance with Riyan's.

Riyan stepped out of the shower. She summoned a towel from the Provider and dried herself vigorously. Ashi squirmed on the bed. Riyan smiled. She slid a finger over her clit and laughed with delight at Ashi's gasp.

While Ashi showered, Riyan amused herself by running her finger across her ring, causing the vibrator within her to speed up and slow down. By the time Ashi was out and dry, she could not stop moaning or rocking her hips.

"You—you—" Ashi sputtered. "You enjoy teasing me!"

Riyan leaned back with a smile. "You only just now noticed? Come here. Let me show you something."

"What's that?"

"I'm not going to tell you!" Riyan said. "I want to show you. Sit down." She patted the bed next to her.

Ashi sat beside her. Riyan tore a strip off the dress she'd worn the night before and wrapped it around Ashi's eyes. "What's your favorite sweet thing?" she asked.

"Strawberries and cream. Why?"

Ashi heard the Provider open. A moment later, her mouth was filled with the taste of strawberries, but subtly different, a complex flavor with just a hint of smokiness.

"Is that how you taste them?"

"Yes." Riyan touched Ashi's lips. Ashi parted them. Riyan placed a strawberry drenched in cream between Ashi's lips.

"Mm," Riyan said. "You taste things a little bit sweeter than I do." She licked the cream from Ashi's lips.

Ashi felt the disorienting, two-places-at-once sensation of both kissing and being kissed. She tasted the cream that Riyan licked up. "You're right," she said. "It's not quite as sweet when you do it."

"I wonder if that's true for everything," Riyan said. "What else do you like?"

Riyan spent the next hour calling forth all kinds of things from the Provider—chocolates, cheeses, fruits, custards. She sampled them herself, making Ashi guess what they were. She fed them to Ashi. Ashi marveled at the differences, sometimes subtle, sometimes profound, in the way they each perceived them.

When Riyan tired of that game, she played another. She summoned textures from the Provider: soft fur, smooth silk, coarse stones, rough burlap. She caressed herself with them. Ashi sighed and moaned and squeaked at the barrage of ever-changing sensations.

She poured oils over herself, running her hands across her body. Ashi writhed, squirming under a phantom caress that felt so real. She touched Ashi, always knowing exactly where and how to bring forth the greatest response. She brought Ashi to the edge of orgasm again and again, sometimes by touching Ashi and sometimes by touching herself, always stopping at precisely the moment Ashi was certain that this time, she would surely come. After more than an hour of this torment. Ashi sobbed with frustration. She writhed, begging Riyan for release.

Riyan tore strips of fabric from the ruins of her dress. She used them to bind Ashi's arms at her side. She tied Ashi's ankles and wound a strip of cloth over her eyes. "There," she said. "Squirm all you want. It won't help you."

She sat on the cushion beside the bed and caressed herself with lazy strokes. Ashi twisted and turned on the bed, bound and blindfolded, feeling Riyan's body beneath Riyan's hands.

Riyan started the vibrator running with a low, throbbing pulse. Ashi wept tears of frustration. "How can you keep doing this to me?" she wailed. "I know you're just as frustrated as I am!"

"I have explored many religions and worshipped many gods," Riyan said, "but the one I always find myself coming back to is the Blesser. Those of us who serve her get used to sex without a goal. The orgasm itself isn't as important for us." She ran her hand over her breast, pausing when she reached her nipple to give it a small tweak. Ashi whimpered.

"Oh, I like that," Riyan said. "You're not as sensitive as I am. Do you suppose I could make you come just by playing with my nipples?"

"Please!" Ashi said.

Riyan laughed. "You're already begging, after only a couple of hours? How in the world will you manage if you are chosen as Sacrifice to the Wild?"

"Oh, and I suppose you think you'd do a better job of...nnngh!" Riyan pinched both her nipples, cutting Ashi off mid-thought.

"You were saying?" Riyan said sweetly.

"It's not supposed to be easy!" Ashi cried. "It's a test of your devotion to the gods!"

"How devoted are you? Devoted enough to bring the blessing of the Wild to all the worshippers?"

"Yes!"

"Then a little thing like this should be easy, I'm sure," Riyan said. She flicked her ring. The thing within her burst into powerful vibrations. Ashi shrieked.

The vibration stopped. Riyan panted, glassy-eyed. Ashi whimpered softly. "Whew," Riyan said. "Almost went too far there. This is fun!"

"Fun?" Ashi said. "I almost hope you get chosen as Sacrifice, just so I can watch."

"And feel?" Riyan said. She laughed. "If I am chosen, would you take the Blessing of Union with me?"

"I don't know if they'd allow it," Ashi said.

"If they did. Would you do it? Feel what I'm feeling? Share in my suffering?"

"Only if you would do the same thing if I am chosen," Ashi said.

"I accept your offer."

"I mean, hypothetically speaking," Ashi added hastily.

"Hypothetically? Oh, no. A bargain is a bargain. If the Priests permit it, we will take the Blessing of Union should one of us be chosen as Sacrifice."

"I didn't mean—"

Ashi never finished the sentence. With a flick of her fingertip, Riyan turned the vibrations as high as they would go. She ran her fingers over her nipples, and they both came in a crescendo of ecstasy.

3.6

"This is an unprecedented request. Never in the history of the Wild has any worshipper made such a petition."

Riyan shifted uncomfortably in her chair, pinned in place by High Priest Yahil's gaze.

Yahil cut an imposing figure. He was short but powerfully built, broad-shouldered and barrel-chested. His brown hair formed four rows of spikes along his skull. He wore nothing but a short red kilt and a leather belt hung with pockets and pouches. Stripes reminiscent of a tiger's decorated his arms and legs, alternating black and deep orange. Thick muscles rippled beneath the tattoos.

He sat on a low podium in an arc-shaped room in a small circular building a short distance from the amphitheater where the annual sacrifice to the Wild was held. The room was the closest thing to an administrative center the priests and priestesses of the Wild had.

Yahil fixed Riyan with bright yellow eyes that had catlike slits for pupils. Riyan blushed and shifted again.

"I know, High Priest Yahil," she said. "But just think! Sharing the experience of the Sacrifice! What better way can there be to understand the blessing of the Wild?"

"You could be chosen as Sacrifice," Yahil said.

"Of course. But vicariously living through the experience is a tremendous show of devotion, isn't it?"

Yahil shook his head. "Being chosen as Sacrifice is not a spectator sport. If anyone who wants it can have the experience of living through someone else's Sacrifice, then it ceases to have any meaning."

"I am competing to be chosen as Sacrifice myself!" Riyan said. "As is Ashi." She wrapped her arm around Ashi, who was doing her best to look small and inconspicuous. "So, in a sense it's like having two Sacrifices in one year!"

"What does the High Cleric of the Blesser have to say about this?" Yahil said.

"I haven't spoken to her yet. I thought it was important to get your opinion first."

"How diplomatic of you. Don't you mostly serve the Blesser?"

"I do, High Priest. Though I find the Wild does have a certain allure."

That brought a smile to Yahil's face, which might have been reassuring if it weren't for the pointed teeth. "Indeed he does." He leaned forward and regarded Ashi and Riyan over steepled fingers. His strange, catlike eyes bored through them. Ashi held her breath, not sure if she was hoping for a yes or a no.

Finally, he said, "I will confer with the other priests and priestesses. In the meantime, I suggest you talk to the High Cleric of the Blesser—Jiialen, is it?—to see what she has to say."

Riyan bowed. "Of course."

"Is there anything else you need?"

"No, High Priest," Ashi said. "Thank you for your time." She stood and took Riyan by the hand. With a bow toward Yahil, she turned and fled.

Outside the office, Riyan broke into a grin. "He's going to say yes."

"How do you know?"

"Did you see the look on his face?" Riyan's eyes glowed. "He wants to watch us suffer together."

"If you say so. What do you think the High Cleric will say about this idea of yours?"

Riyan took her arm. "Don't you mean this idea of ours?" She winked. "Let's find out!"

Half an hour later, they met with Jiialen, the High Cleric of the Blesser, in a small, cozy room with thick rugs and dark wood paneling. She greeted them warmly, her open, friendly face beaming, and bade them to take off their shoes. She invited them to sit in soft cushions around a low table while she bustled about preparing tea for them—made from leaves in hot water, not called up from a Provider. She set the tea before them in delicate cups.

Jiialen was a short woman with long black hair tied back with a silver clip engraved with a floral design. Her simple blue shift dress left her arms and legs bare. "Riyan, it's a pleasure to see you," she said after she had set out the tea. "Your service last week was exemplary, as always."

Riyan bowed. "Thank you, Cleric." She raised the small, fragile teacup to her lips. "This is my…um, friend Ashi. She is a worshipper of the Wild."

"As are you now, if I remember correctly," Jiialen said.

"Yes. I am planning to compete in the selection for this year's Sacrifice to the Wild. We both are."

"Hmm." Jiialen regarded the two of them over her cup. "So, you two are adversaries?"

"It's more complicated than that. Which brings me to why we're here. We would like to ask the Blesser for a favor."

"A favor involving competition to be Sacrifice for the Wild?" Jiialen raised an eyebrow. "This ought to be interesting. Please do go on."

"Well…" Riyan blushed. "I thought…that is, we had this idea, see, that…"

"Don't be so modest," Ashi interjected. "It was entirely your idea. The credit belongs to you."

"Okay," Riyan said. "I had an idea. We—I—thought, if one of us is chosen as the Sacrifice, then the other could maybe share in the experience."

"Ah." A smile lit up Jiialen's face. "And so, if I may fill in the spaces where words have not been said, you would like to receive the Blessing of Union so that both of you might participate, in a manner of speaking."

"Yes!" Riyan said.

"I see. What an intriguing idea." Jiialen's smile turned positively wolfish. "And in exchange for this gift, you are offering…?"

"That's why we're here," Riyan said. "To learn what the Blesser might find appropriate."

"On the surface, it seems a simple thing," Jiialen said. "An offering of three days' service is traditional for those who want the Blessing of Union. I recall you did this recently yourself, Riyan."

Riyan nodded. Beside her, Ashi grinned at the memory. Jiialen's eyebrow raised again.

"But to use the Blessing in so unusual a way is not a simple thing," Jiialen went on. "Have the priests of the Wild consented to this?"

"We've talked to Yahil," Riyan said. "He's thinking about it."

"Ah. And, of course, you're assuming that one of you will be chosen. I don't know a great deal about the worship of the Wild, but I recall that the selection for Sacrifice can be quite competitive."

"Well…" Ashi said.

"Hmm?" Jiialen said.

"I wouldn't call the selection competitive, exactly," Ashi said. "Well, I mean, it is. There are usually a lot of people who are at least theoretically competing, sure. But it's open to anyone who has ever participated in one of the great rituals, and the selection process is quite a lot of fun, so…"

"I see you share Riyan's tendency to leave the most important parts in the space between the words. So, you're saying that many of those who compete, aren't necessarily competing to win?"

"Yes."

"But you are."

Ashi nodded vigorously. "Oh, yes."

"And Riyan? Do you genuinely wish to be sacrificed to the Wild?"

Riyan's eyes glowed. "Very much."

"Both of you want this experience enough to share in it if the other is chosen?"

"Yes!" Riyan said.

Ashi hesitated. "Yes," she said.

"And you want the Blesser's help." She sat back, looking at them with an expression somewhere between amused and raptorial. It sat unexpectedly comfortably on her round face. The moment stretched to the breaking point. At last, she said, "Very well. Here's what I will offer. After the Selection, whichever of you is not chosen as Sacrifice will serve the Blesser for five consecutive days. Three days for the Blessing, and two for using it in such an unusual and uniquely intimate way."

"Thank you, High Priestess," Riyan said.

"What if neither of us is chosen?" Ashi said.

"I like your friend," Jiialen said to Riyan. "She spots the things unsaid. If neither of you is chosen, or if the priests of the Wild decide not to permit it, then both of you will serve the Blesser for five consecutive days. At the end of that time, you will each receive the Blessing of Union, to use as you see fit. Do you agree?"

"I do," Riyan said without hesitation. Ashi hesitated. Riyan poked her in the ribs with her elbow.

"I agree," Ashi said. "Though I don't know what serving the Blesser entails, exactly."

"Oh, I am confident if you're willing to be Sacrifice to the Wild, it will be no problem," Jiialen said.

Ashi turned to Riyan. "Is that true?"

"Err," Riyan said, "sure. No problem."

They left the meeting with Ashi wondering, not for the first time, what it was she had just agreed to. Jiialen's vulpine grin followed them out.

3.7

A SOFT CHIME woke Ashi. A directionless, melodious voice followed it. "You have a visitor."

Vrynn untangled himself from Ashi's legs. His tattoos covered his chest in soft green loops. The covers, half on and half off the bed, twisted around both of them in a knotted mess. Pillows lay strewn about the small living unit. Ashi's shirt, or what was left of it, had ended up scattered in at least three places on the floor. "Who is it?" he said.

Ashi whacked him in the chest. "Hush! I'm trying to teach it to tell me without asking."

"Riyan," said the disembodied voice.

"Send her in," Ashi said.

Ruji crawled out from beneath the covers. "Riyan? You've been seeing rather a lot of her lately."

"I've been enjoying rather a lot of her lately," Ashi smirked.

Ruji crawled across Vrynn and Ashi, pausing only long enough to give each a kiss. He stumbled naked to the Provider. "Coffee, black, sweet, and for the love of the Eight, please make it fast," he said. "What time is it?"

"Six twenty-seven in the morning," the directionless voice replied.

The door opened. "Ashi! Come qui—oh, hey, I'm sorry, I didn't know you had guests. Hey, guys!"

"Hey, Riyan!" Vrynn said. Ruji waved.

"I tried to message you, but you weren't receiving."

"I was—" Ashi waved her hand in the air. "Occupied. What's up?"

"A new forest has appeared! It's time for the Selection!"

Ruji and Vrynn stared at each other. Ashi sat bolt upright. Her sleepiness fled. "How long ago?"

"About half an hour."

"Where?"

"Just south of the Quickener's Garden."

By the time she'd finished speaking, Ashi was already standing beneath the shower.

The pod transit station closest to the forest was jammed with people on their way to visit the Fountain. Ashi fidgeted as they pushed their way through the crowd. "Remind me to always accept messages from you," she told Riyan. "It would be so ironic if, after all this, neither one of us was selected as Sacrifice because we didn't make it in time. Do you think Jiialen would still expect us to serve the Blesser anyway?"

"Oh yeah," Riyan said.

"Well, it's only five days, right? I mean, you said it wasn't that big a deal, right?"

"Yeah, about that," Riyan said. "I may have understated things just a little bit. You know, in the spirit of mutual agreement."

Ashi stopped dead in her tracks. "How bad is five days of service to the Blesser?"

"Let's just say being Sacrifice to the Wild would be easier."

"You—"

"Yes?"

"What have you got me into?" Ashi demanded.

"Nothing, as long as you just remember to do one thing," Riyan said.

"What's that?"

"Move quickly." She grinned at Ashi. "Come on!"

They pushed through the crowd at the bottom of the float tube and headed along a curved path through a park festooned with yellow and red flowers. The path brought them to the top of a large hill in a series of back-and-forth switchbacks.

From the top, they looked down into a bowl-shaped valley. A ring-shaped forest of ancient trees stood where only hours ago there had been nothing but grass. Three enormous trees, breathtaking in their size and width, rose from a large clearing in the center of the forest. Ashi could just make out a complex web of bridges, rope ladders, stairs, and platforms lacing through the trees.

Ashi sighed with relief. A dense row of large thorns still surrounded the forest. A crowd of people waited on the grass just outside the forest's edge, forming a loose, chaotic semicircle around High Priest Yahil. An even larger crowd had formed on the top of the ridge looking down into the valley. The selection ritual for the Wild always attracted an audience.

Ashi raced down the hill. The others followed more sedately. She reached the bottom out of breath.

"...who has ever participated in the Ritual of Sacrifice is free to participate in the Selection," Yahil said. "Ah, Ashi, I had wondered if you'd decided to sit this year out. I'm glad you made it. Now then, those who wish to compete for the role of Sacrifice, step forward."

In typical Wild fashion, the crowd didn't step so much as swarm forward. High Priest Yahil walked to a round silver tray, its lip embossed with images of wild animals, that floated in mid-air about waist high. A large number of small vials of different colors and shapes sat on the tray in five spirals that curved out from the center.

"The Wild offers his gifts to those who would be considered for Sacrifice," he said. His voice boomed over the crowd. "May he guide you in your choice."

One by one, the people vying for Sacrifice chose a vial from the tray. Riyan leaned toward Ashi. "We missed the whole preamble," she said. "What's the story here?"

"We each choose one of the vials," Ashi said. "Each one has different effects. Some of them might make you floaty, or cause you to hallucinate, or make you really horny...well, actually, all of them do that. But each one causes a different effect, and you're never quite sure what you're getting. So, you choose one, and hope for the best."

"We have no idea which one does what?"

"Nope," Ashi said. "That's the whole point. You're placing yourself in the hands of the Wild."

"Is it just random?"

"Not exactly," Ashi said. "The Wild knows more about you than you know about yourself. He knows your favorite color. He knows how you make choices, everything. He creates the vials accordingly."

"You're saying he knows which vial we'll choose?"

Ashi laughed. "No. Well, I don't think so. But he can influence the choice."

"What if I know that the Wild is trying to influence me, and I make a choice that I wouldn't normally make? Like choosing my least favorite color?"

"I reckon the Wild would know that about you too."

"Aha! But what if I know that he knows that about me, so I account for that, and choose my favorite color, knowing that he would expect me to choose my least favorite color?"

Ashi shook her head. "You can drive yourself crazy trying to outsmart a god." She stepped up to the tray. "I just hope I choose better than I did last time."

She reached out and, without hesitation, selected a jeweled bottle of deep turquoise. Yahil bowed to her. "Good luck," he said.

Riyan stepped up to the floating tray. She paused for a long time, deep in thought. About a third of the vials had already been taken, leaving gaps in the spiral design. She reached for a tall purple bottle with a flower-shaped stopper, then changed her mind. She picked up a short, wide vial of yellow crystal cut in facets. She set it back down, then reached for a lavender vial shaped like a swan. High Priest Yahil watched her with open curiosity, making no effort to hurry her.

She took a deep breath, then closed her eyes and snatched a vial at random. It was shaped a bit like an antique oil lamp, made of dark green glass topped with a round stopper with a tiny bird perched atop it, wings spread. Clutching her prize, she hurried over to Ashi. "What now?"

"Strip," Ashi said. She pulled off her dress. "The vial is full of oil. Rub it all over yourself. You'll start to feel it pretty quickly. Then we head into the forest. The Sacrifice is the first person to make it to the center, climb to the top of the tallest tree, and ring the bell up top." She uncapped her vial and held it beneath Riyan's nose. "Do you smell anything?"

Riyan sniffed. "Not really. A little bit spicy, maybe. It's very faint."

"Once you've accepted the Gift, that smell will not seem so faint anymore. It will have quite a strong effect on you."

"What will it do?"

"It makes you go insane with lust." Ashi grinned at Riyan's expression. "It's hard to focus on getting to the top of the tree when you're out of your head and everyone around you wants to leap on you and ravish you. Every now and then, someone who didn't really want to be Sacrifice makes it to the top, just to get away from everyone else, and well…that's the chance you take by being here. Gosh, did I not tell you all the details of the Selection? I'm so sorry about that." A hot flash swept over her, followed by a wave of dizziness. "Whew!" she said. "Careful, it comes on fast."

Riyan stripped off her skirt. When she was nude, she spread the oil over herself. "What now?"

"Now?" A short, powerfully built woman with long black hair looked up from spreading oil on her body to regard Riyan with a quizzical expression.

"Now we wait, of course! When the thorns go down, we go in. Didn't you do any research?"

"Well..." Riyan gave an embarrassed smile. "I've been a bit busy." She glanced at Ashi. "A lot busy, actually."

Ashi looked up at the woman. "Jannon? Is that you?" Her eyes swept Jannon's body. "This is a new look."

Jannon grinned. "I figured I've participated in the Ritual every year for the last five years, might as well throw my hat in the ring to be Sacrifice." She looked down at herself. "You like? I still haven't quite gotten used to it."

"Does the Sacrifice have to be a woman?" Riyan asked.

"Not as such, no," Jannon said. "but it helps. It's a lot to take in a woman's body. In a man's body? Even I'm not that big a glutton for punishment. Most people who are chosen, whether they compete at a man or a woman, will change to a...more accommodating form for the Sacrifice."

"Ha!" Camit paused oiling himself to give Jannon a lopsided smile. "Most people, perhaps, but not everyone. If I win, I'm staying this way, thank you very much. I *like* this body."

"Suit yourself," Jannon said. "The Wild is totally okay if you want to make things harder on yourself." She bared pointed teeth at him. "Just so you know, if you're chosen, I'm going back to my old body for the sacrifice."

"Bring it!" Camit said. He winked at Ashi.

Riyan staggered. "Whoa!" she said. "I feel...I feel..."

"Yes?" Ashi said.

Riyan grabbed Ashi and kissed her hard, tongue pressing against her lips, seeking entrance. Her body pressed warm and slick against Ashi's.

A wave of dizziness surged through Ashi, followed by a hot, desperate longing. Her skin flushed. Her fingertips tingled. Camit pressed himself against Riyan from behind. Riyan ground back into him. She cried out as he entered her. Ashi inhaled the cry, kissing Riyan's lips over and over.

A crackling sound filled the air. The thick vines retreated, uncoiling, pulling themselves into the ground. The crowd roared. People streamed into the forest from all directions.

"Oh!" Riyan said. "I think...uh! I think we should...we should..."

"We should what?" Ashi said. "We should wait until you come?" She took Riyan's lower lip between her teeth. Her fingers caressed Riyan's nipples.

Riyan squirmed. Her eyelids fluttered. "I'm—" she gasped. "I'm going... I'm going to..."

Camit withdrew. Riyan sagged in Ashi's arms. Camit laughed. "See you at the top!" he said. With that, he raced toward the forest.

Riyan made small whimpering sounds. Her hips gyrated in empty air.

"What's wrong?" Ashi said. "Did he stop too soon? You poor thing. Let's go! We have a tree to climb…oh!" For a moment, streamers of light danced at the edge of her vision. The smell of Riyan and the warmth of her body filled the air around her. Ashi shivered. Her body flushed. "I—we should go."

"But—" Riyan shivered. She wrapped her arms around Ashi.

The scent of sweet-smelling oil filled Ashi's senses. Wild lust spread heat through her body. "I—I want—" She shook her head. Little sparkles danced in the corners of her eyes. With some difficulty, she unwrapped from Riyan. She felt a pang of separation as their bodies parted. She took Riyan's hand and made for the forest.

They were nearly the last to reach the line of trees. The forest swallowed them. From somewhere behind them came sounds of pleasure from people who couldn't even make it into the newly-appeared woodland before their desire, fueled by whatever vial they had chosen, overtook them.

Ashi followed a dirt trail beneath the canopy of trees. She was acutely aware of Riyan's hand in hers, the warmth of Riyan's skin, the subtle scent that ignited a fire within her. Sunlight filtered through the leaves. The air around her danced and shimmered.

The forest formed a ring around the wide clearing in the center. It was laced through with a confusing maze of narrow paths. Ashi quickly realized she was lost. The paths forked, curved, and twisted back on themselves, leading Ashi in circles. The dense canopy overhead prevented them from using the tall trees in the middle of the clearing as a guide. Other competitors, naked and dazed, wandered the paths, just as confused as they were.

A tall, muscular man whose crimson eyes sported cross-shaped pupils ran out from a narrow, overgrown trail toward Ashi and Riyan. White hair streaked with red and orange fell almost to his knees. His face was a mask of crazed need, without the slightest trace of reason.

He collided with Ashi, sending her tumbling backward into Riyan. Riyan flew with a squeak back against a tree. The man grabbed Ashi by her arms, pinning her against Riyan, holding them both against the tree. His rigid cock trembled, a bead of white fluid already collecting at the tip.

Ashi came the moment he entered her. Riyan wrapped her arms tightly around both of them. Her teeth sank into Ashi's neck. Ashi squirmed and writhed. Thousands of tiny points of light exploded all around her.

Riyan's lips burned like fire against Ashi's skin. The man in front of her was a raging inferno, blazing hot against her skin. Another orgasm flared inside her. Her scream changed in mid-stream, becoming a moan. Sparks danced before her eyes.

"Yes!" Riyan told him over Ashi's shoulder. "Do it! Take her! Pleasure yourself with her!"

The man let out a groan. His body stiffened. Ashi felt a wet splat deep within her, burning hot.

He released Ashi and pulled away without a word. Ashi mewled at the sudden withdrawal. She wobbled. The man staggered off down the path, as unsteady as she was.

The wet heat tingled inside her. She felt something drip from her, sliding down her leg, burning her skin as it went. The tingle grew, radiating up through her from the space between her legs. Ashi shook her head. It refused to clear.

The sensation rose. Her skin felt prickly. A line of heat ascended, crackling like static on her skin. When it reached her breasts, her nipples hardened. Still it crawled up her body, to her shoulders, her neck, her head...

A howling maelstrom blew all reason away. She felt lost inside a whirling vortex of need and desire. She watched, a powerless observer behind her own eyes, as she twisted around, grabbed Riyan by the shoulders, pushed her up against the tree, kissed her...

"Oh!" Riyan said. "What's gotten into you?"

Ashi shook her head. The fog of frenzy did not clear. "I—I don't know, I—there's something in—in his—" She grabbed Riyan's shoulders tightly and kissed her again.

Riyan pushed Ashi away. "We need to move!" Ashi made a small whimpering sound.

"Come on!" Riyan said. She grabbed Ashi's hand and dragged her down the path.

3.8

ASHI STRUGGLED AGAINST the tornado of need. She wanted to grab Riyan and pull her down on the ground, but some tiny thought nagged at her. There was something else she needed to do. Something important, something that required her attention. Clouds rolled in over her mind.

They passed people writhing together in every combination imaginable, standing up, leaning against the trees, lying on the ground. Sighs and screams rose all around them. People coupled in a frenzy, minds bent on nothing but raw animal sex. Hands slid over oiled flesh.

Ashi felt heat on her face. A tall man with long brown hair tied back in a braid stood by the side of the path, kissing another man with close-cropped black hair frosted with white at the ends. A woman with pale skin knelt at their feet, her shining silver hair flecked with tiny motes of bright colors. She had the taller man's erect shaft in her mouth. Her hand played between her legs.

Ashi staggered. She took a step toward the three of them, visions of soft skin and hard cocks dancing behind her eyes.

"No," Riyan said.

The man flashed Ashi a grin filled with pointed teeth. Ashi's knees trembled. She kept looking back at him until Riyan tugged her around a bend in the path.

"Please," Ashi said, "I need…"

"No!" Riyan said. "Time for that later." She wrapped both arms around Ashi, bodily restraining her from running back to the three people and the promise of ecstasy. "We need—"

Riyan's nostrils flared. Her body went rigid.

Then she was kissing Ashi in a mindless delirium, tongue pushing its way between Ashi's lips. Her hands slid up to Ashi's breasts, glossy and slick with oil. Ashi placed her hands over Riyan's and squeezed. She moaned with pleasure.

Riyan knelt. She grabbed Ashi's hips and pulled them toward her. Her tongue slid over Ashi's clit. Ashi swayed on her feet. The orgasm came fast. Pleasure exploded over Ashi, ferocious and hot. She screamed. Her fingers clamped down on her nipple as she came.

It ended as suddenly as it started. Ashi shook, gasping. Swirls of light danced around her. Her mind cleared. She looked down. Riyan had a look of such naked hunger on her face that it took Ashi's breath away. It seemed that whatever madness had taken Ashi had moved on to find a new home within Riyan.

"We need—" Ashi said.

Riyan bit her. Her fingers slid up to impale Ashi. Ashi exploded into another orgasm, quick and unexpected.

Ashi reached down and lifted Riyan to her feet. This time, it was Riyan's turn to whimper. Colored streamers of light rippled from Riyan's body, from the leaves on the trees, even from Ashi's hands. "Come on," Ashi panted. "We have to go. This way." She pulled Riyan down a narrow, dark pathway that branched from the wider path they were on. "This is the way. I can feel it."

Riyan clung to her hand, making small mewling sounds as Ashi dragged her along. The path closed in around them, dark and forbidding. Branches scrabbled at them.

They emerged into a broad clearing with springy grass so soft beneath their bare feet it felt like walking across a pillowy mattress.

Riyan tugged at Ashi. "You're so pretty," she said. Her eyes were unfocused, her voice dreamlike.

"Thank you!" Ashi said. She blushed. The swirls and patterns of light wavering all around her took on a reddish hue.

"I want to pleasure you," Riyan said. She slid her hand down Ashi's body. "Doesn't that sound nice?" Her voice was still far away.

"It…mmm," Ashi said. "It does. I…oh!" Riyan cupped her breast. Ashi sighed.

Focus, she told herself. She was here to do something important.

More important than this woman pressing herself against you? another part of her asked. *More important than these soft lips against yours? More important than the fingers caressing your skin? More important than the heights of ecstasy—*

Heights! She was here to climb a tree. There was a reason, an important one.

More important than the finger slipping so gently inside you?

Ashi moaned. Riyan's lips touched her neck. Streamers of light swirled all around her...

The Sacrifice! She was here to become the next Sacrifice!

Ashi squirmed free of Riyan's embrace. "Come on," she panted. "If you help me get to the top, you can do anything you want to me."

"Anything?"

"Anything."

Riyan nuzzled Ashi's neck. "Do you promise?"

"Yes!" Ashi said. "I promise!"

Riyan took a long, deep breath. She closed her strange silver eyes tightly. Her body quivered. When she opened her eyes again, they were clear. "I accept your promise," she said.

They made for the middle of the clearing. A line of naked people streamed from the forest after them.

Three enormous trees sprung up from atop a low hill in the middle of the clearing. Small clusters of lesser trees surrounded the titans. Rope ladders, bridges, and wooden platforms connected all the trees together in a jumbled cat's cradle. As they raced up the hill, Ashi saw figures swarming up the rope ladders.

At the base of one of the smaller trees, Ashi and Riyan found a steep ramp made of ropes with slats of wood between. Two rope handrails were all that kept climbers from tumbling off.

Ashi started up the ramp with Riyan behind her. It swayed dangerously beneath their feet. Ashi clutched the rope handrails so tightly her knuckles turned white. She kept her eyes focused on the branch above her. Sunlight filtered through dense leaves, bathing the platform ahead of them with golden light.

She reached the platform with a sigh of relief. It hugged the diameter of the tree, barely wide enough for two people to pass one another, without handholds or rails. Riyan held Ashi's hand tightly and peered over the edge.

Ashi edged around the platform. On the far side, a long rope ladder slanted up toward the lowest branch on the smallest of the three great trees.

She shielded her eyes with her hand and looked up. In the space between the trees, the ladder leaned precariously over empty space.

Riyan's hands slid over Ashi's breasts from behind. Ashi pushed aside a sudden sharp spike of desire. "Stop that," she said, "you're distracting me."

"Good!" Riyan said with a smirk. She pushed past Ashi and grabbed the rope ladder. It bowed alarmingly beneath her.

The climb was far more difficult than it looked. Midway up, Ashi made the mistake of looking down. Far below her, the ground rippled with streamers of green and orange. She clung to the swaying ladder, eyes closed, heart pounding.

When her heart slowed, she carefully opened her eyes. Wind whispered around the leaves. The ladder bobbed. *Look only to the next rung,* that was the secret. *Don't look up. Don't look down. Look only to the next rung.*

Her world contracted: Reach up, grab the next rope, step up, wait for the ladder to stop swaying. The breeze played around her naked body, reminding her how high she was.

Her hand slipped. She clung to the rope with one hand. Her heart threatened to leap from her chest. She closed her eyes and forced herself to breathe slowly. A chasm yawned beneath her feet.

"Come on!" came Riyan's voice from somewhere above her. "You're almost to the platform!"

Ashi kept going, one hand over the other, one step at a time, squeezing the rungs so tightly the rough rope dug into her skin. One step up, and then another, and then strong hands were pulling her onto a wooden platform.

Ashi looked up, expecting to see Riyan. Instead, her eyes met the sideways figure-8s of Camit's eyes. He smiled at her. "You made it!"

Ashi became aware of a tingling where their hands met. Her breath caught in her throat. Her heart forgot to beat for a moment. She found herself transfixed by Camit's golden eyes with their strange pupils. He drew her closer, until their bodies touched. The tingle spread everywhere skin touched skin. She breathed in the scented oil that covered his skin. A warm, pleasant feeling of heaviness took hold of her.

Camit's pupils diminished until they were little more than a straight line of black in a sea of brilliant gold. He clutched Ashi tightly, pinning her body against his. The feeling of warm heaviness spread. Everything but the heat on her skin faded away. She tried to wrap her arms around him, but her arms felt sluggish and unresponsive.

Camit kissed her, urgent and hungry. Ashi tasted his lips. She pressed herself to him, heedless of anything but the kiss that sucked her breath away.

They tumbled off the platform. Riyan cried out.

For a brief moment, Ashi felt herself falling. Then her stomach lurched as a float-field caught them. Her hair swirled. They hung suspended in midair. Camit's arms and legs locked around Ashi. The moment he entered her, her body went limp. She let out a long, shivering moan of delight.

They drifted lazily toward the ground. Time slowed. Camit held her tight, his hips thrusting. They tumbled slowly through the air, their bodies locked together. Beyond Camit's shoulder, Ashi saw sky, then leaves, then ground, then sky again. The warm heaviness spread down her arms to her fingers, down her legs to her toes.

By the time they were halfway to the ground, Ashi was completely paralyzed. She felt no fear or discomfort, just a sense of peace, as though she were sinking into a pleasant warm bath that drained all the tension from her body. Camit bit her shoulder. He pounded hard and fast in his wild need, as insistent as she was soft and yielding.

She felt the tension of an oncoming orgasm. The pleasure climbed and climbed, each slide of his erection lifting it higher. She came just as they settled on the soft grass. Streamers of light rippled all around her, the same gold color as his eyes.

Then he roared, and heat poured into her. She felt the wet deluge of his ejaculation, and all at once, the heaviness lifted. Her body was hers again.

He slid out of her, panting. His pupils returned to their unusual norm. "Thank you," he gasped, "thank you, thank you."

She kissed him, arms wrapping tight around him, savoring the feel of his hot slick body against hers. A thin voice called to her from somewhere high above. "Ashi! If you're finished, can we get back to this?"

Ashi's lust shattered. In its place came an overwhelming need to move, to climb, to rise. She scrambled to her feet and raced for the ramp that led up the tree.

The climb was easier the second time. Ashi dashed up the ramp, ignoring the swaying beneath her feet. She pushed past three other people on the platform, who were eying the treacherous ladder with trepidation. She hesitated for only a moment, then started to climb hand over hand, up and out over the empty space between the trees.

Up and up, the single-minded repetition of reach, grab, step, pull, and she was back on the lowest platform of the smallest of the three great trees. Far below, Camit still lay on the ground with a dreamy smile on his face. Around him, people writhed in twos and threes and fours. Most of them had either not started the climb or, like Ashi, had fallen from the tree and were now locked together in a frenzy.

"There are people ahead of us," Riyan said. "Look." She pointed.

Far above them, dots moved along the spider web of bridges and ladders. Ashi despaired.

"They aren't at the top yet," Riyan said. "We can still win."

She set out across a rope bridge that connected the platform to the second-tallest tree. Ashi followed her. The bridge wobbled with every step. Ashi hung on to the ropes on each side and forced herself to put one foot in front of the other.

At the far side, they started up a swaying rope ladder, Riyan ahead of Ashi. The streamers of light grew brighter and brighter in Ashi's vision, until she could see clearly only in a small circle in front of her. She grabbed each rung of the rope ladder tightly. Step by treacherous step she climbed, while whorls and loops of color wrapped around her.

They reached another platform. Another rope bridge arced back to the smallest of the three great trees. From there, an explosion of ladders, ropes, and bridges branched out in all directions, connecting the three huge trees and the smaller trees around them in a bewildering web. Ashi's heart sank. It was not at all clear which of the many paths would be fastest.

Riyan wrapped her arms around Ashi from behind. She kissed the back of Ashi's neck. Her hand crept up, inch by inch, until her fingers rested lightly against Ashi's nipple.

"That's very distracting," Ashi said.

"I'm thinking about what I might like to do to you," Riyan murmured. "You know, if I can do anything I want."

"That only happens if I win," Ashi said.

"Well, then," Riyan said, "you should win."

"I don't know which way to go!"

"So, think." Riyan nuzzled the side of Ashi's neck. "The maze through the forest ring had obvious paths and hidden paths. The obvious paths just went around in circles. The right path…"

"…is the one that's hard to see." Ashi gazed up at the trees. "There." She pointed to a thin length of rope with knots all along it that ran from a platform on the second-highest tree up to a branch on the tallest. "That's where we need to be."

Ashi walked carefully around the platform, skirting a man who clung to the tree trunk with white knuckles, eyes squeezed shut. She found a V-shaped rope bridge without even a set of planks, just three ropes, two as handholds and one to walk on, that crossed to another of the smaller trees. It bowed dangerously under her foot.

Riyan stepped onto it behind her, causing it to sway. Ashi made her slow way across, breathing hard the whole time.

They climbed a long rope ladder that ascended to a branch on the second-largest tree. From there, they made their way across an unstable rope and plank bridge to a platform high in the largest tree, where a woman knelt on hands and knees with a man behind her and another in front of her. The three of them coupled fiercely, seemingly unaware of anything or anyone around them. Ashi smelled a faint spicy scent. Her heart skipped a beat. Without conscious thought, she kissed the man in front of the kneeling woman. He groaned as he erupted in her mouth. White fluid dripped down her chin to splatter on the wood.

Riyan pulled Ashi away from the trio. Ashi mewled her disappointment.

"There's time for that lat—oof!" Riyan said. Ashi kissed her with blind need, fingers probing between Riyan's legs. Riyan melted into her. Soon Riyan was clutching Ashi's body, head thrown back, crying out in ecstasy.

"That was nice," Riyan said when she had quit shaking. "But we still have a long way to go."

The higher they climbed, the fewer people they encountered. The trees bobbed in the whistling wind, threatening to send them tumbling at the slightest misstep.

They crossed another bridge from the largest tree to the second largest. A rope ladder took them down to a lower platform, where another bridge crossed back to the largest tree and the knotted rope that led to a small wooden ledge near the top. A short ladder ascended to the tiny platform where the victory bell waited.

Ashi looked across and down. Her heart sank. A tall, slender figure with ivory skin, hair tied back in a long black braid streaked with red and blue, edged along the bridge to the knotted rope. Ashi realized at that moment that the race was over. She had no hope of catching him, and certainly no way to pass him on the climb.

Riyan made a disappointed sound. She took Ashi's hand. "Maybe next year," she said.

Ashi stood at the edge of the platform looking down. The bridge below them led to the largest tree, and the long rope that could be climbed to the ladder that brought them to their goal. She saw no other path to the platform and the bell.

"Trust in the Wild," Ashi said.

"Ashi?" Riyan said.

"Trust in the Wild. Let yourself go." She backed back away from the edge of the platform, until her back was against the tree. Ribbons of light swirled all around her. The tree swayed in the breeze.

"Ashi, darling, it's over."

Ashi flung herself off the edge of the platform. She felt a sickening drop as she fell. Then the float-field had her, and she was drifting slowly down, still traveling forward toward the largest tree. The man on the bridge looked up at her as she flashed by overhead, mouth agape.

About three quarters of the way across, she realized she had miscalculated. She flew fast toward the largest tree, with no way to slow herself. She wind-milled her arms and legs in the air just before crashing into the branches. The float-field released her. She fell hard through several branches before striking a tree limb with such force that it knocked the wind out of her. She grabbed hold and hung on, gasping for air.

"Ashi!" Riyan called. "Ashi!" She stepped back and hurled herself into the air.

Ashi forced herself upright and started climbing. There were no ropes or ladders, just branches. Riyan crashed through the crown of the tree a short distance from Ashi. The float field released her. She plummeted, scrabbling frantically, until she grabbed a branch. It bowed beneath her weight.

"Ashi!" she called.

"I'm okay!" Ashi said. "Go!"

The man below them, realizing the danger, raced across the bridge. It bounced beneath his feet. He scrambled onto the platform and reached the rope, where he began to climb.

Ashi and Riyan were still a good distance above him, but there was no easy path to the platform. Ashi climbed as best as she was able, scrambling from branch to branch. Her arms and legs burned. Every breath sent daggers of pain through her side where she had struck the tree.

Riyan made her own way up toward the tiny platform, following a differ-ent course. She reached it first, before Ashi or their competitor. Ashi realized Riyan had a problem: from beneath the platform, she had no way to get atop it. She stood on a long, strong branch and strained upward, but the platform remained stubbornly out of reach. The only path up took her away from her goal. She hesitated, then climbed rapidly, her path carrying her around the tree until she was hidden from Ashi's sight.

Wheezing, Ashi forced her way through the leaves. She stood on a slender branch that bowed beneath her, its bark rough against her soles. She flexed her legs and jumped. The branch cracked under her feet. She grabbed the branch above her one-handed and, with great effort, hauled herself up. Pain lashed through her side. Twigs scratched at her face and body. Her arm groaned in its socket.

At last, sweaty and panting, she found herself alongside the last platform. From here, a short rope ladder ascended to the goal. The man was already standing on it. He grinned at her in triumph.

The branch above the platform cracked. With a cry of surprise, Riyan thudded heavily onto the platform in a shower of leaves and broken twigs. She landed awkwardly on her side and rolled into the man. He stumbled.

In a flash, Ashi flung herself onto the platform. She leaped over him and Riyan both and started up the rope ladder. The man let out a roar and headed after her, too late. Ashi climbed to the top of the ladder, where a large silver bell hung from one of the very top branches. She grabbed the cord that dangled from its clapper and pulled vigorously. The bell rang. A distant cheer went up from the audience gathered at the crest of the hill overlooking the ring forest. Her competitor released his hold on the ladder and dropped back down to the platform, catlike.

Riyan climbed to her feet. She brushed herself off and touched the man who had, until moments ago, been completely convinced he was going to win the role of Sacrifice. "I'm sorry you didn't make it," she told him. "I can offer you a consolation prize, if it will help."

3.9

THE CROWD GRADUALLY dispersed. When the bell rang, the worshippers still in the trees climbed or, more often, dropped to the ground. Ashi stood at the edge of the highest platform for a time, caught in a jumble of emotions. Then, without really thinking about what she was doing, she stepped off the platform into empty air. The float-field caught her. She drifted gently to the base of the tree. Riyan and the man she'd beaten with her last-minute improvisational thinking remained behind, arms around each other, bodies pressed together.

High Priest Yahil greeted Ashi at the foot of the tree, shirtless and wearing a deep red kilt. He bowed before Ashi. "Congratulations," he said. "You will be this year's Sacrifice to the Wild." Then a grin split his face. He lowered his voice conspiratorially. "And might I just say, splendidly played. That was unconventional thinking. Well done."

Ashi flushed. "Thank you, High Priest. What happens now?"

"Now you follow me. This way."

Yahil led Ashi back through the ring of trees. As they walked, worshippers stopped whatever they were doing to bow, whistle, and clap. Cheers followed in her wake.

They made their way through the City to the circular building near the grand amphitheater where the sacrifice to the Wild was held. A massive bruise rose on Ashi's side. Leaves and bits of twig clung to her oiled skin.

Several people stood outside the heavy wood and glass doorway into the Temple. Ashi recognized Priest Hemmis, short, stout, and muscular with crimson eyes and short purple hair; Priestess Wahai, tall and dark-skinned, with amber eyes and long black hair that rippled with subtle, constantly-changing lights; and Priestess Fiha, who towered imposingly over the others, a head and a half taller than the tallest of them, her skin pale, her eyes as black as her hair. There were two other priests Ashi didn't recognize, mirror images of each other, with the same plump build and copper-colored hair, one with bright green eyes, the other with pale blue. All were bare-chested and wore the same red kilt Yahil wore.

They all bowed to Ashi as she passed between them. Fiha opened the door for Yahil and Ashi.

They walked along a hallway that followed the curve of the building. Sunlight spilled in through tall windows. A door in front of them opened into another long hallway that bisected the circular building, with doors on both sides and another at the end.

At the center of the hallway, exactly in the middle of the building, a spiral staircase made of rough-hewn, deeply textured wood descended through a circular hole in the ground. Ashi followed Yahil downstairs, floor after floor, until Ashi felt the weight of stone above her head. The claustrophobic shaft closed around her. The others came behind, single file. They emerged into a dark, cavernous place lit only by the dim glow of phosphorescent lichen growing on the rough stone walls.

Ashi padded along the downward-sloping passageway. It ended in a roughly circular chamber with another passageway to the left and a massive wood door bound with thick iron straps to the right.

Yahil worked the crude iron latch on the door and swung it open. He bowed deeply to Ashi. "If you please," he said.

Ashi stepped through the doorway. The cavern beyond looked natural. The walls glittered with small glowing points of light that cast an ethereal glow. Ashi heard water dripping and felt cold, damp stone beneath her feet.

The ground slanted steeply down toward the back of the chamber. Water flooded a third of the cavern, forming a rough pool that hugged the far wall. In the center of the chamber, a stone column rose to waist height. Atop it rested a silver urn. Liquid dripped from the ceiling into the urn in a slow, irregular *plunk plunk plunk*.

"For the next three months," Yahil said, "we will prepare you for the ritual of Sacrifice. During this time, you will be the living avatar of the Wild. Please kneel."

Trembling, Ashi knelt on the hard, stone floor. Yahil tilted Ashi's head up and held the urn to her lips. The liquid burned pleasantly in her mouth, with a complex flavor like wood smoke and jasmine. She swallowed. It left a sweet aftertaste.

"This is the Blessing of Enticement," Yahil said. "It will keep you sexually hungry." He replaced the urn on its stone column. "You may rise."

Ashi stood. Small hallucinatory ribbons of light still clung faintly to the edges of her vision.

Yahil and the others removed their kilts. Yahil took Ashi by the hand and led her into the pool. Warm water closed around her. Priest Hemmis and Priestess Wahai followed her. The others knelt on the edge of the pool.

Ashi submerged to her neck. Yahil, Hemmis, and Wahai ran their hands over Ashi's body. She closed her eyes and relaxed into their hands, letting the priests and priestess bathe her. They massaged her in the warm water until she found herself drifting, basking in the sensations.

Soon, her skin started to tingle. She felt a stirring inside herself, a spreading warmth between her legs. Without thought, she ran her hands over her body. She shivered with pleasure.

The people in the pool with her seemed to feel it, too. She heard Yahil's breath quicken, felt Wahai's hand tremble on her skin. Ashi parted her legs. Her hand crept down her body, lower and lower.

Yahil stood. He took Ashi's hands and helped her rise. Priestess Fiha dried her with a soft towel. When she was dry, Priest Hemmis gave her a short, pleated skirt of deep red edged with white, a red sleeveless vest of soft leather, and a pair of leather sandals.

After everyone dressed, Yahil led her back through the door, then down the passageway opposite it. The stone passageway opened into an enormous rectangular room, three times as long as it was wide, hewn out of living rock. Glowing orbs floated silently near the ceiling. The stone beneath Ashi's feet gave way to a floor of dark wood streaked with red and black.

Iron bars split the room. On this side, a large collection of soft chairs, couches, and cushions gave the impression of an opulent sitting room.

A barred door led to the other side of the room, which looked like nothing so much as a luxurious, if small, apartment. A massive bed squatted at one end of the long room, dressed in red blankets with an abstract black design of jagged points and swooping curves. A massage table padded in red and black leather stood at the foot of the bed. Ashi saw a table with several chairs around it, several plush couches also in red with jagged black abstract designs printed on them, and the blank rectangle of a Provider set in the far wall.

An enormous screen on the wall above the bed showed the late afternoon sun over the amphitheater. An elaborate glowing chandelier floated near the ceiling. Arms of dark-colored wood extended from a central sphere, each one curving slightly downward, then ending in a sudden upward angle. A small glowing sphere floated above each arm.

"This is where you'll stay for the next three months," Yahil said. "Each morning and evening, you'll be brought out for a ritual cleansing. Members of the Temple will be available to tend to all your needs." He produced a key from a small zippered pocket concealed in his kilt and unlocked the iron door.

Ashi stepped through the gate into the barred-off half of the chamber. She explored, lying on the luxuriously soft bed, trying the plush couches, comfortable to the point of decadence. She ran her hands over the polished wood table. A small opening in the wall led into a spacious, well-appointed bathroom.

"It's nice," Ashi said. "I notice the door has a lock on it."

"You are the Avatar of the Wild," Yahil said. "Many worshippers will visit you. The lock is to keep them separated from you, not the other way around."

Ashi sat on the edge of the bed. "So, I can leave if I want to?"

"Do you want to?" Wahai said.

"No."

"Does it matter, then?"

Ashi laughed. "No, I suppose it doesn't."

She sprawled on the bed. A warm glow enveloped her. Yahil said something, but his words came from somewhere far away.

"I'm sorry, what was that?" she asked.

"We will leave you to settle in. Priest Hemmis will remain with you to start your orientation," Yahil said.

"Mm, that's nice of him," Ashi said.

She felt the bed move as Hemmis sat down next to her. She heard the footsteps of the others as they left, the door clang shut, and the key scrape in the lock.

"Shall we get started?" Hemmis said.

"Oh, please do," Ashi said without opening her eyes.

"The thing about the Wild," Priest Hemmis began, "is that those who worship him must be willing to trust him implicitly. Like you did when you threw yourself from the top of the tree. Absolute trust brings absolute surrender."

"Mmm-hmm," Ashi said. She stretched languidly. The sense of calm seeped into her bones.

"The worshippers will want to visit you in your role as avatar of the Wild," he went on. "Your presence will inspire them to new heights of surrender."

"Is that why there are so many cushions out there? So they can surrender?"

"Yes. It is also why there are bars between you and them. Otherwise they might give you no peace at all."

"My, that sounds terrible," Ashi said. She drew a hand down along her body. "Pleasured again and again by hungry worshippers…"

Hemmis coughed. "Well, yes, about that," he said. "The Blessing of Enticement inspires desire but prevents release."

Ashi sat up. Her calm peace fled. "Wait a minute," she said. "You mean I'm going to spend the next three months without an orgasm?"

"Ah, well, err, yes," Hemmis said. "You do understand how the Sacrifice works, right? You've attended previous Sacrifices."

"Yes, but—"

"The Sacrifice to the Wild is a purging. Before the purging comes the buildup."

"For three months?"

"You need to learn the purity of absolute surrender. That takes time."

"You expect me to be chaste?" Incredulity expressed itself in Ashi's voice.

"No!" Hemmis said, shocked at the notion. "Not at all! Far from it! You will simply be without release, that's all."

"This is going to be a long three months," Ashi sighed.

3.10

ASHI AWOKE THE next morning to the scrape of the key in the lock. Yahil, Hemmis, and Wahai stood outside waiting respectfully for her to invite them in. She shrugged on a simple robe from the Provider and opened the door. "Good morning!" she said to Yahil. "I heard a rumor that I'm not to have an orgasm for months. Is that true?"

Yahil had the good grace to look embarrassed. "It is."

"I wasn't aware of that particular detail."

"Well," Yahil said, "it's not like it's a secret. You've talked to previous Sacrifices, right?"

"The subject never came up."

"You can't exactly blame me for that." Yahil gestured to the door. "After you, please."

The three escorted Ashi to the cavern beyond the heavy wood door. The two priests Ashi didn't know—the ones who looked near-identical except for their hair and eyes—already waited there, nude.

"Ashi, this is Acolyte Emrin and Acolyte Marnin. They'll also be seeing to your needs over the next few months. Now, if you would kneel, please?"

Ashi knelt on the damp stone floor. Yahil picked up the silver urn and brought it to her lips. She swallowed a mouthful of the heady liquid. Her skin tingled.

She disrobed and followed Yahil, Hemmis, and Wahai into the pool. Yahil drew Ashi onto his lap. He massaged her shoulders while Hemmis and Wahai caressed her.

She closed her eyes and drifted, enjoying the warm water and the acolytes' hands on her. The pleasant tingle spread until her entire body glowed. A soft, gentle buzz of arousal started somewhere between her legs, sending little tendrils up her body.

"Let go," Yahil murmured in her ear.

She heard a sigh—Hemmis, maybe, she wasn't sure. Lips, she didn't know whose, touched her neck. She arched her back without opening her eyes. One of her hands reached out and found soft skin. She was rewarded with another sigh. Her other hand crept slowly down her body, over her belly, across the sensitive skin of her mound.

Now there were lips on hers. A tongue flicked against her lips. Ashi parted them to invite it in. She moved her questing hand up someone's leg, exploring, until it encountered an erection. She curled her fingers around it, gently, almost shyly. The lips on her neck became more urgent. Someone's hand caressed her breast.

Then Yahil stood, lifting Ashi up with him. She opened her eyes. Emrin and Marnin helped her from the pool. Emrin dried her off. Marnin slipped the robe around her.

"This way," Marnin said.

Ashi left the room. She spared a backward glance at Yahil, Hemmis, and Wahai, who remained behind in the pool. Yahil and Hemmis kissed frantically. Wahai bit Yahil's shoulder, reaching around him, her hands working somewhere beneath the water.

"They're not coming with us?" Ashi said.

"They have not had the Blessing of Enticement," Emrin said. "The pool's effects on them are stronger than they are on you. They'll be...um, busy for a while."

Ashi returned to her quarters, or cell, depending on which way she looked at it. Emrin and Marnin remained outside, waiting.

"Yes?" Ashi said.

"May we come in?" Marnin said.

Ashi sat on one of the couches. "Depends. Are you going to give me more bad news?"

"No," Emrin said. "In fact, we're here to give you a massage."

"Oh!" Ashi's eyes glowed. "In that case, please do!"

Marnin bid Ashi to remove her robe and lie on the wide massage table. Emrin called up two flasks of oil from the Provider. They set to work on her.

Marnin started with her hands. Emrin started with her feet. Ashi soon found herself drifting off into a dreamlike trance beneath their skilled hands. Her body felt warm and heavy. A deep sense of calm settled around her like a blanket.

Marnin worked his slow, patient way up to her shoulders. Emrin massaged the backs of her legs, his fingers strong and nimble. As Ashi relaxed further into the trance, she felt another presence, some subtle, formless benevolence watching her. She smiled.

Marnin's hands made their way down her back. Emrin moved without haste up her legs. They met at her butt, each of them massaging her muscles deeply. Ashi sighed.

Presently, they helped her turn over. She lay on her back while each of the acolytes massaged one of her hands. She lay still with her eyes closed, soaking in the sensation. Their hands slid up her arms to her shoulders. She purred with pleasure.

Emrin and Marnin moved their hands in lazy spirals around her breasts, starting from the outside in. Ashi wriggled beneath their touch. Her skin tingled pleasantly. Eventually, their fingers found her nipples. She smiled. "Mmm," she said.

Emrin poured the oil down her body and over her mound. Marnin cupped both of her breasts. Ashi's sighs became soft moans. When Emrin reached her mound, Ashi opened her legs for him. He parted her folds with his fingers, then poured a thin stream of oil directly over her clit. The very tip of his finger slid into her, so slightly she could only just feel it. He stroked around her clit, not quite touching it. Little ripples followed in the wake of his fingers. Ashi felt a pleasant sense of longing.

Then they both moved on. Marnin stood over her head and ran his hands down her sides, up across her belly, then back down her sides again. Emrin massaged her legs, his hands somehow finding all the most sensitive places along her inner thighs.

A warm golden glow enveloped Ashi. She reached up and put her hands behind Marnin's head, drawing him down. Their lips met.

Marnin turned out to be as patient and focused when it came to kissing as he was with his massage. His tongue touched her lips politely, asking for entry. She parted her lips for him. The kiss took her breath away. Emrin's hands moved lower, until he was doing something extraordinary to her feet.

When Marnin broke the kiss and Emrin removed his hands from her, Ashi felt a sense of loss. "You stopped!" she pouted. "Just when you were being so wonderful!"

Emrin laughed. "Don't worry, we're not going anywhere," he said. "Our duty to you includes massages twice a day, once in the morning and once in the evening."

"Oh?" Ashi smiled a lazy smile. "I think I could get used to that."

Marnin helped her stand. In the shower, he washed her hair while Emrin washed her body. Afterward, Emrin helped her dry.

She emerged absolutely radiant, with a calm, happy smile on her face. "That was lovely," she said. "Thank you."

Marnin bowed. "You are welcome."

As they left, Marnin locked the door behind him with a key from his kilt.

Ashi instructed the viewscreen to show her a sweeping overview of the City from atop the highest living tower. From this perspective, Ashi thought the City itself looked like a vast living thing. Sleek black towers curved upward like appendages reaching skyward from some great creature buried far beneath the ground. Pods zipped along the tracks that threaded like spiderwebs between the towers. Tiny people filled the courtyard in front of the Temple of the Fiery One. Many of them gathered around priests and priestesses bound to columns.

To the side of the City, nestled against the shield, she could just make out the garden of the Quickener. Tiny dots moved through the hedge maze on their way to visit the sleeping avatar of their god. Ashi had never understood that religion. If you were going to be tied down and ravished, she thought, you ought to be awake to enjoy it.

She watched the goings-on for a while. Eventually, she called up a portable screen from the Provider. She flipped through it, looking for some light entertainment. She sprawled on her back on the bed, positioned the screen to hover above her, and read a new novel in a series she'd been fond of for a while, then lost track of.

Her body still thrummed pleasantly. She ran her hand down over herself, savoring the feel of her soft skin under her palm. Her hand slipped lower and lower while she read. She slipped a finger idly over her clit, not really paying attention to what she was doing.

The key scraped in the lock. She looked up. "Hello, High Priest!" she said.

"May I come in?" Yahil said.

"Of course!"

She stood and summoned a robe from the Provider. Yahil sat on one of the couches. "I just spoke to your friend Riyan," he said.

"How is she? Is she going to visit me?"

Yahil chuckled. "She seems lovely. She was almost hesitant to bring it up, but she says that you made a promise to her?"

"Ah, yes," Ashi said. "You whisked me away here before I could make good on it."

"What was your promise?"

"I may have promised her that if she helped me win the competition to become Sacrifice, she could do whatever she wanted to my body," Ashi said. "Though now that I think about it, that might have been unwise."

"I can't speak to whether it was wise, but that's not for me to decide." Yahil settled back in his chair. "The gods have their ways. We have the rituals, and the Sacrifices, but a promise, well…a promise is a sacred thing. If we don't keep our promises, society breaks down. Even the gods themselves won't stand in the way of a fair promise fairly made."

"Does that mean she can visit me?"

"Of course!" Yahil said. "She can visit you whenever she likes. As for the promise, well… Even though you have been chosen as Sacrifice and you must remain here until the ritual, you will still keep your promise. I came to make sure that what she said was true. Since it is…" He stood and smiled. "I will let the others know."

He stood and left, closing the door behind him but not, Ashi noticed, locking it.

Minutes ticked by. Ashi heard footsteps coming down the hallway. Riyan appeared at her door, wearing a black corset and a long black skirt that shimmered faintly as she walked. She had tied up her silver hair in ringlets and woven small flowers through them. "Ashi!" she said.

Ashi grinned. "Hi! Come in! I just got a visit from High Priest Yahil. He says you told him about my promise."

Riyan looked down, demure, but an irrepressible smile crossed her lips. "I didn't know if he would make me wait until after your Sacrifice, but…"

"But even the gods themselves respect a promise," Ashi said.

Riyan flung herself into Ashi's arms. "How are you? Are they treating you well?" She looked around Ashi's quarters. "I didn't know there'd be bars!"

"Apparently," Ashi said, "they're to keep me from being ravished."

"Oh? We'll see about that," Riyan said. "I have plans for you."

"Mm. Should I be scared?"

"Maybe a little."

"About that," Ashi said. "Apparently I'm not allowed to experience sexual release for the next few months."

"Oh, really?" Riyan's smile grew wider. "That sounds like fun. I might have to change my plans." She put her hands on Ashi's shoulders and looked her up and down. "How's life as a sacrifice to the Wild? Have they done terrible things to you?"

Ashi laughed. "It's been less than a day! They haven't had time. Though it seems I'm fated to receive massages at least twice daily."

"You poor thing!" Riyan said. "Would that I could bear some of your suffering for you."

"Huh. I always had you pegged as the type to inflict suffering," Ashi said.

"Oh, you know, I can go either way." Riyan flopped down on the couch. "Come sit next to me! I want to kiss you."

"Is this you collecting on my promise?" Ashi said.

"No, this is just me wanting to kiss you."

Ashi straddled Riyan on the couch. Their lips met. Riyan's hands wandered over Ashi's body. Presently, Riyan said, "Tell me about this no-orgasm thing."

Ashi shrugged. "They have given me the Blessing of Enticement. Apparently it will help me let go."

"Ooh," Riyan said. She opened the front of Ashi's robe and slipped her hands inside. "How does that work?"

"I'm not really...mmm." Ashi closed her eyes. "I'm not really sure. I suppose that's one of the things I'll have to learn before the Sacrifice. Oh!" She pressed herself forward into Riyan's hands. "You can keep doing that if you like."

"What, this?" Riyan slid her hands over Ashi's breasts.

"Mmm, yes."

"What does it feel like? The Blessing, I mean."

"Warm," Ashi said. "Comfortable. Have you ever taken the Blessing at the Temple of the Fiery One?"

"Yes." Riyan frowned. "It made me pretty desperate. Not really my thing."

"It's kind of the opposite of that," Ashi said. "Mm, definitely keep doing that." She shivered. "This Blessing is gentler. It's like the feeling you get on a lazy afternoon when you're kind of comfortable and kind of hungry, but you don't want to get out of bed to do anything about it, you know?"

"That sounds fun," Riyan said. She opened Ashi's robe further and slid a hand between Ashi's legs. "How about this?"

Ashi sighed. "Oh, that's very nice."

"What happens if I try to make you come?"

"I don't know."

Riyan's eyes lit up. "I think we should find out, don't you?"

She pushed Ashi onto her back on the couch and knelt over her. Ashi looked up into her flat silver eyes for a moment. Two tiny reflections looked back down at her. Then Riyan kissed Ashi's neck, her body barely touching Ashi's. Ashi's eyelids fluttered.

She moved down without haste. Her lips made a path down Ashi's throat, across her collarbone, and down to Ashi's stomach. By the time she reached Ashi's mound, Ashi felt bathed in a sultry glow, as though she were sinking into a warm bath.

When Riyan's tongue touched her clit, it sent not a shock but a gentle ripple of pleasure through Ashi, that she felt from her toes up to her cheeks. She ran her hands over her breasts. "That feels really nice," she said.

"Should I keep going, then?"

"Yes, please."

Riyan's tongue danced over Ashi's clit. Great slow swells of pleasure washed through Ashi. She sank further into the warm glow. She felt the orgasm building gradually within her, but the closer it came, the more slowly it built. *Zeno's orgasm*, Ashi thought. *I will never catch up with it.* The idea made her giggle.

Riyan continued her attention until Ashi found herself writhing on the couch, always closing on the orgasm but never reaching it.

"My goodness," Riyan said. "I like how squirmy you are. This is fun! I could keep this up all day."

She didn't, but she did keep it up until late morning became noon, then early afternoon. By the time she was done, sweat covered Ashi's body. Ashi wriggled and squirmed, eyes closed, unable to reach any kind of release but also desperate for Riyan not to stop.

Finally, Riyan sat up. Ashi let out a sharp cry of disappointment. Riyan laughed. "I like you this way," she said. "Even I have limits, though." She leaned back, lifting her skirt. "Doing this to you has really got me going. Come see!"

Ashi knelt on the floor. She ran her hand between Riyan's legs and found wetness. She slipped a finger easily inside Riyan, then withdrew it. "It has," she said. She looked up into Riyan's silver eyes. "Do you enjoy making me wiggly and needy? Does it turn you on to see me like this?"

"Oh, yes," Riyan breathed. "Yes, it does." She placed both hands behind Ashi's head and pushed her face down. She crossed her legs around Ashi's back, hooking her ankles together to hold her there.

Ashi's tongue moved. Riyan exploded almost instantly. "Don't you stop!" she cried. "Don't even think about stopping!"

Riyan held Ashi's head down through four more orgasms, screaming and bucking her hips to meet Ashi's tongue. Ashi felt her own wetness leak down her thighs as she knelt there. With every one of Riyan's orgasms, Ashi felt herself ache with longing.

When Riyan had had enough, she pulled Ashi up and smoothed down her skirt. "Mm, come here," she said, "I want to kiss you again."

Ashi lunged at Riyan, kissing her with rough, careless urgency. Riyan purred with delight. "Do you think they'll let us have more Blessing of Enticement after the Sacrifice?" she said. "I like what it does to you."

Ashi kissed her again, hungry. Riyan wrapped her arms around her and pulled her close. Ashi tasted herself on Riyan's lips.

Eventually, Riyan pushed her away. "Much as I want to stay here all day and play with you, I have things to do," she said.

"What things?"

Riyan winked. "You'll find out later." She rose and left, pausing at the door to blow Ashi a kiss. She took a key from her corset and locked the door.

"Hey, wait a minute!" Ashi called. "They gave you a key?"

Riyan's laughter echoed off the stone walls.

3.11

THAT EVENING, ASHI spent some time trying in vain to give herself an orgasm. She succeeded only in increasing her hunger. After she gave up, High Priest Yahil appeared at her door with Priest Hemmis and Priestess Wahai, all of them bare-chested and dressed only in their red kilts. Wahai's skin had changed, and now bore subtle stripes, a bit like a zebra's but in lighter and darker brown rather than black and white. Her hair was tied back in a ponytail, the ends frosted in silver, and her ears had been replaced with delicate silver carvings.

They brought her to the chamber with the pool. Ashi's bare feet padded along the stone floor. She knelt at Yahil's feet. He tipped the silver urn into her mouth. She swallowed, the liquid burning pleasantly on the way down. Almost immediately, her body glowed with warmth. A flush touched her cheeks.

"I feel lightheaded," Ashi said. "Did you give me more than you usually do?"

"As time goes on, you will become more and more sensitive to the Blessing," Yahil said.

Ashi smiled dreamily. "I like it," she said.

Emrin and Marnin waited beside the pool. Wahai slipped the robe from Ashi's shoulders. Wahai, Yahil, and Hemmis entered the pool with her.

Ashi found herself slipping into a haze. The water lapped pleasantly at her skin. Yahil caressed her back. Wahai stroked her breasts. Hemmis placed his hand on her knee. Everywhere touch made her skin tingle and buzz with pleasure.

"Did you enjoy your visit from your friend?" Yahil said.

"Mm, very much," Ashi said. She stretched luxuriantly, arching her back against him, pressing her breasts into Wahai's hands. The warmth spread all through her until even her fingers and toes tingled. "I noticed you gave her a key."

"Of course," Yahil said. He kissed the side of her neck.

Ashi closed her eyes and squirmed. "Hello," she said when she encountered his erect shaft, "what's this?" She lifted herself slightly and sat again, impaling herself as she settled back down onto his lap. "Oh!" she said.

She started to move her hips. Yahil put his hands on her waist. "No," he said. "Just be still in the moment. Feel, without desire or intent. Will yourself to calm."

Ashi shuddered. She closed her eyes to focus on the feeling. Wahai's hands sent electric currents of ecstasy through her nipples. Yahil was rigid inside her. With each beat of her heart, she felt herself close around him.

"Yes, like that," Yahil said. "What do you want?"

"I want to come," Ashi said. Her voice was a throaty whisper.

"Part of surrendering to the Wild is giving up your control," Yahil said. "Exist for the purity of the moment. Let go."

"But—"

"Let go," he repeated.

He held her still, hands firm on her hips. Wahai cupped Ashi's breasts. Hemmis leaned forward and, with great gentleness, kissed Ashi's lips. Ashi forced herself to sit still, even though her skin was so sensitive that the hands on her body and the feel of Yahil inside her threatened to overwhelm her. Hemmis kissed her again. Ashi found herself floating, drifting somewhere, untethered to her body. She felt the presence of someone else, a feeling like someone looking over her shoulder...

Yahil stirred. The spell shattered. Wahai stood, sending a cascade of water sloshing through the pool. Hemmis helped Ashi to her feet. She whimpered as Yahil slid out of her.

Emrin had a towel waiting for her. When she had dried herself off, Marnin slipped the robe over her shoulders. He and Emrin led Ashi from the room. Behind her, she heard Wahai gasp.

They escorted her back to her chamber, or room, or cell...she still hadn't decided what to call it. They waited at the door until she invited them in.

"You don't need to wait every time," she said. She floated, slightly disconnected from the world.

Emrin helped her take off her robe. She lay down, and the two of them put their hands on her back.

"The first Greeting of the Avatar is tonight," Emrin said.

"What does that mean?" Ashi said.

"The worshippers will come to commune with you."

"That's nice," Ashi said. Her voice had a languid, dreamlike quality to it. She sighed as Marnin drizzled oil down her back. They set to work on her with skilled hands. She drifted away.

By the time they helped her turn over, Ashi floated in a state of euphoria They worked her until she writhed moaning on the table. Then they led her to the shower, where Emrin bathed her and Marnin washed her hair. She turned to face him, placing a kiss on his lips. Then she sank to her knees, her body sliding against his. He continued to wash her hair as she wrapped her lips around his erection. A tremor ran through his body.

She took her time, just as he had taken his, building him up slowly. When at last she finished him, he came with a deep, prolonged cry. His warm come gushed into her mouth.

She rose, hungrier than ever, eyes fixed on his. She licked her lips. He kissed her, rough and demanding, under the stream of water. Emrin kissed the back of her neck, sandwiching her between them.

Then Marnin commanded the water to switch off. He and Emrin dried her. They dressed and left. The lock scraped shut behind them.

She didn't have long to wait. Her body still buzzed when Yahil appeared. He wore his kilt and nothing else. His face wore a relaxed, happy expression. "The worshippers will arrive soon," he said from outside the door. "They will want to commune in the presence of the new avatar of the Wild."

"What do I have to do?" Ashi said.

"Nothing. Your presence alone is enough. You represent the personification of the god. All you need to do is be here." He smiled. "You may find you want to participate more directly in the events. That's up to you."

"What do you mean? What events?"

"The Provider will provide appropriate dress for you."

"What events?"

"The worshippers will be arriving soon." He bowed. "Avatar."

"Hang on!" she called after him as he disappeared down the hallway. "What events? Ah, I hate when you guys do that." She went to the Provider. "I hear you have clothes for me." The black panel flipped open. A dress slid out. Ashi took off her robe and fed it into the slot.

The dress fit snugly on top and fell to a wide pleated skirt that nearly reached the ground. The top half was black, lined with red. The bottom faded from black to red, with a subtle pattern of jagged geometric designs that flowed and changed as she watched. She slipped it in. The front descended in a deep V all the way to her navel, and had no sleeves.

"Mirror," she said.

The viewscreen changed to a mirror. She turned this way and that, admiring herself. "I think I need different hair," she said. "And maybe different eyes."

The Provider flipped open to offer her a hairbrush. "Black," she said, "with red streaks." She ran the brush through her hair. As she did, the brown melted into to black. Crimson highlights appeared behind the brush. She picked up a device a bit like a pair of binoculars with closed ends. She touched a control on the top, scrolling through colors before she settled on a dark, vivid red that matched the dress. She held it up to her eyes. A light flashed. When she put it down, her copper-colored eyes had changed to a dark crimson. She admired the way her cross-shaped pupils looked against the red. "Yes, much better," she said. "If I'm going to be an avatar of a god, I might as well look the part." She fed the devices back into the Provider. The panel closed behind them.

The chandelier over her head brightened, so subtly Ashi didn't notice at first. At the same time, the glowing orbs outside the cage dimmed, until deep shadows filled the area beyond the bars.

Priestess Fiha walked into the chamber with a huge silver tray. She wore a dress of red and black similar to Ashi's, also cut in a deep V that reached to her navel. A variety of small vials sat on the tray: some tall, some short, some shaped like spheres, others like teardrops, still others like cylinders. Each was filled with a different-colored liquid.

Fiha bowed to Ashi. Ashi nodded back. "So, it's going to be that kind of party, hmm?" she said.

Fiha inclined her head. "You represent the Wild. The worshippers will commune with the Wild in your presence."

"Thought so." She sighed theatrically. "And me not able to have an orgasm."

"Such is the life of a Sacrifice," Fiha said.

The first worshippers arrived. "Ruji!" Ashi exclaimed. "Vrynn!"

Vrynn bowed to Ashi, but there was a hint of mischievousness in his eyes. "Avatar," he said. He and Ruji chose vials from the tray. Ruji lifted his in Ashi's direction. The two of them downed the contents of their vials.

More people came in after them: Camit, Tavin, Shia, Martia, Jannon (who had changed back to his male body), and more. Each of them took a vial from Fiha's tray and drank.

A subliminal hum settled over the people sprawled on the couches and curled up on the cushions, a sense of expectation. Worshippers settled in next to one another, talking in low voices. Electricity crackled in the air.

The mood grew more sensual. The worshippers began kissing one another. Clothing was discreetly moved aside to give access to hands and tongues. Sighs and moans filled the air.

Ashi felt an intense rush of heat. She pressed herself against the bars of the cage, watching what was happening just out of reach. Every soft sound of pleasure set her quivering. Her body flushed with desire.

One of the worshippers, a man with short hair that cycled slowly through a rainbow of colors, approached the bars. His red kilt shimmered with subtle light, nearly invisible even in the shadows. Both his nipples bore vertical piercings from which fine chains of silver metal dangled. A tiny silver weight hung from the end of each chain. He had golden eyes with pupils shaped like crosses. He bowed. "Avatar of the Wild, will you bless me?"

He extended a hand. Hypnotized, Ashi reached through the bars to touch him. The moment their skin made contact, Ashi felt a flash of heat. The man's pupils contracted to crossed slashes. He shuddered with a small "uh" sound.

Then in one fluid movement he flung himself against the bars. He pressed himself against Ashi, reaching through the bars to embrace her. She felt cold iron and warm skin through the fabric of her dress. Their lips met. Ashi felt dizzy and euphoric at once. She returned the kiss with enthusiasm. Somewhere out beyond her cell, Ashi heard a gasp, followed by a long moan.

Ruji and Vrynn came up to the bars. Vrynn bowed low. "Avatar of the Wild," he said, "I beseech your blessing." The corners of his lips turned upward in a smile. His eyes sparkled with mischievous humor.

Ashi extended her hand. He took it in both of his and raised it to his lips. The shock of contact sent a surge of dizziness through Ashi. He stiffened. His pupils dilated, then constricted. He let out a soft, barely audible groan.

The rainbow-haired man fondled her. She took his hand and slipped it inside her dress, folding it over her breast. The feeling of his skin on hers sucked her breath away. She kissed Vrynn through the bars.

Ruji caressed her arm. The touch sent a jolt through her. He sucked in his breath with a shudder. A moment later, his hands were all over her, urgent with his need.

Wild euphoria surged through Ashi. She tried to remove her dress, but the process seemed cumbersome and much too slow. In a fit of impatience, she grabbed the deep plunging neckline with both hands and tore the dress away. She tugged at the waistband of Vrynn's kilt, fingers clumsy with haste.

They pressed together through the bars. A moment later, he was inside her. Cold iron pressed against Ashi's hips. She whimpered as Vrynn thrust against her. Ruji and the stranger groped her breasts. She reached down, fumbling at their kilts. When at last they were out of the way, she curled her fingers around two erect shafts.

Vrynn thrust fast until he let out a roar and erupted within her. She gasped at the sudden, shocking emptiness of his withdrawal.

Ashi guided the stranger into her. He growled as he penetrated her. His eyes seemed fixed on a point somewhere behind her, as though he were looking through her rather than at her. She kissed Ruji through the bars, lost in the feeling of his tongue in her mouth and the stranger's hard cock inside her. She kept stroking Ruji, savoring his small sounds of pleasure. His body stiffened. His shaft twitched in her hand. Warm wetness splattered her side. She raised her dripping fingers to his lips and pushed them in his mouth. He moaned. The stranger threw back his head and howled as he came.

The evening became a blur after that. Ashi quivered with feral energy. People crowded against the bars, seeking her touch. She moved up and down, reaching out to touch them, kiss them, grope them. Every time her skin contacted another person, bodies quivered with need.

The worshippers grabbed and clutched at her and each other. Ashi drifted through a maelstrom of erotic energy. Fingers and cocks and tongues explored her, bringing her ever closer to an orgasm she couldn't quite reach. She felt part of the festivities but also distant from them, gifting ecstasy to others but unable to receive it. The evening went on and on, worshippers indulging themselves in each other all around Ashi while the bars held them separate.

It ended slowly. People gradually drifted away, sated, until there was nobody left. The energy still hummed in Ashi's body. Vrynn was the last to go. She felt a deep pang at his leaving.

Fiha bowed to Ashi. She collected the discarded clothing that remained behind. "Good night, Sacrifice," she said. "You did well. The Wild is pleased."

Ashi stood for a while under the shower. The euphoria gradually drained away, like the tide receding from the shore. She dried and went to bed. She commanded the lights and viewscreen off, then lay for a time in the bed, one hand on her breast, the other between her legs, stroking herself absently until finally sleep carried her away.

3.12

ASHI WOKE JITTERY and vaguely irritable the next morning. The feeling lingered even after Yahil gave her the liquid from the silver flask. Not even the warm water in the pool relaxed her.

She sat on Yahil's lap, eyes closed, willing herself to be tranquil. It didn't work. She felt aroused, and frustrated, and annoyed at her inability to orgasm. The warm hazy glow from the night before had faded into grouchiness.

"I don't see why I have to go three months without an orgasm," Ashi complained. "Especially if everyone else gets to have them."

Yahil massaged her shoulders. Ashi closed her eyes and sighed, then immediately resented it.

"Your Sacrifice will be intense," Yahil said. "You need to learn to surrender yourself to the Wild, to be in the moment without goal or destination. As long as you still desire, your experience as Sacrifice will not be good."

"And I'm supposed to learn this by not coming?" Ashi said.

"Yes."

"That makes absolutely no sense."

Yahil pulled her back against him. He kissed the back of her neck. Ashi shivered with pleasure, then resented that, too. Wahai and Hemmis massaged her hands. She felt a tight knot of need inside her. She ground her hips against Yahil's erection, wanting it inside her but also resenting that desire.

345

"Let go," Yahil said. "Appreciate what is, not what you can't have."

"I want—"

"Don't think about what you want. Think about what is."

Ashi gave an exasperated sigh. "This is bullshit."

"It isn't," Yahil said calmly. "Trust the Wild."

"Trust the Wild," Ashi repeated. "Right."

The grouchiness lingered even when she returned to her cell, despite the wonderful things Marnin and Emrin did to her back.

They rolled her over. Emrin poured a stream of oil between her breasts. He and Marnin slid their hands over her. Ashi felt herself clench in a sudden burst of intense need. "I'm not sure if I like that," Ashi said.

"Oh?" Marnin said. He took his hands off her. "Does it not feel good?"

She grabbed his hand and placed it back on her body. "No!" she said. "That's not the problem. The problem is—"

"Yes?"

"It feels too good. I know it's not going to go anywhere, and you're only going to leave me hanging."

"Ah." Marnin's hand slid over her breast. "Isn't it enough to enjoy it for what it is?"

"You sound like Yahil," Ashi said.

"Well, yes. He is the High Priest."

"Why do you do this, anyway?" Ashi said.

"Do what? Join the temple of the Wild?"

"No, get me all worked up like this. Twice a day. I mean, don't get me wrong, I'm not complaining—"

"But you are," Emrin said.

"Okay, yes, I am complaining. Why do you get me...oh! Mmm." She closed her eyes and angled her hips up. "See? Like that! Why do you get me all worked up when you know I won't be satisfied?"

"You have attended a Sacrifice, yes?" Marnin said.

"Of course!" She smiled at the memory. "If I hadn't, I couldn't be this year's Sacrifice."

"So, you know what will happen to you, and how long it will take."

"Yes."

"Only by enjoying what's happening in the moment can you hope to make it through," Marnin said. "If your mind is on what will happen instead of what is happening, well..." He shrugged.

"How would you feel if I did this to you?" Ashi said.

"Did what?"

"Got you all worked up and left you hanging."

"We are not Sacrifices," Emrin said. He slipped a finger easily into Ashi. She groaned.

"That...mmm. That doesn't answer the...uh!" She raised her hips, forcing his finger deeper. "That doesn't answer the question!"

Marnin shrugged. His fingers closed over Ashi's nipples. "We all have our own struggles."

"Come over here and say that," Ashi said.

Marnin moved obligingly beside Ashi. "We all have—" Ashi reached down to wrap her hand around his cock. It hardened beneath her fingers. "Our own struggles!" The last word came out a squeak.

"I'm sorry, was that bad of me?" Ashi said.

Marnin made a strangled "urk!" sound. His hands continued to massage Ashi's breasts as though nothing were happening. Ashi took his noise as a small victory.

When they finished, Ashi felt even more frustrated. They brought her to the shower. Nuts on this, she told herself. Instead of detaching from desire, let's see how they like living for the moment!

Marnin washed her back. Ashi kissed Emrin. She curled her hands around his cock, encouraging it to hardness. She stroked him in long, slow strokes, savoring every little gasp and tremble. She increased her speed slowly, until his eyes grew unfocused and his breath quickened. He threw back his head. She released her grip. "Do my hair," she said, turning her back to him.

While Emrin washed her hair, Ashi turned Marnin around and leaned him against the wall. She reached around him with soapy hands to stroke his cock. "How does it feel to know I'm not going to let you come?" she murmured. Her hands slid rapidly up and down.

He pressed back against her, breathing, hoarse. "By all the gods!" he rasped. "I—I—" His body shook.

Ashi released him and rinsed herself. "Okay, you two can go now. Get!"

They left, whimpering. Ashi smiled.

There was no gathering of the worshippers that day. Nor did Riyan come to visit her. Instead, after she had had lunch and spent a frustrating time running her hands over herself, always getting closer to that orgasm that remained forever beyond reach, Yahil came to see her.

He waited outside the cage door until Ashi invited him in. "Are you here to torment me?" she said.

Yahil laughed. "No. I'm here to teach you some meditation techniques that will help make these next few months less frustrating."

"I know something that would make them less frustrating," Ashi said.

"I imagine so," Yahil said. "Still, you did volunteer."

"And you had to remind me of that."

Yahil inclined his head. "Being a Sacrifice is always challenging."

"You're here to make my challenge less so?"

"If you like."

"Have you ever faced this...challenge?"

Yahil smiled thinly. "Oh yes. I was a priest of the Fiery One before I became High Priest of the Wild. I know at least something of the frustration you face."

"Prove it," Ashi said.

"Beg pardon?"

"You want to teach me meditation to help me manage being frustrated? I want to see that it works."

Yahil looked puzzled. "I'm not sure I underst—"

"Take off your clothes."

"I'm...I..." he stammered, flustered.

Ashi smiled. "Surely the idea is simple?" she said, her voice sweet as honey. "If you want to teach me ways to manage frustration, it's reasonable to demonstrate your own mastery, is it not?"

"I—"

"Get undressed."

Yahil stood. "You are the Avatar," he said. He removed his kilt and his simple red shirt.

Ashi placed her hand on his shoulder. "Sit down. Put your hands behind your head."

"What—"

"Call it a demonstration of competency."

Yahil sighed. He sat in the chair and, with an exaggerated motion with his hands behind his head.

"Now then," Ashi said. She knelt in front of him. "Don't move. Don't say a word. Don't make a sound."

"I—"

"Shush! Not a word. Show me that you know enough about mastery to teach me."

She stroked his cock, very gently, her fingertips barely brushing it. When it started to harden, she leaned over and placed a tiny kiss on the head. Her warm breath caressed his skin. He tensed up slightly.

Ashi extended her tongue. She flicked the head of his cock very lightly. Yahil took a deep breath and closed his eyes.

She worked on him with all the skill she had, teasing him with lips and tongue. A drop of wetness formed at the head of his cock. She took it slowly into her mouth, allowing her tongue to play over the sensitive underside. Yahil remained still, breathing slowly.

She moved faster, letting him slip in and out of her mouth, tongue dancing across the head on every stroke. She ran her hands along his thighs as she sucked. His cock thickened. She tasted drops of salty liquid. He remained calm, hands behind his head, his breathing deep and even.

She brought him to the edge of orgasm again and again, feeling the tension in his body, the thickening of the cock in her mouth. He neither moved nor made a sound.

Finally, after well over an hour of this, she admitted defeat. "Okay, you have pretty good control," she admitted grudgingly. "How do you do it?"

"Thank you." Yahil opened his eyes. "It is largely a matter of appreciating each sensation for what it is, without thinking about what I would like it to be. To do it requires a clarity of focus that only comes with surrender."

"That's not really all that helpful," Ashi said. "It sounds nice and all, but it doesn't tell me how to do it."

"Start by breathing," Yahil said. "Sit down and breathe."

Ashi expected him to tease her, or run his hands over her, something, but he didn't. He simply sat in front of her and instructed her to breathe. She closed her eyes and looked for the center of calmness that might indicate surrender. She didn't find it.

Finally, he said, "That is all for today, I think."

"I thought I was supposed to learn to surrender to the Wild," Ashi said.

"The first people to come here did not arrive on this world in a day. We did not create the gods in a day. That is why there is time between the Selection and the Sacrifice."

"Oh? I thought that was so there was plenty of time to have parties in front of me."

"That too." Yahil smiled. "For right now, I suggest you surrender to dinner. I will be back in a bit for your evening cleansing."

Later that evening, when she swallowed the liquid from the urn and then sat on Yahil's lap in the pool, sliding onto his erection as she did, Ashi tried to focus on breathing. She took joy in Yahil's moans and the shudder that ran through him as she impaled herself on him.

She felt hyper-aware of the feel of Yahil inside her, the touch of Wahai's hands on her sensitive breasts, the feel of Hemmis kissing her. These things intruded on her awareness, a constant reminder of the desire she could not slake. She trembled and whimpered. Her head spun.

She found herself unsteady on her feet when Emrin and Marnin led her back to her cell. "Whew!" she said. "I feel strange."

"It's the Blessing," Marnin said. "You'll learn to handle it."

"Everyone keeps telling me that," Ashi said. "Are you two going to put your hands on me now?"

"Yes," Emrin said. He summoned two flasks of oil from the Provider.

"You realize I'm going to tease you also."

"Yes," Marnin said. He poured a line of oil down her back. His strong hands worked her muscles.

Ashi sighed. "After the Sacrifice," she said, "is there any way I can get you two to keep doing this?"

"Perhaps," Emrin said. He ran his hands up her legs. "If you ask nicely."

"Mmm, good," she said. "If you do, perhaps I'll even let you come."

She teased them without mercy while they massaged her and went to bed that night with a self-congratulatory smile on her face.

3.13

Riyan did not appear the following day. Ashi half-expected her to, somewhere after the day's first massage, but there was no sign of her.

She teased Marnin and Emrin, but while there was some joy in their squirming, she still felt vaguely irritated. Her heart wasn't really in the torments she inflicted on them, even when Emrin had difficulty walking as he left her cell.

She watched the goings-on in the City from her viewscreen for a while. She read for a while. She ran her hands over herself for a while, but that only made her more frustrated. When Yahil came to collect her for the evening's cleansing, she found herself glad of the company.

"You know," she said as they walked down the passageway, "this isn't really all I had hoped. The Wild wants us to be out under the sun and stars, not cooped up in…" She waved her arm. "This. Being underground feels unnatural."

Yahil opened the massive wooden door. "Becoming Sacrifice means learning new things," he said mildly. "Kneel, please."

She slid to her knees in front of him. "Why, High Priest Yahil," she said in her most innocent voice, "is there something you'd like to put in my mouth?" She gazed up at him and opened wide, tongue extended.

Yahil put his hand under her chin. "Yes, there is," he said. He picked up the urn from its place on the stone where it collected the slow *drip, drip, drip* from the cavern's ceiling and brought it to her lips. She drank, her eyes not leaving his. When he had replaced the urn, she said, "Is there anything else you'd like to put in my mouth? You know, as long as I'm here."

Wahai laughed. "She is spirited, isn't she?"

"That's one word for it," Marnin said.

The Blessing took effect quickly. A hazy golden glow spread through Ashi. Her knees wobbled as she stepped down into the pool. She melted into Yahil. Wahai kissed her. She returned her kiss with slow intensity, moaning. Hemmis explored her body with his fingertips. His touch left little tingling whorls of sensation on her skin.

The buzz persisted as Marnin and Emrin massaged her back. Their hands sent delightful ripples through her skin. When they helped her turn over, she moved up, so her head hung off the edge of the table. Emrin stood above her, running his hands over her breasts. She put her hands on his hips and pulled him forward, guiding him into her mouth. She held him there, neither moving nor allowing him to thrust his hips, just holding him in her mouth, caressing his shaft with her tongue. Marnin ran his hands up her legs. She parted them for him, allowing him access. He poured a bit of oil directly over her clit. She moaned. Emrin quivered at the moan.

The buzz persisted when Marnin and Emrin washed her. In the shower, she directed them to spread their legs and lean against the wall. Then she moved back and forth between the two of them. She started with Marnin, standing behind him and reaching around to stroke him with soapy hands until he groaned, trembling. She left him hanging just before orgasm while she did the same to Emrin, running her hands over his shaft until his body trembled. She released him and returned to Marnin, hands working his cock while she kissed the back of his neck until he whimpered. Then she moved over to Emrin, stroking him with short, rapid motions to the point where he quivered at the edge of release.

"Aren't you two glad you have this job?" she said.

"Yes!" they both gasped in unison.

"Hm. No accounting for taste," she said. "Off you go, then."

She floated out to the main room. The Provider had already disgorged a dress for her, identical to the one she'd worn, and destroyed, at the first gathering of worshippers. She picked it up. "I guess there's another party tonight," she said.

That suspicion was confirmed when Fiha arrived in the room outside her cell, holding a tray of small vials. "Time for a party again?" she said through the bars.

Fiha bowed. "Yes."

"Everyone's having fun but me," Ashi said. "Well, and you, I suppose. You just stand there holding that tray."

"Are you inviting me to participate?"

Ashi looked Fiha up and down. "Are you allowed to?"

"If the Avatar of the Wild wills it, it is allowed," Fiha said.

"What's allowed?" Ruji said. He and Vrynn walked into the chamber holding hands. Each selected a vial from the tray. They uncapped the vials and drank, then kissed.

"Ruji! Vrynn!" Ashi said. "We were just talking about whether Fiha here should join the party instead of just standing there with a tray in her hand. After all, it's not like she's stuck in a cage or something."

Ruji's eyes swept over Fiha's form. "I endorse this idea," he said.

"Seconded," Vrynn said. He bowed toward Ashi. "Greetings, Avatar of the Wild, Sacrifice to his service, representative of a living god, bearer of his blessings, carrier of the secret knowledge."

"Have you been planning to say that all day?" Ashi said.

"Why? Does it show?"

"'Carrier of the secret knowledge'? Really?"

Vrynn broke into a broad grin. "What? I thought it sounded good."

Ashi snorted. "The only secret knowledge I have is what it feels like to be teased without being allowed to come."

"I don't think that's secret knowledge," Ruji said. "I hear you've been spreading that knowledge, in fact." Fiha suppressed a laugh.

More people arrived, and more after that. The lights outside the cell dimmed. Soon Ashi stood in a pool of light from the chandelier above her, with shadows all around her. Soft moans and sighs, punctuated with the occasional gasp or squeak, came from the darkness outside her cell.

Jannon was the first to approach Ashi's cell, back in his old body. He bowed in front of her. "Avatar of the Wild, will you bestow your blessing—"

"Oh, get over here," Ashi said. She reached through the bars and dragged him close. She kissed him roughly, forcing her tongue into his mouth. He tensed up. Then, with a growl, he was grabbing her, squeezing her breasts, tearing at her dress.

The room spun. Ashi allowed the feeling to sweep over her. She offered no resistance as Jannon tore at her clothes. He kissed her bare breasts through the bars. She ran her fingers through his hair. He struggled with his kilt, clawing at the waistband with such haste that it took him several tries to unfasten it. Then he put his hands on her hips, pulling her forward so hard the bars dug into her skin, and with one thrust he was inside her. He let out a roar. Ashi felt a wave of pleasure so intense it took her breath away.

His orgasm started small but grew until, by the end, he was breathless and shaking. Almost before it had ended, Ashi grabbed his hair and pushed him down onto his knees. She pressed his face between her legs and thrust herself forward as far as the bars would allow. Every movement of his tongue against her clit sent shivering heat up her body.

"Would anyone else like to receive my blessing?" she called.

Worshippers swarmed around her. Hands pressed through the bars to touch, squeeze, and fondle her. She held Jannon down, forcing his face between her legs while the other worshippers pawed and groped her with increasing urgency. With every touch, the warm glow spread, until Ashi was lost in a haze, inundated by sensation but unable to focus on specifics. Hands touched her, but she couldn't really tell who they belonged to. When she released Jannon, someone else entered her. She felt lips on her lips, but she wasn't sure if they belonged to whoever was inside her.

Time expanded and shrank at the same time. Every kiss, every thrust went on forever, but before she knew it, the evening ended, and worshippers headed for the door, leaving their clothes behind.

Ashi leaned against the bars, panting. Her body thrummed. The world around her seemed just slightly out of focus. Fiha approached her. "Would you still like me to participate?" she said.

Ashi nodded. "Yes," she rasped.

Fiha set her tray on a nearby cushion. She picked up a tiny jeweled vial and downed its contents. She stood still for a moment, blinking. A soft sigh escaped her lips. Her pupils dilated.

"May I—"

"Yes!" Ashi said.

Fiha walked up to the bars. Ashi put her arms around her and kissed her. Fiha stiffened for a moment.

"Let me pleasure you," Ashi said. She knelt. "Just be still." Her hands moved up Fiha's long legs, pushing her skirt up. "Enjoy me."

She pulled Fiha's hips against the bars and explored Fiha's folds with her tongue. Fiha grabbed the bars and held on tightly as Ashi brought her to pleasure over and over again, each orgasm accompanied by a long, gentle sigh.

When Ashi opened her eyes the next morning, the grouchiness settled back around her. As much as she had enjoyed the previous evening, her inability to orgasm left her frustrated and irritable in the morning light. Not that she could see the morning light, she thought bitterly as she followed Yahil down the corridor. An underground cage was no place for a worshipper of the Wild.

The Blessing from the urn burned away a little of the irritability, but a stubborn residue clung to her like a bad aftertaste even while Marnin and Emrin massaged her. Her body responded to their touch, but her mind remained elsewhere.

After they had washed her, she stood between them in the shower. She curled a hand around both men's cocks, coaxing them erect. "Do you like it when I tease you?" she asked.

"Yes," Marnin said.

"Oh," she said. "Well then, I imagine it must be quite frustrating if I don't." She released them. "Go."

Yahil came to visit her later that morning, accompanied by a short, pale woman with large gray eyes. She was barefoot and wore a simple white dress of silky fabric. Waves of deep burgundy hair spilling across one shoulder provided her only color. Tiny gems glowed faintly in rows along her arms. "May we come in?" Yahil asked.

"Yes," Ashi said. "I never thought I'd miss a disembodied voice telling me 'you have a visitor,' yet here we are."

Yahil smiled. "Thank you, I think." He opened the door. The two of them settled on a couch. Ashi sat on a chair facing them.

"Who's your friend?" Ashi said.

"This is Orias," Yahil said. "She was Sacrifice to the Wild...oh, a long time ago. Before I joined the Temple. Maybe before I was born."

Orias extended a hand. "I went by the name Patillas then," she said in a gentle, melodious voice. "I am pleased to meet you. I hear you are having difficulty adjusting."

Ashi's eyes darted between Orias and Yahil. "You could say that."

Orias smiled. "I understand. It's paradoxical, isn't it? The Wild tells us to abandon ourselves completely. So why, then, would he want his Sacrifice to be locked in a cage abstaining from pleasure?"

"You see?" Ashi said to Yahil. "She gets it! It makes no sense."

Yahil inclined his head. "I will leave you two to your conversation." He rose and left, without locking the door behind him.

"Maybe I can offer some insight into the paradox," Orias said once he was gone. "You have participated in a Sacrifice ritual before, so you know what happens."

"Yes," Ashi said. "I changed my body for it and everything. Having a penis is interesting." She smiled at the memory.

"So, you know what the Sacrifice must endure."

"Mm, yes. Yes, I do."

"It's no easy thing, what you will experience. Your path through it requires you find a source of calm and surrender within yourself. That's what this will teach you."

"That's what Yahil said."

"Did he try to teach you breathing exercises?"

"Yes."

Orias smiled. "That's a load of rot," she said. "It won't help."

"He also said something about being in the moment…"

"Ah," Orias said, "now that does help. Service to the Wild is about total abandon. Being a sacrifice to the Wild is about total restraint. Those do not necessarily have to be in opposition to each other. In both cases, what he teaches us is to give ourselves entirely to the experience of the moment." She leaned forward and took Ashi's hands in hers. "What do you feel?"

"Your hands."

"Go on."

"They're warm," Ashi said. "And soft."

"What else?"

"I imagine they might feel nice on my body."

"Ah, you see? There. That is where you went from feeling what is, to thinking about what might be. You left the moment."

"But I—"

"Come back to the moment. Feel my hands without attaching to ideas about anything except what you feel right now."

"I don't understand how this helps," Ashi complained.

"It does. During the Sacrifice, you become a vessel through which the worshippers experience a purging. A vessel exists, without goal or desire, like a cup holds water without wishing the water was higher or lower."

"But why?"

"Why what?"

"Why be a vessel? Why any of this?"

"Because," Orias said, "complete abandon all the time doesn't work. In order for some to experience that total surrender in safety, others must have total awareness. A wheel that spins too fast flies apart if the center doesn't hold. As Sacrifice, you are the center. It's not your task forever, but it is your task now."

"That sounds like a complete load of rubbish," Ashi said.

To her surprise, Orias laughed, a full, deep laugh without restraint or self-consciousness. "I thought the same thing," she said, "though I wasn't so brash as to say it out loud. I like you, Ashi."

"I've never seen you around," Ashi said. "Do you still worship the Wild?"

"No. I did for a time, after my Sacrifice. Then I worshipped the Quickener for a time. I wanted something different. She didn't call to me the way the Wild had. Now, the Lady speaks to me. I have worshipped her for many years." She turned Ashi's hand over in hers and ran her fingers across Ashi's palm. "Shall we focus on breathing?"

"Why? You said it doesn't help."

"Yes, but Yahil doesn't know that. He asked me to help you with your breathing. I told him I would. While we're doing that, I can tell you about some things that really will help."

Orias's finger on her palm awoke a powerful awareness of how her body tingled, of the hunger in her skin. "Are you sure there's nothing better we might do?" she said.

Orias laughed again. "There you go, leaving the moment. Close your eyes and breathe with me."

3.14

ASHI FELT A little more grounded the next day. Grounded enough, anyway, that as she lay face down on the table after her morning dip in the pond, enjoying the feel of Marnin's and Emrin's hands on her back, she didn't bother to open her eyes when she heard the door open. She didn't even open her eyes when a third pair of hands joined the ones on her body. She relaxed and let the warm glow envelop her, remaining in the moment.

When they helped her turn over, Riyan grinned down at her, entirely nude except for a fine chain with a key dangling from it around her neck.

Ashi grinned. "I almost thought you'd forgotten about me!"

"Never," she said. "Though you seem to be doing pretty well without me. I thought I'd surprise you by crawling into bed with you. I didn't know you'd be busy. Is this a bad time? Shall I come back later?"

"No!" Ashi said.

Riyan burst out laughing. "I'm teasing you. I still haven't forgotten your promise. I intend to collect tonight. I just had some things to do first."

"What things?"

"Shush." Riyan put her finger over Ashi's lips. "Nothing you need worry about. Much." She poured some oil into her hands. "Now close your eyes and don't move. Let us do wonderful things to you."

They did, for quite a long time. Ashi sighed and moaned and squirmed under three sets of expert hands that seemed to know exactly where and how to touch her. After a time, lips and tongues were added. Ashi cried out when Marnin and Riyan took her nipples between their lips while Emrin's tongue moved over her clit. She arched her back so violently that Marnin and Riyan held her down. Emrin put his hands on her hips to pin her to the table while his tongue kept moving, until Ashi felt so lightheaded she feared she might faint.

Afterward, in the shower, Riyan held Ashi's arms behind her back while Marnin and Emrin washed her. She looked at the two of them over Ashi's shoulder. "Do you see how excited she is? Do you feel how she quivers? Can you tell how she longs for it?"

"Yes," Emrin said, his voice hoarse.

"Today, she must do whatever I say," Riyan said. "She may be the avatar of the Wild, but a promise is a promise." She kissed the side of Ashi's neck. "Take her, if you want. Pleasure yourselves with her. Every part of her cries out for it."

Marnin groaned. He entered Ashi hard. Ashi's knees buckled.

"Yes," Riyan said. "Like that. Don't stop until you're satisfied."

Marnin howled, pounding into Ashi over and over until he swelled and released a hot torrent inside her. His body shook.

When he finished, Riyan turned Ashi toward Emrin, still holding her arms behind her back. "Would you like to pleasure yourself with her?"

"By the Wild, yes," he said. He wrapped his arms around Ashi and Riyan, pinning Ashi between them. He kissed her as he entered her. He took her slowly but not at all gently, forcing himself into her again and again. Riyan encouraged him until he, too, screamed and shook.

"Okay, you can go now," Riyan said.

She dried Ashi, helped her dress, then led her to the couch. They curled up for a while together. Ashi basked in Riyan's closeness. "That wasn't a very nice thing you did to me," she said.

"I understand you weren't being very nice to them," Riyan said.

"I'm allowed!" Ashi protested. "Haven't you heard? I'm the avatar of a god!"

"I'm allowed too," Riyan smirked. "Haven't you heard? The avatar of a god made a promise." She stuck out her tongue at Ashi. "Tonight's going to be fun. I invited Luron."

"Who?"

"Remember that fellow who almost made it to the top when you did your leaping-recklessly-through-the-air-to-crash-into-the-trees thing?"

"Oh."

"Oh yes, 'oh.'" Riyan unwrapped herself from Ashi. "I'm hungry. Fancy a bit of lunch?" As she busied herself with the Provider, she said, "What does the avatar of a god do all day, anyway?"

"Less than you might think," Ashi said. "A lot of it involves breathing."

"Oh?"

"Yeah. Apparently it helps with the—you know. Or so Yahil says. I have it on expert opinion he might be wrong." She curled her feet beneath herself on the couch. "In all honesty, though, I don't really feel like the avatar of a god. It's not like he talks to me or anything. I'm just me, you know? Only less mobile. Speaking of Yahil, he'll be by in a bit to collect me."

"For what?"

"Giving me a blessing, groping me in a pool, and then sending me back here for another massage before the party tonight."

"Ooh, sounds like fun!" Riyan said. "Can I watch?"

"If you want. The avatar of a god wills it so."

"What else does the avatar of a god will?"

"Bring me lunch and snuggle me."

"As you will, oh avatar."

Yahil found them curled up on the sofa together. He and Riyan exchanged a look. Riyan winked.

Ashi was instantly suspicious. "What are you two up to?" she said.

"This way, please," Yahil said. Riyan smirked at Ashi.

In the cavern, Ashi knelt while Yahil poured the liquid from the urn into her mouth. She stood unsteadily, putting her hand on Riyan for support. "Whew!" she said. "Are you sure that isn't getting stronger? It went straight to my head!"

"You poor thing," Riyan said.

She helped Ashi into the pool with Yahil, Wahai, and Hemmis. Ashi giggled as she sat on Yahil's lap. She draped her arms across Wahai and Hemmis. "Which of you wants to kiss me first?" Ashi said.

"I do," Hemmis said. By the time he finished speaking, Wahai was already kissing her.

Riyan chuckled. "What did you just learn?" she said to Hemmis. He rolled his eyes at her.

Riyan sat by the edge of the pool with Marnin and Emrin, watching Ashi sigh and whimper. After a time, Yahil helped her rise. Emrin dried her, and then he and Marnin escorted Ashi and Riyan back to the cell. Ashi looked over her shoulder to see Yahil and Hemmis kiss. Wahai ran her hands over Yahil's back.

In the cell, Marnin summoned flasks of oil from the Provider. Emrin and Riyan helped Ashi onto the table. The three of them went to work on her. Marnin massaged her shoulders, Riyan massaged her back, and Emrin massaged her legs until she felt herself drifting. "If you keep that up," she mumbled, "I am going to melt, and then I'll miss the party."

"We can't have that," Riyan said. "I have plans for you. Shall we turn her over and wake her up again?"

"Of course," Emrin said.

They rolled her over. Emrin set to massaging her breasts while Marnin worked on her legs. Riyan leaned over to kiss Ashi. "What will it take to get you ready for the evening?" she said. "What will excite you?"

"Emrin could use his tongue on me," Ashi said.

"You heard her," Riyan said. "Put your fingers in her while you're at it."

Ashi moaned when Emrin's fingers slid into her. The moan grew louder as she raised her hips to meet his tongue. Marnin squeezed her breasts. Riyan stroked her nipples. Ashi squirmed.

"Do we have your attention yet?" Riyan said.

"You're getting there," Ashi said.

Riyan nodded to Emrin. "A couple more fingers, I think."

Ashi cried out, bucking her hips as Emrin pressed two more fingers into her.

"How about now?" Riyan said.

"Oh!" Ashi said. Her eyes closed. "Oh, that feels nice."

"Harder," Riyan instructed Marnin. He squeezed her breasts more tightly. Riyan's fingers tightened on Ashi's nipples.

They continued their steady assault until Ashi panted and writhed, unable to stay still. Wetness dripped around Emrin's fingers. Riyan did not call a halt until Ashi was begging, barely coherent, for more.

She ground her hips against Marnin while they bathed her. "Would you like them to pleasure themselves with you again?" Riyan said.

"Please!" Ashi said.

Riyan laughed. "Not this time. I like you this way!"

Riyan sent Marnin and Emrin away. She dried Ashi, then took her by the hand and brought her into the main room. The Provider disgorged a dress, neatly folded.

Riyan helped Ashi dress. She summoned a dress of her own, cut similarly down to her navel, but in white, with a simple blue ribbon tied around the waist. "Now then," she said. "Do you agree to do whatever I say, as per the terms of your promise?"

"Yes," Ashi said.

"Oh, that's lovely." Riyan turned to the Provider. She called up another blue ribbon, identical to the one she wore around her waist, and a slender curved vial bent into a spiral. "Here," she said, handing the vial to Ashi. "Drink this."

"Is this the Blessing of Union?"

"Yes."

"You want to feel what I feel?"

Riyan grinned. "No. I'm not taking it. I gave myself in service to the Blesser to get this, but it's not for me. I've already given the other half to someone else."

"Who?"

"Well, that's for you to figure out. It will be someone who is present tonight. You'll know when you find the right person. Now drink!"

Ashi drank the contents of the vial, with more than a little trepidation. She had a brief, dizzying moment of being in two places at once, but it was over too quickly to tell where her other half was.

"Good," Riyan said when she finished. "Now turn around. Put your hands behind your back."

Ashi obeyed. Riyan used the blue ribbon to bind Ashi's wrists.

With that done, she fussed with Ashi's dress. "No, no, no, this won't do at all," she said. She summoned a pair of scissors. With a few quick snips, she cut holes in the front of the dress to reveal Ashi's breasts. "Much better." She fed the scissors back into the Provider and called up two broad clamps connected by a length of chain. She steered Ashi over to the bars of the cage. She placed one clamp on Ashi's nipple, looped the chain around one of the bars, and placed the other clamp on Ashi's other nipple. "There!" she said. "That will keep you from trying to move away!"

"The clamps are very tight!" Ashi complained.

Riyan shook her head. "That also won't do," she said. "I can't have you complaining." She returned to the Provider and came back with a padded metal ring attached to two straps. "Here," she said. "This should stop you from complaining, but still let you moan and scream. Open your mouth!"

She placed the ring in Ashi's mouth and fastened the straps behind her head. As she was finishing, Fiha arrived with her tray of vials.

"Perfect timing," Riyan said. She left the cell and inspected the variety of vials on the tray. "Do they all do the same thing?"

"No," Fiha said.

"Ah, of course not. I like…this one." Riyan chose a short teardrop-shaped vial in dark aquamarine. "Thank you." She went back into the cage, drew out the key that hung on its chain around her neck, and locked the door. "Whew!" she said. "I'm ready. Are you ready?"

"Dus it hatter?" Ashi said.

Riyan stuck her finger playfully into Ashi's mouth. "You're drooling," she said. "I like it. Look! Your guests are arriving. Time to be an avatar of a god!"

"Hunherhul," Ashi said.

The room filled up quickly. Word had gotten around that something unusual was on the agenda, and everyone wanted to be there. Worshippers streamed into the chamber, selected a vial from the tray, and found a space on the chairs or couches or sprawled on the cushions that littered the floor. An excited buzz filled the air.

Riyan ran her hands over Ashi's shoulders. "Good evening!" she said. "As you know, Ashi here will be this year's Sacrifice. What you might not know is she made a promise to me that if she succeeded in being named Sacrifice, she would give herself to me to do whatever I said. Even the gods themselves respect the power of a promise. Tonight, I'm making good on it. Since she has given herself to me, I am sharing my good fortune with all of you." She kissed Ashi on the cheek. "And since she has to do whatever I say, I say she shall have her hands tied behind her back and her nipples clamped to the bars so she can't get away from you lot." Riyan ran her hands lightly down Ashi's arms. Goosebumps rose in their wake. "Tonight, there's no need to ask the Avatar for her blessing. Just come on up and take. Have fun!"

Worshippers surged forward, eager to place their hands on Ashi. She tried to shrink back away from the bars. The clamps tightened on her nipples.

Hands touched Ashi all over. Her nipples swelled in the clamps. The world went hazy, unreal, as if she were seeing herself in a dream. Her mind filled with fog.

Someone grabbed the bottom of her dress and pulled. Fabric tore. More hands reached through the bars, grabbing at her legs, her breasts, her sides. Fingers penetrated her, bringing pleasure so abrupt she felt dizzy. She struggled to free her hands. The ribbon held them fast behind her back.

A hard penis slid into her. She let out a cry, feeling a wave of pleasure so intense that for an instant, she was certain she would come. She trembled on the edge of orgasm, a hair's breadth from the release she had been craving for days, as her unknown lover, lost in the haze, held her pinned against the bars and thrust into her with furious abandon. A tall, willowy woman with brilliant golden eyes pushed her tongue through the ring that held Ashi's mouth open.

Her lover came. When he pulled out, Ashi let out another cry, this one of shock and disappointment.

Now someone else was in front of her. Ashi had a quick impression of broad shoulders and long black hair streaked with white, red, and purple before he pushed his fingers into Ashi's mouth. Ashi ran her tongue over his fingertips. He grabbed the chain that connected the clamps and tugged it downward. Ashi yelped with pain. She sank awkwardly to her knees. He reached through the bars to grab her head. He forced his erect cock into her mouth. Ashi welcomed it with her tongue, swirling it around the head, then running it back and forth along the underside.

He took her mouth with quick, short strokes, until he roared with pleasure and great gouts of warm salty goo filled her mouth. The slick wetness poured right back out again, splattering what was left of her dress.

He stepped away. Another man took his place, his cock already engorged, feeding it to Ashi...

...and as it slid in, she felt it, not just against her tongue, but between her legs, as though a mouth were enclosing some phantom penis she didn't have.

Ashi looked up. He was tall and thin, but muscular. His black hair hung in two braids over his shoulders, one streaked with red, the other with blue. His eyes were slate-gray, the cross-shaped pupils shrunken until they were just thin, crossed lines.

"I'm Luron," he said. "I don't believe we've met. Those clamps on your nipples really hurt, don't they?"

"Hurnf," Ashi said.

"Oh, right. Continue."

Ashi moved her head, playing her tongue against his erection. She felt every motion, every bit of pleasure he felt. The shared sensation told her exactly how to pleasure him, exactly where he was most sensitive.

Her head bobbed. Tension coiled in him, creating an identical tension in her. She built him up quickly, seeking his orgasm, feeling it build in her own body.

He came, howling with pleasure. Ashi felt his orgasm through her body, but it was a pale thing, an echo of an orgasm, a phantom as insubstantial as mist. White goo dribbled down her breasts.

The evening blurred. Ashi was aware only of snippets: hands on her, fingers and cocks entering her, warmth splattering her face and body, her tongue extending through the ring to find a clit, and all around her, moans and cries of pleasure.

Luron visited her five more times. Every time, she felt the echo of his orgasm in her body, as vague and pale as a shape seen through a dense fog. She wept with frustration. Some echo of her frustration seemed to resonate

367

with him, because his own orgasms failed to sate him, and he returned again and again.

Eventually, the worshippers had had enough. In ones and twos, and occasionally in threes, they left, until none remained except Fiha. She smiled at Ashi. "This has been a night to remember," she said. She gathered up the discarded bits of clothing left behind by the worshippers on her way out.

Riyan unfastened the strap that held the ring in Ashi's mouth. She released the clamps from Ashi's nipples. Ashi gasped in pain as the blood rushed back into them. Riyan helped Ashi to the couch. "What did you think?" she said.

Ashi looked up at her with dazed eyes. Riyan seemed enveloped in a golden haze. "I…" she said and stopped. No words seemed adequate.

"You're a mess," Riyan said. "I could help you clean up and then put you to bed. Or…"

"Or?"

Riyan reached down into her dress and took out the vial she'd chosen from Fiha's tray. "Or I could drink this. And then I could touch you. I am already quite aroused, and I'm told that touching the avatar of the Wild after imbibing his blessing is quite intense. If I do that, I will not be able to control myself." She walked toward Ashi, hips swaying. "I will not be able to stop myself from ravishing you." She stopped just out of Ashi's reach. "It's quite likely I'll be very rough. And unlike the others, I have no bars standing between you and me. What do you think, Ashi dear? Shall I put you to bed, or shall I drink this, and we will see what happens next?"

Ashi blinked. Her body thrummed. Her nipples bloomed with pain. The scraps of her dress that still remained were plastered to her body with slick wetness.

She stretched out a hand toward Riyan. "Drink it," she whispered.

Riyan beamed. "Oh, I like you." She took the stopper from the vial and swallowed the liquid inside. Then she reached toward Ashi. Their hands touched.

3.15

THE LOCK SCRAPED open. Ashi untangled herself from Riyan, blinking away sleep. The scraps of what had once been a dress still clung to her body, glued in place by dried semen. Riyan snored softly.

"You had an interesting night, I see," Yahil said.

Ashi rubbed her eyes. She crawled out of bed without waking Riyan and ordered a large glass of water from the Provider. Yahil waited.

She padded silently after him down the hallway. The others already waited in the bathing cavern. Yahil directed Ashi to kneel, then brought the urn to her lips. She drank. The pleasant heat spread through her body, chasing away the fatigue. She floated to her feet.

Yahil and Wahai helped her into the pool. She closed her eyes and sank gratefully into the water. Wahai and Hemmis gently removed the scraps of her dress. Wahai ran her hands over Ashi, cleaning away the last traces from the party. "How are you doing this morning?" she asked.

"Frustrated," Ashi said. "I still haven't had an orgasm."

Wahai nodded. "Understandable. I hear you've been talking to a past Sacrifice."

"Does everyone know everything I'm doing?" Ashi said.

"Of course. You're the avatar of a god. You're also wild even by the standards of the Wild. You've become a bit of a legend. A lot of people are talking about you. Like what you're doing to poor Emrin and Marnin here."

"Hang on," Marnin said from where he sat by the edge of the pool, "I wouldn't exactly say 'poor Marnin.' Serving the Wild in this capacity has its...um, benefits."

"Okay, fair," Wahai said. "And after last night, well..."

"What about last night?"

"Riyan has a bit of a fan club."

"Maybe she should have been chosen as Sacrifice," Ashi said. "I still don't feel like an avatar of a god."

Wahai shrugged, a graceful motion that sent ripples along the surface of the pool. "You grow into it, I think."

"Hmph," Ashi said. She found herself relaxing under Wahai's caress in spite of herself.

Riyan was awake and sipping from a mug of tea when Ashi got back to her cell. She beamed at Ashi. "Did you have fun last night?"

"I'm sore," Ashi grumbled.

"And whose fault is that?"

"Yours, I think."

Riyan smiled wider. "Then my work here is done. Unless you'd like me to stick around and help these two gentlemen massage out all the kinks I put into you."

"Mm, yes, please," Ashi said.

They worked on her for a long time, three sets of hands caressing and massaging her, before they turned her over. Riyan urged Marnin and Emrin to tease Ashi until she wept with frustration. "Don't fuss!" she said. She caressed Ashi's cheek. "If you fuss, I will let them pleasure themselves with you again. And after what I did to you last night, you might be a little too sore for that. Besides, they're being nice to you. You should be grateful. If getting a massage every day is the worst thing that ever happens to you, you're doing pretty well, aren't you? Now say thank you."

"Thank you," Ashi whimpered.

"That's better," Riyan said. She poured oil over Ashi's breasts and put her hands on them. "I think we can do this for...oh, another hour or two at least, right?"

"I have nowhere to be," Emrin said. He spread Ashi open and applied a stream of oil directly to her clit.

Ashi wailed. Riyan smiled.

They made good on the threat to tease her for hours, and indeed were only just finishing bathing her when Yahil arrived with Orias. Ashi dressed before she invited them in. Marnin and Emrin excused themselves. Emrin gave a small bow to Yahil as he left. "High Priest," he said.

Orias smiled at Riyan. "You must be Ashi's friend, the one who agreed to undergo the Sacrifice along with her," she said.

"Does everyone know about that?" Riyan said.

"Word gets around, I'm told," Ashi said dryly. "Apparently the whole damn City is talking about us."

"It's nice to be appreciated," Riyan said. "I'll leave you to talk about important avatar stuff." She squeezed Ashi's hand and winked.

"Stay," Orias said. "Since you will be participating in the Sacrifice, you might find what I have to say useful."

"I'd love to, but I have other things I need to do," Riyan said.

"As you wish."

When Ashi and Orias were alone, Orias took Ashi's hand. "Have you been practicing finding your center of calm?"

"No," Ashi said.

"You sound frustrated."

"I am frustrated! I'm supposed to be the avatar of the Wild and I'm the most constrained of all!"

"Yes," Orias said. "Think of the Wild as a lever, lifting people up to greater surrender to what is, and thereby to greater joy. Every lever needs a point of stillness upon which to move. You are that point."

"Ha!" Ashi said. "That doesn't really help."

Orias smiled calmly. "I'll wager every Sacrifice before you has felt the same way. You are giving a lot to the Temple. That's why it's called a sacrifice. This, too, shall pass."

"Well, it can't pass soon enough."

"Oh, I don't know about that," Orias said. "But then, I have the benefit of hindsight."

"When you were Sacrifice, did people tell you all these things?"

"Yes."

"Did you listen? Did it help?"

"Of course not. You won't understand until the moment you need it. Now close your eyes and breathe."

In the weeks that followed, Ashi became more convinced that the business of being selected as Sacrifice involved a lot of busywork and nonsense. Orias spent every afternoon with her, talking about fulcrums and breathing and finding stillness within herself. Ashi didn't see how all of that made one whit of difference to the fact that she was being teased constantly—not the least by Riyan, spent quite a bit of time with her, and seemed to relish exploring the fertile fields of new and ever more devilish ways to tease her.

Still, she was forced to admit, there might have been something to what Orias was teaching her. Or maybe she was just getting more sensitive to the Blessing of Enticement, as Yahil said she would. Whatever it was, as the weeks went by, she found herself less grouchy and more easily able to bear the constant teasing.

She also found herself spending more and more time in that hazy glow of intoxication, where she felt like she was floating just a little bit above the floor and the world seemed just a tiny bit out of focus.

The haziness helped her to relax into the moment, to enjoy what was happening to her without needing it to be more than it was. She found that she looked forward to the three-nights-a-week parties when the worshippers would gather outside her cell. She would flit to and fro, blessing them with her touch, enjoying the way it drove them to a frenzy of need. Afterward, Riyan would drink from a vial herself, and then touch her, abandoning herself completely to the madness that followed. Ashi would surrender to Riyan's need, as compliant and yielding as Riyan was frantic and demanding, offering herself to Riyan's pleasure however Riyan wanted.

One evening, Riyan and Ashi lounged in bed nibbling on small round pastries filled with fruit. There was no congregation of the worshippers that evening. Marnin and Emrin had just left, and Ashi was lying with her eyes half-closed and a dreamlike, faraway smile on her lips. Her body still thrummed from what Riyan had done to her in the shower while the two men held her arms.

"You're fun," Riyan said. "I really enjoy playing with you. But…" She kissed Ashi's cheek.

"But?"

"I'm worried about you."

Ashi's face folded like a complicated bit of origami into a puzzled frown. "Why?"

"You seem…I don't know. Out of it. I feel like you're moving away from me. You're going somewhere else. Somewhere I can't follow."

"I don't understand," Ashi said.

"Well, it's like…" Riyan hesitated. She gathered the scattered threads of her thoughts and continued. "I really like teasing you when I know you can't come. And you seem to like it too. But lately, it doesn't seem to affect you as much. I don't…" She paused, frowning. "I don't mean physically. You're wonderfully responsive. And I love the sounds you make." She kissed Ashi's cheek again. "But you don't seem to mind."

"Should I mind?" Ashi said. "Are you saying I shouldn't enjoy what you do to me?"

"No! That's not what I mean at all! I mean, you don't seem to get, I don't know, quite as desperate as you used to."

"Is that a bad thing?"

"It's…I'm just worried, that's all. I see you changing. I'm worried you won't change back."

Ashi smiled. She wrapped her arms around Riyan and placed a small kiss on the tip of her nose. "Thank you."

"For what?"

"Worrying about me. Being engaged with me."

Riyan snuggled down beside Ashi. "I know that what's her name—"

"Orias."

"Orias keeps telling you to surrender. I just don't want you to surrender so far you can't come back."

Ashi stretched languidly. "I thought you liked it when I surrender."

"Stop it! I'm being serious."

"I know. I'm fine. It's probably just the Blessing. Well, that and the massages. And, you know, that thing where everyone goes crazy when I touch them. Through the bars of the cage. That I'm living in. For months. Where I can't see the sun."

"Ah," Riyan said. "When you put it that way…" She wrinkled her nose.

Still, as Ashi slipped further and further into the haze, she could tell, with that small part of her that remained aware, that Riyan worried. In her more lucid moments, Ashi could see a look of hesitation in Riyan's silver eyes, particularly before the thrice-weekly gatherings of the worshippers, when she slipped especially deeply into the warm golden haze.

Ten days before the time of the Sacrifice, Riyan woke Ashi with a kiss. Ashi dragged herself up from a dream in which she was poised on a log over a raging torrent of water far below. She knew, with dream logic, that a fall would sweep her away to be dashed on unseen rocks that lurked beyond a bend in the turbulent river, but she felt no fear. A calming presence, felt but not seen, hovered somewhere behind her, and she knew it would catch her if she fell. She made her way across the log, balancing against the gusts of wind kicked up from the seething water. She had almost reached the far side when she felt Riyan's lips on hers.

She forced her eyes open. "Oh, good morning!" she said. "Has Yahil come to take me to the cavern?"

"Not yet," Riyan said. "I…have something I have to do. I will not see you again until the night before the Sacrifice."

"What do you need to do?"

"I have to serve the Blesser to earn the Blessing of Union. Five days is…" She hesitated. "It's more than I've ever done before. I've never served longer than three nights in a row."

"Will you be okay?"

Riyan smiled. "Yes. I will need some time to recover, I expect. I will come back before your Sacrifice. Our Sacrifice." She kissed Ashi again. She climbed out of bed, summoned a dress of blue and gold from the Provider, and slipped it on. Then, with one backward look at Ashi, she left, locking the door behind her.

That afternoon, after Ashi had accepted the Blessing from Yahil, bathed in the pool, and received her massage, a tall, slender man with long black hair and copper-colored eyes came to visit. Tiny points of light danced in his hair. "Are you going to invite me in?" he said. His voice was low and throaty.

"Shia?" Ashi said.

Shia laughed. "In the slightly altered flesh! What do you think?" He ran his hands down his body.

"Is that for me?" Ashi said. "You shouldn't have! No need to change on my account."

"Mm-hmm," Shia said. "I attended my last Sacrifice in my usual body, but Vrynn says it's so much more fun when you have an outie rather than an innie, so I thought, what the hell? I'll give it a try. Hallia changed too. He's looking forward to the Sacrifice. So how about it? Are you going to invite me in?"

"I don't have a key," Ashi said.

"Oh really? You mean you're trapped in there, all alone and helpless?" Shia licked his lips.

"Mmm-hmm," Ashi said. "If you went to any of the parties, you'd know that."

"I keep meaning to. Vrynn and Ruji say they've been having a good time. Are you nervous about the Sacrifice?"

Ashi considered the question. "No," she said after a while. "Not really."

"I'm surprised."

"So am I," Ashi said.

"You're a far braver person than I am," Shia said. "I've only attended one Sacrifice as a worshipper, and I have to say, I'm impressed you're willing to put yourself through that."

Ashi felt the warmth from the Blessing and the arousal from the massage swirl inside her. She walked over to press herself against the bars. She looked Shia up and down. "Would you like to try out the new hardware?" she said. "You know, make sure everything's working?"

Shia laughed again. "You're so eager!"

"You'd be eager too, if you'd spent months caged up down here without an orgasm," Ashi said.

"And whose fault is that? If you want a taste, you'll just have to wait. It won't be long now, hmm?"

"So, you came here just to tease me, then?" Ashi said.

"Yep! And now that that's done, I will see you at the Sacrifice!" With a wink, he turned and walked away.

"You're terrible!" Ashi called after him, laughing.

"I know!" he said.

With a week to go until the Sacrifice, Orias stopped visiting Ashi. "You have learned what I can teach you, or you haven't," she said. "Either way, the Sacrifice will go on."

Ashi blinked. She felt entirely surrounded by warmth, as though she were still in the pool even though she had left it hours ago. "Will the worshippers be visiting me tonight?" she said.

Orias shook her head. "No. There will be no more assemblies before the Sacrifice."

"Oh," Ashi said. She was surprised to find she was disappointed.

"For what it's worth," Orias said, "I think you'll be a brilliant Sacrifice."

"Thank you!" Ashi glowed. "Will you be there?"

"I have duties to the Lady," Orias said. She saw Ashi's crestfallen look and added, "Perhaps I will stop in. You're unlikely to remember me."

"I may not," Ashi said, "but I would still like you to be there anyway. If you can."

"Okay." Orias put her hand on Ashi's arm. "Since you asked me, I will be there."

Ashi smiled. "Thank you."

Time disappeared in the golden haze. Riyan reappeared the day before the Sacrifice, exactly as she said she would. She arrived just as Ashi was receiving her evening massage. Ashi wriggled on the table when a third set of hands joined the two on her body. "Welcome back. Have you served the Blesser?"

Riyan ran her fingers down Ashi's back. "Yes." She shivered slightly, a motion that communicated itself down her arms, through her fingers, into Ashi's sensitive skin.

"You will be there, with me, when…"

"Yes," Riyan said. Her hands slid up Ashi's sides. "I will feel everything you feel."

"I am lucky to have you," Ashi said.

3.16

THE DAY OF Sacrifice started like any other. Ashi woke curled in Riyan's arms. She rose, had breakfast, and followed Yahil to the cavern. The air hung still around her. It took her a moment to realize what was different: there was no steady *drip, drip* of liquid falling from the ceiling into the urn.

When she knelt, mouth open, to receive the Blessing of Enticement, Yahil said, "This will be the last time you receive this before your Sacrifice." He touched the tip of the urn to Ashi's lips and poured, draining every last drop into her mouth. Ashi swallowed. Heat burned inside her.

She felt a quiver in her belly as she stepped into the pool. Her heart beat faster. Months of repetition had made the little ritual normal, part of the background of her life. She knew the texture of the stone beneath her knees when she accepted the Blessing, the feel of the water on her skin as she sat in the pool, the taste of Hemmis's lips on hers, the softness of Wahai's hands on her skin. It was strange knowing this was the last time she would be experiencing these things.

Ashi swallowed nervously as she settled on Yahil's lap. He slid his hands around her body.

"Are you afraid?" he said.

"No."

"Are you lying?"

"Yes."

"All this will be over soon. Being confined down here, not being allowed pleasure…"

"I know. It's just…" Ashi hesitated. "After all these months, it's just how things are now. I'm not sure I want it to be over." She settled back against him, basking in the pleasant blurriness. "Maybe I've gotten used to this."

"Humans are adaptable." He kissed her shoulder. "You'll be okay. In fact, I think you'll be better than okay. I think you'll make a splendid Sacrifice."

If Riyan, Emrin, or Marnin noticed her nervousness during her massage, they didn't remark on it. In fact, there was very little conversation at all. They all seemed aware that this phase of things was drawing to a close.

After they had washed Ashi, Emrin and Marnin bid her goodbye. "We will be at the Sacrifice tonight," Emrin said, "though of course we will be… different. It has been an honor to serve you, Avatar." He bowed.

"Oh, cut that out," Ashi said. She hugged him fiercely. "I still don't feel like an avatar." She embraced Marnin. "I will look forward to seeing you both tonight."

They left without another word. Marnin locked the door behind him.

"Are you scared?" Riyan asked once they were alone.

"Yes."

"Me too."

"I'm not sure which one of us should be more scared," Ashi said.

"Oh, definitely you," Riyan said. "I'll be feeling everything that happens to you, but you'll be the one it's happening to."

"Are you sure you don't want to trade places?" Ashi said. "I bet we could convince them—"

Riyan kissed the tip of Ashi's nose. "No." She put her arms around Ashi.

Ashi leaned against her. She commanded the viewscreen to show her the City. Riyan regarded it thoughtfully. "Why do you like looking at that?"

Ashi shrugged. Her shoulders wriggled against Riyan's warm skin. "I don't know," she said. "It just calms me."

The sun was setting over the City, sending long fingers of shadow across the massive ziggurat of the Fiery One, when Fiha and Yahil came to the door. They both wore kilts of deep red, and simple harnesses of black leather on their chests. Yahil stood outside the barred gate. "Avatar, are you ready?" he said.

Ashi's heart thudded. "Yes," she said. Her voice sounded thin in her ears. "Riyan, are you ready?"

"I am." Riyan stood gracefully. She smiled at Ashi. "Let's do this."

Yahil unlocked the door. Hand in hand, Ashi and Riyan followed Fiha and Yahil out.

They climbed back up the long, twisting set of stairs and out into a warm, clear evening. Ashi stopped, eyes closed, breathing deeply. The air carried the scent of growing things.

She opened her eyes again. "Okay," she said.

Yahil and Fiha led them along a tiled path toward the amphitheater. Flowers lined both sides of the path. People wandered about, enjoying the evening. They bowed and stepped out of the way when Ashi and Riyan passed.

The amphitheater was a large, round structure, several stories high, made of stone so white it seemed to glow in the last rays of the sun. Large dronelights hovered over it, illuminating it with a soft warm glow.

Yahil and Fiha led Ashi and Riyan up the ramp that climbed the outside of the amphitheater to a platform at the top, where Hemmis and Wahai already waited. Jiialen, the High Cleric of the Blesser, stood beside them, holding a tray with two curved, spiral-shaped glass vials interlocked together. Hemmis held a large bundle of thin, filmy robes over his arm.

A pedestal on the platform held a tray bearing a large number of small, identical vials and two larger, delicately fluted vials. Amber fluid filled with tiny flecks of glittering green dust filled the small vials. The larger vials held a clear liquid in which swirled tiny flecks of red and gold. Behind the pedestal was a small, ankle-deep pool filled with honey-colored liquid.

Another ramp spiraled down from the platform into the amphitheater. Iron cages lined both sides of the narrow ramp, each one just large enough to hold a person. Every cage held a naked prisoner, all watching Ashi with hungry eyes.

The bottom of the amphitheater was rough stone, sculpted into many small pools connected by little streams, filled with the same honey-colored liquid as the pool. The center of the amphitheater rose slightly to a smooth, featureless rectangular pillar of stone, about waist high. A long, low cage of black metal sat on the ground behind the altar. Heavy chains connected to the cage hung slack from two large curved arms that extended gracefully over the open, roofless top of the amphitheater.

Hemmis and Wahai bowed deeply to Ashi. Excitement passed like a physical thing through the people in the cages.

"Avatar," Wahai said. "Are you ready for the Sacrifice to the Wild?"

"I am," Ashi said.

"Riyan, as representative of the Blesser, are you also ready to participate in the Sacrifice to the Wild?" Jiialen said.

"Sure, why not?" Riyan said. She flashed Ashi a quick smile.

Jiialen separated the two entwined vials. She handed one to Ashi and the other to Riyan. "The Blesser grants you, Ashi and Riyan, the Blessing of Union," she said. "This Blessing is more potent than the regular Blessing, so as to last for the entire duration of Ashi's Sacrifice."

Riyan uncapped her vial. "Well, here goes," she said. She threw back her head and tossed it down. Ashi drank the liquid in her vial. She felt a flash of disconnection, quickly gone.

Wahai picked up the two larger vials. "These contain the Lord of Light's Ambrosia," she said. "You will feel no need for food or sleep while the Sacrifice goes on." She gave a vial to Ashi and Riyan, bowing as she did. Riyan looked at Ashi. Ashi noticed a small tremor in Riyan's hand as she uncapped it and raised it to her lips.

Ashi uncapped her own vial. They drank simultaneously. For an instant, Ashi felt as though she were standing in two places at once, feeling the liquid slide down two throats at the same time.

Wahai nodded to Fiha. "Priestess, if you will distribute the Blessing of the Wild, please?"

Fiha nodded. She picked up the tray and walked down the ramp. As she passed each cage, she gave a vial to the person locked inside. Ashi watched the people closest to her open their vials and drink. Their bodies went rigid, vials dropping from shaking fingers to roll away undetected. Reason left their eyes, replaced by a feral wildness.

"If you will stand still, please," Yahil said. He moved behind Ashi and removed her dress, leaving her naked atop the platform. He then removed Riyan's dress, leaving her bare as well. Riyan looked down, a small smile on her face.

Wahai took one of the robes draped over Hemmis's arm. She spread it out across the surface of the pool, careful not to touch the liquid. The tissue-thin fabric turned transparent. She took another robe and placed it in the pool, then another and another, until sixteen robes floated in the shallow liquid.

Wahai and Hemmis stood on either side of the pool. Each of them took a pair of tongs from their belts. They lifted one of the robes from the pool, holding it carefully with the tongs, and moved over to Ashi. Ashi held out her arms. They draped the robe over her body.

It clung to her skin, warm and wet. The instant it touched her, a fierce, burning arousal crashed over her, so hot and fast it felt like a physical blow. She sucked in her breath. Beside her, Riyan made a soft "unh!" sound.

They removed another of the robes from the pool and layered it over Ashi's body, and another after that, until eight of them lay draped across her.

382

They lifted another robe and slipped it over Riyan's body. She moaned.

They repeated the process until Riyan also wore eight of the filmy, insubstantial robes. They clung to her body, highlighting rather than concealing every curve.

"Let us begin the Procession of Sacrifice," Yahil said. "Follow me."

He started down the long spiral ramp that led down into the amphitheater. Riyan followed behind Ashi. With every step, Ashi felt that weird sensation of being in two places at once. She felt the smooth stone floor beneath Riyan's feet, the wet robes that clung to Riyan's skin.

Growls preceded them down the ramp. Hands reached out from the cages to clutch at them. Ashi saw Vrynn in one of the cages. She smiled at him. There was no recognition in his eyes, nothing but raw animal need. He grabbed at her as she walked by. She pulled away. One of her robes tore like tissue in his hands, leaving him clutching a scrap of wet cloth. His body went taut. His cock sprang to attention. He threw back his head and howled.

Ashi and Riyan battled their way down the ramp through seizing, grabbing hands. The caged worshippers snarled and roared as they tore the robes away, flinging themselves forward, beating their hands against the iron bars.

By the time they reached the bottom of the amphitheater, all the robes had been ripped off, leaving Ashi and Riyan nude. Fiha waited for them on the small rise in the center. She opened a door at the end of the cage. "Riyan, if you please," she said.

The cage was about the size of a narrow bed, much too low to sit in. A plush cushion lay in the bottom. Riyan got on her hands and knees and crawled inside. Fiha closed the door behind her. It latched with a loud clank. The chains tightened, lifting the cage into the air high above the altar.

Ashi approached the short, slender column of dull, featureless stone in the exact center of the amphitheater. As she drew near, the altar came to life. Faint lines and curls rippled across its surface. The gray took on an iridescent sheen. Subtle colors played in its depths.

She took another step closer. All at once, its shape changed. The stone moved and flowed like a thick liquid. Two depressions appeared in the top. The corners softened and rounded. Shackles materialized at its base. Ashi's heart skipped a beat.

She took a deep, trembling breath. Then, with just a moment's hesitation, she bent over the altar.

The stone moved beneath her like a living thing, warm and fluid, molding itself to her body. The two depressions shifted and flowed until they exactly conformed to her breasts. She spread her legs and placed her ankles in the cuffs. They snapped shut. The edge of the stone lifted to raise her hips until she stood on her toes.

The sides of the altar rippled. Two more cuffs sprang from the surface, one on each side. Ashi placed her wrists in the cuffs. They closed around her, locking her wrists in place.

She took a deep breath and lowered her head. Curved bands sprang from the top of the altar, wrapped around her neck, and locked closed. Ashi found herself bound securely, bent over the altar with her hips up and her head slightly down, cuffed at wrist and ankle, head held in place.

Yahil took a flask from a pouch at his belt. He poured its thick, slippery contents down the cleft of Ashi's ass. He worked it into her with her fingers, pressing the slick stuff into her anus. When he was finished, he said, "The Avatar is ready. Let the Sacrifice begin."

He and Fiha left the center of the amphitheater. Ashi drew a shuddering breath. The cage doors sprang open. A roar went up from the worshippers. They poured down the ramp toward Ashi, snarling with hunger and intent.

They swarmed around her, growling and barking, every one of them consumed with the desire to take her. Someone, she couldn't see who, grabbed her hips and shoved his erect cock into her. She yelped. Above her, Riyan cried out.

People clustered around the altar, pushing and shoving, battling each other to get close to her. More frenzied worshippers piled up beyond them, and more after that, fighting and jostling to reach Ashi. Bent over as she was, unable to lift her head, she could not see the faces of the people in front of her, only hips and legs and hard, demanding cocks.

An erection was shoved down her throat, so abruptly she choked. Tears welled in her eyes. The burning need within her flared higher. She pushed her hips back against the worshipper behind her, desperate to drive him deeper.

The man in front of her thrust hard, shoving himself down her throat again and again. There was no finesse in it. Ashi was not a participant, merely a receptacle for his need. There was a mindless urgency to his use of her mouth, a wildness that would not be contained.

Ashi sputtered and coughed. The man behind her leaned over, pressing her hips against the altar as he took her in his frenzy. Waves of pleasure crashed through her, higher with every thrust, building toward an orgasm she'd been denied for months. Her body tensed, tightening around the erection inside her...

...and then, just like that, the oncoming orgasm faded and was gone. Above her, Riyan mewled with frustration.

The cock in her mouth erupted. A thick torrent of come poured down her throat. Ashi coughed. White fluid leaked from her mouth.

Deep inside her, she felt the cock swell, then twitch. The man behind her let out a long, loud yell as he released into her. Ashi felt fingers on her clit and realized Riyan was touching herself, consumed by the same heedless mania that gripped everyone else.

Both cocks withdrew at once. Ashi panted. Turbulence swirled through the people clustered around her as the worshippers fought each other to be the next to use her. Another cock, thick, and rigid, pressed into her mouth. Ashi felt pressure on the pucker of her ass, a sense of stretching, then a sudden, shocking inrush. Riyan screamed. Her fingers worked her clit, sending echoes of pleasure shivering through Ashi.

The cock buried itself deeper in her ass. Ashi felt the tension of an orgasm building inside her, and knew it was Riyan's. It approached, closer and closer, then disappeared. Riyan let out a whimper of frustration and denial.

The two men ravaged Ashi's mouth and ass, overwhelming her. From somewhere off to her left, a thick, sticky gout of wetness splattered the side of her face. Another spurted warm across her hips. She heard groans and cries and snarls all around her as people struggled to get closer to her.

The cock swelled in her ass. She heard a roar, then jet after jet flooded her rectum with slippery goo. Her cry was choked off as the cock in her mouth plunged down her throat. Another eruption of warm wetness splattered the side of her face and neck.

The man behind Ashi kept driving into her ass, still erect despite his orgasm. The man in front of her moved faster, thrusting more and more quickly in her mouth until he groaned. Thick saltiness spurted into her mouth. Up in her cage, Riyan twisted her nipples. The sudden stab of sensation drew a cry from Ashi. "Buh!" she said. Goo dripped from her chin.

She sensed rather than saw a scuffle behind her. The cock slid from her ass. She heard a commotion, filled with growls and yelps. A new person shoved himself into her, coming as he impaled her. Wild aching pleasure filled her. She howled, hands balled into fists. Riyan let out a cry of her own. A blast of wetness spattered across Ashi's face. Thick streams of come shot into her hair. Another orgasm built and built, then faded into mist. Riyan screamed with helpless frustration. She squeezed her breast tightly.

More people used her, and more after that. Insistent, forceful cocks shoved their way into her, frenzied and unrelenting. Women grabbed her hair and ground themselves against her face. Chaos swirled around her as people shoved at each other to relieve their need with Ashi's body. Riyan writhed in her cage, moaning and screaming, chasing orgasms that collapsed into nothing just at the moment when they seemed inevitable.

The sun settled low. The floating dronelights bathed the amphitheater in light. Surreal, twisting shadows danced around them. Ashi felt her mind drifting with the shadows while maddened worshippers tussled over her.

Worshippers driven crazy by the Wild's blessing forced their cocks into her. Less patient worshippers ejaculated on her, until her face, neck, arms, and legs dripped with slick warm come, matting her hair and clinging to her skin, dripping from her onto the ground. Time and again, the relentless use of her body brought her to the edge of an orgasm that simply collapsed and disappeared, leaving her without release.

The bands held her tightly to the altar. The shackle around her neck kept her from moving her head. Her bonds forced her to remain entirely passive, a repository for the ferocious desires of the worshippers who crowded and squabbled around her, a recipient of their need but not a true participant in it. She was merely a fixture, conveniently placed for others to pour their desperation into.

Riyan thrashed so violently that her cage swung on its chains. She ran her hands over herself, squeezing her breasts, stroking her clit, pushing her fingers into her mouth. Ashi felt all of it, just as she knew Riyan felt the frenzied worshippers using Ashi's body.

The last light faded. As worshippers released their needs upon Ashi, they staggered backward, splashing through the pools surrounding the altar. The liquid in the pools re-ignited their wild, unthinking lust. Ashi was the center of an ever-circulating storm of people who fought their way to the altar, sated themselves in or on her body, then were carried away by the jostling crowd into the pools, where the golden liquid inflamed their cravings once more.

Orias, with the self-control of a previous Sacrifice, waited until Ashi was dripping and panting before she fought her way to the center of the maelstrom. She yanked Ashi's hair, rough with need, and pushed Ashi's face between her legs. The angle made it difficult for Ashi's tongue to reach her clit, and uncomfortable too. Orias pinned her there anyway, holding Ashi by the hair with both hands, until she screamed with pleasure.

A thick cock forced its way into Ashi's ass. Ashi and Riyan cried out simultaneously. Strong hands pushed Orias out of the way. Frantic fingers pried Ashi's mouth open. A cock erupted before it could enter her mouth. Hot blasts of white fluid spurted onto her face. Then he, too, was shoved out of the way by yet another worshipper, who thrust himself into Ashi's mouth with urgent abandon. Semen flooded into her mouth and rectum.

Ashi gurgled. Riyan's fingers flew over her clit. Another orgasm built and vanished. Riyan wailed.

The night went on. The storm of frenzied desire around Ashi continued. She whimpered and moaned, cried out and gasped, wept with frustration and longing, and still the worshippers used her body as a vessel for their needs. Even after every part of her overflowed with come, the worshippers still returned to use her again. Through it all, she and Riyan did not come, no matter how their bodies ached for release.

Then, as the shadows paled with the early light of dawn, Ashi found a sense of peace. The frenzy swirled around her. She felt the thrust of rigid cocks within her, hard and demanding. She felt her own pleasure swell and then fade, swell and then fade. She was aware of every throb, every moan, the wet slap of every ejaculation inside her or on her skin, but she had passed beyond need or desire. She observed each sensation for what it was. She savored the buildup of pleasure without disappointment when no orgasm came.

In that place of peace, she felt something else, too, a presence that was separate from her, separate from everyone else in the amphitheater. A strange, alien mind moved within her thoughts. She looked at it, and knew it approved of her.

She also felt Riyan, and knew all the ways Riyan's experience differed from hers. Riyan wept with every failed orgasm, pursuing release in a frenzy. She bucked her hips and drove her fingers deep into herself, trying to force an orgasm that wouldn't come.

Ashi accepted this, too, without trying to change it. She turned inward, studying each new sensation, witnessing every grope, every thrust, every pulse and throb and splatter. She stopped keeping track of time. She observed the shadows growing shorter, the light brightening, the warmth of the sun on her back, the shadows lengthening again, all without considering what it meant. She was here to offer herself as a receptacle for the energy of the worshippers, and a receptacle does not concern itself with what it receives.

The storm, impossibly, subsided. The urgency faded. Gaps appeared, small intervals of time in which nobody was using Ashi. Almost imperceptibly, the crowd thinned around her. People lay on the ground, too spent to move, exhausted beyond the capability of the pools to incite them any further.

The amphitheater quieted except for Riyan's cries. Ashi panted. Slick wetness ran down her body and dripped from her face. She felt herself leaking between her legs.

Finally, there were no more people making demands of her. Ashi waited, bent over the altar, breathing deeply. Ryan's cage swayed back and forth. The chains squeaked. Worshippers lay in exhausted stupor about her.

Hemmis and Yahil walked up to the altar. The ground beneath them began to rise, until the small hill on which the altar was mounted became a wide column of stone half again as tall as a person.

Hemmis stood in front of Ashi and removed his kilt. Yahil stepped behind her. In her cage, Riyan lay on her back whimpering, legs apart as wide as the bars allowed, fingers working inside herself.

Yahil and Hemmis sank into Ashi at the same time. Riyan cried out. The two men thrust with the same careful tempo, gradually breathing faster. Ashi felt Hemmis quiver, felt him holding back.

At some unspoken cue, they both came simultaneously. Hot fluid rushed into her. At the exact instant they came, a torrential rain poured down from the sky through the open roof of the amphitheater.

The moment the deluge struck Ashi, whatever force had blocked her orgasms vanished. She came, harder than she ever had before. Riyan shrieked with ecstasy at the same instant.

It didn't stop. Not for Ashi, not for Riyan, not for Yahil or Hemmis. Every orgasm that had built up only to fade away, every pleasure that had been denied her during the Sacrifice, came roaring over them.

Riyan screamed and thrashed. Ashi fought with all her strength against the shackles that bound her to the altar. Yahil and Hemmis roared, gushing into Ashi in great spurts until they had both run dry. Still it didn't stop. Ashi's vision blurred. Riyan's screams took on an edge of despair. The orgasm went on and on, every single moment of denied release now returning to her with the ferocity of a wildfire.

Riyan sobbed. Yahil and Hemmis groaned. Ashi's body shook. The rain stopped. The orgasm didn't. It rose higher, pleasure unlike anything Ashi had ever felt before. It unraveled her until she couldn't do anything but surrender to it. The world faded away, leaving nothing but a tiny spark of Ashi's awareness that knew only immense, indescribable ecstasy.

And then, it was over. Hemmis reeled. Yahil collapsed over Ashi, panting. The stone column retreated back into the earth, lowering the altar to where it had been. Riyan wept softly in her cage.

The shackles snapped open. Fiha and Wahai lifted Ashi from the altar. She looked at them with incomprehension. Her mouth worked. No words came out.

With a rattle, the chains lowered Riyan to the ground. The cage opened. All around them, worshippers climbed wearily to their feet, faces blank.

The large doors at ground level slid open, releasing them into the warm peaceful night. Without a word or a backward glance, they staggered out of the amphitheater on unsteady legs.

Ashi collapsed. She crawled on hands and knees to where Riyan lay on her side on the ground, weeping. Ashi gathered her in her arms. They clung to each other until Riyan's sobs quieted and the trembling in Ashi's body stilled.

Fiha and Wahai waited respectfully until Ashi stirred. Wahai helped Ashi stand. Fiha helped Riyan to her feet.

"Thank you, Avatar," Yahil said. His body glistened with water. He too was unsteady on his feet. "You have facilitated the great purging for all who had things in their lives to let go of. Thank you for your sacrifice on our behalf." He bowed low. "If you wish to join the ranks of the priesthood in whatever capacity you desire, we stand ready to receive you. If you need anything from us, we are at your service."

"I—" Ashi blinked several times. Already, the sacrifice was fading, like something that had happened to someone else. Riyan hugged her close and buried her face in Ashi's neck. "I think...I think we need to go home."

"Of course," Fiha said. "I will help you."

3.17

A soft chime filled the air. A pleasant, directionless voice said, "You have visitors."

Riyan, snuggled against her, said, "Who—"

Ashi put her finger over Riyan's lips. "Shh! I'm trying to teach it."

There was a pause.

"And?" Ashi prompted.

"You have visitors," came the voice. "Vrynn and Ruji."

"See? That wasn't so hard, was it? Let them in."

The door opened. Vrynn and Ruji walked in. The tattoos on Vrynn's chest formed swirling designs of green and blue, signaling excitement. "Ashi! Riyan! There's a new forest! Looks like a big one. Want to go?"

"Mm," Ashi said. "I think I'll pass."

"That's what you said the last three times," Ruji said. "Some folks are starting to wonder if you're ever going to come out and play again. You and Riyan are sorely missed."

"That's sweet," Riyan said. "And thank you for thinking of us. I don't—I don't think we're ready to play in the forest just yet."

"Nobody's seen you in months," Vrynn said. "You haven't even gone to any dances. What are you doing with all your time?"

"Debating theology," Riyan said.

"What?"

Riyan smiled. "I've finally convinced Ashi to try her hand at being a Greeter for the Blesser. It's...well, it's kind of the opposite of being Sacrifice to the Wild, in a way."

"Ah, I see," Vrynn said. "Taking her away from us, are you? I see how you are." He waggled his finger at Riyan. "Swooping in and snatching our Avatar right from under us. It's dastardly, it is."

"Oh?" Riyan raised an eyebrow. "What are you going to do, reprimand me?"

"Don't give me ideas," Vrynn said. "Stealing our Sacrifice might warrant a stern...stern...something."

Ashi laughed. "It's nothing like that. My heart will always belong to the Wild, I think. But it's only fair. Riyan endured a lot to be with me. Didn't you, darling?" She kissed Riyan's cheek. "A bit of reciprocity seems reasonable. Besides, if I go with Riyan to serve the Blesser, we can both get the Blessing of Union. That's two pairs of doses."

"What are you going to do with them?"

"Well, you know," Ashi said, "we thought it might be fun to share it with you two, next time a new forest opens up. What do you say?"

We met at an orgy in a castle in France in 2010. On that fateful day, neither of us ever expected that ten years later, we would write a book together. We spent a lovely time with each other, then went our separate ways.

We saw each other rarely, perhaps every year or two, but with the number of overlapping people in our social and romantic circles, it was inevitable that we kept brushing across each other's lives. Over time, that developed into the seeds of a genuine friendship.

In 2017, Franklin invited Eunice to his wedding to his wife, Shara. During the rehearsal dinner, Maxine, one of Franklin's romantic partners, said, "Hey Eunice, did you know Franklin has a crush on you?" (It was true.) With those particular beans well and truly spilled, we started properly connecting. We soon realized we had even more in common than we initially realised, and a spark of something curious and unexpected started to grow.

Eunice built the world of the City as a space for play and exploration, a mental playground of fantasy and philosophy. She told Franklin about this magical place one evening after dinner, and Franklin said, "Hey, that might make a lovely setting for a book!"

We started working on the book you now hold during our polyamorous group vacation in Lincoln, England. Franklin wrote the first paragraph of the first draft of what would eventually become *The Brazen Altar* on Eunice's naked back with fountain pens. The seed had become a sapling, and in the time since that moment, it has grown into a full tree.

We hope you enjoy visiting our forest of delights as much as we enjoyed tending it.

London, England and Portland, Oregon, March 2020.

Explore the world of

The Passionate Pantheon

The Brazen Altar
Published by Luminastra Press May 2021

Welcome to the far future utopia of the City. Here, benevolent AIs rule as gods, worshipped in rituals of sex and connection that weave tapestries of divine experience.

In a culture where sex, pleasure and serving others are the highest good, how do you find meaning and purpose? As willing sacrifices to their gods, three women endure extremes of pleasure and sensation far beyond what they could ever have imagined.

Divine Burdens
Published by Luminastra Press Fall 2021

The far-future utopian ideals of the Passionate Pantheon is twisted into horror. In this new City, with no scarcity and no money, the only thing worth trading is your own body.

Lija trains with ferocious determination to be sacrificed to the god of the Hunt, driven to exhaustion and terror as she is hunted for three days. Rajja, exiled from another City, is captured to be bred as the horrified vessel for the new tentacled incarnation of the God of the Deep. The sacred parasite of the mysterious Gleaner burrows deep into Erianna's body, using her flesh to develop the Blessing that drives all who take it wild with desperate sexual desire.

The Hallowed Covenant
Published by Luminastra Press Spring 2022

Celebrate the Festival of the Lady, a month-long fiesta of creativity and joy, where a group of friends who worship different gods come together in erotic adventures in service to the City. Their choices affect themselves and each other, and the ripples spread out through the entire City.